DON'T TELL A SOUL

ALSO BY JAY STRINGER

The Eoin Miller Trilogy

Old Gold

Runaway Town

Lost City

The Sam Ireland Mysteries

Ways to Die in Glasgow

How to Kill Friend and Implicate People

The Marah Chase Adventures

Marah Chase and the Conqueror's Tomb

Marah Chase and the Fountain of Youth

A SWAG TALES PAPERBACK

First published in the United Kingdom and United States in 2021.

This edition published by Swag Tales, Glasgow, G40 4TR..

All works copyright Jay Stringer 2021.

All rights reserved. No part of the book may be reproduced in any form or by any electronic or mechanical means, including information storage and retrieval systems, without written permission from the author. Reviewers may quote the text for reviews, students may quote the text for educational purposes, but cannot be used for profit.

Cover design by Jay Stringer.
Book formatted in Affinity Publisher.

Standard Paperback Edition ISBN: 978-1-9168923-0-9
Dyslexic Reader Edition ISBN: 978-1-9168923-1-6
Ebook Edition ISBN: 978-1-9168923-2-3

DON'T TELL A SOUL

A Mystery

Jay Stringer

PART ONE

"If you're a fool for truth,
I'm a fool for you."
-The Doormats

Episode One: Where Were You When?

Audio Clip: Hot Take ident.

Ad: *Don't Tell A Soul is part of the Hot Take network. For more information visit hottake.com and subscribe to Hot Take Plus to hear all our shows with ads and plugs removed.*

Audio Clip: News Bulletin: *"...from outside the sixth precinct, where we understand Louisa Mantalos has just been arrested in connection with the disappearance of her husband, David Ash, six months ago..."*

Audio Clip: News Bulletin: *"...suicide, suspected to be in order to avoid the murder charges..."*

Audio Clip: Crowd outside Sixth Precinct: *"I told you, I said all along, told you, she did it."*

Theme tune plays.

    Dee: Hi, I'm Dee Buana. This is Don't Tell A Soul, the podcast about secrets, lies, and the truths we think we know.

Theme tune fades out.

    Dee: Okay. So you think there's no mystery here.
    You've all seen the news; you already know what happened. If you don't, you will the moment you type the names *David Ash* or *Louisa Mantalos* into your search engine. The mystery of the year. Rock star goes missing.
    Wife suspected of killing him.
    Social media goldmine.

Things like this, they're why the internet was invented, right?

And yes, the rumors are true, I do have a copy of the taped confession. I'll play it for you in a later episode. I record this on the day of the second funeral. It feels bittersweet right now even talking about this.

So, why am I still doing the show?

The truth is, I'm not sure. It feels like I need to.

The first rule I always observe in my work is not to interfere with the story. But on this case, I couldn't help it. I became part of the story. And I think I need to see that through. Go back to who I was before I got hurt, relive the moments, then follow through on what happened.

Like therapy, I guess.

And also, because it's my job.

Hot Take funded this whole thing, which means you funded this whole thing. And you got to give the people what they want.

If you've listened to the first two seasons, you'll know I'm obsessed with truth and lies. The small things we all know, but agree not to know, and the big things we all don't know, but agree to know. True crime podcasts have been the perfect vehicle for that, because I get to explore the gaps between the things people *mean* and the things people *say*.

And that was my plan.

I started out by interviewing people from David and Louisa's past, trying to figure out who they both really were. I didn't know how close we were to getting the answer, I didn't know that I'd be sitting here, talking to you, about a whole different kind of show.

The one it has turned into.

The other thing I had no way of knowing was just how much this was all going to play with my other big obsession.

Memory.

I've mentioned this before, but when I was thirteen, I was knocked off my bike in a hit and run. I suffered brain damage as a result of the accident, or the trauma, and for about six months afterwards I lost large chunks of my memory.

It took a lot of hard work and patience for them to fade back in.

And ever since then, I've wondered, did I become a different person? Memories shape who we are. They define us. If our memories change, or go away, do *we* change with them?

This season gives me a chance to test that out on myself. I get to go back and listen to who I was before I got involved in the story, and before we all found out what happened to David Ash. Is that version of me a different person? And of course, the shared memory that drew me to this case in the first place. Those cultural moments. *Where were you when...?* They're always followed by a story. A shared story. Somehow, we all agree who did what, and why, and how, and then, regardless of the facts, we've agreed that this is the truth.

But if that shared memory changes, does the truth change? Do *we* all change?

This season is an experiment.

Most of what you will hear was recorded in the moment, during the investigation, as things happened. In a way, I'm going to be having a conversation with myself. And with you, too. We all know what happened, but you didn't know back then. If I present these episodes in the order I intended, before we all knew, then maybe you'll learn things about yourselves, too. *Your* assumptions.

Hindsight is an interesting thing. Even until the last couple days, when I was wrestling with what to do with all the hours of recordings, I told myself a lie. I was saying that I'd not intended to involve myself in this story, I was there to observe and report.

But listening to the first episode, all I can hear is me talking about... *me.*

For some reason, even before events forced my hand, I was already taking this story personally. And I hope putting these episodes out will help me figure out why.

And, like I said, you all think there's no mystery here. But I still have a few tricks up my sleeve.

And so, over to Dee... in the past.

Theme tune fades in.
Theme tune fades out.

Dee: Where were you on November eleventh, last year? Not sure? No, me neither. I was probably sitting on my couch, staring at my phone. Or sitting on my couch, staring at my laptop. Or sitting on my couch, watching Netflix, while alternately staring at my phone and laptop.

If I were to ask you what you were doing four days later, on November fifteenth, you might be able to answer. I can guess that with some certainty, because you're listening to this podcast, which means you're already interested in this subject. You know what I'm going to be talking about. But, for anyone at the back who came in late – that's totally how podcasts work – I'll ask a different question.

Where were you on the night they announced David Ash was missing?

And you'll know. Or you'll tell yourself you know. Like the alibis and fake memories we've explored in previous seasons, you'll make an educated guess, and over time your memory will solidify that into fact.

It felt like the whole city stopped that night, to take in the news. Whether you liked Ash or not. Whether you'd ever heard of him. (I was only vaguely aware.)

It was just one of those perfect storms. A semi-famous person, a possible murder, and an empty news cycle.

For me, Ash was just that guy who covered a song over the closing credits of Frozen 3.

I would never have been interested in his old band, *the Doormats.* I'm still not.

Sad boys singings about being sad, with a premium on references to alcohol. I would probably have been a fan of his solo career, if I'd heard much of it before the news broke. But overnight I became obsessed with the man. And with his wife, Louisa. You all know who she is. And you think you know what happened, right?

So, to the facts:

Fact one. David Ash left his home in the Meatpacking District on November eleventh and went across the river to Greenpoint. We have surveillance camera footage to prove that.

Fact two. On November twelfth his wife, Louisa, called 911 and reported that Ash never came home. They referred her to the 6th Precinct, who sent a patrol unit to knock on doors in Ash's building, but said they needed to wait another day before they could do anything else with the report.

Fact three. Louisa called the precinct back on November thirteenth. The case was officially picked up by Detective Henry Elizondo.

Fact four. The media reported the story on the evening of November fifteenth.

Fact five. The hashtag #DidSheDoIt predates the David Ash story. It's been used for political debates, book marketing, two soap operas, and a TV show about an animal rights activist accused of killing her husband. But there's an undeniable link. Tweets started using the hashtag in relation to Louisa on November sixteenth, in the early hours, less than a day after news broke about Ash's disappearance.

That's it, really. Fact-wise.

Everything else seems to be guesswork.

Looking at it here, at the start of the project, it seems like nobody's story really adds up.

Can everybody be telling the truth?

No.

But could everybody be lying?

Maybe.

ONE

LOUISA

"They want to take my kids."

I feel the familiar desperation. The panic. My voice is a higher pitch than I intended. It sounds like I'm shouting at Ally. I see her take a step back.

Like she's–

What's the word?

Like, she's surprised but—

Startled.

That's it. I've startled her. I put my hand out and scrunch my face up in an apology. Ally smiles it away and sits down on the couch. I can't afford to have Ally mad. She's become everything to me. A combination of my manager, my agent, my best friend and–

There's another word.

It's about the way she helps me with my problems.

Damn.

Anyway, I need Ally. Couldn't cope without her. She's stuck with me long after I stopped being a profitable client. I've had good offers for TV appearances and interviews, but they're from people I don't trust. I'm not going to make a profit off what's happened with Dave. Ally supports my decision. Even though I'm now burning through residuals, and turning down money for both of us, she's standing by me. You can't buy loyalty like that, and we've both learned the hard way.

I turn my attention back to the phone. My lawyer is talking. Ramona Cross.

She's speaking fast and using words I don't always understand. I think I used to know them, but some days it's not so clear.

On my good days, my best days, I know I'm forgetting things. I can see the gaps. Big fuzzy spaces where words and concepts used to be. I know I'll wake up one morning and find faces and names occupy the same space, and it scares the hell out of me.

Ramona is still talking.

"....and David's not's legally dead yet."

Yet.

I haven't mourned for Dave. He's not dead yet. Not in any sense I can hold onto or build my life around. My heart won't settle. I wake up in the morning certain he's alive, and we'll be reunited and forget all of the problems. By bedtime I'm convinced he's dead.

The whole world thinks I killed my husband.

Maybe I did.

I just don't know.

He left for work six months ago, and never came home.

I'm not a killer.

That's what I tell myself. But how do any of us ever know, unless we've been tested? I bet everyone has it in them. Deep down. In the heat of the moment, if we're backed into a corner.

Maybe he finally asked for the divorce from our cold war of a marriage. Maybe he'd threatened to take the kids. Even thinking about it, I can feel the dark bubble deep down in my gut.

The capacity for violence.

The minute I looked into my baby's eyes, I knew the lengths I would go to. You bring a life into the world, you know you'll do anything to keep him here, and to stay next to him.

And there's the other side of it.

The one we never admit to.

Your baby cries for three days straight, and it's 3am, and you can't sleep....

The breaking point comes into view.

You don't cross the line, because your kid is crying, and you feel bad. But you see it. You feel how easy it would be. I know I'm capable. The violence is there. It's there for all of us. Maybe I'm just more honest than most people. I admit to my problems. I see my own dark side; and everyone else has seen it too. My life has been lived on the front page of the tabloids. On Facebook. Twitter. Interviews from fifteen years ago are still in circulation, as if they have any relevance to the person I've become. If you're not famous, you get to make mistakes and grow. But once the public feel like they own your identity, you can only ever be one thing.

Dave was smarter. He kept his mistakes secret. Right up until he met me, and the rules changed for both of us. A celebrity couple. The poster boy of indie rock, and the has-been reality TV star, out to ruin his life and steal his money.

David's not's legally dead yet.

Yet.

It's not Ramona's fault the word hurts. I'm paying her to be blunt. When she first took the case, she would talk around the issue. The conversations would be vague, and Ramona would walk on eggshells rather than come right out and say it.

I asked her to be direct.

Talk to me about Dave the same way she does to everyone else. So now she talks about him in the past tense. We discuss how long it will be before the state can declare him legally dead.

When the game will change.

Dave's creditors might go away. Most of them. Some will come looking for his estate, but I won't have to worry about the monthly bills in his name. I'm still paying his life insurance. They won't cash out until it's official, but if I stop paying, they'll say I voided the agreement.

I don't have access to most of Dave's money.

We kept things separate. Bank accounts. Savings. It was the wise move. Two people with addiction issues, two people with trust issues. There's a house account we both paid into, but for the past six months it's only been me. Dave's music sales have soared since he went missing, but it goes into accounts I can't get to unless he's dead. The mortgage we took on this place is covered by insurance, too. Once he's officially dead, the apartment is paid off.

That sounds cold.

I want him to be alive. He can walk through the door now, I'll shout at him, scream at him, and demand answers. But he'll be here. I can hold him. I don't want to be thinking about money and paperwork, but this is the world I'm left with. I have to look at the future for me and my children. Our children. Petey, the son I had before Dave, and Johnny, the boy we had together. Johnny looks just like his dad.

Oh, hell. That gets me crying.

His parents think I killed him, just like everyone else. And now they want the kids. Right now. Right now, while the world is spinning and I just can't get five minutes to think. It feels like mothers usually get the custody in a legal battle, but I'm not a usual mother.

The court of public opinion would be in their favor. The court of law? Wouldn't be any different.

On the one side, the judge would see two retired teachers, kind old people, who raised a good and famous musician. On the other? Louisa Mantalos. Famous for being famous. The corrupting influence who led the nice boy astray. Sex tapes. Public drug addiction. No surviving relatives.

They want the kids, and everyone will help them.

David's not's legally dead yet.

Yet.

It's not even about him being legally dead.

I don't know if he's *actually* dead. I assumed he'd left me. Shacked up with someone else. Slumped in a corner somewhere, shooting up. He took things from our apartment, cash and his favorite guitar. Dave went everywhere with that stupid thing. But nobody knew our marriage had been in trouble. We kept it hidden.

The secret protected our careers.

A very happy marriage, we'd say. *Planning to renew our vows.* The whole deal. Nobody else needed to know we were falling apart.

The police were the first to mention the word.

Death.

The detective let it slip in the middle of his questions. I've become an expert at reading people over the years, I could see his game. He wanted to catch me in a lie. Trip me up, so I'd admit what I'd done.

Hell, maybe I should just accept popular opinion. The papers. The TV. The internet. They didn't even wait for a trial. Not even for the cops to build a case. I've read so many theories on how I could have done it.

And why.

I was raised Greek Orthodox. Guilt comes easy. I'm hardwired to carry the can for sins someone else committed.

If there's even a chance I killed him… I feel like I did.

Someone is making a podcast. *Don't Tell A Soul,* a true crime show that's already had a couple seasons, been a big hit both times. They're talking to the cops, to lawyers, to Dave's parents, and his old bandmates. Some Brit from the BBC is asking around, trying to put together a documentary. He's even asked Dave's band for permission to use their music. I'm learning there are a hell of a lot of people willing to pay to hear gossip about me.

And I can't even tell them they're wrong.

Recent events are jumbled.

I'm spending time each day trying to piece together all the moments that make me who I am.

For the most part I think I'm getting them right, but what if I'm not? Am I still the same person if I have different memories?

I don't question I could have done it.

But there's no body.

Dave vanished. It's like he caught a rocket ship to another planet.

And now I'm losing everything. Dave's parents are petitioning to get access to my medical records, to have me assessed on whether I'm fit to be a mother. Once they discover my illness, it'll be game over.

Ramona says something else and I have to backtrack. "What?"

She's learned to be patient with me. "I can delay them," she says. Her tone tells me she's repeating something. "It won't last long. We'll need a plan, and I don't have one. But in the short term, I can delay them from getting access."

"How?"

"I'll divert the issue. Hire an investigator, say we believe Dave's alive and we're trying to locate him. I'll say it's not fair to use your medical records against you while you're on medication for stress because of Dave."

It's not even a way to win. Just to delay losing.

"But we already tried finding an investigator."

"I…" Ramona pauses. "I know a guy."

TWO

CON

I was hiding in a closet when Ramona Cross called.

My cell wasn't on silent.

I'd been listening to the two frantic lovers on the other side of the door. Now all three of us were listening to my ringtone.

The Spider-Man theme song.

(Queens represent.)

Being in the closest hadn't been part of the plan. I was there to steal a ring. Well, steal it back. It belonged to my client. Elaine Blatt. She'd been dating a personal trainer from her gym, a guy named Sammy Leonard. Sammy wasn't exactly what Elaine called a long-term bet, but fun was fun. Right up until he left her for a younger model, fresh off the treadmill, and took a ring that belonged to Elaine's grandmother. The ring was the only thing she had to remember her by. That, and irritable bowel syndrome.

Elaine didn't have much of a criminal record. Not in my league, anyway. She'd been busted once at school for possession and picked up one DUI as an adult. But she knew the first rule.

Never call the cops.

When someone like Elaine had a problem, they came to me for a quick fix. I help people, for fifty dollars an hour.

Sometimes thirty.

Depends if I like them.

The ring had been easy to track down. Sammy's new squeeze hadn't been shy in wearing it. She lived over in Prospect Heights and getting into the apartment had been easy for someone with my background.

I found the ring on a dresser by the bed. But the two of them came in the front door, laughing and flirting, and the closet had been closer than the window. And I'd forgotten the most important part of hiding in someone's furniture;

Always put your phone on silent.

So now I waited, to see what happened next.

The mattress squeaked, and footsteps came toward me. The closet door flew open and Sammy Leonard glared down.

He had about four inches on me.

Height was the least of the differences.

"This probably looks bad," I said.

My cell rang again. *Perfect.* I answered it and put my finger out toward Sammy, in a way that said, just a minute, this is important.

Sammy looked at my hand, then at me, and bit down on whatever insult he'd been about to throw. I was more worried about the fist he would follow with. It used to be that a clipboard and a confident wave could get you out of any situation. Now all you need is a cell phone and a touch of arrogance.

Ramona started talking right away. "Hey, I've got a job for you."

"Okay," I made it sound as official as I could. "Interesting. Yes, I'm doing it right now."

"Doing what?"

I looked at Sammy and rolled my eyes, pretending we were on the same side. "That's right. Oh, you said the closet in number 32? Marlon told me 54."

"You're doing the telephone thing again, aren't you?"

I grinned at Sammy. He was realizing he had no reason to back down here. "Yeah. Say—" I looked to the woman on the bed, covering long limbs with the sheets. "Is that Beyoncé?"

Sammy's face creased in confusion. He looked at me, then the phone, then back toward his sex buddy. "Is—?"

I used his confusion as a chance to bolt. By the time he turned back to grab at me, I was out the bedroom door into the hallway. I heard him swear and start to give chase, but I got to the front door and pulled it open, slamming it shut just before he reached me. I heard him thud against the other side and swear again.

I lifted the phone back to my ear. "Meet me at the bar, thirty minutes." The door opened and Sammy stepped out toward me. He wasn't done yet. I turned and ran for the stairs. "Make it an hour," I said, killing the call.

I didn't have to run far.

The merciful gods of Uber were kind, and I got picked up three blocks away. Sammy might have been built for power, but I have a lifetime of running away. I headed straight for one waiting on Bergen Street.

I was dropped off outside my stepfather's bar on 28th

Sharkey's had been a run-down Irish bar when Frank bought it. Complete with neon clovers on the wall and terrible Guinness in the pumps. It came cheap, and Frank had dreams of being a small business owner after receiving a payout from an accident at work. We renovated the place together. Frank, me, and Frank's brother, Liam. It was just about the only thing we'd ever done without trying to kill each other. Frank and Liam had never really got on with each other, and I tended to agree more with Liam thank Frank. Liam saw life the same way I did. From the other side.

We stripped out the Irish props. Cleaned the walls. Fitted a new bar and converted the basement to a gig venue. There were comedy shows down there three times a week, and student bands used it the rest of the time.

Frank was behind the bar when I walked in. He was doing paperwork and pretending to look busy.

I slid the ring across the bar toward him without a word. Frank rang up a no sale on the register and slipped the ring in beneath the cash tray. Elaine would stop by to pick it up later. Frank went back to the paperwork, as if nothing had happened. He didn't like to talk about my cases. Most of my clients were criminals, or ex-cons, and Frank thought it was only a matter of time before I'd get mixed up in something that would land me back in prison.

Ramona was sitting in the back, waiting at the table I used as an office, two Cokes in front of her. I waved for her to stand up as I walked over, and we hugged.

Ramona wasn't much into things like that, but she made an exception for me. Two mixed-up kids at high school. Both raised Catholic by adoptive fathers, both wondering who the hell we really were.

Ramona's mother was Puerto Rican, her father had been Irish Catholic. An old school friend of Frank's, but he split before Ramona was born.

We'd both grown up with the gift of talking our way out

of trouble. Thinking on out feet. Being persuasive. The difference was what we did with our skills. While I was learning all the best short cuts on the other side of the law, Ramona was putting herself through college and law school.

When I was adding sleight-of-hand, card mechanics, and lock picking to my toolbox, Ramona was learning to use her hands to write legal documents.

We'd fooled around off and on for years, but she broke things off permanently when I went to prison. It was the wound we couldn't heal. Having a criminal as a boyfriend had never been good for her career but dating a convict would have been the end of it. More than one big law firm in the city had been attracted by her grades, only to shut the door when they found out about me.

Ramona's cases usually ended in settlements and plea bargains. She rarely went to court. She came to me for small-time investigation work.If something went all the way to trial, she would refer the job over to a more experienced attorney, and I would be replaced by a licensed PI.

"Hey," she said, fixing me with the kind of smile that used to slay me. "Did you have fun?"

I nodded. "I guess."

"Ready for a challenge?"

"Almost never."

"I have a client, she's in some trouble. Her husband is missing."

"Sounds like it would be-"

"An open investigation, yeah."

"Mona-"

I had a rule never to get mixed up in anything the cops were actively pursuing. It was my way of avoiding what Frank feared, getting in deep into something that could wind me right back in prison.

"It's a big case. This could be the one puts me back on the map." She gave me a full blast of her brown eyes. There was no need to say, you owe me this after costing me all those jobs, because I heard it in everything she said. "Plus, it'll be good for you. Log some hours on this, and maybe we can get you licensed."

"I'm doing fine."

"You like hiding in closets?"

"Who is she?"

"First I need you to say you'll do it."

"Mona, who is she?"

"If I tell you first, you'll say no." She fixed me with the look again. Equal parts big eyes and mischief. "Say you'll do it?"

Not a chance.

"Fine, fine. I'll do it."

When she gave me the name, I understood why she was nervous.

Louisa Mantalos.

Oh, *hell no.*

THREE

LOUISA

"No way." Ally's turn to raise her voice. "He's a criminal. He's done time."

Ramona sent me the name of the guy she's bringing over. Con McGarry. We find a couple of old news stories. He's done time.

Ally continues. "This is a bad idea. We can't trust him, not with your…"

She stops short of finishing the sentence. We both avoid putting a name to my problem. It doesn't feel real.

It's past Johnny's bedtime, but he's still crawling around on the floor playing with superhero toys. We're both using the children as an excuse not to talk too much about real issues. Six months later, and I still have no idea what to say to them about Dave.

Petey's in his room, reading. He's older and remembers the time when it was just the two of us. He already sees father figures as temporary. Dave was supposed to be the fix. The guy who would stick around and give Petey someone to look up to. He's old enough to notice the way people look at us when we're out. He goes to an expensive school, and the teachers promise me nobody is talking to him about Dave, but who can control what the kids say at playtime? He has to know something, and each day I go by without talking to him about it is a day that eats away at his trust in me.

When Johnny was born, we'd agreed to always treat him like a grown up. Reason with him when he cried.

Especially when one of us left the room, and the tears would be explosive.

"Daddy's gone," I would say. "But you know what happens next? He comes back."

The tears would stop. Johnny would nod, sniff, and look forward to Daddy coming home.

I've been using that line ever since Dave disappeared, but we have to be careful what news we have on the TV.

At some point very soon, I'll need to find a way to tell Johnny the truth, and he'll realize his mom is a liar.

"I just think we should try someone else," Ally says.

"We've already tried everyone."

"I know." She sighs. "Yeah."

Ally doesn't trust people easily. Not after being screwed over by her own parents. They took all of her money from the films and TV shows she made as a kid. She sued them, and they all went to court in a battle that kept the tabloids happy for months. Now she works as an agent and manager, protecting other people .

"I can't judge someone else based on a quick Google," I say. "Chances are, he's read far worse about me."

"Yeah, but most aren't true."

"Totally. But if he knows a hundred things about me, and ninety of them are false, the ten that are true still outnumber the one thing we know about him."

She shakes her head and eases into a smile. "Did any of that make sense?"

Johnny touches my leg. "Mom, you're on teevee."

Ally and I both look up at the screen. It's muted, but the channel is turned to one of those bland daytime shows. Small-time local celebrities talking about the crazy things their dogs do, or whatever news story Kanye has whipped up. I recognize they've had me on as a guest several times. It looks big on the screen, but the studio is the size of a shoe box. A leather sofa in front of a large window overlooking Central Park, but the view is fake.

The host is a twenty-something with a hipster beard, holding an iPad to give the impression news could happen at any moment. What's his name? Jax? Jarrod? I don't know. It hadn't been important to me even before my memory became a problem.

He has two guests. One was a contestant on *The Biz* a few seasons after me, and modeled her look on mine. Now she's on TV stabbing me in the back to take my place. It takes me a few seconds to place the second guest. Twenty-something, black glasses. It's the host of the podcast. Don't Tell A Soul, the one focusing on me and Dave for their third season. I can't remember the host's name. Maybe I can. Dee? Dee something?

They've tried to contact me a bunch of times. Claiming they want my side of the story.

Yeah, right.

My photograph is on the screen, along with a caption underneath saying "Six Months On. LoJay. Killer?" There's a hashtag beneath it, #didshedoit?

LoJay. I hate that. It's a mashup of Louisa Jade, my first and middle names. Everyone else in the world these days has the right to decide how they identify themselves, what their own name or gender is, but once you're famous? Forget it. They own your identity.

Johnny isn't a great reader yet, so he won't know what the screen says, but I don't want to take any chances. I pick up the remote and turn it off. My hands shake. I've started having panic attacks lately.

A nice new complication to add to everything else. Sometimes I can feel them coming, and calm down before the worst of it kicks in. Other times all I can do is ride it out.

I close my eyes and breathe slowly. It doesn't help. The world closes in around me.

"We'll meet this guy," I say. "I need to do something."

And then, the other shoe drops.

The old itch.

Drugs.

They would solve all of this.

For just an hour, nothing else would matter.

Is that wrong?

FOUR

CON

"Didn't you used to have a thing for her?"

Ramona was playing with me. She knew the answer.

"Me and half the city."

Louisa Mantalos and David Ash had both been a big part of my life.

Louisa had been a contestant on *The Biz*, a show I had pretended not to watch. Young men and women who imagined themselves future tycoons, running around the city on a different task each week, competing for a large investment from the hotel mogul who hosted the show.

At thirteen, I got two things out of watching. On the one hand, it was a chance to see rich kids and arrogant Ivy League types get ritually humiliated. On the other, I got to see hot women in business suits. I was probably the exact demographic the producers had in mind. And Louisa was my favorite. The local girl, trying to make it. A single mother, running some kind of bakery business out of her parent's kitchen, while caring for both of them through illnesses. She would shout to be heard over the manicured voices, with a real Rockaway accent. A voice with something to prove.

It drove me crazy. I tuned in every week to see her taking on the trust funders who'd grown up with nannies and credit cards.

I wasn't alone.

Most of the city fell for her.

She came in second, losing out to a guy who was related to a congressman, and went on to host a business show on CNN, but it was Louisa who everyone remembered.

At first she did the circuit of the local stations, appearing on lifestyle segments to talk about food, music, whatever celebrity gossip people where caring about that day. She was given her own show, cooking large meals on a budget, showing the rest of us ways to get by, how to get the best ingredients, how to prepare food like a professional chef.

Somewhere along the way, Louisa started to change. She was wearing more makeup and posing in raunchier pictures. Playboy came calling. I still wasn't complaining. That issue might have been the only one I ever paid for. It was equal measure local pride and blood rush. I noticed the way the media talked about her started to shift, and there were always rumors about which clubs she would fall out of at 4am.

Then she met David Ash, and two separate strands of my teenaged life came crashing together. Ash had been the front man for my favorite band.

The Doormats.

They were a ragged group from Minneapolis and Brooklyn, with songs about beer, failure, and unrequited love. They released albums that almost crossed over into the mainstream and their songs became anthems of failure for mixed-up kids like me. Years later they evolved into the hipsters' band of choice, and everyone would pretend to have seen one of their original shows.

David Ash had always been destined for bigger things than the band. He launched a solo career while the band was on hiatus. Sell-out music, with all the rough edges sanded off. Layers of polish and gloss. He started to show up on TV soundtracks, and people who had never even heard of The Doormats were claiming him as their hero. And then he was hooking up with Louisa. The hip rock star and the mainstream celebrity. One magazine paid for the wedding photos, and another for the baby pictures. A news website didn't pay them anything to run a snap of Louisa doing drugs while pregnant.

The media storm that followed was enough to get the cooking show canceled.

Somewhere in there, it was also announced The Doormats had officially split. Fans blamed Louisa.

I did, too.

And then the whole city blamed her for Dave's death.

And again, so did I.

"I'm not the guy for this," I said to Ramona. "It's too big."

I help locals. Friends. Criminals. People with small-world problems. This was an open police case with media coverage.

"Nobody knows what happened." Ramona got her defense in before I could actually say no. "The cops didn't bother to look at any other suspects. The minute he was reported missing, everybody decided she was guilty. *Everybody.*" She paused, giving me a 'you too' look. Making me complicit. "Not one other lead has been followed up."

"Are there any? Other leads?"

She paused again. The long one that told me I wouldn't like what she said next. "I don't know. Nobody looked for them."

"You need a real PI for this. Someone with a license, office. Fedora. Voiceover. I don't even drink."

"What I need is you. She needs our help. Everyone's given up on her."

Ramona knew all the right buttons to press. I'm a sucker for a lost cause. I'd chosen Saint Jude for my confirmation name. I've never been sure if it counted as nominative determinism if you chose the name yourself, but the pattern was locked in. From the playground on up, I couldn't walk away from a fight with a bully.

Even still, Ramona was holding something back. A wise man once said there were only three certainties in life: death, taxes, and the ability of Ramona Cross and Constantin McGarry to see through each other.

"We tried real PIs on this one." She paused again. "They all said no."

"Why? Even if they find nothing, a case like this, they could make a fortune."

"A couple started to talk to us, then backed off. Isn't that weird? One of them said this was more than their license was worth. It's intimidation."

"From who?"

"The ADA, I think. Carl Waltz. He's applying a lot of pressure. It's bullying, pure and simple."

She was playing me perfectly. She pressed the advantage by leaning in closer, letting our shoulders touch.

"Help me out," she said. "You don't have a license to lose. Can't be pressured. We just need you to start looking. Try and find a sign. Anything. If there's something solid, we can get the cops to change their approach, maybe get the media off her back, and you get to raise your profile. Besides." She paused. Holding back the trump card for one more moment. "If nobody else wants the money…"

I raised my glass. "To lost causes and last resorts." I didn't add, *to a paycheck.*

FIVE

CON

Ramona said Louisa lived in a penthouse in the Meatpacking District, a clean and lifeless place to shop for craft beer, iPads, and high-end shoes. But she led me to a red brick walk-up on the corner of 8th Avenue.

"First," I said. "A building like this doesn't have a penthouse." I turned and pointed west. "And second, the Meatpacking District is over there."

"The boundaries are shifting," Ramona said, like, *what are you gonna do?*

"I remember when it was cool enough just to say someone lived in the Village."

"And cool to say you were arrested in the Village."

Ramona hit home with that one. I'd gone away for filling in as the getaway driver on a robbery over on MacDougal.

Ramona smiled as she pulled open the main door. "It's not even the top floor."

We climbed the stairs and Ramona rang the bell.

The door was opened by an attractive blonde. I recognized her from somewhere, but couldn't place it. Her hair was pulled back, showing a small brown mole at her temple. She was dressed mostly in white. It takes confidence to dress like that. It means she lives in a world without stains. Blondie looked me up and down then turned to Ramona. "This the guy?"

Ramona stepped between us and made a hasty introduction. "Con McGarry, Alison Oliver. Alison, Con."

I knew who she was now, and why it had taken me so long to place her.

Ally Oliver had been all over TV when I was a kid.

There was a series of Teen Agent films where she would get separated from her family in different location and solve crimes. She stopped a bank robbery in one, and foiled terrorists on a boat in another. I'm pretty sure the third involved a space station. She had a sitcom too. *Ally Tells It Like*

It Is. Back then she'd been a redheaded girl-next-door type with a big smile and cute freckles.

I offered my hand. Ally paused before taking it. I was getting the feeling she didn't want me there. She nodded back into the apartment behind her and said, "Come on in."

Ally led us into a large room, with windows lining two walls looking out onto the small park across 8th Avenue. A streetlight in front of the park was blinking. The exterior walls were bare brick, painted white to match the smooth interior. There were multi-colored post-it notes attached to the electrical appliances, like the TV and a games console.

There was a large sofa in the middle of the room, and Ally waved for us to sit down. She asked if I wanted anything to drink.

"Water. Just water, please."

Ally stepped out through a door opposite where we'd come in. I took a second look around. There was another sofa beneath the windows, and a large TV on a stand. There was an assortment of three or four coffee tables, and a dining table by the windows. I could see a few toys scattered around.

Ally came back in with two glasses of water. She handed one each to me and Ramona, then said, "She'll be with us in a minute."

"How's she doing?" Ramona said.

"Okay." Ally took a seat beside me. "It's not a great day today, but she wants to do this."

There was something I wasn't in on. They were talking as if Louisa was an elderly relative.

Ally spoke again before I could ask what was going on. "We looked you up."

That wasn't a good start. My own fifteen minutes of infamy.

The real key to making it as a criminal is to know your strengths. Stay in your lane. I'm good with my words and my hands. I've never liked guns and I'm a terrible driver. It's no surprise, really, that the one time I got behind the wheel of a getaway car in an armed robbery, I messed up and went down for it. Along with two of the three thieves.

A door opened behind us, and a star stepped into the room. That was my first thought when I saw Louisa.

She had *it.* The magic quality that draws in all attention. She moved with an ease I couldn't master with a lifetime of practice. Her dark clothes folded perfectly around her, clinging and billowing in all the right places. For a moment I was thirteen again, seeing her on TV for the first time. Then I was older, picking up the copy of Playboy. I pushed that one out of my mind.

I stood up to greet her and she took my hand before offering a cheek to kiss.

"Mr. McGarry?"

"Yeah, uh, Con."

"I'm Louisa."

She smiled at me, but up close I could see something was wrong. Those big brown eyes were holding something else. There was an uncertainty there. I saw a change. This time it looked more conscious. Putting her guard up.

"So, Con, did you do it?"

Wait, what?

"Wait, what?"

"We looked you up. Saw you did time. So, did you do it?"

Wasn't that supposed to be my line? I was standing in front of a woman suspected by just about everybody of killing her husband, but it was my guilt being questioned.

"Depends on who you ask," I said.

"Well, I'm asking you."

She gave me a small smile. Just enough to let me know she was testing me.

"Yes," I said. "I did it."

"Do you regret it?"

My head twitched, just a little, but enough for Ramona to notice it and turn to watch me. The robbery was the thing we'd never moved past. The one part of our past we never talked about.

I'd never really been asked that question. Sure, the parole meeting talked around it. I mentioned contrition. But in truth, my lawyer had done most of the heavy lifting in getting me out. I had never really needed to directly express any regret.

"I try not to dwell on the past." I said, and then aimed for something I hoped sounded cool. "I do regret getting caught."

Louisa cocked her head to one side and watched me for a

moment. She seemed to like that answer. "I know the feeling. So you were a getaway driver?"

"Just that once, usually I did other things."

Her eyes flashed. Interested. "Like what?"

"Lies, mostly."

Louisa repeated her line: "Tell me about it."

She motioned for me to sit down but seemed distracted, bending down to pick a toy up off the ground. A superhero. I saw uncertainty in her eyes again, and then she looked around the room.

"Sorry about the mess." Ally spoke loud. "The boys went to bed late."

"Yeah." Louisa's expression changed as she nodded along. "I'm too soft on them."

I took a chance while her guard was down.

"How about you, did you do it?"

She met my gaze without blinking.

"I don't know."

SIX

LOUISA

Truth is something I have to hand out in small portions. *Honesty* could destroy me.

"It's the drugs," I say. "My memory is all messed up."

Con nods. He doesn't look convinced, yet. He turns to Ramona. This is key. Ramona knows the truth, and we hadn't told her we would lie to Con.

Will she back us up?

Ramona gives Con an encouraging smile.

Just a few degrees above neutral. She's still making her mind up.

"How do you mean?" he says.

I go for an edited version. "I've always been forgetful. Numbers. Like money, dates. I've always had difficulty with them. But then a couple years ago we noticed I was getting clumsy. Falling over, losing my balance. Conversations I'd forget right away, or I'd leave the faucet running. Just little things, but they built up." I wait, give a nervous laugh. "Dave said I'd snorted my brain away. Then, I had, uh…"

Ally fills in my silence. "About eighteen months ago, they were on vacation. Louisa, Dave, the boys. Louisa had a small incident."

I remember the word I was looking for earlier.

Caregiver.

Ally is pretty much my caregiver.

I depend on her.

"I lost my temper. Over nothing. Like, it was about tissues on a table in a restaurant, or something. I've always had a temper, but not like this. For a minute, it was like I was a different person."

"Did you go to a doctor?"

"Yes." A half-truth. I have been diagnosed. "They confirmed it. I've damaged my short-term memory, my coordination skills, a whole bunch of things. Last week I saw one of my dad's favorite films on TV, and I picked up the phone to call him. And it was, it was like, I knew he wasn't around anymore, but I was still trying to call him."

"That must have hurt."

I stop. This is more than I want to give. Forgetting my daddy had passed? That's not a short-term memory issue. "So, when I say I don't know if I did anything to Dave, I really don't. The night he left is just... gone. I can see it's gone. I can see the day before it, and after, but the one I need is just a big blank space."

"Is that normal? For your condition, I mean?"

I look down at the floor for a second. Is this symptom normal for the condition I've totally made up? It's hard to stick to a lie when things in my own mind keep moving. "I don't know," I say. "I can't really ask anyone without giving away the secret."

"Why does it need to be secret? People would understand."

He's right, of course.

They probably would.

I laugh. I can hear the edge to it. The raw nerve. "It's gotten so big. I mean, you're right. I should have just admitted all of this up front. But I've been kicked around so many times by the media, you learn... I learned... to not give anyone anything. I want to be in control of my own story. And now, Dave's family, his parents? They think I killed him, and if they find out—"

He nods. "They'll take your kids. Okay. What about the cops, are they still on you?"

"There's this one. Elizondo. He's from the 6th Precinct, where I went to report Dave missing." I notice Con smiling. "What?"

"How can this town always be so small? He's the cop who arrested me." He's fully onboard now. We have a connection. "Okay. What do you think happened to David?"

"I really don't know. I didn't even think of it as a crime, not at first. I thought he'd split."

"What made you think that?"

I hold back on telling him the marriage was failing. It's something else I haven't gotten used to saying out loud. Another reality I keep trying to hold off with silence.

"Money," Ally says.

I nod. Yes. Good save. "We kept five thousand in the sock drawer. It was emergency money. When you're an ex, well, when two people have both had drug problems, having 'go money' is kind of a habit."

"And it's gone?"

"It went missing at the same time he did," Ally says. "We told the cops about it, but without any proof the money was there in the first place, they ignored it."

"And his guitar," I say. "He has this Les Paul Junior, it's from the fifties. He always used to joke, wherever he put it down, that was his home. And it's gone."

"So you think he's maybe just hiding out somewhere?"

"I hope so." I swallow. "I mean, it wouldn't make sense, would it? Someone would have heard from him by now. But it's better than-"

"Yeah. Okay. First thing anyone does is follow the money. You've said there was a stash, but how about the rest? I don't really know how money works for people in your... world."

Neither do I.

I thought it was something that would come with age. Adults always used to look so sure. But I've never figured it out. There was a moment, a couple years after I got famous, when the money was running out. I thought about getting a job, a normal job, in a call center.

But the thought of working for other people, I just couldn't do it. And the money turns up. Somehow. From somewhere. The money always just about turns up.

"Dave, me, we kept most things separate. His earnings go into his own accounts, mine go into mine. We have a family account in both our names, and we've always paid in an equal share, but since he went missing..."

"So his money is just piling up?"

"Yeah. Should be. I mean, I don't see any of it."

"But the police will have looked at it, and if he was withdrawing, somebody would have noticed." He pauses. Shares a look with Ramona. "But if I find out David is dead, that money comes to you."

"I know how it looks."

He shares another look with Ramona. "What's the last thing you do remember?"

"We argued. Over the phone. Just something silly. Another mood swing. He'd eaten some leftover pasta I'd been saving, I got really angry."

"This was on the day he disappeared?"

"Yeah. Like six or seven."

"Do you know where he was? When he called?"

"Said he was at the studio."

"Could he have taken the guitar there? To record?"

"Nobody there saw it, they all said he never took it in. We'd all taken it as a sign he wasn't enjoying the album, he wasn't taking in his baby to record the songs."

"I'll check out what they've said."

I look at Ally. She nods and says to Con, "It's in Greenpoint. I'll get you the address."

"I've got the details," Ramona says. She pats her bag for Con's benefit. "I'll show you the file."

Con turns back to me. He has a look I recognize from the police interviews. The Columbo expression. Just one more thing. "You mentioned mood swings. Ever get violent?"

"I was here that night," Ally says. "There was no violence. I've told the cops, too. Me and my boyfriend. We rented a movie online, streamed it, watched it here."

"Were you here when they argued?"

Ally waits a beat. "No. We came after."

"What time?"

"I don't know," Ally sounds frustrated. She does know, but we've been over this a dozen times with the cops, given them the whole timeline. "Seven-thirty? Eight?"

"How long did you stay?"

"The film, plus maybe three hours? We left around one. Got a cab."

Con nods. He's silent for a moment. His lips purse. Then, to Ally again, "Can I talk to your boyfriend?"

"I'll arrange that, but it's complicated."

"How?"

"He's married."

"Okay. Whenever you can figure it out, then. And you guys haven't hired anybody to look for David before?"

"We've tried. We tried hiring a PI, but nobody would help us."

I judge the last line right. It's the hook. I have nobody else, *please help.*

"Okay. So you don't remember whether you killed him, I believe you. But I need to know what you think." He stares straight into my eyes. "Do you think you did it?"

I meet the stare. "No."

Con pauses before he speaks, but I can tell he's already in. "If this turns into something else, like if the cops find anything on you, I'll need to walk away. I can't risk getting caught up in something, with my record."

"Of course."

Con stands up. We all rise with him.

I give him a hug, and say thank you.

I sit back down on the sofa and look at the plastic thing in my hand while Ally walks Con and Ramona to the door. After they've gone, she comes back to sit next to me.

"What do you think?"

"I think he almost fell over when you walked in the room." Ally waits a beat before adding, "What happens when he realizes we've lied to him?"

SEVEN

CON

"This is the last place he was seen," Ramona said, pointing. "Right out there."

We were in a bar on the corner of 8th and West 12th. Sitting on high stools in the window, looking out onto the street. The area was full into the swing of Friday night. This bit of town shows off its diversity during the day, with local kids playing in the parks, but goes full-on hipster at night. The room behind us was full of young people ordering cocktails named with so many levels of irony that they formed a black hole. The space where irony used to be.

Ramona paused to check a message on her phone. She smiled and typed out a reply, before turning her attention back to me. She slipped a leather folio onto the black table, opened it, and started leafing through papers.

"He showed up on three cameras."

"Ash."

"Yeah, here's the first. It's from out front of a restaurant in Greenpoint."

Ash was standing across the road, opening the back door of a cab. There was a nondescript redbrick wall behind him, with a darker storefront at the edge of the frame.

"This one is from the Williamsburg bridge. Same cab."

The yellow cab was passing by the camera, and a figure could been seen in the back, in profile. The image was too dark and grainy to make out details.

"This is the one you'll have seen," Ramona said, tapping the third picture. "It's the one the press have, taken right out there at the curb."

Ash getting out of the cab, with this bar in the background of shot.

I looked from the picture to the curb and back again. "And from here?"

"Nothing. He didn't make it back up to the apartment, but didn't go anywhere else. Cops canvassed the whole area, I've seen the records. They checked all the businesses, looked at security cameras. There's a lot of them around here. But this is the only time he showed up."

That would have been hard work.

"Like he wanted to disappear," I said.

Louisa had me all mixed up. I'd gone into the meeting already believing the gossip. She'd killed him, and the whole world was watching her get away with it.

And yet—

There was something else there.

An extra level. She'd trusted me with private information. A secret about the damage done to her memory. Why would she do that if she'd been lying about Ash? Why would she hire me to find a missing person, if she knew there was no chance he could be found?

I used to be a conman. I guess I always will be, deep down. Playing on people's ego, on their confidence, their assumptions. One of the oldest tricks in the book was telling someone a small truth to blind them to a bigger lie.

And yet—

Those big brown eyes.

So familiar to me from years of seeing them on TV screens. I want to believe them.

I don't want to think she's capable of lying.

Con, are you being fooled by those eyes?

"You're thinking about Louisa," Ramona said. She moved in close, without touching me, almost a nudge. "I knew it."

"Knew what?"

These are the games we play.

"You still like her," she grinned. "It's why you're taking the case."

"I'm taking the case because you're paying me. What about you?"

"Same."

"But why? The thing I don't get is how, why you, and why me? Two stars like that? They can throw a stone in any direction and find a celebrity lawyer. A licensed PI. How did they pick you?"

"Obviously for my mad skills."

"Sorry."

"I know. And you're right. I asked the same thing, back when Ally first hired me. She said Louisa wanted someone from back home."

"You buy that?"

"Not really. I think, and this is cone of silence, right? I think Ally likes to be in control. And I think hiring a small-time lawyer like me, that lets her feel like she's still the biggest part in all this."

"I could tell she doesn't like me."

"She'll come around."

"And she's got her own lawyer, right?"

"Yeah, met him a couple times. I can set up a meet, if you need it."

"Just wondering, if she already had one of her own, why not just get him to take on Louisa?"

Ramona's phone buzzed again. I noticed how quickly she turned to it.

"Who's that?"

"Nobody," she said.

Her tone told me the opposite.

This was *definitely* somebody.

I had no right to feel hurt. My rush of jealousy was completely out of line. Ramona and I hadn't been an item in years. We had separate lives. Her work was really the only way we came together now, aside from the occasional night when she would turn up at Sharkey's for a drink. Her private life was her own, whether I was part of it or not.

I changed the subject. "Can we get his financials? A man can't go six months without touching his bank account, so if he's alive, there'll be something there. If he's dead, maybe we'll see something from before he died. A trail."

"Difficult. The cops have them, but they don't need to hand anything over at this stage. And with Ash not officially dead, there's not much I can do about accessing them."

"I'll sort it."

There were options. I had a few friends who were good at hacking bank accounts, and other forms of personal information. But the less I said to Ramona, the better. She was bound by her job. An officer of the court.

I waited a beat as she decided to let that one go. Then continued with: "Do you have Louisa's financials?"

"Yeah. A lot of it, anyway. Wanted to cover all bases. Anything I thought was relevant to the case."

"One last thing." I leaned in, saying it like Columbo. She smiled. "You said the ADA is applying pressure. What kind?"

"Threats. I mean, not threats, you know. But his office keeps making it clear they want this done. Anyone I've used for help, they back off after contact from the ADA's office. I think maybe Louisa had that problem before me, too. Other lawyers she tried. Everyone decides the trouble isn't worth it."

"Why is he applying the pressure?"

"I guess he's confident in the case."

"If he was confident in the case, it would have been closed six months ago."

She nodded, sighing. "Yeah. He's just such a hard ass now. He used to be fine, I met him a few times, he was okay. After his son passed away…"

"I remember that. Suicide, right?"

"Yeah, it's a shame. So many young guys these days. I guess something like that, it changes you. He's been crazy about the job since then, really going for it."

I picked up the third picture. Ash had gone missing on this block, on a busy Friday night, six months before. Short of hopping in a time machine, this was the closest we could get to recreating the moment. I motioned for Ramona to keep our seats, and headed out onto the sidewalk with the picture.

Standing in the same spot as Ash, I could see people all around. Passers-by. Shoppers. Diners. Drinkers. Ash would have been visible to at least a hundred people, maybe more. The street was full of cars, which added to potential witnesses. The cops would have canvassed as many as possible, in theory. But, if Ramona and Louisa were right, they'd pre-judged what had happened. Maybe they hadn't put in the necessary legwork.

One thing the movies always get wrong is the idea of crusading cops who bend the rules to set someone up and close a case. That's way more effort than anyone wants to put in on any job. Cops, like everyone else, play a numbers game. Time versus money. They have targets to meet. Reviews to sit through. Assessments. Save your ass from cutbacks, protect your 401(k). Go for the easiest options. If a case isn't working out, find one that will.

Ramona's job should be easy enough, playing by those rules. Just stall the case long enough, make it just too inconvenient, and the cops move on.

Except the case found its way to a worrier like Elizondo. He's the exception you get in all jobs, the one who can't let anything go. He doesn't stop. If any other cop in the office had pulled my case, I wouldn't have been caught. But not Elizondo. He worried away at the facts until he made me for the crime, and it sounded like he was doing the same to Louisa.

But I was guilty.

Was that the difference here?

If Louisa was innocent, Elizondo wouldn't set her up. He wasn't that guy.

But why would the ADA be taking such an interest? Unless they were sure there was something here. But if they were sure...

Neither side of this made sense.

Back inside, I called the server over. She looked to be in her early twenties, with a permanent smile hinting at deep boredom. "Hey, how long you been working here?"

"Started at twelve."

"No, I mean, in total. How long you had this job?"

She took a step back and tilted her head. It wasn't a defensive gesture, more of a confused move, a question she hadn't expected. "About a year, I think. Why?"

"Were you working here November 11th?"

"That's an odd...I don't know."

I gave her some help. "The night David Ash disappeared."

She was still smiling, but I could see the wall going up. "Why?"

I needed to pick the best lie. It was a skill. Say the right thing, and she'd give me what I needed; say the wrong thing, and I'd never get anything more. I took a look at Ramona. She was dressed exactly like a cheap lawyer. I'm an unlicensed part-time PI. Nobody's going to be impressed by us.

I leaned in closer to talk quietly, keeping this on the down low. "We're researching for a podcast,"

Her eyes flashed. "*Don't Tell A Soul?*"

"*Don't* tell a soul, okay? We're looking into the murder of David Ash."

I leaned on murder. Wanted to see the reaction. Did she agree? Had she seen anything to make her push back?

"Wish I'd seen something," she said. "Oh my god. That show. I love Dee, they're so cool. The one about Watergate, did you listen to that? I tried the one on Manson but it got too grisly." She paused, remembering the question. " I was off that night. Nuno was working. He talked to the cops, but he's off tonight."

"When's he due in?"

"Monday, I think."

I thanked her and headed back outside with Ramona. We stood on the spot from the photograph again. This was where David Ash had slipped off the planet. I was willing the concrete to tell me something. Anything.

"Can you stop her losing the kids?"

Ramona hesitated. "I don't know."

EIGHT

CON

I caught the L to Greenpoint to start retracing Ash's last steps.

Headspace Recording Studio was on the end of Greenpoint Avenue, next to Transmitter Park. It was a square building with a view across the river to the towers of a Con-Ed plant.

There were no signs on the front. Just a plain brick wall with garage shutters on the ground floor and windows up above. One of the shutters was raised up high enough to walk under. The second one was down, with 'no parking' painted on it. A black van was sitting there defiantly, with two guys on the back, smoking joints. I recognized one of them as the bass player from a local indie rock band. I nodded a greeting as if I had a reason to be there, then headed inside.

I found a large open reception area, with doors at the back and crates stacked along the sides. A tall black kid was sifting through a box of cables.

"The boss in?"

I had no idea who the boss was, but the kid didn't know that. He looked up at me for a second, playing the game in his mind of whether I was someone he should recognize from the scene. "Uh, yeah. Main studio."

I walked through the first door, into a narrow hallway lined with framed albums.

I followed the sounds of a musical instrument being tuned up. I pushed through a door to find three people sitting in a studio space.

A short guy with curly brown hair was hunched over a mixing desk, and another member of the band was tooling around with an accordion. He was playing the same notes repeatedly, and I recognized it as part of a familiar song.

There was a wiry guy facing the musician, with his back to me. It looked like they'd been in conversation, but turned as I walked in. The musician wore a crumpled trilby and had a close-shaved beard. The slim guy's face was pulled tight into a gaunt expression.

"Help you?" Slim said.

"I was looking for whoever's in charge."

I didn't offer a name or reason. The basics of being a private investigator were the same as being a conman. Use people's attitude against them. His reaction would tell me what kind of a guy he was, and what approach I needed.

He straightened. "I'm the producer."

There was attitude there, but it looked fragile. He was an arty type who liked to project authority, but he would cave to emotion if I challenged him. I could picture his face flushing red as he tried to push back against anyone who didn't go along with what he said.

"My name's Con, I'm-"

"Oh you're the guy." I swear he almost rolled his eyes at me. "Ally called."

Damn. I'd wanted to meet people on my own terms, figure out the best way to get information from each of them. If Ally had tipped everyone off, they had a chance to get their defenses up and straighten out their stories.

"Where you here when-"

"No, it was Joss. Dave didn't think I was good enough for his album."

Just like that, the conversation was over. He stepped over to the music desk and started asking the curly haired guy about the levels.

The musician smiled at me. "Zeke's still sore about Joss getting the gig, don't worry about it." He lifted the instrument's straps off his shoulders and set it down on a sofa beside us. "I played on Dave's album. He was doing some good stuff."

"It was recorded here, wasn't it?"

He nodded before answering. His expression was friendly, but the wheels were turning on whether to trust me.

"Sorry." I offered him my hand. "My name's Con McGarry, I'm an investigator."

"Franz." His grip was strong. Fingers hard from years of guitar strings. "Yeah, Zeke told us you'd be over. Hope you can find out what happened to him."

"How did he seem to you, before he went missing?"

"Worked up. Excited. But I was only in for two days doing some tracking, so I don't know what he was like the rest of the time."

"This Joss, is he around?"

"No. Last I heard, he was working on the Faulkner Detectives album, they're over at Soundworks. I think."

"Is there anyone I could talk to about the day he went missing? Anyone who would have been here?"

Franz nodded to the mixing desk and called out, "Nik, did you do all the sessions for Dave Ash?"

Nik, the curly haired guy, answered without turning. "Yeah." He pushed a few faders on the soundboard then waited for Zeke to utter an agreement to the changes before speaking again. "While he was here, anyway."

Zeke turned to leave the room.

"While he was here?"

Nik turned to face me. His eyes were lazy and unresponsive. He was blind, operating the board by sound and touch.

"He wasn't doing the whole record here," Nik said. "He was supposed to. Put a whole backing band together, rehearsed the songs. Then, I don't know, he changed his mind. Fired the players, started going for a different sound."

"And he was recording somewhere else?"

"Yeah. Showing up with pre-recorded tracks, things he'd written and cut at this other place, and getting Franz to add layers."

"But he was here on the night? November 11th?"

"No." His tone was clear. Unwavering. "Like I told the cops, he wasn't here on the 11th."

"But he was on camera."

I regretted saying it right away. As much as it was true, it still felt tactless to mention the security footage to a blind guy.

"I've been told," he grinned. "Down on the corner, yeah. But he wasn't in here, so I don't know what he was doing."

"Louisa said this is where he called from."

"Yeah," Nik bobbed his head. "I know. Believe me. We checked the logs, to make sure I didn't forget, but he definitely wasn't here."

I thought back to what Louisa had said. There had been no mention of the studio's name, he could have been calling from a different one. The place he'd been working up the songs.

"Do you know what other studio he was using?"

"Nope. He didn't say, I didn't ask."

"You said you checked logs? But I didn't sign in when I came here, so what would you be checking?"

His patience was wearing thin. "We keep records of any work done." Nik turned back to face the faders. I saw his fingers twitching, waiting to get back to work. "Recording. Individual tracks. Dates and times. We have a record of everything we do here, and Dave wasn't in that whole week."

I had the feeling there was more there.

Were they protecting Ash? Probably. But it could be nothing more than a professional code of silence, not wanting to share Ash's business with an outsider. I wouldn't be able to get to it straight on, I'd need to find another way.

The kid who had been sorting through the cables appeared to have given up in a fit of anger. The box was on its side, and the contents were strewn across the floor. He was standing outside smoking a rolled-up cigarette.

I walked over and nodded a greeting. "Losing the fight?"

"Yeah." He spoke calmly. He was a big guy, and I imagined he'd grown used to managing people's expectations, speaking quietly to avoid being tagged as aggressive.

I offered him a handshake. "Con."

"Jayar."

He relaxed. Introducing myself was the tipoff that I wasn't famous. Jayar didn't need to worry about not recognizing me. His accent wasn't local, but he'd lost any regional edge to tell me where he was from originally.

"You're the detective, right?"

Dammit. "Zeke told you?"

"Yeah. Told everyone."

"Still got you doing the cables?"

"Yeah," he said it with a snort. "They treat the intern better than me."

"They never change."

He snorted again, and followed it with, "Been here for two hours already, I'll be here an hour after everyone's done. Never even get mentioned in liner notes."

This was good. He felt slighted. All I needed to do was show some interest in him. "When did you start here?"

"Oh, like a year ago?" There were some hints of California in his voice for the first time. "Nine months maybe."

The bass player walked past, and I nodded, saying "hey," as if we were old friends. Then to Jayar: "I bet he doesn't even remember your name."

He gave me a look that said, I know, right?

"They could sound so good, if Nik would let me at the desk. He keeps saying it's the mics in the room, but they're in the right place. He's just letting Zeke have too much say on the mix. Just five minutes. All I'd need."

"Nik was telling me about the work he was doing on Dave's album."

He shook his head. Smiled, can you believe this? "Total mess. They talked him into hiring this whole band. I think they just wanted to trick him into making something like a Doormats album. He wasn't happy with it."

"He tell you that?"

"Yeah." He was warming to the subject. I'd hit a vein. He wanted to make sure I knew he was friends with the rock star. "He was writing good stuff, but it needed to be tight, like claustrophobic? Moody. Atmospheric. Not a full band thing."

"What was he writing about?"

"Addiction, I think. You could tell he was struggling."

Jayar motioned for me to follow him. We walked through to a small room at the back, where he went through a pile of paperwork and CDs on a desk. He handed me a disk with "*D.A. MIX*" written on it in sharpie.

"I tried remixing them after everyone went home. Give 'em a listen."

I felt sorry for this kid. He was trying to make it in New York, but he was learning to resent the people he worked with while trusting a stranger who walked in off the street. He was going to get eaten alive. I pocketed the disc without putting him right. I'm not a fool.

"You said he was struggling?"

Jayar nodded. "Yeah. He was back on the stuff."

"When was the last time you saw him?"

"The night he went missing," he said.

"He was here?"

"Nah. Zeke was here, hanging out with his girlfriend and Joss. Dave wasn't in the mood, headed to the Star."

There was a bar one block over, called Dark Star Lounge. It had blacked out windows and a big red sign above the door. Perfect place for musicians to hang out if they wanted to stay out of sight.

"Did you tell the cops about this?"

"I didn't talk to them," he said. "Nobody listens to me."

I thanked Jayar and headed up the block. The bar was on the corner of West Street and Greenpoint Avenue. I looked in through the door, but it was full of customers and the music was loud. Two bartenders were on. I didn't want to head in without a plan. Ally calling ahead had made things difficult. If there was any chance people inside the bar were expecting me, I might run into more brick walls.

The bar could wait.

I checked my email. Ramona had sent me copies of the photographs. The building behind Ash, in the first picture, looked the same as the one next to the Dark Star Lounge. I took a few paces along the sidewalk, until I was standing in the same spot as Ash, and spotted the camera across the street, above a closed restaurant.

The place looked like it had been out of business for a few months. This was the spot. His last known journey started right here.

I had the feeling I was being lied to. That was fine. It was the second rule of life in the criminal lane. *Everybody lies.* Big lies. Small lies. Innocent lies. Guilty lies. We all do it. Every time you meet someone for the first time, there is some form of performance going on. We don't walk round telling the truth.

The trick was spotting the important lies.

And I wasn't there yet. I needed to know more.

NINE

LOUISA

In moments like this, I hate my parents.

And miss them like hell.

They were always there for me. Encouraged me. My mom was the disciplinarian. Mary Mantalos kept me in line with harsh words and strict lessons. But she always did it with love. She wouldn't pick me up when I fell over, because she knew I could be better. I could do better. I would walk a million miles just to try and earn her approval, and life never felt better than those small moments when she would give me a nod or a smile. And after she started to change, when her mood swings became more severe, and her words grew more cruel, there would still be those breaks in the cloud. On her death bed, after her illness had taken away so much of the person I knew, I still wanted the small gestures.

My pappi, Stav Mantalos, was the gentle touch. He would always tell me he loved me. His words would be the soothing cream to the harsher lessons. His strong hands were the ones that would pick me up when Mom wasn't looking. He taught me to bake, and installed a larger oven in the kitchen for me to start my business. His heart was so big, it could float away like a balloon. Without his wife to keep him tethered to the ground, it had only been a matter of time before he did just that. He passed in his sleep three months later.

They're in a better place. Looking down on me, getting the kitchen ready.

The relationship never changes. From when you're a small child looking up to hold their finger, to when you're nursing them through the last days, you never stop looking to them for answers or approval.

And they're both gone when I need them most.

I hate them for that.

I miss them for that.

I miss Dave's parents, too.

In a different way.

They're still around, but they hate me now. They used to like me. Or they pretended they did. I should be able to lean on them now, send the boys round to stay when I need time off. Dave bought them a nice house over in Jersey, so they cpould be near when we needed them.

Should be able to, but can't.

They'd never give them back. I'd get a letter, some kind of summons or demand, and that would be that, my children stolen away from me by handing over paperwork.

Or friends.

I remember them. Friends. A thing I used to have plenty of, now none. Only Ally. Basically in the whole world, only Ally.

She left not long after Ramona and Con. She always offers to stay, but I don't want her to. I know, soon enough, I'll need to have someone around me all the time. I watched it happen to my mother. But I'm not there yet. I'm still me, and I want to hold onto me for as long as I can.

The door buzzes. It'll be my prescription delivery. Usually I let Ally deal with it. She's set up an account under another name at the Duane Reade. But I lost track of my pills, and I was running low, called in a delivery.

A small Asian man holds out my package when I open the door. He nods curtly, doesn't mention my name. I hand over the tip and he's on his way.

I open up the bag and find my medication, but more importantly the pack of smokes I'd asked them to throw in.

I haven't touched a cigarette since I stopped doing drugs. I cleaned up everything at the same time.

But god, with all that's going on, I need this one thing. Just this. The one vice. I already know cancer's not going to kill me, so what the hell?

That thought makes me laugh.

Hey, I'm one of the lucky ones.

I know what's going to kill me. I know how. I have a rough idea of when.

Louisa 1. Everyone else 0.

Petey and Johnny are asleep. They'll be okay alone for five minutes. I pull the door shut behind me and go up to the roof. There's a small terrace only people who live in the building can access. Dave and I used to love coming up here, when we still loved doing anything. It was a joke that only we were in on, sitting here, underneath the sun or the stars, doing whatever we wanted, while people down on the street couldn't see us. I could stay out of sight tonight, but if I lean on the railing, I can look down at the lights coming from my apartment. It feels like I'm checking on my boys, somehow.

I light up and suck the smoke in. First I taste the chemicals. My throat feels scratched as I hold it. Then my lungs grab at it, and the soft buzz hits my brain, and oh, yeah, I needed this.

Daddy hated me smoking. He caught me doing it once, and tried the trick of telling me to smoke the whole pack in front of him. I did. It was great. He was worried . So many of my friends were giving in to drugs, or boozing too hard. But he never saw me at my worst.

Both of my parents were spared that.

I didn't see it in the moment. I was too busy having fun and drinking. Learning all about the great advances in science for things I could snort, smoke, or rub on my gums. But maybe if the hacks had taken a moment to do their jobs, and to see how soon it was after my parents had died, maybe if they'd pulled the cameras back instead of pushing them in….

Never mind.

What's done is done.

There might come a time when I don't remember my parents. There were so many days near the end when my mom didn't know who I was. There was always a love there, always the feeling I was important, but she didn't know why. I know, at some point, this thing that's eating away at my mind will make me forget that they're dead. Deep down, there's a bit of me that looks forward to that. To the certainty that comes from knowing there are people above you, who know how the world works.

I crane my neck to look down 8th Avenue, imagining I can see all the way to the spot where Dave was dropped off by the taxi. The last place the world saw him. What was he doing? Where did he go? Why didn't he come back up and watch the movie with us?

I feel something. Dave used to call it my *celebrity sense*.

I'd always tell him, no, it's my *woman* sense. The survival mechanism that can tell the difference between someone taking a casual look at me in the street, or staring just too long. It's tingling away at me now. In my peripheral vision I catch a shape across the road. The dark outline of someone standing down the street, beneath the blinking light in front of Jackson Square.

Not walking.

Not moving.

Standing.

Watching.

But what am I, from down there? In the dark, maybe a stranger would see the glow of the cigarette. But it would need to be someone who knows what they're looking for.

His face isn't clear, buried beneath a hat and a shadow cast by the streetlight, but something about the stance is familiar.

Black T-shirt.

Scruffy hair.

Wallet chain.

Dave?

Jack?

Why did I think that name? Who is Jack? It feels like there's someone in there, in my memories. But they trip me up so often now. Jack? Who that even be? I turn to face the figure. It looks so much like Dave. I bolt, taking the back stairs. It's an exit I've used many times, bringing me out through a metal gate on the corner, away from the front door where the paparazzi like to gather. There's nobody around tonight. The door gate shuts behind me.

I turn the corner, to face the streetlight across the road.

There's nobody there.

TEN

CON

"Bet you she did it," Frank said. "Hundred bucks."

He set a glass of Malbec down on the counter in front of Ramona before topping up my Coke. I'd never been much of a drinker. I'd seen the damage it can do close up, on Frank's brother, Liam. He never met a mistake he couldn't make, and alcohol was his crutch. In my old life, it paid to have a clearer head than everyone else. To be able to think quicker, concentrate on what I was saying. Keep the lies straight. My time in prison had soured me to booze further. My stomach still turned at the memory of the hooch, pruno and bootleg cans.

Ramona put her hands up. "I'm out, obviously."

"What's going on, Frank, you want to take an interest in my cases now?"

"Well, this one's different."

"This one's famous, you mean."

"Well." He busied himself wiping down the clean counter.

"So you think she's a killer, but because she's a star, it's better than when I help an innocent friend?"

He stopped wiping. "When was the last time one of your friends was innocent?"

"Hey." Ramona put her hand up like she was in school, looking for attention.

"You don't count," Frank said. "You're a lawyer."

That was Frank's way. He would talk trash about authority figures, and always claimed not to trust cops, lawyers, or politicians, but still resented me for not playing by the rules.

"Your mother likes that podcast, they're covering the story," he said. "She'll be excited about this one."

"How do you guys know about the podcast?"

"We're old," Frank said, "Not dead. Your mom likes to listen to them when she goes for her walks. And besides," he slapped a piece of paper on the counter, it had a name and number written on it. "The kid who hosts it called for you."

"How do they already know I'm involved?"

"Don't tell her," Ramona ignored my question, getting back to the topic of my parents. "This is supposed to be a secret."

"Don't tell her yet," I said. The half-measure. "Let me get a feel for it first."

"My feel is a hundred on guilty. Come on. I won't tell your mom about the case, if you don't tell her I'm gambling."

I wasn't ready to take the bet.

Was David Ash dead? Or was he holed up somewhere, trying to cover his tracks? Had Louisa lied to me? If not, why had the cops been so sure she was guilty? If she was playing me, then she was fooling Ramona, too.

But Ramona wasn't the best judge of character. She'd been in love with me once.

I offered Frank thirty.

He counted three tens out onto the bar, and I matched them. He took the bills and slipped them in the cash register, beneath the drawer.

"What will you spend your winnings on?" Frank said. "I think I'll buy a good whiskey, something from the home country."

Frank was Queens born and raised. The closest he'd ever been to the *home country* was singing rebel songs when he was drunk.

"I'll buy a swimming pool for my hamster," I said.

Ramona snorted. "You don't have a hamster."

"I'll buy a hamster, to go with the swimming pool. This is America." I took the chance to change the subject. "Maybe I could buy something for your sister. Her baby's due soon, right?"

"Any time now," Ramona said.

Frank beamed and patted the bar. "Congratulations."

"I didn't do anything," Ramona said. "I'm not sure I'm ready to be an aunt. Babies freak me out."

"Come on." Frank stretched out the words. "You'll be great."

"I don't know. They can't talk, they just make a mess. I'll check back in when he gets interesting."

I saw a chance to keep the conversation away from the case. "Were you attacked by a baby once or something?"

She glared at me. "Don't even joke about that."

We sipped in silence for a few beats. Letting the jokes rest. Sometimes you can just tell when a conversation is about to turn serious again, and none of us wanted to rush it.

Once she was ready, Ramona said, "What's your next move? Going to talk to Reah?"

Reah Kanellis.

The head of a local crime family.

Frank shook his head, sighed, and moved away down the bar to get back his paperwork. The Kanellis name wasn't as powerful as it used to be. Back in Frank's day, they'd controlled half of Queens. Reah was still important in Astoria, and I'd worked for her when I was a teenager. She'd encouraged me, partnered me up with mentors who developed my skills, turned me into the conman I became. Frank blamed Reah for all my bad choices. In truth, deep down, I think he felt I'd chosen her over him.

Since getting out of prison I'd avoided visiting Reah. My detective work hadn't strayed into her business, and I wanted to keep it that way.

But I'd found myself standing outside her shop on more than one occasion, at night, staring up at the second floor windows where she kept her office, trying to decide whether to step inside. Go back in time. From the news reports, I knew Louisa had close ties with Reah too. At some point the investigation might take me there, but I hoped not.

After reading from silence that an answer wasn't coming, Ramona slid off the stool, heading for the restroom.

A table full of drunks turned to watch as she passed by. They were new faces. The bar was quiet, with only a few regulars dotted about the place, but these guys had been in for the comedy show, and stayed to get wasted. They were talking loud, cracking terrible jokes. I could see Frank was keeping an eye on them.

He smiled at me, both of us thinking the same thing.

"He's definitely dead," Frank said.

"Ash?"

"Dead. He's in the foundations of a Starbucks or something."

"Is that how you'd do it? A building site?"

"There was a guy in here last week, said he used to work at the zoo. Bronx, I think. He said they covered up a few deaths every year."

"You're making that up."

"No. Well, maybe he was. But he said they'd get a few crazies climbing into the grounds after dark. Fetishes, wackos. They'd climb in with the animals, and if it was a lion, or a bear, well."

"It wouldn't be pretty." I took a sip of my drink and tried not to picture the scene.

"This guy said if the news got out, there would be charges, civil suits, and the animals would have to be killed. It would be the Harambe thing all over again. So the zoo just makes the whole mess go away."

"You're getting ideas for how to deal with drunks in here, aren't you?"

Frank grinned. Ramona came back carrying her phone. She made a show of checking her sports watch. "I'm turning in." She checked her screen. "My ride's here."

Ramona picked up her jacket and bag and blew Frank a kiss.

"Hey, is this your new man?" I aimed for sounding casual, but even to my own ears it was edgy.

"Maybe." She gave me a slow smile. "But you stay here."

She pushed out through the door. I heard a car open and close, and the engine revved. My hand tightened around the glass, and Frank smiled.

"What?"

"You want to know? Why don't you ask her?"

"None of my business."

He smiled again.

I waited until the sound of the car had faded into the distance and called it a night myself. There were two cars waiting at the lights down the block. The brake lights and evening darkness combined to blur the details, but one was red and the other silver. I tried not to wonder if Ramona was in one of them. The lights changed to green, and both pulled away.

The first punch caught me unawares.

I saw the second one coming, but it still took me off my feet.

The dark shape loomed over me.

My vision blurred for a second. First I focused in on the fists, then on the huge shoulders powering them. The person between the two shoulders appeared to be a sasquatch squeezed into a dark jacket and ski-mask. His frame blocked off the street light from half a block down.

I heard someone across the street shouting.

Sasquatch stepped in and kicked me. Hard.

I heard more shouting. Somewhere in there was Frank's voice. I looked past the giant's legs and saw Frank moving toward us at something approaching a run, carrying his baseball bat. Sasquatch bent down and grabbed my neck. Or, I think he was aiming for my neck, but he got a mix of my shoulder and the lapel of my jacket. It hurt just as much.

"Back off Ash."

He spat the words at me before taking off at high speed. He was surprisingly fast for a big guy, but then, they do say that about Bigfoot.

PART TWO

"I make you richer, every day.
I make you richer, you just make me pay."
-The Doormats

 **TRANSCRIPT**

Episode Two: The Appearance of David Ash

Audio Clip: Hot Take ident.

Ad: *Don't Tell A Soul is part of the Hot Take network. For more information visit hottake.com and subscribe to Hot Take Plus to hear all our shows with ads and plugs removed.*

Audio Clip: Interview: *"Yeah, you know... David was the last person we would ever have thought would become a rock star."*

Audio Clip: Interview: *"Thing with Dave was, you could always tell. Always. The minute you met him, this guy is going to be a rock star."*

Theme tune plays.

Dee: Hi, I'm Dee Buana. This is Don't Tell A Soul, the podcast about secrets, lies, and the truths we think we know.

Theme tune fades out.

Dee: This episode was the most fun to do. This is me talking now. Dee from the future. Or the present. Whatever. This is confusing. This is me *now*, where we all know how this mystery turned out. I want to take a minute to thank you all for the feedback.

On the first two seasons, all the episodes were edited and ready before the first one was released. This time, with the... well, you know... everything, I'm editing this episode now, a few days after the first one dropped. And mostly, you're all being incredibly generous. It feels like this is group therapy, maybe?

We all followed the story, and we all still have questions about what happened, and we need to talk about the hurt.

I'm seeing the criticisms, too. And I'm listening.

To the people who think I'm being exploitative, that this is wrong, and it's all in poor taste... I hear you, you know? I think anyone involved in true crime podcasts has to think about these issues all the time. And this case is extra weird, with me getting involved in the story.

I guess... I don't know what the rules are here.

But keep your thoughts coming in, and I'll address all of this in a future episode. Maybe we can figure it all out together.

Full disclosure, I had a lot of fun recording this one. I remember it. I'd not really been aware of David Ash or the Doormats before the news broke about his disappearance, so it seemed like the best place to start, learning his history, trying to figure out who he was. And while I was doing it, I got to forget he was missing, for a few moments in each interview, and feel like I was recording some kind of rock biography.

It was the most fun. The *most* fun.

But that brings a curse with it. This extra emotion I'd not expected. For everything we now know, there's an extra sadness hidden away in here, too.

But I had no way of knowing that at the time. I listen to this person talk, this slightly younger version of me, and think, are they a different person?

Theme tune fades in.
Theme tune fades out.

Dee: It's impossible to dislike David Ash's parents.

Living on a quiet and leafy street in Upper Monclair, you could mistake Phillip and Bethany Ash for retired teachers. In fact, it wouldn't be a mistake. Phillip taught at community college and Bethany taught high school English for thirty years. They welcome me in with a smile and cookies. Bethany looks a lot like her son. The slightly elfin features that took the edge off his rock persona. I see David in Phillip's smile.

An older version, worn down by the worry.

I wasn't sure what I'd find when I contacted them.

The parents of musicians always seem to fall into three groups. Overbearing, absentee, or abusive. At least, that's what I thought. And that's before taking into account the circumstances. Meeting them to talk about a son who has been missing for six months.

Bethany does most of the talking. Phillip drifts in and out, making eye contact occasionally, just enough to stay in the room with us, but rarely adding to the conversation.

Dee: Tell me about David as a boy.

Bethany: Oh, you know. He was shy. I think he took after Phil a lot at that age, he didn't like to say much, was more interested in doing things.

Dee: What kind of things?

Bethany: Climbing things. Breaking things. He wasn't very patient, if you said we'd do something later, he would just go and do it now. I remember – do you remember the treehouse, Phil?

Phillip nodded.

Bethany (Contd): He wanted a treehouse. One of his friends had one, so he just came home one day and said he wanted one. And Phil, Phil's always been good with his hands, he said they could make one together the next day, the weekend. Later on, we noticed we hadn't seen David for a few hours. We looked out the back, and he was sat in the tree, in a big cardboard box he'd found somewhere, carried it up, balanced it on two strong branches. He was just smiling at us, like he'd won.

Phillip: Fell out of that tree.

Bethany: Later on, yes. Broke his arm, was it that summer?

Phillip: I cut the tree down.

Bethany: That's right, yeah. I forgot that.

Dee: Because he fell?

Phillip: It blocked the light to our kitchen.

Bethany: It was because David fell, really.

Dee: How early did you know he was going to be a musician?

Bethany: Yeah, you know... David was the last person we would ever have thought would become a rock star. He was just so shy as a boy.

Phillip: He was always a writer.

Bethany: Yes, I knew he'd be a writer. He got my interest in books and stories.

Dee: But not a singer?

Bethany: There just wasn't anyone in our family for him to look to. None of us were musical. He'd spend hours in the basement and later on we learned he was practising guitar.

Phillip: That's how he got over the shyness. He just got really good in private, waited until he was the best, then just started playing in front of people. An instant player.

Bethany: Him and Eddy.

Phillip: Yeah, Eddy after a while, they spent hours down there together. I didn't go down until later on, saw they'd soundproofed the walls with egg cartons and old clothes. Set up a drum kit, guitar.

They're talking about Edgar Malmon, David's best friend, who would go on to be the drummer in the Doormats.

Dee: What did you think they were doing down there?

Phillip: They'd both been really into comedy. That's how they met, both checking out the same albums from the library. So I guess...

Bethany: We thought they were watching comedy.

Phillip: Yeah.

Bethany: Or, you know... two teenage boys, we didn't want to intrude...

Phillip: Yeah.

This is a theme that plays out across my conversations with people who knew David as a boy and teenager. Different people knew different versions of him.

David, the shy, bookish son of two teachers, too scared to perform. There's David the sensitive geek, over-thinking everything, wanting to write jokes and poems. Then there's Dave, the flirty, edgy, born-musician, who just appeared fully formed on the local scene one day as the best guitarist in town. Nobody seems to have seen the transition from one to the other. Nobody saw the hours of practicing.

Except for one person.

Sally: Eddy and Dave, they were inseparable.

This is Sally, one of Dave's high school girlfriends.

Sally: They kinda loved each other, you know? Like, it was intense. I knew Dave liked me. But the thing he had with Edgar...

Dee: Were they...?

Sally: Oh no. Nothing like that. It was just... you know? Sometimes teenage boys, they have this thing, almost romantic, but not, you know? I think Eddy is the only person who ever got to see all the different sides of Dave.

Dee: Which one did you see?

Sally: Oh, an early version of the one you know. The famous one.

Dee: What was that like?

Sally: Exhausting, really. It's like he couldn't talk to one person. He could talk to a room full of people, but he couldn't really hold a conversation with me. I remember he wrote a song about us, played it live, and he was saying all the things he'd never said to me.

Dee: He was in bands before the Doormats?

Sally: Oh sure. Him and Eddy. I mean, I always think really the Doormats started here, and they just added the new guy when they moved.

Completist fans circulate tapes of the bands Ash and Malmon played in back in Minnesota. I've listened to a few songs. You can hear the through line.

Dee: And when did you...

There's an awkward pause.

Sally: Well, he left me for a friend of mine.
Karen. Karen Jesperson.

ELEVEN

LOUISA

Johnny and Petey are running around Washington Square Park, dressed as superheroes. I would prefer Abingdon, or the playground at the back of my building, but the boys like coming here to watch the dogs. They've never been allowed to have one at home, because Dave was allergic to them.

No, *is* allergic.

Saturday mornings have always been our time. Me and the boys. Dave would be gigging on a Friday night, and would sleep late into Saturday. Johnny, Petey and me would always find something to do. We've settled into a routine. There's an ice cream place they like on Greenwich Avenue. If they're good, we walk down from the apartment, stop off for ice cream, then come here to watch the dogs.

I love seeing the boys together. Petey takes care of his brother. He's patient. Doesn't get annoyed when Johnny acts his age.

I treasure these moments. I like to come here and let them play. Life has always been lonely for them. Being the children of celebrities is tough, but at least they used to get invited to parties. It all stopped the minute Dave went missing. No parents want them now. Hating on me, by proxy.

Part of me thinks their lives would be better without me. But then I remember that'll happen soon enough.For right now, we're just a family. A mother out with her boys. That should feel like the most natural thing in the world, not a treat.

I touch the map in my pocket. It shows the way back home. I've never needed it, but I like being prepared.

Back at the apartment I have other cheat sheets. Ally has written out how to make coffee and cook pasta. We made a game with Petey and Johnny, going round with post-it notes labeling things. They wrote the names, and in the case of the TV and Blu-Ray, I let Petey write out instructions on how to use them, pretending it was for his benefit.

I haven't needed any of them, but I feel better knowing they're there. Half of the things I'm forgetting seem to be because of stress. The more relaxed I feel, the more I can hold on to.

"Mommy, look," Johnny calls over to me then tries to do an action roll, landing with his arm out like Spider-Man shooting a web.

He wobbles and falls to the side, but Petey catches him.

I love it here. Everyone else grouses about the tourists, or the trust-fund NYU hippies. But if I didn't want to see those people, I would've stayed in Queens. At least here, around the Village, I can blend in. Anywhere else I get stopped or photographed. But around here, people are too busy looking at the actors or musicians. Everywhere you look, there's a famous landmark from film or television. Nobody cares about some reality TV has-been.

Talking about myself in the past tense. Has-been.

My phone buzzes. I've been tagged on social media. I usually have notifications turned off, because they can go crazy, but when I'm out alone with the boys it can be a good early warning system. One time, before I was ill, I took them to the Statue of Liberty because Petey had seen it in a film. While we were there, I got notifications people were talking about me on Twitter, someone had posted a picture of me with the boys. I took them straight home.

I look down at the phone's screen now. It's a photo of me sitting on the bench, taken from across the park, the other side of the fountain.

There's a hashtag with it: #didshedoit? Someone who may still be standing in that spot, taking more pictures.

That rattles me.

I take a deep breath.

This is supposed to be my safe place. The TV show last night. The gossip mags commenting on the six-month anniversary. *Monthaversary*. Whatever.

My phone buzzes again and again as the message gets shared by other people.

"Are those your boys?"

A young man sits next to me. Black glasses. I know his face. "What?" I say.

"Spidey and Iron Man?"

Iron Man. "Yeah."

"They look happy."

I nod and give a smile.

There's already a small bit of panic building. I don't cope well with new things, or unexpected conversations. I never have, really.

Even back on that damn TV show. Arguing with the rich kids and the lawyers. It was all a front. I was scared every minute of every day. On the very first episode, the director called me to one side off-camera to tell me to stop looking into the lens. "It's reality TV," he said. "Don't let the audience know the crew's here." They started giving me Valium to calm me down. The more we did to fake things, the more real it looked.

"Must be hard raising them alone," Buddy says. "Without their father."

I look at him again. Something in me is saying, not him. And now I know the face. It's Dee. Dee whatever. Dee Buenea? Dee Boo- something. The host of the podcast. And they're non-binary. I remember that much.

Then I think, is that your pressing concern right now?

You're alone in a park with your boys and now...

The tremor builds.

Panic.

"Petey," I call over to my son. "Time to go."

I can hear the fear in my own voice.

"I'd just like to talk," Dee says.

"I've got nothing to say." Then to Petey. "Now. Come on."

"But Mom—"

Now other people are looking. I'm not blending into the background anymore. I can hear whispering. Look at the crazy murderer, she's shouting at her kid. Did she shout at her husband?

Over and over, the hashtag is spreading into words.

#didshedoit?

I stride across and grab Petey's hand, then turn and start to run out of the park. I can't breathe. Petey is pulling back against me. I'm almost dragging him. He's getting strong.

He's yelling something, but I block it out.

Think.

Concentrate.

We stop on the corner.

"But Mom—"

"Quiet, honey."

Where are we? What's the street?

Oh god, I'm losing it. I can feel the world slipping—

Breathe.

The map. I have the map. I pull it out of my pocket. I can get us home. Me and Petey and—

Oh god.

I look down at my oldest son. Petey. He's crying. Trying to pull back toward the park.

Where I left Johnny.

TWELVE

CON

Prison changed many things about me.

My timekeeping wasn't one of them.

I knew a lot of people who became accustomed to the schedule in Watertown. To uniforms deciding what time we woke up, when we went to bed. Having my freedom taken away made me even more determined to live by my own rules once I got out. No office job. No set hours. No times set by anyone other than me.

Which is the long way of saying I like to go to bed late and sleep in.

It was rare for me to be up before noon. I usually only saw morning if I needed to fix something for guests. My apartment has three bedrooms, and Frank had talked me into using two of them for an AirBnB. On weekends my mom, Maria, would come round and cook breakfasts for the guests. It wasn't covered in their fee, but she liked to do it. She's Jewish, from a Greek family, the two things she does best are guilt and food.

Maria McGarry had worked hard. First as a secretary for an accountant here in Astoria, and then, after putting herself through college while Frank covered the house bills, she became a bookkeeper for local business owners. I think, deep down, some part of her felt I wouldn't have gone off the rails if she'd just fed me a little more. I could talk to her about that, but then I might miss out on the free meals.

The smell of cooking was often what woke me up on a Saturday, so she was surprised to find me already up and dressed when she let herself in.

Her face registered surprise, then disappointment. "You haven't been to bed yet."

"Sure, I got up early to get some work done."

"You have a case."

The excitement in her voice made me feel better about losing sleep. Mom's reaction to my side-career was the complete opposite of Frank. She loved any idea of me having projects to invest my time and skills into. And, secretly, I think she found the idea of having a private investigator for a son cool.

The excitement soon washed away as she noticed the impressive bruise on the side of my face, where the fist had delivered its message the night before.

"You're hurt?"

Frank had kept his promise of not telling her what happened. For all her support in my work, she was still a mother, and I was still a son. I tried to shield her from the worst parts of my life. Not an easy thing to do when you've served time for armed robbery.

One of the witnesses last night had called the cops. Last thing I'd wanted. Even when I was the one being attacked, the first rule still applied. *Never call the cops.*

I brushed them off, saying it was all a misunderstanding and nobody was hurt. How would I have explained it? I was threatened to stay away from a missing rock star?

The threat swirled around in my head.

What did it mean?

Who was it from?

Why was it delivered to my face and gut?

I'm a reasonable guy, they could have tried delivering it to my wallet. But now? Now they'd annoyed me. I just didn't know who they were.

I loaded the CD Jayar had given me onto my phone, and listened to it with my earphones as I researched the case online. Read up on Ash and Louisa. The first track felt like a throwback to the earliest Doormats songs.

Old school garage rock with a high tempo.

"I used to love her, but now she's blonde, then she waves like a magic wand, I don't believe it."

As with many parts of their story, it was hard to know the truth of how the Doormats were formed. Their early adventures in myth-making had thrown up a number of different stories.

David Ash would tell interviewers the three-piece came together when they lost a bet. The drummer – Edgar Malmon - told people that they had originally formed as a Celine Dion tribute act. His claim was supported by a particularly raucous version of My Heart Will Go On which dominated their early gigs. Todd Flambé, bass player and official bringer of attitude, spun a yarn involving them meeting up to go and case a liquor store, before deciding to jam instead.

What I did know for sure was two Minneapolis kids, Ash and Malmon, had come to New York for college. Somewhere in there they hooked up with Flambé, a New York native, and the band was formed. Malmon had always given the impression music was something he was doing to tide him over, like an office temp. He left the scene after the band split and became an artist. He had a reputation for being difficult. I was happy to save him for later.

I'd start with Todd Flambé. He was easier to find.

Flambé came from Long Island, but in the band he'd been billed as being from New York City. He played the role of an old-school street punk, dressing like Johnny Thunders and talking like he'd never been to school. Wikipedia told me he'd done session work for Soul Asylum, Foo Fighters and Ryan Adams. I learned his real name was Anthony Preston Jr. Flambé owned a dive in the East Village, named after the last Doormats song, and was well known for sitting at the bar and letting music geeks buy him drinks in exchange for stories and rock gossip.

I called and arranged to meet. It was easier to tell the truth, in case I needed to follow up with him again.

The second track on the CD was a sloppy power-pop number, with a repeated riff and a loud euphoric chorus that sang of two people who were "*meant to be.*" It had the feel of someone who was head over heels in love, and made me want to feel it, too. Things changed with the third tune. A mood swept in on a melancholy piano, and the guitars were there to provide background ambience. Dave's voice was different. Without having to sing over the sounds of a band, he was able to whisper and mumble, and to draw out words for a greater effect.

"*Here and now the game begins, pounds on my door I wanna let it in, swore off you and the trouble you bring, you look in my eyes and I'm gone again.*"

I didn't need to have heard Jayar's description of the material to know Dave was singing about addiction.

It would be good to find his dealer.

If Ash was still alive, and hiding, there was a chance he was still in touch with his source. Supply and demand. If a gambler is laying low, talk to the bookies. If a drug addict is missing, find their supplier.

The closing song was raw and haunting. A solo cut, with a single electric guitar and Dave's voice, sounding distant and eerie.

"It's so easy, so easy, so easy to die."

His vocals were hoarse by the end, repeating over and over, *"When you lose your days, when you lose your days."*

He sounded seconds from falling apart.

THIRTEEN

LOUISA

Johnny.

I left him behind.

He's on his own. Right now.

Okay. Calm down Louisa. Breathe. It wasn't your fault. The illness did this. It's eating away at everything. Don't let it take your boys.

No. You did this. You were panicked. It was that creep. He showed up and I got flustered. I got scared and I ran. I didn't even think.

Get it together.

Go find him.

I squeeze Petey's hand, let him know things are going to be okay. We start off back down the block, the way we came.

"It's okay, Mommy," Pete says.

Right there, my son is more grown up than me. Parenting win, right? Shows I'm raising him okay.

We cross the road and head back into the park the same way we left. Past the patch of grass where Pete and Johnny like to have picnics, straight to the fountain in the middle. I can see most of the same children and parents who were there before. Some of them have gone back to whatever they were doing. Some turn to watch me.

My heart beats in my ears.

Johnny isn't here.

How can he be gone?

Where can he be gone?

I haven't been away long. Two minutes. He wouldn't have walked off. Johnny and Petey both know the drill.

He would stand here and wait for me to come back.

Unless -

- What if he panicked and ran after us?

There are other gates. He could have gone through one of the others. Out on the street.

He could be under the wheels of a car.

You're doing it again, calm down.

What if the creep took him?

CALM. DOWN.

I need to call 911. Will that blow my secret? I can say we just got separated. They don't need to know the rest. If anyone pushes too hard, it'll come out. Dave's parents will find out I'm sick, and they'll take my boys away.

But I have to. Johnny's out there. I'm going to have to lose him to get him back.

Petey starts to pull away. I grip tighter and pull back, but then he shouts, "There."

He points to the left, in the direction of MacDougal Street.

Johnny is walking toward us.

He's holding hands with Detective Elizondo. The cop who investigated me, who believes I killed Dave. If he wasn't a cop in real life, he could play one on TV. He's broad shouldered but walks with a stoop, and his jowly face is always fixed in a hangdog expression. He talks in one of those old accents that have died out in the city, rough and dirty, like a seventies movie.

He's the last person I want to see. But he's holding the hand of the first person I want to see.

My gut turns over.

My heart swells.

I think I want to throw up.

Johnny waves at us and smiles through tears. Then Elizondo lets go as he runs toward us. Pete leaves my side to meet Johnny in the middle, and immediately starts parenting him, talking about not going off with strangers. They both bury their faces in my side. Johnny's face is wet.

"Lucky I was passing," Elizondo says.

I know there's no luck to it. Elizondo is a dog with a bone. He thinks I'm the one that got away. Keeps finding ways to be in the same place as me. I could complain. Accuse him of harassment. But what does that do? It would make him pay even more attention. On anyone else it would be stalking and I could press charges, but on a cop it's just "determination". But right now it's paid off, because he saved my boy. I don't know what to feel.

Angry?

Relieved?

Grateful?

"Thank you," I say.

Elizondo smiles. He's got something. "Johnny said you've been forgetting things?"

Johnny speaks, but his face is still pressed into me, and it comes out muffled. "Mommy forgets."

Oh no.

Cover for it –

I give a laugh. It's not hard to sound genuine, as the relief is washing through me. "Don't we all? I can never remember where I've left my house keys."

"Oh sure. My wife, she forgot she was married." Elizondo smiles and nods, but his eyes are saying he doesn't buy it. "And you've had a rough time. All the grief."

He pauses on the word grief. One of his games. Waiting to read my response. That's fine. I'm well practiced in putting up my defenses. There are so many different versions of me. There's the real Louisa, the one's my parents knew. Then there's the version I played on *The Biz*, the wide-eyed little Queens girl. There's LoJay, the media celebrity who falls out of nightclubs when paparazzi are around. I play her with a little bit of a guffaw, and an I-should-know-better-smile. I'm trying hard to push through the emotions of the last few minutes and find one of my go-to acts.

"Listen," he says. "You've all had a scare. Why don't I walk you home?"

It's a trap, of course.

We've had over a dozen of these meetings since Dave went missing. Each time, he's fishing to find something, to get the hook to build a case. I should say no, but he did just help us, and I can see the wheels are already turning on what's just happened. Why was I running out of the park? Why did I leave Johnny? I need to play the same game. Keep calm, talk my way out.

"Sure," I say.

FOURTEEN

CON

The third rule of crime is *never show off*.

Don't start getting arrogant. Don't call attention to yourself. Don't make it obvious.

The bigger the job you've pulled off, the lower your profile should be. And absolutely, under no circumstances, let anybody know you have money.

Most criminals who get caught have broken this rule.

My friend Ray Yorke, for instance, watched his whole life fall apart because he hadn't known about the third rule. Before we'd met in Watertown, he'd been a trader in the city. He was living his best life. Two hours in the gym every morning. A corner office. And then as much sex and cocaine as he could fit into his studio apartment in the evenings.

These days he lived in a cramped single storey house on Hallets Point, right down at the end of 26th Avenue. He was about thirty pounds overweight, and answered the doorbell in cargo shorts, a movie T-shirt, and with breakfast cereal dripping from his hair.

I could hear a child crying in the house behind him.

"Whatever you want," he said. "If you can just get him to shut up for five minutes."

"Hi Ray." I leaned past him to call into the house. "Matty, what's up?"

The crying almost stopped.

There was a definite moment when the kid thought about letting up, and took a breath, but then he continued as loud as before.

Ray nodded for me to follow him in. The boy, Matthew, was sitting in the epicenter of a disaster zone. The breakfast cereal was all over the floor and wall, and must have been thrown with an impressive force. There was chocolate milk in a pool by his feet. A cartoon was playing on the TV, but Matty wasn't paying it any attention.

"I swear," Ray said. "I just. Can't. Keep. Doing. This."

It would be easy to feel bad for the turn Ray's life had taken, if it wasn't all his own fault.

Back at the height of his success, he'd told people numbers were his first love. It was a half-truth. He *understood* numbers. It was a language he spoke fluently. But his first love had been hacking. He used his skills to get insider information, and occasionally try and influence deals and share prices. He'd been so good, the 2008 crash hadn't made a dent in his career. He'd continued on for years, still living the same life.

He'd been caught by chance.

A friend had struggled after the crash. Ray helped him out by covering his rent for a few months, long enough to get back on his feet. Later, it turned out the same friend had been cheating on his taxes. When the IRS auditors asked Ray a few innocent questions about the rent, they picked up the scent. Six months later he was in handcuffs, negotiating a deal. He got a reduced sentence by rolling over on some of the dirtier dealers on Wall Street and was banned from taking any jobs in the financial industry. After getting out from Watertown, he settled in Queens and tried to rebuild.

He launched a tech startup, and was just starting to find his feet in the new economy when the corona crash happened. Now he was a single father living in a house which was, as far as I could tell, held together by tape. Half the buildings around him were marked for demolition, in a redevelopment that kept getting postponed.

Hallets Point was the part of Queens closest to the city, but in many ways, the farthest away.

"Hey Matt." I put my hand out. "Fist bump?"

The kid continued to cry. I knelt down in front of him and pulled out a deck of cards from my jacket pocket. I pretty much always carry a deck, just out of habit. Card mechanics were one of the first skills I picked up, and cheating at poker was one of the first hustles I perfected. Word got around early, and that was how I learned the second rule, never show off. It had been years since anyone was willing to let me join a game, and in this city there is always a game.

"How about a magic trick?"

Matt didn't stop crying right away, but there was a clear reduction. It was now more of a curious sniffling. He nodded his head. I shuffled at half speed, letting him see each step. I cut the deck twice. Then split it into three piles, laying them next to each other on the floor. I tapped the piles on the left and right.

"Turn the top card over on that one, and that one."

Each was a 3. Clubs and Spades.

"Okay, now take the top card off this middle pile here, and don't show it to me, but show it to your dad."

He picked the card up and turned it for Ray to see, putting his chubby hands around it to keep it away from me. Ray nodded encouragement at his son but knew what was coming. He'd seen me do this trick before.

"Okay, now put it back in, and put all the cards back together, and shuffle them."

He gathered them all together into a messy stack and started shuffling them slowly. He did it in clumps of five or six at a time. I made a note to teach this kid how to do it properly, some day.

"Now let your dad do it, too."

Matt handed the cards to Ray, who was almost as bad. I took the deck and reshuffled. I cut it again twice, and then into three separate piles. I tapped the top card on the left and right, and Matt turned them over.

Three of clubs.

Three of spades.

Matt squealed, then swore. He realized what he'd done, and looked to Ray, waiting to be shouted at. Ray was just happy the crying had stopped.

"That's not the trick," I said. "Ready for the real magic?"

Matt nodded, then followed up with, "Yeah."

"Okay. Those are threes. So I get three attempts to find your card, okay?"

Matt nodded again.

I pulled the top card of the middle pile. "It's this one."

He laughed and shook his head.

"Okay," I pulled the second card. "It's definitely this one."

He laughed even louder. "You're bad."

I leaned in close, and motioned for him to do the same, to hear a secret. "You wanna know the truth? I'm not really any good at magic. But I think you are."

"No I'm not?"

"Sure you are. Give me your hand."

He held out his right hand, and I palmed the card into it. I pulled my own hand away, then feigned surprise as Matt saw he was holding the correct card.

He squealed even louder and clapped his hands.

"Again."

I handed him the cards and said, "Maybe in a few minutes. I need to talk to your dad. Why don't you see if you can figure it out?"

Ray nodded for me to follow him through to the back room. There was a desk piled high with wires, computer parts and dirty coffee cups. Through the window I could see billboards covering a vacant lot, showing signs for the redevelopment plans. Promises that were broken before they were even made.

"Thanks, man." The relief in his voice was clear.

"I don't know. He's going to expect that every time now."

"I'll think of something." He settled into a worn out old office chair and lifted the lid on his laptop. "What do you need."

"Financials. Bank records, savings, the usual."

He started pressing keys, nodding as we went. "Sure, who's the target?"

I hesitated. "David Ash."

Ray stopped typing and lowered the lid. He looked up at me. "The musician?"

"Yep."

"No way. He's still in the news. His wife killed him, right?"

"Well, she still hasn't been -"

"Con, it's an open case. If I hack his financials, the banks will be looking for it. The cops. They'll see it."

"I thought you were the best?"

He waved that way. "Think I'm so easy to play? No chance. Can't be done. I could access his records, but they'd notice it. And he's still missing, right? You see what happened to those journalists in England who hacked the voicemails of the missing girl? No way."

He had a point. If the cops were still convinced Ash had been murdered, and someone hacked his financial records, there was no telling where we could end up.

"Okay. Other people have his records. How about the cops?"

"Easy. But no. Same reason."

There had to be another route. I thought back to my conversation with Ramona. She had some of Louisa's records....

"His lawyer," I said. "Maybe his lawyer would have something. They won't have the kinds of security measures as the banks or cops, right?"

He cracked his knuckles. "I like the way you think. Yeah. If they have them stored digitally, I can probably get at them."

He opened up a web browser and searched for 'David Ash' and 'lawyer'. The results came back with a number of news stories.

"Leave it with me."

I showed Matt the trick again on my way out.

FIFTEEN

CON

The Last Drop was sitting on the corner of Avenue A and East 6th. The outside walls were covered in murals of old rock stars. The window held gig posters for bands I'd never heard of. The door was locked, but I rapped on the glass and a young woman with sleeve tattoos and a pixie cut opened the door wide enough for a conversation.

"Hey. I'm looking for Todd?"

She gave me an appraising look. "You the PI?"

"'Fraid so."

"Cool." She opened wider and nodded backwards. "Take a seat, I'll let him know. Get you anything?"

Inside the place looked like it was trying too hard to re-capture something that didn't exist anymore. If it ever had. The bar was a faded brown, with a variety of liquor on glass shelves behind the bartender. The walls were painted a light cream, with messages and doodles drawn in sharpie. There was a small stage area at the back with a stool and solitary mic stand.

I took a coffee and picked a booth. The table had graffiti on it to match the walls, and on closer inspection it all seemed to be done with the same hand. This was all a bit too practiced.

I heard Todd Flambé before I saw him. The sound of a chain chinked across the room toward me. He was dressed all in black, with tight jeans, boots, and a vest over a T-shirt. The chain hung down close to his knee before looping back up into a pocket.

"Hey, you the gumshoe? Cool. Cool" He took my hand in the thumb-clasp greeting. "I bet you got loads of stories."

That's what I was to him. Another tale to add to the collection. I was fine with it. Whatever got him talking.

"A few," I said.

"Cool. Cool. Yeah, man."

"Thanks for taking the time to talk to me," I said, easing us back in the right direction.

"Yeah. Yeah. No problem. Dave, Jeez, man." A grin spread across his face. "You know he took a vow of silence once? We'd signed this major label deal, spent three months writing songs. Had all this pressure, from the fans, you know? They said we'd sold out. So we took it serious, spent all this time writing songs. Our first day in the studio, me and Eddy get there, and this guy from the label is running around screaming, he's in tears. And there's Dave, sitting on the floor, head shaved like a Buddhist, legs crossed, grinning like a loon."

There was a rehearsed element to the story. It was a comedy bit. I could tell Todd had repeated this, word for word, beat for beat, hundreds of times.

"Just to mess with the label?"

"To mess with all of us. He couldn't take the easy route. You ever seen the music video to *Nothing Always Happens?*"

"Yeah, he's not in it."

"Right, yeah. He refused. But not like, 'no I'm not doing this' - he played along until the day, then sent a roadie in a clown costume in his place."

"He did music videos when he went solo, though."

"Yeah." There was a bitterness in his reply.

"When was the last time you spoke to him?"

He paused before answering. There was a lie coming. "You know, I don't know, man. I tried to think about that for the last guy."

"Last guy?"

He blinked.

This time the pause wasn't a lie, it was confusion. "Yeah, the other PI. He was fun. Had loads of stories."

There had been another PI working the case? Had it been the other side? Ash's parents? I needed to stay on topic.

"And what did you tell him?"

Flambé's eyes drifted away. He was in a different place for a moment, then he said, "Hey, you want a drink? I'm getting a drink."

"I'm good with my coffee."

His head bobbed in a nod and he walked over to the bar. While Pixie fixed him a drink he cracked a few jokes I didn't hear, followed by a snort. Then he shouted out, "I'm gonna go talk to my gumshoe."

Todd slapped a glass full of red wine on the table and slid into the booth.

"So you wanna find Dave?"

"Yeah."

"What if he don't want you to?"

He caught me off guard. "What do you mean?"

"Well, see, this other time, we was touring England, it was Glasgow I think, and he went missing. Just went out drinking one night and didn't come back. Tour manager went nuts, we called the cops. Looked for him for three days, cancelled a bunch of shows. Later on we get a postcard, one with the Eiffel Tower on it. He'd taken a break."

That gave me hope.

Dave lived in a goldfish bowl with Louisa, and it was clear he'd been feeling the pressure on the album. Combined with his slide back into substance abuse, maybe he'd just decided to take a break?

"How long did he stay away?"

"Three weeks."

Three weeks is plausible. Six months? Not so much.

"Do you know who his dealer was?"

He shook his head. "Dave's been clean for years."

Another lie.

"Who did he buy from before he cleaned up?"

Flambé waved at the air with both hands. "They could form a line, man. He had a notebook full of 'em, names, numbers. I never mixed with any of that stuff, though. Don't remember any names."

"You guys met in college, right?"

"Yeah." He grinned, but it looked practiced. "Both of 'em. Dave and Eddy. They was just these two scared kids, from niceville, looking for someone to talk to. I think I was more their bodyguard than anything else. Their way to look cool. They handed me a bass..." He waved at the bar. "And here we are."

The story felt fake.

Another piece of the mythology wrapped around the band. A tall tale that no real person could match up to.

I was sensing I wasn't going to get past his act on this first meeting. He wasn't going to open up to me here. The Last Drop was his home turf. If I wanted to get at the truth I would need to find a way to talk to Anthony Preston, not Todd Flambé.

"Looks like he'd been recording some of his own stuff at a private studio, any idea where that might be?"

"Nah." His eyes drifted away again. He snapped back. "He didn't tell me shit like that."

I tried playing into his act rather than attempting to break through. If he wanted to play the rockstar, and spin legends of the life, maybe I could creep up on the truth. "I saw you guys a couple times."

"Oh yeah?" His eyes brightened. "When?"

"Around the time of *Legends of the Mall*. I was big into that album, man. Loved it."

"Yeah, it was fun. Real fun, you know? Just messing about, playing good songs. None of the crap."

"Your bass solo on that one song, what was it?"

"*Runaway Town?*"

"Yeah, great. Just, the way it moves, like an engine."

His ego beamed. "First part of the song we laid down. Then Eddy put a beat next to it. Dave messed around for ages trying to find the words, but the song, I always said, the song was there from the moment I put that bass down. We knew it was a single."

"I read you guys always shared the writing credits on the singles?"

"Yeah, totally."

"How would all of that work if something's happened to Dave? Would you guys still be okay?"

"Oh, I don't know about the money stuff. I leave all of that to Danny."

Danny Stewart. Their manager. His name had come up a few times in my research.

It was time to see if I could get back to his first lie. "And when did you say you saw Dave last?"

He grinned. He'd caught my own tell. One liar to another. "No idea, man. Like I said. You're working for Louisa?"

"Yeah."

There was a distant spark in his eyes. An old memory of some kind. "Say hi to her for me."

"You can't call her yourself?"

"Nah." The memory had gone. It was replaced by something bitter. "We don't talk."

"Why not?" He gave me an odd look in place of an answer. There was a story there but, like everything else, he wasn't going to give it to me. "I need to talk to Edgar, could you give me his address?"

"Cool. Cool. He lives in Williamsburg."

Oh hell, I needed to go *there*.

SIXTEEN

CON

From everything I knew about Edgar Malmon, I expected to meet some half-crazed cross between Andy Warhol and Salvador Dali. Crazy eyes and a short fuse. The figure who greeted me on the doorstep of his Humboldt Street townhouse was slight and balding, with a sleepy smile.

"Hey man," he said, with a breeze in his voice. "Todd called, said you were coming."

Edgar Malmon was dressed in paint flecked-jeans and a long-sleeved red tee with *Enjoy Capitalism* printed to look like the Coca-Cola logo. The look reminded me of his signature drum kit in the band, which was bright red and coated in drops of paint.

Malmon stepped inside and nodded for me to follow.

He yawned as we climbed the stairs.

"Did I wake you up?"

He laughed. "No, don't worry. I've been up about an hour, but I wake up slow. I won't really be awake for a couple of hours."

"Rock star schedule?"

"I've always been this way. I go to bed around three or four, get up around eleven. My family used to say I lived on *Eddy Time*."

We took the stairs up to the top floor. It looked like everything except the supporting walls had been knocked through, creating an open space. There were canvasses and easels resting against the walls, and a desk was covered with large computer screens and cables.

Edgar offered me a drink and I declined. He got right to it. "You're looking for Dave."

"Yeah."

"Maybe he doesn't want to be found?"

That chimed almost exactly with something Todd Flambé said. Were they in on a secret, or had Flambé primed Malmon when he called?

Malmon got in a follow up question before I could respond. "What did you make of Todd?"

I figured it was a test. He wanted to see how honest I was, or how perceptive.

"I don't know," I said. "He seemed to be playing a part."

He looked at me again, and this time I got the feeling I'd just gone up in his estimation.

I wanted to take this one slowly.

Between the recording studio and Todd Flambé, I felt played. Everyone knew I was coming, and they were keeping their guard up, protecting secrets. I figured Malmon would be the most difficult, based on his reputation. I'd need to sneak up on the subject.

I pointed to one of the paintings. "Nice. I have no idea what it is, but I like it."

"A representation of the soul of a dying caterpillar as it liquefies, and turns into something new."

"Okay."

He grinned. "Just kidding. I threw a bunch of crap at the canvas, experimenting with some new paint mixes. But, hey, if the caterpillar line worked I can probably get a fortune for it in the city."

"Is that how it works?"

"Yup."

Along the opposite wall I saw much simpler, cleaner pictures. Sports cars on mountain roads, space-age apartment buildings, a few sports stadiums. They looked digital. The lines and colours were too crisp to be done by hand. Some paintings of playing cards, chips, poker games.

Malmon followed my gaze. "The commercial jobs. Every artist's dirty secret. That one was for a sports car, they turned the picture into an ad for magazines. I do a bunch of stuff for film and TV, too. Production art, storyboards. The poker stuff was for a film."

"The buildings?"

"When you see news stories about redevelopment, urban renewal, those things? They've got someone like me to do the graphic. I mean, I was part of the gentrification of Brooklyn, so I might as well make some money off it, right?"

"The music doesn't cover everything?"

"The band? Nah. The money's okay, but we were in debt for most of the time we were together. It was really only after Dave's solo career took off, we started to sell to his new fans. It's, uh," he hesitated. "It's picked up more since he went missing. The money's getting good now. But, you know, I don't want to think about that."

There was a fun contradiction between the man standing in front of me wearing an anti-capitalist slogan on his T-shirt, and the idea of an artist cozying up to car companies and architects. But I took money to help people, so I wasn't fit to judge.

There was no sign of any music memorabilia. Not even an acoustic guitar to sit in the corner and never get played. "No instruments?"

He blinked. It seemed to take him a second to understand the question. "Music? No. Got it all out of my system."

"You never miss it?"

He gave me a look, like I'd just asked the most naïve question imaginable. "What's there to miss? Hotels. Buses. Planes. The way security is now, we'd spend most of our lives in airports. Need something to get your body to sleep after a show, then something else to get up in the morning. I'm forty-six, I just don't have the energy for it all." He laughed. "The gig economy. We lived the real thing."

"How about those guys who just play a couple shows a month?"

"Sure. You know," he grinned, "Billy Joel has a regular thing, once a month at MSG. I wouldn't be caught dead there. But I heard he had staff out on the doors who pick out attractive women, and give them tickets for the front two rows."

"Kinda sleazy."

"Well," he said. "I mean, most people do something like that, when they have the power. But it made me think, what would we see, in our audience now? It'd be a toss-up. We'd have middle-aged men, wearing checked shirts, or we'd have the young women who went to Dave's solo shows. And you know, we'd probably want to pick the latter."

"Something you'd talked about? You guys playing together again?"

I heard something else in my voice. I wasn't just an adult asking questions about my case, for a second I was a teenager asking about my favorite band. I'd managed not to think about that side of it while talking to Flambé or Malmon.

"Oh, hell no. Not serious. Todd tried to talk us into it. He saw guys like the Hold Steady doing what you're saying, a few dates here and there. He'd worked out our costs, and how much we could make."

"Todd?"

"Yeah, he'd always been the money guy in the group."

That didn't mesh with what Todd had claimed, but I wasn't surprised to learn just how much of an act it had been.

"Todd's the only one who pushed to get back together?"

Malmon lifted a bottle of water out of a small fridge beneath the computer desk and took a long sip. "I've moved on, like I said. And Dave had no need for it. His career was in a different place, wouldn't really make sense to take a step backwards, lose half his audience. Doormats fans would keep buying his solo stuff, out of loyalty, but I don't think his solo audience would want to come to a Doormats show. Todd's the one who was still in love with the idea of the band. Which is kinda ironic."

"Why?"

"He was the one split the band up."

"I thought it was because of Louisa?"

"Yeah."

Malmon paused. So did I. He looked at me, and I read the tell in his face, like we were playing poker. I'd been talking about the band splitting up because of Ash's relationship with Louisa. Malmon had been talking about Flambé being the one to call time. But his *yeah* had been an answer to both.

I waited a few more seconds to see if Malmon was going to follow up. When he didn't, I said, "So, Todd and Louisa?"

Malmon sighed. He shook his head. "Yeah. Todd was crazy about Louisa. They went out a few times, before Dave swooped in."

SEVENTEEN

LOUISA

"And your boys still don't know?"

We're sitting in my apartment. Elizondo invited himself up for coffee. He has a certain way about him, never forces anything, but never really makes it feel like no is an option. I'm going to take him on. I'm sick of hiding. Sick of running. That mess back at the park, nobody should have to live in fear. I've already had to mute my social media accounts again. The hashtags are going crazy, and now people have a new thing to jump on.

She tried to abandon her kid?

Obviously the actions of a killer.

#DidSheDoIt?
#LockHerUp

I'm pretty sure they'll have a psychological "expert" on one of the news channels within the next few minutes, to talk about my body language. This is how the game goes for me now. Every single thing is analyzed, each moment is owned by other people.

I'm taking my life back.

Starting with Detective Elizondo.

"No. They think he's away on tour."

"Is it to protect them?"

I give him my most confident smile. No need to show I've been questioning that decision every minute of every day for the past six months.

"Yeah. Dave'll be back at some point, apologizing for everything he's done, and they'll have their daddy back."

He leans forward and smiles. Unnerving. We've played this game many times, and he's never really smiled. "It must be hard for you, keeping it going with them, when everyone wants to talk to you about David."

"It's not easy."

I don't know how he's done it, but suddenly I want to trust him. I want to start creating things to tell him, truths to give up. It must be all the years of interrogations, he can switch this on at will. I put my own defenses up by slipping into the *The Biz* version of me, younger and hopeful. This face usually gets people on my side.

His smile stays in place. "But they trust you?"

I see the trap just in time. He's playing on my honesty. Well, if you lie to your kids... Time to change to another mask. My favorite is the businesswoman. Dave used to call it my House of Cards face. I play it cool and calm, giving nothing away. And if Elizondo wants to try and play me, this is the one he's going to get.

"Of course they do," I say. I slip a little of the political cool into my voice, let him read it. "Why wouldn't they?"

"You like Lou Reed? I bet your husband did. He had this song, blew me away when I heard it. It's got this one line about how you can't trust your mother. Part of growing up, isn't it?"

"I suppose it is."

"And your boys will be growing up very soon."

I don't rise to it. This is my home. My game.

"My whole life has been in the media for ten years now, Detective. I'm followed by paparazzi everywhere I go. US Weekly knows when I get my roots done. Twitter can tell me everywhere I've been. I once saw someone selling one of my bras on eBay, and I still have no idea how they got it. So, you tell me, where in all this do you think I would have time to carry out and cover up a murder?"

He leans back and sips his coffee. I see his eyes scanning around the room. Pausing to take in the Post-It notes scattered around the place. What does he make of them? Maybe this was a mistake.

"Those for your boys?"

I nod. "I'm teaching them how to use things. Petey writes them out as we talk."

"Good idea," he says. His tone is mild. Playing nice. "When was the last time you spoke to Reah Kanellis?"

"You already know. Not since I moved to the Rockaways."

Most people knew me as a girl from Rockaway Beach, but

I'd grown up on Newton Avenue in Astoria. My parents moved us out to the beach when I was fourteen, or fifteen, to get me away from the Kanellis family.

He changes lanes again, trying to throw me off balance. "Does your boy know how to rent movies? Do the instructions cover that?"

Nice trick. Really nice. "He doesn't know the PIN."

"Right. Right."

I feel a flush of anger. Elizondo is annoying, but this is something pure. Pure aggression, out of nowhere. My hands flex, tensing into fists. I'm ready to snap, shout, swear. I bite it back. Stay in control. This is just another of the changes I'm learning to live with. Sometimes I choose to be someone else, but other times my illness makes the decision for me. I can lose my temper. Lash out. But most times I catch myself in time. I'm still in control.

I breathe in deep, then out again, like I'm doing yoga.

Elizondo watches my hands.

Did he see the fists?

"Moms are still important though, aren't they?" He changed lanes again, back to where we'd been. "I still miss mine. Everyday. Fourteen years last month, and I still pick up the phone every night."

"You didn't call you mother every day."

He smiles. "You got me. Maybe once a month. But if I could have the time back, I'd do it every day. I read up on what happened with your parents. I'm sorry. It's a terrible disease."

"Yes."

"You must worry about it?"

He pauses to read my eyes again.

Does he know?

He knows.

Does he know?

He knows.

"That podcast keep leaving me messages," he says. "The one doing a show about you."

"You should take the call, make you famous."

The front door opens. It's Gyul, the nanny. She takes the boys until nine on weekends, gives me time to go to meetings and pretend to have a normal life. Gyul starts to say hello and tell me about her morning in a stop-start mix of Russia and Jersey, but stops when she notices Elizondo.

"Oh, sorry," she nods at him. "I didn't see."

I make a show of checking the time, standing up to hide how flustered I feel.

"I have a meeting," I say. "Is there anything else?"

"No. No. Thanks for the coffee." He puts the mug down on the table. "It was nice chatting to you, Louisa."

We walk to the door together. I hold it open and he nods a goodbye, then pauses and says the same thing he does every time. "Don't leave town."

I shut the door after him, and breathe in and out, slowly, controlling my panic.

He saw me. He saw my fists.

I swear.

Then, for just a second, I slip again, and I'm not here.

Then I feel fear.

EIGHTEEN

CON

"How did this never get out?"

There had been many rumors surrounding the Doormats. Particularly toward the end, as Ash's star started to rise. If you were a woman in a band, anywhere near New York, somebody would be saying you'd hooked up with Ash. The other guys got some rumors of their own, but nothing ever seemed to have substance.

"None of it ever did," Malmon said. "All that myth-making we did? It's the same as me letting people think I'm a freak. It was planned. We used it like a shield. Our real lives never got out. Until Dave and Louisa, then the rules changed."

"But with you guys being on the local scene, somebody must have seen something?"

That was a double-sided question. As someone who'd been a fan of the local scene, I wanted to know how they pulled it off. But also, it might help me find Ash. If there were people out there who were good at keeping the band's secrets, maybe they were still doing it.

"Pretty easy, really. We protect our own. All the communities do it. Art, music, I bet actors and comedians do, too. We know each other's gossip, but we don't spread it outside of the group."

There was a chance other local musicians might know something important, but I couldn't make that line of thought too obvious to Malmon. He might put up the defenses.

"So, Todd and Louisa?"

"Yeah. Well, more probably Todd, to be honest. He's always been a bit needy. Casual stuff on the road, easy. But actually talking to people? He didn't have a clue."

"How do you mean?"

"Well, I got the impression he thought they had something. But I'm not sure she saw it the same way. From the way she jumped to Dave, I don't think she even thought of it as jumping."

"Did they all meet at clubs?"

"No. Well, Louisa and Dave did. That's probably a sweet story. But Todd and Louisa met at a charity thing. Alzheimers."

"Alzheimers?"

I felt something spark in my mind. A connection I hadn't known I was looking for.

"Yeah. Both of their moms had it, I think. I mean, I know Todd's did. He's terrified of it, gets an annual check-up to see if there's any signs of it passing on. But I think Louisa's mom had it. They both donated money to a place in the city, Upper West Side somewhere."

I remembered the news stories, of Louisa's mother growing seriously ill not long after the TV show. It had been something the gossip mags used to grow sympathy for her, showing this hard-working single mother supporting a son *and* her sick parents.

"So they met at this charity thing, and then Todd thought they had something."

He nodded. "Pretty much, yeah. They went out a few times. But it would be done the way people like us always do it, turning up to the same club separately, leaving separately, and being discreet inside. But then she met Dave outside one of the clubs. I swear," Malmon laughed. "He just had this thing, he just looked at some people, and they loved him."

I noticed the past tense. He'd said Ash *had* this thing.

"How did Todd take it? Had to be hard."

"Yeah." He looked down at the floor for a moment. "And Dave left his own girlfriend to be with Louisa. It was... tense."

"He had another girlfriend here, in New York?"

"Karen, yeah. Half our love songs were all about her."

"Do you know where I can find her?"

"No, but Danny will, our manager. He keeps tabs on everybody."

"Even exes?"

"*Everybody.* Reality changed after Dave got famous. There were always people trying to claim they'd written one of the songs, or he'd slept with them, had a baby. Even when we could prove we were in Europe at the time. So Danny kept track of everyone."

"I'll need to see him."

"I'll give him a call. Put in a word."

It was time to try and steer it back toward the main questions. Start putting everything together.

"When was the last time you saw Dave?"

"Couple weeks before he went missing. Todd had been pushing for a new 'best of' compilation, so we needed to go over the contracts."

"And Todd was at the meeting?"

Malmon nodded. That contradicted what Flambé had said. Unless he'd genuinely forgotten meeting with Ash and Malmon. That was possible, six months later, but didn't ring true. I wasn't buying he'd forget the last time he saw his friend. So why would he be lying?

"You and Dave went back a long way, didn't you?"

He sipped his drink and nodded. "Best friends growing up. Same street. Same school. We got to New York within a few weeks of each other."

"How about Todd and Dave?"

"Todd *worshipped* Dave. You gotta understand, Todd was classically trained. His parents were kinda rich, paid for him to get all kinds of lessons. He grew up on jazz, blues, all that stuff. He was this beatnik-wannabe when we met him. Then, it was like he fell in love with Dave. Next time he turned up, he was a whole different person."

"His whole Johnny Thunders thing?"

"Exactly."

"But Dave was different?"

He laughed to himself. A fond memory. "Always. As annoying as he could be, there was no pose. He always wanted to be *real,* and he wanted his music to be real, too. People saw it as pretentious, I think, but he was just being honest about it. That's who he was."

"And you?"

He paused for a long time, then gave a nervous laugh. "Man, you should be a journalist or something, I opened up here. I was the same as Todd, I guess. The band was an act for both of us."

I looked around the studio. I couldn't help but like this guy. Todd was trapped. He was stuck in a role he'd created. But Edgar had moved on, he was out of the scene and comfortable with who he was.

"You're not what I expected," I said. "I thought you'd be, I dunno…"

"Scarier?" He laughed. "Yeah. Best way to get fans to leave you alone. It's like a force field, keeps people away."

"I've been told Dave was recording on his own.

He had a private studio somewhere, and I'd like to check it out. Any ideas?"

"No. I mean, I know you're right, he told me he'd found a spot, but I didn't push."

"Because you've left it all behind."

He made a noise. It was slightly above a sigh, but below a 'well'. There was something there he'd held back. "What is it?" I said. "It might help."

"Feels like I'm betraying him," he said, more to himself than to me. He sighed again. "Whatever. Dave was off the wagon. He didn't tell me, but I knew. I was the first one to know he had a problem back in the day, so he's never been able to hide it from me. When he said he had a new studio, to be honest, what I heard was he had a new place to get high and drunk, and I didn't want to know."

"You know his dealer?"

"No."

"His old one?"

"No, but I might remember. I can think about it."

"You talk about Dave in the past tense. But right at the start, you said he might not want to be found. What do you think happened to him?"

He left eye twitched. It was the first time I'd seen it, and couldn't read what it meant. Was he thinking of a lie, or a painful truth?

"I don't know," he said. "My gut says he's dead. But he could be hidden away somewhere. With Dave, you just… I don't know."

"Todd said there was another guy asking around, a PI."

"I heard about him, yeah."

Only heard about? "Did you meet him?"

"No. Sounded like an ass. I kept stalling on meeting him, then he stopped asking." He shrugged. "I guessed he'd stopped working the case."

I stood up to leave.

There were still a million questions, but I felt like I was at the start of the maze, waiting to take the first step. Each time I spoke to someone, I only got more confused about which way to go.

"Hey, one more thing. You mentioned all three of you needed to sign off on Todd's 'best of' project? If something has happened. To Dave. If he's gone. What would happen to the band's music?"

Malmon breathed in and out, deep and heavy. It felt like the gesture carried a lot of history.

I nudged him along. "Sore subject?"

"Always is. Show me a band, I'll show you an argument over royalties. For us, the band itself is a three way partnership. Well, four. The three of us got an equal share, and we gave ten percent to Danny. So we all get that split of the name, the merch, all those things. And we all get paid off the songs based on what we played on the recordings. But Dave was credited with most of the songwriting. We only shared on the singles, so the royalties and publishing rights, mostly his."

"And if something has happened to him?"

"His estate."

"Louisa?"

"Yeah. She'd pretty much control the band's music."

NINETEEN

CON

The Dark Star Lounge was quiet. It was a Saturday afternoon, and I guessed the drinkers all had better places to be. There were more bars farther up the street, and they'd all been much busier on the walk past.

The Dark Star was a narrow bar with a wooden floor and brown walls that held a reddish glow. A door at the back had a sign above it for the washroom. A TV was mounted to the wall in that corner, near the door, showing a British soccer game.

There were no customers, and I got the impression the place had just opened for the day. There was a big guy behind the bar. He was tall with a broad frame and a square jaw. I recognized him from somewhere.

"Hey," he greeted me with a British accent. "How you doing?"

I still couldn't quite place where I knew him from. I ordered a ginger beer to ease into the conversation. He set the drink down in front of me and turned back to the TV screen. One of the teams on the screen behind me scored a goal. Players in blue and white stripes celebrated. The other team was wearing orange. The big guy shook his head slightly, his lips pursed in a look of frustration.

"Not your team?" I said.

"Nope."

He sounded heartbroken.

"Isn't it late for a game? It's like eight over there, right?"

"They moved it for TV."

"I never get this game," I said. "It's all the ties. One one, zero zero. And all those guys who flop."

"It's all part of the drama. Anything can happen."

I thought of the Doormats song Todd Flambé had mentioned, *Nothing Always Happens.*. "But it doesn't."

"Look at these guys." The camera was panning across the crowd, they were on their feet, cheering and shouting. "That's what it's about. The spectacle. Especially now they're allowed back in. It just feels even bigger now."

"But there's only been one goal."

"Doesn't matter. It's the story. The rivalries on the pitch, the build-up play, even the cheating. That's what sport is. I don't remember anything about who won medals at the '92 Olympics, but I'll remember Derek Redmond walking to the finish line until the day I die. You a baseball guy?"

It was my turn to sound heartbroken. "Mets."

"Okay." He gave me a sympathetic nod. "Look, I like baseball, I think. But it has all these dumb unwritten rules. Like, don't celebrate, don't throw the bat. Sport should be drama. You need to get people up out their seats."

"Baseball's different."

"No it's not. Look, your Mets, who was the kid who cried?"

"Flores."

"Right. Flores. So he cries during the game. You ever going to forget that? And then he wins, what the next game, the one after? That's when the season got magic. That's when all you guys around here started to believe. Everything happened after, it was the drama that kicked it off."

"I get what you mean about the spectacle. They should be allowed to celebrate more. You know how you can tell an unwritten rule is stupid?"

"Because if it was any good, they would've written it down."

"They would've written it down. Right. But the thing is, I bet your team ties it up, and it finishes one each. Or, these guys in blue score again, and then they kill off the game."

"It's looking like it."

"Your team, these orange guys-"

"Gold."

"These gold guys. Who are they?"

"Wolves."

"They a big team?"

"No. They were, in the fifties."

"So they've been no good for sixty-something years, and you still follow them?" I raised my glass. "I think you and me are going to be friends. My name's Con, by the way."

"Con, like a criminal?"

In more ways than one.

"Short for Constantin," I said. "My mom's side is Greek."

"Jake." He raised a glass of water at me in a repeat of my toast. "Short for Jake. My mom's side were boring."

"I know you from somewhere," I said.

"Nah." Jake bent down to do some work below the counter but kept talking. "Not me."

While he was down out of sight I took a look at the ceiling. There were two security cameras. One pointed toward me from the door, the other was behind the bar, covering the cash register.

As Jake came back up I pictured him younger, jumping off the top rope of a wrestling ring.

The memory clicked.

"You were a wrester," I said. "Lord something. Lord Sterling? I remember you."

"Henry Sterling." He looked distant for a moment. "Long time ago."

"Yeah." I warmed to it now. "You had the spoiled rich kid act, women in business suits coming down to the ring with you, throwing money into the crowd."

He smiled. "Yeah."

"What happened?"

"Wrestling, man. It's a crazy business."

That seemed to be as far as he wanted to go on the subject, but he didn't close down. I felt like we'd got an easy thing going, and took my chance. "I'm trying to find someone. Dave Ash."

"You're a PI?"

I liked that his first guess hadn't been cop. And for the second time, I got the feeling he wasn't shutting the conversation down.

"Unlicensed, but yeah. Did you know him well?"

"Nah." Jake bent down again for a second, dealing with something out of sight. "He'd been coming in a few times a week. He'd sit and drink, we'd talk football or politics."

"And he was in here the night he went missing?"

He bobbed his head to the side. "Guess so."

I pointed to the camera behind him. "Was he on that?"

"Yup."

"Could I see it?"

"We don't have it anymore. Cops took it. We had a second copy, but we gave it to the other guy."

"The other guy?"

He looked at me like I didn't get it. "The other PI. The one his wife hired."

TWENTY

LOUISA

"It's okay. Kelly-Anne? It's okay, honey, you're here with me, okay?"

The old woman looks at me. The confusion is like a gray mist in her eyes. I put my hand on hers and say again, "We're having a nice lunch, you're with me."

Kelly-Anne smiles. Her eyes change. She's back in the room with me now. I look round at the other people seated at the table. Aged between sixty and eighty, they're all here for the same reason.

Hearthstone is a care facility specializing in Alzheimer's. They have a floor to themselves in the Esplanade, West End Avenue. After my mom passed away, I felt helpless. All my fame, all my money, and there was nothing I could do except hold her hand, change her sheets and tell her stories. I watched her fade, flicker away and go, and I couldn't do a damn thing about it.

So now I come here, once or twice a week, and eat a meal with some of the residents. I listen to their stories. Wait them out when the connections aren't there, don't press them when they can't find the right word.

There are so few of these places. Even fewer are affordable. We hide them away. Especially in the city. Everything has to be new, fresh, exciting. Old age is scary enough, but dementia? No way. It's like admitting death.

There's another out in Brooklyn. The crowd there is more diverse. Most people are on Medicaid, for whatever that's worth now.

I get out there as often as I can, but Hearthstone is usually easier. I can get the train uptown, and Ally lives near here.

Ally can't come in. She goes and gets coffee, or makes calls. Right now I think she's meeting with her own lawyer, Lori. Anything to avoid coming inside and seeing death. I get it. I used to be the same way. Old people scared me. I was going to live forever, so why would I want to be around people who reminded me I wouldn't?

But after Mom…

The rules changed.

These people are my friends. That's what I call them, anyway. Kelly-Anne is only twenty years older than me, but the disease has been harsh, she looks eighty. In her good moments, she's sharp and funny. In her bad moments, she's a confused child. She wears each state of mind on her face, easy to read.

She used to work for a publisher. Had a role in some of the smartest, funniest books I'll never read. Now she's here. Around the table are a couple of retired doctors, a housewife and a janitor. The janitor, Dennis, is the oldest. Pushing eighty. He's fading fast. Used to joke about how he didn't belong here, and maybe he was supposed to clean up after everyone else. Worked himself into the ground to put his children through college. They're all teachers and lawyers now and return the favor, paying for him to get care close to them. The housewife, Jessica, she's new. I was here the day she moved in. She's lived fifty years with her husband. High school sweethearts. Never apart for more than a weekend, and now she lives here, and her husband visits every day. Jessica cries in her room. We all know it, but what can we do?

One of the carers is cutting up food for Dennis. Helping him eat. His children often come and do it, but I think they're all out of town. A family holiday, minus one member.

Like me, this morning. Leaving one member of my family in the park.

Just *leaving* him there. Like a memory I don't need.

Walking away.

Kelly-Anne pulls her hand out from under mine, to place it on top and squeeze.

"Friend," she says.

The memories aren't quite there. I can see she's struggling today. But she knows I'm here to keep her company; she remembers the emotional connection, if not the details. Most days, that's good enough.

I smile, and don't let her see any tears. "Friend."

One of the carers hands me a plate, asks if I need a hand with anything.

"No, thanks. I'm good."

Looking across at Dennis, I wonder if it's easier for his

family than it was for me. I stayed with her until the end. They get time off. I don't judge them. It's important. But I wonder sometimes, is one approach easier than the other? Are the emotions any more or less with distance?

I pick at my own food.

Ally and I are booked at another place after here, to talk business. We could do it in private, at my place or hers, but I'm stubborn. I like to be seen out sometimes, talking business, acting like I don't care what people say about me.

But that's a lie, because I already know if I'm seen eating my food, people will think I'm getting fat. If I'm seen picking at my food, someone might report I have an eating disorder, or question whether I'm on a diet.

I want to be seen, but I don't want to be seen.

My public persona is my career. I need to maintain it to make money. But somewhere along the line, we accepted giving people a little of yourself means that they want to own all of you. It's exhausting.

I need to eat *just the right amount* when I'm out with Ally, so I shouldn't really be eating this. But I don't want to upset anyone at the table. I don't want them to think like I'm not caring about being here, about them.

I can skip the food later. It's only a business meeting.

Who cares?

I do.

That's the problem.

TWENTY-ONE

CON

"Who was the other guy?"

Ramona looked up at me from behind the desk. She was talking on her cell. She mumbled something about calling back, an ended the call.

I'd headed straight to Ramona's office from the bar. She operated out of a small storefront on Steinway, between a pharmacy and an insurance firm. She ran a drop-in clinic from noon until three on Saturdays, but I'd called and told her to wait for me before locking up.

My tone hadn't left any room for debate.

The front door had been unlocked, but she'd already sent her assistant home for the day. I walked straight through the small partitioned waiting area at the front, to the back of the room where Ramona's desk faced the street.

"What happened?" She started to stand up out of her chair, pointing toward my bruised face.

"Bigfoot sighting. Who was the other guy?"

"Did you try and wrestle Bigfoot?"

"Mona. You already hired a PI."

Ramona's eyes gave the game away. She could never lie to me, and she was about the only person I could never fool. We always saw through each other. Or, so I thought. But she'd done a good job of stringing me along here. She let out a long breath. Her shoulders sagged, which made a few creases stand out in her suit.

"Yeah."

"Tell me what's going on."

She waved for me to sit down across the desk.

I paused. I'd stormed in, full of anger and betrayal.

The kind of righteous indignation only a professional liar can summon up when lied to. But now she wanted a calm conversation, and it was taking the heat out of my gut.

It was all too civil.

No way was I going to sit.

I sat.

Ramona pulled a face. "It was Matt Halliday."

Oh great.

There were three tiers to the investigations game in this city. Decent people, with money and common sense, went to the licensed PI's who showed up in phone books and on the internet. Criminals, with no time and limited resources, could come to people like me. Matt Halliday lived in the area between. Old women who didn't know how to use the internet. Fraud victims who compounded their first mistakes by calling on the wrong person to fix it. If he found something juicy enough, he extorted his own clients. Other rumors had him as a bagman for criminal organizations, taking blood money for violence. He'd been linked to at least one murder that I knew of.

Ramona read my expression. "Yeah, that was me, too. I told Ally he was the wrong choice, but they'd already been burned."

"How?"

"He said he'd found proof Louisa was guilty. Knew about her memory. Tried to blackmail them, but they said to get lost."

"What did he do?"

"He backed off."

No way.

If Halliday had something, it made no sense for him to back away. There was something else that continued to eat away at me.

"So it was Ally who hired him?"

"Yeah, she's running the show, so..."

"Ally who hired you."

"What do you mean?"

"I still don't see it. Still doesn't feel right. I mean, I can buy that Louisa feels like she has nobody to turn to. But she does, she has Ally. *Ally* isn't accused of anything, she has her own lawyer, and she's got to have a book full of contacts all over the city. So why does she end up with a lawyer from Astoria who never goes to trial, and the world's sleaziest PI?"

"Ally says Louisa knew Halliday, I think. From when she was a teenager, her parents moved out to the Rockaways and -"

"So same answer both times. Ally says you were hired because Louisa wanted someone from back home, and now it's the same thing with Halliday."

"Louisa's very private, she doesn't trust easy."

The truth finally laid itself out in front of me, obvious.

"This isn't about drugs, is it?"

"I think that's for Louisa -"

"She's not here. You are. I'm asking you. See this? I got attacked. Someone warned me off the case, told me to back away."

Ramona had started to reach for the phone, but pulled back. "Warned off? By who?"

"Bigfoot."

"That's not funny."

"Guy in a mask, hit me and told me to stay away from Ash. So far, I've only spoken to a handful of people. There are only so many people who could've known to attack me last night, and none of them looked like the guy who jumped me. If I don't know the full story, how am I supposed to figure out who it was? And now I know my client isn't even on the level. Did you know she stands to gain, if Ash is dead? She gets control of his music."

"She doesn't want him to be dead, she's not after the music."

"Well, that's what she says, but sitting right here, it's looking like she's lying to me about everything else, so why not that? And you, too, Mona. You're holding out on me. I got warned off the case, and I don't even know what the case *is*."

"Okay, you're right." She reached for the phone. "But this is Louisa's choice to make."

TWENTY-TWO

LOUISA

Tribeca Grill is busy. The Saturday afternoon rush is transitioning into the Saturday evening melee. Chatter, the clink of glasses. The crisp white tablecloths have been laid out with surgical precision, and the staff are picking up your plates the second you set the fork down.

Times like this can be great for listening in. You'll get snatches of other people's conversations. Hear intimate moments, or secrets, or silly jokes. A flash of emotion, or a moment off-guard, when they don't realize how much they're giving away.

But taking in the room means I haven't been listening properly to Ally.

She leans in and repeats herself, her voice low.

"We need to look at these offers. With cashflow being what it is…"

"We have the emergency fund."

There's money nobody knows about. A cash reserve. When all the madness started, I handed it off to Ally to manage. To help her troubleshoot. Pay people to go away. Cover bills I forgot about. Do things I might not need to know.

Ally shakes her head, just once. "We've had six months of emergencies."

I know she's right. There has been a steady flow of offers since Dave went missing.

People who want interviews. Publishers who want to lay down an option on book rights. Film producers who want to lay down an option on the option. Everyone wants a piece of the drama. I get the feeling it's better for all of them if I'm guilty.

I've been turning down each and every one.

I don't want to profit off this.

And I don't trust them. I've been burned too many times. Sure, they'll say, we'll be fair, we'll make you look good in the edit. Then the final product comes out, and you're packaged, processed and sold.

Enough of my life is spiralling out of control without handing more of myself over to someone else.

But Ally is right. She is. I know it. I need to think of the boys. Of finding some more money to look after them, and of cash for the legal battle with Dave's parents. Something for my half of the mortgage.

I could stop paying, I guess. The mortgage comes out of Dave's account. I pay in the value of half, always have. But he'll have cash reserves, all that built up royalty money. I could stop paying my half and the mortgage would continue to be paid from his side. But how would it look?

That's the key.

Suddenly, the crazy woman who killed Dave starts to use his money to pay off the mortgage. No.

"Okay, what options do we have?"

"Well, the guys who did *The Biz* are looking for a new show."

I wave it away. "Not happening. No more reality TV."

"If we're in control of it, might be a good way to show you have nothing to hide."

I smile. I do have something to hide. "No, I don't want to give cameras that much access into my life."

"Okay, well, I've been talking to people at Warners. They're launching a new service, on demand, and want some premium shows to go out with. They're using the Amazon and Netflix model, so all the episodes could drop at once, or we could delay them, put them out weekly. They're talking serious development money."

"What for?"

"A show about you. But scripted. Drama, or comedy."

"Comedy? With everything we have going on?"

"Well, you know, one of those shows that's a bit of both, some drama, some laughs. Season one would be about your first year on reality TV. Then second season would be you meeting Dave. They'll change a few names, but everyone will know it's about you."

"Still feels like a trap."

"They want you involved, you can produce it. If we get a rush on, we could find a ghostwriter, sell one of the books, get extra money. You know if you're producing it *and* it's based on your book, double money."

My gut says no.

My brain says no.

Everything about me says no.

But my mouth says, "Set up a meeting."

"They'll be at the DeNiro party tomorrow. I can talk to them, line a few things up there."

"Wait. No, it's a mistake. Yeah, it's wrong. Look, we don't know what my head's going to be like in a year, two. I might not be up for the fight, and they could twist the story any way they want."

Ally makes a noise saying, *yeah, good point.* She sits back in her chair and thinks. I can see her chewing the inside of her mouth.

"Okay. How about this? We get someone else we trust to come on with you as a producer. We'll let Warners pick the showrunner, but you and someone else come on as part of the deal, and both of you have creative control. So if anything happens to you..."

"There's nobody I trust enough."

"I'll help, we'll find someone."

Wait.

There is one person I trust. "You."

Ally wasn't expecting that. "What?"

"You know how TV works, you had a show. I trust you. We can be the producers. Then if I need someone to have my back, it's you."

"I mean, well, I'm flattered, but..."

"Just think about it."

She smiled and nods, says she will.

My internal alarm goes off as someone walks toward us, clocking in my peripheral vision with a purpose. This isn't a casual passing. I turn to see a slight man, in a finely tailored suit. He has blond hair and just the right amount of stubble. I don't think anything on him is ever out of place.

"Excuse me," he says. His voice is soft. Controlled. "I'm sorry to interrupt."

He's breaking one of the unwritten rules of this part of town. You can stare at the famous people. Talk about us. Say hello in passing. But don't do *this.* Don't walk up on a meeting.

"I saw you from my table and wanted to introduce myself."

He slips a business card out of his inside pocket in one smooth movement, barely opening the jacket to do it. He places the card on the table between me and Ally, makes no move to shake our hands, which is wise.

"Charlie Starr," he says. "I would very much like to talk to you, see if we can work together."

I've never heard the name. He's giving off something that sets off all of my alarm bells. That feeling I get when someone is wearing a mask, hiding something else beneath the surface. That makes him either a psychopath or a film producer.

Ally pulls the card across the table toward her.

"Thank you Mr. Starr -"

"Charlie, please."

What's that accent? It sounds almost southern, but not quite. Just around the edges. Louisville? Somewhere around there?

"Charlie. I'll give you a call when we have some free time."

Ally's phone rings. She looks at me like, *are you okay if I take this now?* I smile up at Charlie Starr and say it was nice to meet him. He returns my smile, and my skin crawls. Maybe he's an executive producer. He tilts his head to acknowledge the end of the conversation and turns, walking straight out of the restaurant, rather than back to a table.

Ally grunts a few times at whatever's being said on the phone, then says okay, twice, and mentions Tribeca Grill.

"Ramona's on the way over with Con," she says to me after killing the call. "He knows."

"He knows what?"

"He *knows.*"

TWENTY-THREE

CON

There was some debate about where we should go. Louisa wanted some place private. Her nanny was in the apartment with the boys. Ally lived on the Upper West Side, but none of us wanted to go that far.

We flagged down a cab and Louisa directed the driver north up Greenwich Street to a shuttered storefront in the Meatpacking District.

She pulled out a set of keys and unlocked a metal box to the side of the rollers. She put another key into a small lock inside the box and turned. Nothing happened. She did it again, then sighed.

"Always takes a few tries."

On the fourth attempt there was an electronic hum, and the metal shutters started to lift up.

Louisa waited until they were shoulder height, and ducked underneath to unlock the door. She stepped in and held it open while we each followed.

Ally said, "I didn't know you still had this place."

"What is it?" I looked around in the darkness as Louisa headed to the back of the room.

I heard Louisa fumbling around, and overhead lights blinked on. We were in what looked to be a café though, from the dust on the furniture and stains on the floor, it hadn't been used in a while. The walls were decorated in pinks and browns, with large chalkboard paint in the shape of cupcakes.

There was a cartoony picture of Louisa in the window, and a smaller version of the same image near the counter.

"Another version of me," Louisa said. "Another mistake."

"You ran a café?"

"Cake and ice cream. Thought I could get back to basics when everything went nuts, start again."

"Looks nice," Ramona said.

"It was. Used the money from the wedding photographs to take out a long lease. Used the same logo as before I was on

The Biz. We did cupcakes, bread, coffee, frozen yogurt and homemade ice cream."

Louisa started pulling chairs down from where they were stacked at the sides of the room. I joined in, and arranged them into a small circle for the four of us. "What happened?"

"Businesses fail in New York every day." Louisa shrugged. "People weren't ready to see me any other way." She paused and laughed at something she'd thought of. "Unlike now, where they all see me as a killer. I got my wish, I guess."

"You could sublet," Ramona said. It was the tone she used when she thought she'd come up with an idea nobody else in the room had considered. "Bring in some money."

Louisa didn't answer, but I recognized the look in her eyes as she glanced around the room. She wasn't ready to let go of this idea, even thought it had failed. It was another piece of who she was.

We settled into the circle. I watched everyone's body language. Louisa was leaning back, wary, while Ally pitched forward a little and looked down at her feet.

We were sitting in silence for longer than any of us was comfortable with, before Louisa said, "So…"

Ramona cut in. "Con was attacked last night. Warned off the case."

"And I know about Matt Halliday."

"He was a mistake," Louisa said.

"Mine." Ally coughed, leaned in. "He was my decision."

I wanted to ask a question before Ramona could give away that I already knew the answer. "How did you find him?"

Ally paused. "My boyfriend's in the music business, said they used Halliday sometimes when people were having problems with drug dealers. Said he could be discreet, and was used to dealing with things others wouldn't touch."

Ramona flashed me a look. This wasn't the reason she'd been given.

Why was Ally's story changing?

I met Ramona's gaze and hoped she read my intent.

Not now.

I wanted to know what game was being played before showing my own cards. We might need it later. And I still didn't know who her boyfriend was.

I asked a question before Ramona could say anything. "He turned on you?"

"Yeah," Louisa said. "He started saying I was guilty, and he had proof. Tried to extort us, so we fired him."

Louisa was telling the truth, but I noticed a tell on Ally's face. I turned my attention to her and waited. I saw the sign again. It was a flick of her eyes, followed by biting the inside of her cheek. Louisa followed my gaze, and turned to face her friend.

"Al?"

"You fired him," Ally said. "I paid him off. He told me all his evidence would go away for fifty K. And he did, for a while. Go away. Then he started contacting me again, said my 'insurance policy' was running out, and I should renew it."

Ramona jumped in. "How much did he ask for?"

"Hang on," Louisa said. "First, where did you get the fifty? Is that why I'm short?"

"I was protecting you. I had to." Ally said quietly.

Louisa's cheek flexed as her jaw tightened. She breathed out, a long slow sound. "You should've told me. We could have managed it."

Ally had easy access to Louisa's money? On top of lying to us about Halliday? This was good information, but I didn't want to lose track of the reason we were there.

"So when he asked for more money," I said, "what did you do?"

"He called yesterday, asked for another fifty. I swore at him and hung up. He called back a bunch of times, but I didn't answer."

"Was this before or after you spoke to me?"

"After," she said. "Right after."

Another obvious piece of the puzzle fell into place. Halliday was big. Linebacker big. Sasquatch big. I shared a look with Ramona as I pictured how Halliday would look in a black jacket and ski mask.

I looked straight into Louisa's eyes. "And he was blackmailing you about Alzheimer's?"

She paused before answering.

"Yes."

TWENTY-FOUR

LOUISA

It never feels real to hear it out loud.

Even now, it sounds as strange as when the doctor first said it. Like being told I have a *spaceship*. Not information I can use or relate to. Not something that should exist in my world.

But it does.

"I have Alzheimer's."

I watch for Con's reaction. He's angry, and has every right to be. I lied to him. He trusted me, believed me, and I lied to him. I would be angry too.

Except *no*.

He has no right. Where does he get off? This is happening to *me*.

It's my problem. My condition. Who the hell is Con McGarry, or Ramona, or the cops, or anybody else, to say how I'm allowed to handle my own secrets?

I watch as he scrolls through reactions in his head. Some of them show in his face. Anger, confusion, doubt. He looks at Ramona, who is also waiting to see what he does next.

"I'm sorry," he says. "That sucks. Can I ask about it?"

"Sure. First, how did you know?"

"Edgar Malmon mentioned your mom, that she had it. And you met Todd through a charity because of it. And that just filled in a blank, I guess. I knew you were holding something back, and I'd been trying to place what it was. I remembered reading about your family back in the day. It just made the most sense."

I can't remember the last time anything felt like it made sense. Good thinking, though. He's smart.

"Aren't you too young?"

"Early onset. There's a gene. Can't remember what it's called." I catch myself with that line, smile. I would never have remembered what it was called, even before. "It only affects, like, three percent, something, but if it's passed on, you've got it."

"What..." He pauses, looks to Ramona, then to me. "I'm sorry I don't want to jus t-"

"It's okay. Just ask the questions."

"How advanced is it?"

It's funny. Doesn't matter how many times you give someone permission to be blunt, it never stops hurting when they are. He's honing in on questions I've been asking myself. How far advanced am I? How long do I have? When do I lose myself?

"When I was diagnosed, the doctor said it would be faster than this. He told me, by the time we start to show symptoms, it's already time for a caregiver. But I've been showing symptoms for a couple of years now, and between Dave and Ally I've been managing fine. And the meds are holding me together. But it feels..." I pause. I don't break. "It feels like it's speeding up."

"And what is it, I mean, how does it..."

"I'm losing the small things. Words. They just move. Sometimes they come back, sometimes they don't. I lose the connections between memories, the links between them. Or sometimes I'm in a different time for a few seconds, like I'll wake up and think I'm late for school, then I snap back to where I really am. Last week I saw one of my dad's favorite films on TV, and I picked the phone to call him. And it was, it was like, I knew he wasn't around anymore, but I was still trying to call him."

"She falls over," Ally says.

"Yeah, my coordination goes. It comes back, but there can be a few seconds where it just doesn't exist."

"When was the diagnosis?"

"I'd been putting off the tests for years. I was too scared. I'd seen it too much, too many people in my family. I used to be scared of old people, you know? Because the old people in my family were all weird. To my eyes, when I was young. They were these scary things, they looked like people but..."

Emotion wells up.

I can't help it.

I flash to seeing my aunt, a wonderful and caring person, stripped away into being someone cold and mean. Her dark eyes, someone else's eyes, flashing before she lashed out. My nanna, always a clever person, needing to be reintroduced to me every time I saw her. My mom, my own mom, who was always strong and independent, turning into someone emotional and helpless. Each of them changed, eaten away by this thing, and turned into new people.

And me.

The face I see in the mirror sometimes just isn't me. For a second. Like I'm wearing someone else's skin. Or I'm thinking through someone else's brain. The thing I know is coming. Not even creeping up on me, it's walking straight toward me, and smiling. I can't stop it.

"The stuff about the vacation is true," Ally fills in for me. "They were away as a family, and Louisa had her... incident."

"You mentioned losing your temper." Con's voice is tender, but he's getting right to the point. "I read that, in some people, the illness can lead to violence."

"I got angry. Really angry. Irrational. There was no reason, it was just, one minute I was me, and the next I was this angry person, someone else. Then it passed, and I was calm again, but... but I'd already done it."

"Done what?"

"I hit Dave. The boys saw it."

We sit in silence for a moment. I feel like I want to cry, but I don't. I've already been living with that punch for too long. It's just a fact now. A memory I can't seem to forget. This illness, it takes away the things I want to keep, but leaves me with the ones I'd be happy to lose.

The boys.

My boys.

The one I left in the park and the one who looked after me. The children I'm lying to. Losing track of all the lies. Of all the pieces. I'm sick of this game.

"Has that happened again?"

"Hitting people? No. I do get really angry. And sad, and happy. I can cycle through emotions, and they're raw, they're like the way a baby reacts to things."

He hits me with the key question. The one I keep coming back to.

"Is there a chance it happened on the night Dave went missing?"

I have no answer.

"Is it usual?" Con says. "To lose a whole evening?"

And here it is. The other thing. My own final piece of failure. The illness is something being done *to* me. But this….

"There's something else," I pause. I breathe. "I got high that night."

…this, I did to myself.

Ramona's eyes widen.

Yes. Judge the junkie. Take note of how weak she is. How out of control.

"The thing with the phone? The burner the cops say I called? I did, I know who it was. I called my old dealer."

"You'd kept the number?"

"There's a system. I don't even really think I knew I was doing it. Just another of those things we don't really notice. Like, 'here's the number for our insurance, here's the number for my accountant, here's the number for my drugs.'"

"Why though?"

Because I'm a drug addict.

"We argued. Me and Dave. We'd been not arguing for a long time, it was getting like a cold war. Then we argued, over the phone, and I think…I don't know if it was an argument we wanted, or if it was my illness, just a flash of anger maybe, but we argued. And he hung up, and I needed to feel something else. Anything else."

Because I'm a drug addict.

Because I fail my boys.

Because I fail.

Ramona's more upset than Con. He seems to have calmed down now we've talked out the illness. What's a few drugs after that? But Ramona's the one who wants to chase this down.

"What did you take?"

"I don't remember. I ordered a 'go bag'. Like a snackbox from a takeout, it comes with a selection. Heroin, Vitamin K, coke and painkillers. I paid for it, and then everything gets foggy. The medication, plus the pills, plus my memory. I remember flushing most of it. Somewhere in there, I realized what I was doing and flushed it. But everything else is gone. If it wasn't for Ally being there, I wouldn't even know which planet I was on."

"Vitamin K," Con says. "You mix that with the cocaine?"

"I mean… I used to? Did I do it that night? I can't say."

"It leads to memory loss." Con turns to Ally. "You were there that night. Did you see what she was doing?"

Ally pauses. "No, she was already high when I got there."

"With your boyfriend."

"Yeah."

"So you weren't there for the phone call, like you told the cops?"

"No."

"You could tell all of this to the police," Ramona says. "A pre-existing medical condition, plus intoxication. There's enough here. Even if they still think you did it, we could plea for diminished -"

"Come on. You've seen the press I get. They all want so badly for me to be guilty. And this is while they think I'm clean and sober. And I am—I was clean for years before, I've been clean since. I messed up on one night, and everything went wrong. I'll need to come clean about the illness. And soon. I don't have a choice. But I want it to be on my terms, and I want to be in control of what happens to my boys. And before I do any of that, I want to know what happened to Dave. If I come out with this while everyone thinks I killed him, I'll have no control over what happens next."

No control.

Everything is out of control.

I'm losing myself. My boys. My mind.

I just want to not care, for five minutes.

Con leans forward. "I just need to know. Again. Do *you* think you killed him?"

I blink.

I start to answer and stop.

The same question I've been asking myself for six months. But the answer is simple.

I'm an addict.

I'm a bad mother.

But I'm not a killer.

"No," I say. "I don't. I just don't."

TWENTY-FIVE

CON

Things were finally moving. Now I had a case to work.

Up until that meeting, I'd been chasing nothing more than a vague idea. David Ash was missing, nobody knew why, and his wife had no memory. He stepped out of a cab and off the planet, with no trail.

But now I knew where some of the lies were.

And why.

I needed to talk to the drug dealer. Louisa agreed to arrange a meet.

And there was Louisa herself. Everything I learned made it more, rather than less, likely she could have killed Ash. She stood to benefit financially from his death, and now had a history of hitting him.

But I still believed her. I don't know why. Maybe just because I wanted to. But when she'd told me, back at the café, that she didn't think she'd killed him, I went with her.

I wasn't sure Ramona had done the same.

She was behind the wheel of her silver Mini, on the way over to Matt Halliday's place in Rockaway Beach, and I could tell she was stewing. I'd come away with more belief, she seemed to have come away with less.

"Want to talk about it?" I tried for a light tone.

"About what?"

I bit back on my first seven responses.

Play nice, Con, *she's hurt.*

I'm used to people lying to me. On the street. On the job. On AirBnB profiles. I didn't take it personally when someone lied to me. It was all part of the game.

Ramona was different.

She'd gone into law because she wanted to defend the truth. She believed in honesty, and the justice system.

When real life started to chip away at that belief, she'd scaled back on her dreams, and now only insisted her clients be honest with *her*.

"My other big case this week?" she said after another mile of silence. "A drug addict who stole a computer, to pay for a birthday present for a son he remembers twice a year. He's guilty. He told me he's guilty. The cops know he's guilty. He's come to me to get a deal, to negotiate a plea bargain. Not to get him off. Not to help an innocent man. Just to help a loser lose a little less. That's what my life is now. I thought this one would be different. Just once, I thought maybe we could pick the right one. Look at myself in the mirror. Go home at the end of the day feeling like I'd done something."

"But you still think she's innocent?"

She drummed her fingers on the wheel. "Yeah. I do. I do. But she lied to me. Wasn't part of the deal."

"You didn't know about the drugs?"

"No."

"And Ally is lying, too. She has access to Louisa's money. And she's changing the story about Halliday. Do you know who her boyfriend is?"

"No, she keeps stalling on that. It always slips through, something else comes up."

"Have you asked Louisa for his name?

"Why would I…" A pause. "That's clever. See if Louisa knows the name, if he even exists. But why would Ally be lying about that? If we both believe Louisa, if she's innocent, then what would Ally have to gain by lying? What else is she doing?"

I parked the questions about Ally. I could ask Ray Yorke to sniff around her finances, see what he could turn up, but Ramona didn't need to know that.

"Her life just seems so small," I said. "Louisa's. No friends? No other family?"

"She does seem lonely. Just her and the boys, Ally."

"I always figured famous people have millions of friends, they all know each other, hang out."

"I guess not."

Still, though. Something didn't sit right with me about Louisa's complete lack of friends. Even an asshole has a couple of people who care about them, why did Louisa only seem to have her manager?

Ramona's cell buzzed a couple times in the silence.

She checked the screen when we stopped at lights and slipped the phone back into her pocket. Her body language shifted slightly, like this was something furtive, secret. I guessed it was her mystery man.

"Mona, this drug addict, the computer thief."

"I shouldn't have told you."

"I know, don't worry. But this guy, why did you take the job?"

She kept her eyes on the road. "He walked in my door."

"Plenty of people walk in your door. You don't take them all on. Why this guy?"

I saw something approaching a smile at the edge of her mouth, in profile. "I think he's trying. He's a terrible father, and he can't kick the drugs, but I think he deserves a break."

"Because you see the best in people. Always have. And then, when you get him that break, get him a good deal, aren't you going to go home feeling like you've done something?"

The smile spread. She took her eyes off the road long enough to look at me. "You're good."

"I have my moments."

"And thank you. All my stuff about honesty and feeling good, and you haven't thrown it back at me for lying to you about Louisa."

"Oh, I'm saving that for a special occasion."

We fell back into silence as we crossed Jamaica Bay.

She had lied to me. I took it as another part of the game. Ramona and I went back a long way, but she was also a lawyer representing a client. And, hell, I had a couple of secrets I'd kept from her for years, so I couldn't judge. Ramona had always been an expert at blaming herself for things she hadn't done. My own speciality was not caring all that much about things I *was* guilty of. But now she had genuine reasons to feel bad. I knew it would be eating her up.

I watched planes coming into land at JFK.

"I don't think he'll be at the office," Ramona said. "Halliday. It's late."

"Don't be fooled by the word office. He works from home."

I could have also added, don't be fooled by the word home

. Halliday lived and worked out of a trailer overlooking the beach, in the corner of a vacant lot where someone had pulled down a building and then never replaced it.

"You think he's the guy, don't you?"

I nodded.

We turned onto Rockaway Beach Boulevard. I directed her the rest of the way, through the residential part with nice houses and American flags, onto the more uneven road surface as we got to the commercial part, the bodegas, takeaways and bars. We turned off at a Chinese restaurant, onto 115th. Down to the end, past an empty warehouse, to the vacant lot nestled between the buildings and the beach. It would have been a prime spot for redevelopment, if the sea view wasn't obscured by the public toilets rising up above the sand on wooden supports. Halliday's trailer was in the corner, in the shadow of the toilets. It looked old and tired, half of it sagging a little lower than the rest. One light was on, shining out dimly against the shadows.

Ramona parked up in the middle of street, wanting to keep her tyres from the rocks and broken glass that spilled out from the vacant lot onto the curb. While we were both looking at the car, we heard the trailer door slam shut. We walked across the lot, the glass crackling beneath our feet. I knocked on the trailer door, to no answer. Ramona took a turn a few seconds later.

I raised my voice, "Halliday. Open up."

Ramona said, "Maybe he's not in?"

I nodded off to the side, towards the beach, "What was that?"

While Ramona turned to look, I stepped forward and turned the handle, opening the door. She whipped back to me with a smile, knowing the game I'd just played. The door swung out and I stepped up into the trailer, hit straight away by the smell of raw beef, urine, and human faeces. The trailer had been ransacked. Papers strewn across the floor, clothes pulled out of drawers, furniture tipped over. The wall and some of the papers were flecked with blood, and something more solid. Halliday was sprawled on the floor. His mouth was slack, open wide, and there was more blood mottled around a hole in the top of his head.

Ramona started to speak, but the words died in her throat as she took in the scene, coming out as more of a mumbled *yip*.

Out in the darkness of the vacant lot, we heard the crack of a footstep on broken glass.

TWENTY-SIX

LOUISA

I head up for a smoke on the rooftop terrace.

Ally is downstairs, with Gyul and the boys.

I don't know what I'm feeling. Is it anger? Suspicion? Every time I think back to our conversation at the café, I hear Ally talking about paying off Halliday. I hear her talking about money. My money. The money I trusted her with.

My life is falling apart.

My *brain* is falling apart.

And the one person I've trusted with everything, everything, is spending my money behind my back.

But -

I already knew that, didn't I?

What was the point of the emergency fund, if not for Ally to fix things without me knowing? To pay paparazzi to go away, bribe a reporter into turning up at an agreed time. It's there for bail, if the cops seize my assets, and to look after the boys if the worst happens and my estate gets tied up in legal issues.

And Ally is my caregiver in everything other than name. Haven't I already accepted she'll be making decisions for me? That she will be moving my money, my assets, and my life around, as I start losing touch?

Am I mad at Ally, or myself?

I don't know anymore. Like I don't know if the argument with Dave was genuine, or because I'm ill.

Like I don't know if our marriage was failing because of us, or because of the disease.

Or because of Jack.

That name again.

My brain just does this to me now. Throws things at me, with no explanation. I'll suddenly smell a cake my mom baked when I was six years old. Not just any cake, that specific one. A memory stored away somewhere untouched for almost forty years.

Or I'll suddenly be back in the middle of an argument I had at school, with Elsi Tanner. Probably over Ricky, a boy we both dated. And it will feel so fresh. I'm right there, in the middle of it, even though neither of them are in the room with me.

The most common one recently has been walking down a booze aisle in a shop, looking at all the different colored liquids. And it's a specific store. A specific memory. I just can't place where it is, or where it belongs in my head.

And now the name.

Jack.

Is it someone I used to know?

Why would my brain throw it at me in relation to my marriage failing? Is he someone I...

No, I'm still pretty sure I would remember sleeping with a guy.

Nothing feels certain anymore. Things are meant to be fixed in place at my age. Right and wrong. Yes and no. Dead or alive. Instead I'm just a walking mood ring.

I'm done hiding. Done waiting for the sky to cave in, or the world to end. I'm taking control back. I won't let this thing win. It's going to have to take me kicking and screaming. I'm going to the party, I'm making the deal, and I'm doing it on my terms.

I head downstairs. Gyul has gone, Ally is on the sofa, drinking water. I can hear the boys in their rooms, playing, talking to themselves. Ally doesn't meet my eyes at first. I grab a glass of water and sit across from her.

"I'm not mad," I say.

"You are."

"Yeah but forget it."

She sips, thinks for a few seconds, then nods. "You're taking too much on. Way too much. Hiring Con. The meeting today. These are the things I'm supposed to manage for you, but you need to let me do them. I've been putting out fires all day about your stunt in the park. We both know Dave's parents will..."

She stops when she can see I'm upset. There's no need to remind me I left Johnny behind at the park. I've been thinking about it every minute. Flashing back to the horror, and the pain, and to the creeping feeling, maybe I *should* let Dave's parents take the boys.

Maybe they'd be safer.

Every time I check my social media profiles, I'm hit with the hashtag #didshedoit? And people cracking jokes about what happened in the park. There's already a thing, what's the word, when they edit a picture and mix it with a joke? A meme? A meme. I'm a meme. Again.

"We're both acting like I'm seventy. I'm in hiding, giving up, and you've been enabling me."

"Now, come on -"

"When's that party?"

"Tomorrow?" She checks her cell. "Yeah, tomorrow."

Who has a party on a Sunday? Yeah. Normal people. I sometimes forget real adults can go to a dinner or a party without needing to stay out all night and get wasted. Most people probably just see a party on a Sunday night as code for *behave*. A DeNiro party will be perfect. I've been to a few before. I'm not in the same league as most of the people at those things, but it doesn't matter.

Simply *turning up* will send a message: open season is over.

"Ask Gyul to stay later tomorrow," I say. "I'm going to the party."

"What are you trying to prove? The thing at the park, the meeting with Elizondo, these are reasons for us to take it slow, not speed up. The whole city thinks you killed Dave." Her voice drops to a whisper. "And you want to start turning up to a party? Like you don't care?"

Like you don't care. There's an extra emotion to the words here. I've touched a nerve, I'm just not sure what it is. Concern for me? Concern for Dave? Concern for PR?

"I want to live. And this isn't living. Look —" I feel a flush. I recognize the signs; this is one of my emotional waves. My heart is pounding. But I'll ride it out. I'll control it. "Look, I know you're right. Probably. I'm making more mistakes. It's coming. But I don't want to just hide, what good is that? I sit up here, day by day, waiting to die? I need more."

She pauses again. Looks at me. "This is maybe one of those times when I cross the line, but am I talking to you, or to one of your mood swings?"

I give Ally my it's happening look. It skilfully hides how right she is.

"Okay," she says. "Let me set up a private meeting. We'll get them to come here." She watches my reaction and caves a little more. "Let's make a deal. You want to turn up to be seen, and make a deal? Let's do that. In, out. Find her, talk it out, see a few people, and leave."

"Okay. And if I'm struggling, we bail right away."

We both know this is all lies.

She's talking to me the way a parent talks to a child. Making a deal, expecting I'll forget about it when my mood changes. And I'm playing along because...

Because I know she's right.

"Hey." I change gears fast, but it's deliberate this time, not the result of a random brain fart. "Your boyfriend, the one who was with us that night?"

Ally's mouth opens and closes, she shrugs, "Yeah?"

"Was it Jack?"

She laughs, nervous, like *where is this going.* "Jack? Why would... no, Louisa, we've talked about this. My boyfriend's name is Zeke, you remember? He's in the music business. He knows Dave, you've met him a bunch of times, but we keep it quiet, we don't admit to it, because he's married. You do remember him being here, right?"

No, not one bit.

But I say, "Yes, *yes.* Sorry. Just confused there for a minute."

She watches me for a while, not saying anything, then grabs her coat and says goodbye to the boys heading on out the door. I pick my laptop up and start looking through the day's news. The usual fluff. A local Democrat involved in a scandal. A Republican from a town I've never heard of has apologized for a sexist remark. Stories about me in the park. More coverage of the, the thing. The picture thing. The meme.

There's the soft ping of a new email.

My inbox has over three thousand unread messages. Most of them will stay that way. But I try and scan fresh ones as they come in, to see if it's important. Occasionally I think one might be Dave, or an urgent email from him might be buried in the pile. But that's not how he would try to reach me after all this time.

The subject heading pops up on my notifications bar:

I Know Where He Is.

My heart stops. No, it doesn't, it goes nuts. A crazy
rhythm.
The email loads up.

He's alive.
I can take you to him.

PART THREE

"The hotel's the same.
We can use other names.
They'll never see,
That we're meant to be."
-David Ash

Episode Three: Little Ditty Bout Jack And Dee

Audio Clip: Hot Take ident.

Ad: *Don't Tell A Soul is part of the Hot Take network. For more information visit hottake.com and subscribe to Hot Take Plus to hear all our shows with ads and plugs removed.*

Audio Clip: *"What? Wait... how... no get... no please..."*
Loud noises. Scream.

Theme tune plays.

Dee: Hi, I'm Dee Buana. This is Don't Tell A Soul, the podcast about secrets, lies, and the truths we think we know.

Theme tune fades out.

Audio Clip: *"What? Wait... how... no get... no please..." Loud noises. Scream. Crying. "Please."*

Dee: What you're hearing is me. My attacker didn't seem to care that I was recording the incident as they broke my arm.
I know it's hard to listen to.
Here's some more.
Audio Clip: *Whimpering. Crying. "Please."*

Dee: I keep putting this episode off. I had planned to just do the episodes in the order I'd originally mapped out, and fit this one in later on. But it's started to feel like a con. I keep telling you all I got involved, and then I never say why. But this is the whole reason I've needed to complete this season. This is the one about me. The part where I got mixed up in the whole thing. I've not been able to listen to this recording since it happened. Until now. My hands are shaking as I speak. Can you hear it in my voice?

Just listening to that clip, I'm right back in the moment and I feel...

No.

(Audible blip.)

Dee: Sorry, I had to stop recording there. But I'm leaving the moment in. I want to report this as is. Mistakes and all. And to do that, I need to back way up to the start. Every year, we receive hundreds of suggestions for the next season of Don't Sell A Soul. We can't do them all, of course. But I'll admit, I was already interested in this case. As I said in episode one, that weekend, that news cycle when nothing else was happening, I think we all got a little obsessed with this story, didn't we?

So, when the suggestions to cover this story came in, well, we figured, of course.

The original plan was to take six months. We knew this would be a big one, lots of coverage. I started researching it about three months ago and started interviewing people a month after that. The plan was to release all the episodes in the run-up to the anniversary. But then, well... life happened. Louisa was arrested. Then the truth came out. The confession tape. And then... everything went a little crazy.

You know all of this, but I need to say it.

We had meetings, me and my bosses at Hot Take. Meetings for like ten days straight, about what to do with the recordings. The way I work is, I'll put together loose edits of episodes as I go along, in real time. I like to see the structure come together. Get out ahead of myself and get an idea of what the narrative needs next.

Narrative, right? Like I'm telling a story, and not reporting it. But I guess that's always been true, until now. I sit on things, hold them back for episode ten or eleven, leave a trail of hints, knowing it'll keep listeners coming back, like a game. Until the day it wasn't a game.

I guess there's always been an edge of exploitation to that, but I never...

Anyway...
(Laughter.)
I'm still talking round it. Avoiding it.
(Deep breath.)
Okay.

I got attacked. Partway through recording. Long before all the meetings I'm talking about there. Kind of the real reason for the meetings, let's be real. And I've been living with the effects of that ever since. And the people at Hot Take, well, they wanted to know what the right and wrong of this situation is.

So, we got the usual suggestions to cover the case. But what I didn't know at the time, one of those suggestions was coming from someone involved in the case.

The name they gave was Jack. I had no idea at the time that this was fake. Emails at first. We talked back and forth. I thought I was making... well, I thought we were getting close. I don't know. Friendly. We exchanged numbers so we could message each other on a secure app.

As I researched, we continued to talk. And then the hints started. Some of the things you've heard on the series already? Some of the people I tracked down to speak to? The information came from Jack. And there was more. Things I haven't told you about yet. In the last episode, I mentioned Louisa hired two associates of Reah Kanellis, and I said I'd Googled their backgrounds. That's only partly true. I did Google them, but only after Jack had already tipped me off.

And did I question it? I mean, yes. Of course. But only to myself. This was a great source, and it was going to get me a great story, why would I want to stop that?

So here's an example. Right around the time I was researching Louisa's past, and taking trips over to Astoria, I got this message.

Jack (Dee reading): You need to talk to her drug dealer?

I responded, asking if Louisa was still taking drugs.

Jack (Dee reading): Not now.

I asked, was she taking drugs when David went missing?

Jack (Dee reading): Warmer.

I asked if they knew how to contact the dealer.

Jack (Dee reading): I can set it up.

So the next day, I get a call on a different number. My cell is set up to record all calls.

Dee (recording): Hello?

Voice: You've been looking for me.

The voice is disguised, as you can hear. I've played around with it in editing a few times, to try and clear it up, but it doesn't work.

Dee (recording): Who am I talking to?

Voice: Someone you want to meet.

I know, all very vague, right? Truth is, I'm used to calls like this. They come with the gig. But they never stop sounding like a silly 70s paranoia film.

Dee (recording): Are you Louisa's drug dealer?

Voice: I'm sending you details. Don't be late. Come alone.

Dee: I just had to redo this bit. Originally I said I didn't think anything of it, the idea that this was Louisa's dealer. Jack had set up the meeting, and I was going to follow the instructions. But then I went back on that, went on a long tangent for, like, five minutes, about cognitive dissonance and how of course I thought something of it, but doing my job means you have to roll with things that you wouldn't normally accept.

But you don't need that whole speech.

So, the message came through. Rockaway Beach. A time. A repeat to come alone.

Now, I should say here, to head off some complaints, that Hot Take have procedures in place for this. Mine isn't the only investigative show. Across the network, there are a few of us who get messages like '*come alone*' or '*don't call the cops*'. And there's a support system in place. We notify two other people of where we're going, and when, and we record a message explaining why. But I guess, in a weird way, all of this worked against me. Because this, combined with my previous experience, really meant I walked into the meeting with no real fear.

I was wired up to record. I mean, I figure, if you tell a podcaster to come alone but don't specify anything about recording, you know what you're getting, right?

The directions lead me to the public washrooms on Rockaway Beach. If you've been there you know the ones. They're these wood and metal pods, standing up off the sand on poles. You can get down beneath them, in the shadows.

I would suggest you never do that. I don't know how often it gets cleaned down there. It was hard to tell in the dark, at night, but it didn't smell clean, and I didn't want to think about what my foot kept nudging as I walked down there.

(cough.)

(Sniffing sound.)

Sorry. So that's when it happens. I still never saw anything. Or don't remember seeing anything. I didn't hear anything. There was nothing at all to suggest someone was behind me until I got hit in the head. I felt someone strong grabbing my right arm. And then the audio picks up, the clip you've already heard, with the warning right before.

Unknown Male: Back off Louisa

Dee: What? Wait... how... no get... no please...

Loud noises.

Scream.

What you're hearing now is me, crying. If you listened really closely, you might have heard my arm snapping. My shoulder dislocated, too. Popped clean out. I'm still on painkillers.

Dee: Please.

Unknown Male: Where are your tapes? I want to know who you've talked to.

Dee: Wh... what? You want...

Unknown Male: Stop jerking me around.

Scream.

That was him twisting my broken arm.
That might even be the moment my shoulder dislocated. I can't be sure. But there... if you listen... I've tried to bring the audio up as high as I can, you hear this?

(Metallic clicking.)

I think that's a gun. Because then there's this other voice. I don't really remember any of this. I'm not sure if it's trauma, or if I was blacking out, but this bit is just gone from my memory, but not my tape.

Second Unknown Male: I suggest you stop what you're doing.

First Unknown Male: The fuck?

Second Unknown Male: Follow me.

Note the accents. The first guy was local.
The second sounds different, southern maybe.
Then it's footsteps away, you can hear them here.

This is guesswork, just based on the sounds on the tape and things I learned since. But I think the second man turned up and pointed a gun at my attacker.

My attacker, he's local, best I can figure, was a man named Matthew Halliday. He was a corrupt PI, hired by Louisa.I say *was* because he died that night. That's what I think this is, listen close...

(Gunshot.)

I know for sure I blacked out around here, you can hear my heavy breathing on the tape. I picked up a concussion that night, a big lump on the back of my head that took ages to go down. I don't remember where in all of this I hit my head, but somewhere, I did.

I'm out of it for quite a while. I must have come around and then blacked out again, because there are a few times I'm moaning. I'll skip past that. But then about ten minutes later you hear footsteps coming back towards me and then this...

(Rustling sounds.)

Second Unknown Male: Ah.

That's someone pulling at my clothes. When I woke up, the mic had been pulled out of my coat pocket.

It wasn't disconnected.

And then this, again I'm bringing the audio up to help.

(Banging.)

Third Unknown Male (distant): Halliday open up.

(Footsteps running away.)

And then a little a little later, I seem fully alert, though I still don't remember this...

Dee: Wh... hey, help. Help. Can you... puh... help.

Unknown Female Voice: It's from down here.

TWENTY-SEVEN

CON

There was someone else in the lot with us.

I planted my hand between Ramona's shoulder blades and pushed her forwards. She tripped on the step and fell face forwards into the trailer. I turned on my heels, searching the shadows for a solid shape. I had no plan for what I'd do when I found one. The crackling came again, farther away now, and repetitive. Long, running strides.

I caught movement from the corner of my eye, back near the road. Someone turning out onto the street, rounding the corner of the warehouse. My first instinct was to give chase, and I shifted forwards onto the balls of my toes. Then my second, third, and hundredth instincts all kicked in, and I looked back to Ramona. She'd tripped on the step and planted onto the carpeted floor of the trailer.

Face to face with the dead body.

"He's... did he... that's..."

She gave up trying to find words and started typing a number into her cell. Three digits. I put my hand over her phone and said to wait.

Ramona stared up at me at me for a second, then looked around the trailer, at all the papers and upturned furniture, and said, "Oh, no."

"Mona -"

She looked around again, then let her eyes settle on the body. She coughed, stood up, taking a step back out into the lot.

"This is a crime scene."

"It will be, the minute you call the cops."

"He's just, he's right there, he, why would he..."

The color had drained from her face. She looked the way I felt. But this was the only chance I would get.

"We'll call them." I touched her arm gently. "Of course we will. But when we do, everything changes. They'll be in here, looking at the scene, they'll close all of this off, and if there's anything here to help our case, we'll never see it."

Ramona took a step back and lifted the phone again.

"Look, we're not covering for anything. We're not moving him, hiding him. We're going to do the right thing. I just need us to do it a little later. He knew something we don't. It looks like he's been killed for it. There might be something here."

"You don't think he…"

She didn't finish the question, but I knew what she meant. I touched her arm gently, whispered: "The gun isn't here."

I pulled a pair of gloves from my jacket pocket.

Ramona said: "Why do you have those?"

"Because you pay me to do things you don't want to know about. Wait at the car if you have to, but give me five minutes. Just five, that's all. Then we do the right thing."

She hesitated, nodded, and turned to leave.

I stepped back up into the trailer. The weight shifted beneath my feet every time I moved. It was a strange feeling, stepping around him, looking through his things. The trailer felt empty. I was alone, but there was someone with me. Almost the exact opposite feeling of a moment earlier, out in the lot, when I'd felt like we weren't alone but didn't see anybody.

I focused on the task at hand. No need to worry about leaving things as I found them, it was already a mess. I sifted through papers. Turned over drawers. I used my cell to take pictures of the documents, trying to focus in on any names or dates, but nothing was feeling relevant. There was a pile of receipts and old post-it notes in the corner, where they must have fallen when something was moved. One of them had Ally's name, and "50k" written next to it. There was another with my name and address. I pocketed both. I didn't want to leave a direct link back to me.

I found power leads and USB cables, but no computer.

Where was it?

I took a deep breath before bending down over the corpse and checking his pockets. I found his wallet. Receipts, credit cards in a variety of names. Several loyalty cards for the same coffee shop. I took the cards that weren't in his own name. I'd probably be able to talk Ray into hacking them, if there was no direct link to Halliday. Maybe something would show up.

I looked closer at the wallet. There was a gap in the lining. And old trick of the trade, known as a safe sleeve. Unpick the sewing, or unstick the glue, and slip things into the slim new sleeve you've created. There was a business card. Just a name and a number. *Charlie Starr.* Never heard of him. Pulling the card out, I felt something else move beneath it.

A slip of folded paper.

Another post-it.

C Waltz.

100K.

I stared at the note. *C Waltz.* The assistant district attorney, the same one applying pressure to get the case wrapped up, was *Carl Waltz.* Why would the ADA's name be hidden away in the safe sleeve of a known blackmailer? It seemed like Halliday had been finding dirt on everyone involved in this case. Did that include Waltz? What could the ADA have to hide?

And with that, another creeping feeling. The wallet was easy to find. Right there, in the pocket. Whoever had killed him hadn't gotten round to it yet. They'd still been tossing the place when we turned up.

They might be coming back.

I pocketed the wallet.

Someone called for help outside. It was distant, but sound carried near the beach at this time of night. I looked out the doorway and could make out the edges of Ramona, a shadow mixed in shadows, near the concrete barrier in front of the boardwalk.

She called out: "It's from down here."

I hesitated. There was still so much to do here. But then I saw Ramona's shape off and moving, and I wasn't leaving her alone if there was still a killer out there. I jumped down out of the trailer and ran after her, over the barrier, onto the boardwalk, and to the low fence circling the washroom supports.

The groaning was coming from down there, in the weeds and sand. We climbed over the fence and slipped down the bank, almost tripping over litter and probably worse. Using the torch settings on our cells we found the source of the sounds.

A young black guy, huddled at the base of one of the support struts. His face was almost vacant, the semi-blissed out stage that only comes from a mix if shock and extreme pain.

Ramona paused, looking down at his face. "I know him, er, them. This is the podcaster."

"The one investigating Louisa?"

I knelt down, looking in a little closer. Their eyes focused slowly on me.

"You okay?"

They breathed in deep, out, a little jagged. "My arm."

The shoulder looked wrong. The arm was too long, and twisted in an odd angle.

It looked like a pretty bad dislocation. Sometimes you can pop them back in, be fine five minutes later. Sometimes you feel it for the rest of your life.

"We shouldn't move them," Ramona said. "We should get some paramedics down here, not risk it."

I nodded, but said, "What happened here?"

They were more alert now, eyes focusing on me and then lingering on Ramona. "You're the lawyer."

Ramona knelt down beside me. "Yeah. What happened here?"

"Jack set me up."

I said: "Who's Jack?"

They mumbled the name a few more times and then started to sound drowsy.

I was worried about a head wound and nodded for Ramona to go ahead and call 911.

I asked again, "Who is Jack?"

"Don't know. Somebody..." A sleepy pause. "Thought they were helping me with the... story."

"A source?"

"I shouldn't be talking to you."

"You shouldn't be lying here all beat up, either, but we are where we are." I smiled, hoping it showed in the light given off by our phones. "Tell me what's going on."

"I've been getting tip offs from Jack. By text. They told me…" The kid paused, looked up at Ramona, thought it over. "They told me Louisa was still taking drugs and promised to set up a meeting with the dealer for an interview. That's -" a loud scream of pain as they tried to readjust their sitting position. "Fuck. That's what I thought this was, the meet."

"Jack did this to you?"

"There were two different…" Another yelp, a grunt. "People. I think… did I hear a gun?"

I waited until Ramona finished her call. She'd been half listening in. "Do you know any Jack?"

"Not in relation to this."

I turned back to the podcaster. "Hey, ambulance is coming. Cops, too. We should talk. Once you've been checked out, and this circus is over. We'll both -" I shared a look with Ramona, who wasn't happy at the promise I was making, "give you an interview, okay? Do you have a phone? I'll give you my number, or take yours."

They started fumbling with their good arm to reach a jacket pocket, but it came with more squeals and grunts. I put up my hand to signal they should stop, then slowly reached into the pocket myself, pulling out a smart phone and placing it in their good hand. They unlocked it.

"Here," I said. "I'll do it."

I added myself as a contact, and then took a quick look at their texts.

In a secured messenger app I could see a conversation with Jack. I clicked on the name, which loaded up the phone number linked to it.

I took a quick picture of it with my own cell, making it look like I'd forgotten my number and was getting it off my contacts list, then placed the kids' cell back in the pocket.

They said: "Why are you here?"

I didn't answer. A new distraction had taken over. The sound of burning. There was a glow coming from above us, back on the boardwalk. I shouted for Ramona to keep the kid talking and ran back up the bank, up and over the fence, and across the wooden walkway to what I'd known I would find.

Halliday's trailer was engulfed in flames.

The killer had circled back, to get rid of the evidence .

TWENTY-EIGHT

CON

The uniforms from the 100th Precinct turned up, along with paramedics and fire trucks. The holy trinity. The firefighters got to work putting out the blaze, the paramedics took the kid away to the nearest hospital, and the uniforms asked us the same six or seven questions over and over. Ramona told them we'd come to see Halliday in relation to one of her clients and found the trailer this way, and then heard the kid calling for help. She was leaving out details, but she wasn't lying. I knew they'd checked my name in the system. There were a tense few moments when I worried they might arrest me, search my pockets. In all the drama I'd forgotten I still had Halliday's wallet.

After a while, a detective turned up. A woman named Irene Doyle. She had an Irish name, but looked to be Indigenous. We went over the story a couple more times with her, Ramona doing most of the talking. The story held up just enough to get us through. Reading between the lines of what we both picked up, it felt like the cops were going to be happy to connect the half-formed trail and chalk this one up as a suicide. How the podcaster would fit into that was a much larger question, their statement could mean they would have to do some actual police work. But it wouldn't be hard for them to massage the podcaster's statement, if they wanted to. It would be easier than actually investigating.

We were quiet on the drive back. Rattled. Ramona was upset and trying not to show it. That worked for me. I could ignore how shaken I was and focus on reassuring her.

"The blood…" She shook her head.

"Yeah."

The image was going to stay with me, too. I was amazed by how much it had spread out. The pattern on the wall. I started to think of the way it was still moving when we walked in.

I shuddered in my seat and Ramona noticed it. "You okay?"

"I'm a bit freaked, too, I guess."

"And the kid. Dee. What was that about?"

"We need to talk to them. Maybe they know something."

"And this Jack."

I swiped through the camera roll on my cell, loading up the picture I'd taken of Jack's contact details. I read the number out loud so we could both remember it for a few seconds, then we both recited it as I typed it into my cell and dialled.

It rang through to an anonymous voicemail, then went dead.

I remembered the other number I'd taken that night. Leaning to the side, I pulled out Halliday's wallet.

Ramona looked at it briefly, taking her eyes off the road, "Is that?"

"Don't ask."

I opened the sleeve and pulled out the Post-It with the apparent Waltz marker on it, turned it for Ramona to see. Then retrieved the ones with Ally's and my names on, stored them all away back in the wallet.

Ramona pulled up outside my building on 44th. There was a pause, like we were waiting for each other to make a move.

Ramona shook her head again. "This is getting nuts."

"Yeah." I waited. Hoping something more intelligent would come to me, but I kept flashing back to the dead body and the words wouldn't come.

Ramona left me alone with my thoughts for a few seconds as she typed out a few messages on her cell. From the buzzing, I could tell she was getting instant replies. Someone had been waiting to hear from her.

She looked back up at me. "Do you really think that's why I hire you? What you said back there, I pay you to do bad things?"

"I didn't say *bad*. I said you pay me to do things you don't know about. I cut corners. I get into buildings, steal wallets, I tell lies. You want the end result."

She stayed silent for a long time. Stewing. Just the sound of the car's hazard lights filling the silence. I could tell I'd said something wrong, I just wasn't sure what it was.

"Is that really what you think?" Her voice was subdued.

"I didn't mean -"

"I need to go." She nodded for me to get out.

Ramona keyed the ignition. I climbed out and watched her taillights down to 30th Avenue.

The lights were on in my guest rooms. I looked up at them and thought for a moment about checking in on the guests. It could be fun to hang out with them, talk to people from different backgrounds and countries. I thought, too, about heading to Sharkey's.

I was lit up from behind by car headlights. An engine revved. There was a red Porsche at the curb, behind where Ramona had pulled in. Must have been sitting there the whole time. I couldn't make out who was behind the wheel through the glare of the lights.

The car pulled forward, into the space Ramona had vacated.

The side window was down. It was Ally.

"I think we should talk," she said.

TWENTY-NINE

CON

Ally had been drinking. I could smell it as I sat in the passenger side. She had the look. Not a full-on drunk, but something had taken the edge off. She wasn't as stiff as she'd been the last couple times.

"We can't go upstairs?"

I pointed up at the lights. "My guests are in. I'm guessing you don't want -"

"No." She pushed back into her seat, smiled at me. "Where can we go?"

This was a different side to her. I'd already seen a few different versions of Louisa as the story had changed, but Ally had been consistent. Cold, and annoyed at me for existing. Now she was almost playful.

"You shouldn't be driving," I said. "How much have you had?"

"Only a couple. You blame me, after the day we've had?"

I felt like explaining all the ways my day had been worse, but thought instead about how many bad evenings she'd been having in the last few months, and wondered how many couples she'd been drinking each night. Was this a regular routine?

She waved from me to the wheel. "You drive."

"Don't have a licence. They took it away."

"After your Steve McQueen impression." She gave me a knowing look. Like she was after some fun. Any other time, I'd have played along. But I didn't know what the game was. "Now you're interested in the rules?"

"I'm interested in not getting arrested."

"Or not getting caught?"

She was fast. I started to wonder how much of the drunk was an act. Just another way of manipulating me.

"Well, you choose," she said. "Am I going to drive drunk, or are you going to drive without a licence? I bet you've always wanted to take one of these for a spin."

The sane option was to get her a cab home and head up to bed. Take the case up again in the morning, after a chance to sort everything out in my head. But I haven't always been known for taking the sane option.

I got out and walked around, while she climbed across into the passenger seat. The Porsche begged me to rev the engine. I could feel it as I put my hands on the wheel. I pulled away from the curb, and up into traffic at the top of the road. We were both holding back, me and the car. I wanted to floor the pedal, see what she could do, but I couldn't risk being pulled over.

"Nice car."

"Really? I don't really like it. It's a piece of junk that goes fast. And I don't even get to do that, not living in the city."

"If you don't like it, why not sell?"

"It was my father's." She paused. Stretched the silence out, until I was thinking that was meant to be explanation enough. "His midlife crisis, or whatever. He loved this thing more than me, so I made my attorney throw the car into the demands."

"It's a good trophy."

"All trophies are good." She leaned back into the seat again, making a show of it, stretching her limbs out. "So, where are we going?"

I took my eyes off the road for a second to look at her. She was watching me. Her eyes were more sober than her voice. I could feel the edges of her game. The attempts to sway me, direct my thoughts.

"Halliday's dead," I said.

Her reactions were honest.

I saw the shock register on her face. The way she stiffened, throwing cold water on her act. There was booze there, but now I could see the real amount. Maybe one drink. Maybe only a couple of sips. Enough to relax her, and to pick up the smell. But she hadn't known Halliday had been killed unless she was an Oscar-worthy performer.

"What happened?"

"Made to look like suicide."

"*Made to look?*"

"Not very well. We interrupted whoever was doing it, so they couldn't neaten it all up."

"Someone killed him?"

"Or someone had him killed." Left that in the air, seeing if she would pick up on the inference, before adding: "The podcaster was there too."

"Dee?" Her voice peaked a little, concerned more now than when I'd mentioned Halliday was dead.

"Yeah. Someone's been feeding them information, lured them out to the beach, beat the crap out them."

She echoed what Ramona had said, "This is getting nuts."

We passed Citi Field on the Parkway, and I realized where I was taking us. In focusing so much on figuring Ally out, I'd left the driving pretty much to instinct and my subconscious. Now I knew where that was leading, I smiled.

Ally caught it. "What's funny?"

"Nothing."

She made a noise somewhere beneath a snort. Not annoyed enough to call me on it. She reached beneath her feet and pulled out a flask, opening the lid and taking a long pull. She offered it to me, but I shook my head.

"You talked to Halliday last night," I said. "Right before he attacked me, if I've got the times right. How did he sound?"

"His usual charming self." The tone in *charming* was anything but. "He was angry, aggressive."

"Anything sound out of the ordinary?"

"Not for him, no."

I took a right, onto Jackie Robinson, following it down to Forest Park Drive. Looping through the park, I knew where we were going, and went with it. Pulling us to a stop in the parking lot at the other end.

"Where are we?" Ally looked around at the trees, mostly just shapes in shadows at this time of night.

"Forest Park," I said. "Used to come here when I was a kid."

I left off the extra details. How this was the place Ramona and I would come to when we wanted someplace private. How climbing onto the carousel after dark was an adventure for Ramona, and a chance for me to show off about breaking rules. Back in the days when we'd both wanted those things from each other. Before life got in the way. I couldn't help but wonder who it was Ramona had gone to when she left me standing outside my apartment. Where was she now, and how far away had we drifted?

The rush of jealousy hit me again.

I pushed it away.

Ally was smiling. "Who were you thinking about there? Ramona?"

I got out of the car and headed toward the carousel. Ally walked behind me at first, then strode to catch up. Out in the darkness we could hear kids laughing, calling out to each other, being young.

"You wanted to talk," I said. "What about?"

She shot me a look that said, *spoilsport.* "I think we got off on the wrong foot."

"You don't like me."

"Tell you a secret, I don't like anyone."

"That's not a secret."

When the metal fence came into view at the top of the path, and the carousel beyond, Ally laughed. "Oh, I do know where we are. Filmed here once, I think. Or I've seen it in a film. I don't know, they kinda blur after a while."

The gate was locked. It would have been easy enough to climb over, and I could probably get the lock open even quicker, but I didn't feel the need to show off.

"Why did you hire me?"

"*I* didn't hire you. For the record. That was Ramona and Louisa. I said no."

"I bet you hated that."

She stopped walking. "Really? We've met twice, you got me all figured out?"

"I've been trying to figure it out. I mean, Ramona, Halliday. I couldn't get it. Why would you hire them? You've got all your contacts in the city. Probably a load of favors you can call in. But you hire a cheap lawyer from Astoria -"

"She know you talk about her like that?"

"And a conman from the Rockaways. But I get it now."

"Okay." I had her annoyed now. Defensive. "What's your professional opinion? As my psychiatrist?"

I leaned back against the fence.

"You're a control freak. You need to be the one in control of the situation. And I get that you've got reasons. The family thing and all. So you hired a lawyer who you thought would be grateful for the work, someone you could control, be intimidated by you and Louisa. And you hired a lump of a PI, figuring you could manipulate him however you wanted. But then he turned on you, and Ramona went rogue by hiring me."

"That's not bad." She produced the flask and took another drink. Pausing for a second after, pretending to be hit hard by whatever was inside. "My turn. I've been trying to figure you out. I get Ramona. I know who she is. How she works. And I get - got - Halliday, too. Okay, so I didn't see him turning on me, but I knew who he was, how he was wired. I know Louisa. I know that cop, too. Elizondo. I feel like I know who everybody is in this thing, except you. You're the one thing I don't understand."

I read that as, you're the one I can't control.

"Real talk now. Louisa's not here. Ramona's not here. You can be honest with me. Do you think she killed him?"

She blinked. "What? No." She waved in the air between us, pushing the idea out of the way. "I know her. Like I say. Okay, you're right, I'm a control freak. I like to have everyone pegged. But that means I have Louisa pegged, too. I know she's not a killer." She leaned back next to me on the railing. I almost saw an invitation in the move. "And I think you know it, too. I think maybe we're the same."

"You and me?"

"Yeah. You read people. For you to figure me out so fast, I think it means you're seeing yourself. Was that what you did? Read people so you could scam them?"

I didn't say yes.

Neither of us needed that.

"If you're so good at it, why'd you stop?"

"Who says I did? Same set of skills, then and now. Just a different outcome. You know that old joke, that being an alcoholic is the only hobby that takes away things? Everything else you build up a collection of stuff, but as an alcoholic, you slowly lose it all. My old life I took things away from people, now I bring them back."

"For money."

"Of course."

"Why did you get involved in the robbery?"

I shrugged. "I was helping a friend."

She tilted her head toward me. "See, that's exactly what I mean. Who are you? I don't get you at all."

"What's to get?"

"You want me to believe you'd do time because you were just helping a friend? I don't know what's crazier, that line, or that I think I believe it."

I could feel the pull. Her lips were right there, and I knew I was reading the invitation right. She wanted to control me, but in the moment, why not let it happen? She was attractive, and we were both adults. Who cared if it was a trap, as long as I could walk away after?

If Ramona could be off right now with her new life, why couldn't I?

"Who's your boyfriend? The mystery man we haven't met yet?"

"Do we need to talk about him?"

Somewhere in there, I found whatever it was I needed to push back.

Self-respect, maybe?

"So you think, pretend to be drunk and I'll play along?"

Ally snorted for real this time. Pushing off from the fence, she handed the flask to me. I could smell rum. It was so close to one of the sickly prison hooches, my stomach turned over. I went back to my first guess, about Ally self-medicating with booze.

"Maybe I just wanted to talk." She started back the way we'd come, toward the car. "You think of that?"

THIRTY

LOUISA

I stare at the computer.

Lunchtime, and I'm still waiting for another message. I've been refreshing my inbox since the sun came up. It's automatic, but still I keep pressing the button. I check my spam folders every five minutes, convinced that the all-important message will somehow end up in there. Meanwhile, *actual spam* keeps coming through. I jump each time I hear the ping, thinking this is the one.

It's been a sleepless night.

The first email last night had been clear enough. It was followed instantly by another.

> Do not tell anybody. Do not show anybody. Do not
> call the cops. I will contact you with details tomorrow.
> If you try to trick me, you will never see him.

Is this a kidnapper? I can't tell. I read and re-read the words. There's a threat in there, for sure. But is it from someone who is holding Dave to ransom, or someone who knows where he is?

Or what if -

I'm used to hoaxes. When I first got famous it would be fake offers of work. People emailing me, or leaving voicemail messages pretending to be from television companies, magazines or movie studios. When Dave and I got together it changed to women claiming to be his long-lost lovers. Possessive fans of his music who felt I was stealing him away. And since he went missing, Ally has started intercepting most of my messages. She checks my voicemail. The contact details on my website all route through to her, and all but one of my email accounts are filtered through her computer.

All but this one.

The Hotmail account I opened when I was twenty. Only a handful of people know this one still exists. Friends from back in the day. A few Nigerian princes. Dave. This was how we would get private messages to each other. I've been checking it regularly to see if he was going to get in touch.

Or what if -

They say it's the hope that kills you. Well, for me and Dave, it was addiction that tried to do us in. The little voice saying go on, have another. The whispering doubts. The hole deep down inside which needed filling. Hope is what kept me alive. Hope is what made me think the withdrawal would be worth it.

But this version of hope? Yeah, I could see how this can kill.

The song in the bottom of my gut, telling me Dave is out there, and I'll see him once I get this email.

I can't believe it.

I won't believe it.

Or what if -

Sleep has been impossible.

Just when I was accepting Dave is dead.

He's out there?

Can I get to see him?

Will it be today?

Is he coming home?

I take a sip of water and down my pills before wiping breadcrumbs off the bed. Toast is the only thing I've been able to keep down. If I let the boys see me eating in here, they'll think they can have food in their rooms, too. It's one of the few rules I really insist on. No food in the bedrooms. My mom used to say that. Food was for the kitchen and the dining table. Maybe the yard on a hot day. Never for the bedsheets.

Aside from food, I let Pete and Johnny get away with murder. They're usually up at the crack of dawn on a Sunday. I've always longed for the day they turn into teenagers and want to sleep in. I don't mind them playing around the apartment, or turning on the TV. It's only if they come into my room they get shouted at.

I can hear them outside, the noise of a cartoon, the clack of toys on the floor. I want to go and join them. Spend all my time with them. But then the email might come through, and what if I get emotional?

No.
I'm staying in here.
A kid at Christmas.
A *very strange* Christmas.
The computer pings. A new message hits my inbox. My heart stops.

> Have you told anyone?

Typing back as fast as I can. My email software tries to predict what I'm saying, I have to go back twice and rewrite the words.

> *No, you said not to. What do you want me to do? Do you really know where Dave is?*

I wait for the response. It comes within a few seconds. One word.

> Yes.

Followed a moment later by another.

> I know where he is.
> For seventy thousand dollars. Cash.
> I will take you to see him.

THIRTY-ONE

CON

Is it possible to be hungover without having a drink?

I woke up after a weird series of dreams, only half-remembered in the morning light. I'd been spending time with Sofia, an old woman who was some vague relation to my mother. She'd scared the hell out of me as a child. Her old skin, paper-thin and cracked, her gums, the smell that lingered in her apartment, that I still associated with age. Her memory had been fading toward the end of her life, and I dreaded the times she would try to talk to me, forgetting who I was, or mixing me up with children she'd known decades before.

One time, my mom needed to rush out to run an errand and left me alone with Sofia. Looking back, as an adult, I know nothing bad happened. She was just a distant relative who kept an eye on me for thirty minutes. But as I boy, I was terrified. I felt trapped, locked in with a monster.

And in my dreams now, part of me was trying to bond that feeling to Louisa Mantalos.

Physically, I still have the hots for her. The brown eyes. But beneath the surface, she's struggling just as much as Sofia. And what did it say about me, that my brain needed to go to these places? To decide whether I still liked her because she's hot, or was scared of her because she's ill?

A fresh cup of coffee pushed the dreams to the back of my head, where they could fade away, and I got on with the job. What had happened the night before? Halliday? Ally? Every single step I took led to more confusion.

I wanted to go back to finding a missing ring, or a lost bodega cat.

But the questions were wired into me now. I needed to answer them.

I got two calls. The first, bright and early, was from Ash's manager. Danny Stewart. He worked at Modello Talent Agency on Park Avenue. I hadn't expected people like Danny would work on a Sunday, but he was in the office and happy to see me.

The second call made hell freeze over. Detective Elizondo. The cop who was working Louisa's case. More importantly for me, the cop who caught me all those years ago. He wanted to meet for coffee. Why the hell would I do that? Ignored him at first, to return Danny Stewart's call and set up the meeting. Then I reconsidered. What could it hurt to meet Elizondo? He would have an angle, naturally. He'd be trying to get information from me. But I could work the same trick on him. He'd been working the case for six months and was still convinced Louisa was guilty. Maybe I could get something out of him.

Meeting the guy who put me away for a social chat.

What was this case doing to me?

Sundays are the days my guests usually check out. My mom turned up at her usual time to start offering food and turning over the rooms, letting me get on with my work.

I did a quick google of the Modello Talent Agency. The company was formed by a series of corporate buyouts which absorbed literary, music, and film agencies. Their website carried a list of their clients, including stadium bands, bestselling authors, Hollywood A-list talent and even a couple of politicians. They were owned by the same multinational as Ash's record label.

I caught the L into the city. The journey gave me time to listen to some of Ash's album again. My mind kept catching on the joyous, upbeat sound of the love song, the chorus singing about two people being "meant to be." There was such celebration in the song. Such certainty. Had I ever been as sure about anything?

Well, I was fairly sure I didn't want to go through with what came next.

I'd arranged to meet Elizondo in a coffee shop across from the Union Square Greenmarket. It was close enough to Modello's 5th Avenue office for me to fit both into one trip, but the hustle and life of the market might be enough to distract him from the reason I was there.

I ordered a green tea with honey, and settled into a booth near the fire escape. My subconscious clearly still telling me to get the hell out and run. The detective was late, so I kept my earphones in and listened to the album.

I'd gotten through a few songs by the time Elizondo walked in. I almost didn't recognise him. The man I'd known before was someone in denial of middle age. He'd worn leather coats, a goatee and, I'd suspected, dyed his hair. He'd tried to relate to me through music, talking about the New York scene, trying to show me how cool he was. But the version of Elizondo that entered the coffee shop now looked fifteen years older, and like he was born in a previous era. Shirt and tie. Long coat, with a few stains. His beard was full now, mostly gray, covering jowls and a pockmarked face. His hair was thinned out to the point he really needed to make a decision. Shave it off, or run for president.

He paused at the counter to order a coffee, and chatted to the server long enough to wait there for the fill up. He then nodded at me, and walked over with a slow roll to his shoulders as he moved.

He started with a lie. "Good to see you, McGarry."

I responded in kind. "You're looking well."

He smiled, spotting the subtext. "Thanks for agreeing to it, I know it feels strange."

"Sure. How you been, Detective?"

"They say teachers never forget a student. It's true, you know that? I was thirty eight, thirty nine, attending a robbery homicide on a block near where I grew up. This little old lady sticks her head out of the apartment opposite, calls me by name. Turns out, she was my high school math teacher. Mrs Bennett. Remembered me, started asking my whole life story. I'm stood there trying to work a case. Dead body at my feet. *His* bare feet sticking out into the hall. But I had to stand there and catch up about old times with a teacher who hadn't seen me for twenty years. And straight away, I was like her student again, doing whatever she told me."

"I don't think my teachers would want to talk to me."

"You'd be surprised, I don't think they ever give up on you. The good ones. But my point is, it's the same. Cops and teachers, I never forget a case."

"Are you one of the good ones?"

"We'll see." He paused, downing the coffee, half the cup in three thirsty gulps. "I've been keeping an eye on you. Since you came out. Fancy yourself as a detective now?"

Fancy yourself as a detective.

The insult was clear, but I ignored it. "I help people out, when I can."

"For money."

"You don't put people away for free, do you? I mean, I heard cops were underpaid, but..."

"It's all relative, isn't it?"

I was thrown off by the tangent. "What is?"

"You asked if I was one of the good ones. But that's all relative. Good. Bad."

There was a real sense of weight to the air around him as he talked. His words felt tired, heavy. We'd first met as a cocky young criminal and a cocky middle-aged cop. I'd come out of prison in better shape than I went in, and liking myself a lot better than I did before. He seemed to have gone the other way, slowly falling apart in the intervening years.

I set my drink down, aimed for feigned shock to lighten the mood. "You're the cop, telling me, the ex-con, this?"

"Not like that." He dismissed the thought with an irritated wave. "At a job, I mean. You stay long enough in one career, you see everything comes in cycles. Different regimes. Different priorities. The idea of being good or bad at your job becomes irrelevant. It's just about whether you can keep *doing* it. You pick your own version of good, focus on that."

"Sounds like what I've always done."

"You always confused me, you know that?"

"Me?"

"Why did you get behind that wheel? Made no sense. That's what your local cops told me. They almost convinced me you were innocent. Him? No, he's not a driver. He's a talker. Card player. Fraud, maybe. A heist? No way. Everything they said pointed me away from you. You almost got away with it because of cops."

I leaned in, lowered my voice like I was giving him the big secret. "The problem you have, your job, is you need things to make sense. Your cases rest on it. Proof. Selling logic to the jury. Lining things up in a sequence that feels right. But crime doesn't need to make sense. People take what they can take, in the moment they can take it."

"Everyone has a motive."

"There's a difference between reason and motive. There's a reason for everything to happen. Doesn't always mean it's a motive. Not the way you guys worship the idea of one, anyway. I walk out of here, I see a piece of fruit from the market on the street, it's available, nobody has spotted it. I pick it up. What's my motive?"

"It's there."

"Exactly."

He smiled and shook his head, repeating the dismissive wave. "I guess this is why you're only an amateur detective."

"I get paid okay."

"Mantalos must be paying you okay, to waste her time."

Now we were getting to it. For all the distractions, all the fake nostalgia, he wanted to talk about the case. "You're worried about her time?"

"I'm worried about mine."

We were both silent as the server came by and refilled Elizondo's cup, asking if I wanted another tea.

I asked for a glass of water, and we kept the silence going as he grabbed me one from the counter and filled it from a jug.

"You get to my age, time becomes important. You start to realise, you don't know your last day. Your last good sleep -"

I nodded, cutting in, "When was your last good sleep?"

"Not since David Ash went missing. Things just get in my head that way, and stay there. That's how I caught you. We knew who two of the three kids in the masks were. We didn't need them to name the third, and if they were willing we could offer a deal. There was already enough of a case there for conviction, and for another dot on my record. But you know what it was?"

"What?"

"Cars don't drive themselves. That's what I kept telling myself. I'd lie awake at night, mumbling it. We had the gunmen, but cars don't drive themselves. Drove my wife crazy."

"How is she?"

"No idea."

Okay. That explained at least part of his late life collapse.

He continued. "I didn't care about the third masked guy. Still don't." He paused, giving me a look, wondering if I finally wanted to say, after all these years, who the third robber had been. "But it didn't sit right with me that we didn't know who was behind the wheel. So I kept working away at it, way past my captain's patience. He didn't care. Nobody cared. We had enough."

Rule number four, *never name names*.

"That doesn't sound at all obsessive."

He laughed, genuinely amused by the sarcasm. "You're not wrong. I wish I could switch these thoughts off. Everyone else seems to do okay without these worries, But me? I latch onto something, can't stop thinking about it."

I was seeing a new side of the boogie man.

I'd never hated Elizondo, really. He was a guy doing a job, and it came up against a job I'd done, and he'd caught me because I was guilty. There was no more to it than that. But when I was younger, fresh after the conviction, there had been elements of fear and anger. I'd spent nights staring at the ceiling thinking, why couldn't he just let it go? Why did he have to come after me? Now I could see him for what he was. Another man trapped in his own wiring.

"Why are you taking her money, when you know she's guilty?"

I decided to play into his impression of me. "Because it's there."

"Like the fruit."

"Exactly."

"But you do know she's guilty?"

"Do I?"

"A wife gets killed, it's almost always the husband. A husband gets killed, it's almost always the wife. Why should this case be any different, just because the wife looks good on TV?"

"You're jumping straight to *dead*, not thinking he could be shacked up somewhere else, living his best life?"

"You think he could find a better life than living in the Village with Louisa Mantalos, getting paid millions to sing for three minutes at a time?"

"If their life is so great, why would she kill him?"

He smiled, leaned back into the seat and took more deep gulps from the cup. Wiped his beard with his thumb, "Well, you being the master detective, you have it all sorted. The rest of us still look for motive. And motive makes it pretty clear, she thinks she gets all his money if he's dead."

"If the motive is all important, like you say, then you would have the case closed by now."

"Why would a kid known as one of the best talkers in town get behind the wheel of a getaway car?"

"Why would a wife kill her husband for money, then cover up his death so that she can't get the money?"

He wiped his beard with his thumb again. I recognised the gesture this time.

He'd done it before, way back in the interrogation room, right before he'd tripped me up in my own words. I realised we were in that room again now. He was playing me. How much of his tired old man routine was just an act, to catch me out?

"You used to work for Reah Kanellis, didn't you?"

I nodded.

"I find it interesting. The one connection that's always stood out to me is Louisa coming from that background, knowing Reah. It's the one thing. The person she could have called to help her do all of this. I learned a long time ago, people don't change. And now Louisa hires someone else who used to work for Reah. She just keeps digging the hole."

The front door opened. I turned my attention from Elizondo to see Carl Waltz walk into the coffee shop. The ADA. The man whose number Halliday had hidden in his wallet, and who was also applying pressure across the board to get this case wrapped up.

"I may have played dirty here," Elizondo said.

"He asked you to set this up."

Elizondo shuffled across the cushion on his booth and stood up. "Yeah, but I did want to talk to you. I'm still looking for something."

"What?"

He stared at me for a moment. It was uncomfortable. "I'll know it when I see it."

Elizondo walked out, nodding at Carl Waltz as they passed each other. Waltz was tall and slim with fine features that had given over to craggy with age. *Weathered* was probably the way a magazine would describe it.

As he settled into the spot vacated by Elizondo, I saw his clear blue eyes up close. There was a haunted look that only showed up when you really examined him. Lines around those eyes. Maybe the grief Ramona had mentioned, or maybe my own imagination, looking for something that wasn't there.

I tried not to feel intimidated. But at heart, I guess I'll always be an ex-con from Astoria. And now I was sitting face to face with one of the most influential people in the city.

"Thanks for agreeing to meet me," he said.

"I didn't."

His mouth formed the word *ah*, but he didn't say it. "Detective Elizondo played you a little dirty."

The exact same phrase. They'd rehearsed this right down to coming up with a term to describe the trick.

"I read your file yesterday," he said, gliding across to a new subject with full control.

I needed to push back. "Did you ask Matt Halliday about me?"

He stared at me.

I followed up with the other name I'd found in the wallet, just to see his reaction, "How is Charlie Starr doing?"

Waltz tilted his head slightly. It was probably meant to show he was thinking, but just made me think of Michael Myers. "I don't know who that is."

"Okay."

He smiled. "You're a fighter. You should have been a lawyer."

"Why are we here?"

"I read your file yesterday." He repeated it with the exact same tone, almost ignoring everything that had been said since. "If I'd been ADA when you were arrested, you wouldn't be out on the street now. But I think we could have had some fun in the court, throwing punches." He paused to check his watch. It was expensive. "And you're an unlicensed private investigator now?"

"I help people."

"You know, you're talking to someone who could easily help you with that '*unlicensed*' part. I make a couple calls, put in a good word. It would be good publicity, proof of rehabilitation in the New York justice system."

"Help you pretend that's a real thing."

He smiled.

I pushed on. "Why do you have such a thing for this case?"

"The opposite is true, too. I read the terms of your parole. This unlicensed work you're doing, it wouldn't take much for me to make a case you've been violating your terms. And you were at the scene of a crime last night, from what I understand."

"You couldn't do that."

"Is it something you'd really want to test?"

"Why do you owe Matt Halliday one hundred grand?"

He paused, scratched at a spot just above his eyebrow. If I was still a poker player I'd suggest it was his tell, but I'd need more of a chance to test it.

I tried pushing from a different angle. "Why do you care about this one so much?"

He nodded. He formed another silent word, okay. "It's not so hard. District attorneys don't last forever. They have term limits. And when one goes, it's good to have someone popular enough to take their place."

"A sexy media-friendly case like this would help you run for office."

"It would."

I mimicked his silent okay. "But I don't respond well to threats."

"I don't make them," he said, matter of fact. "I make promises. Staying on this case would be very bad for you, Mr McGarry. And your step-father."

"What?"

"The same person who could offer you a private investigations license wouldn't have much difficulty getting a bar's liquor license revoked. It's all the same contact book."

He stood up with far more grace than Elizondo, leaving his business card on the table.

"Walk away, McGarry. Or should I say '*get away*'? That's more your style."

THIRTY-TWO

CON

Modello's front door was between two banks, and the doorman in the narrow foyer waved me on to the elevator. The offices were on the fourth floor, behind a large glass door bearing the company logo in silver frosting.

Danny Stewart was a small guy. He had reddish hair and a goatee. He wore light brown slacks and a black shirt, holding a pair of glasses in his left hand. He walked toward me and offered a quick shake in greeting.

"Pleasure," he said. "Let's go somewhere quieter."

I took it as a figure of speech. Aside from Danny and the receptionist, it didn't sound like there was anybody else in. I followed him down a narrow corridor between more glass doors. He bobbed as he walked, as if to claim some of the air above him and make up for his lack of height. We stepped inside an office and he shut the door.

The walls were lined with photographs.

Danny with Springsteen, De Niro, Hanks and half the cast of Friends.

Maybe if he'd had Seinfeld, I would've been impressed.

"Edgar asked me to help you any way I can."

"Appreciate it. And seeing me on a Sunday."

He dismissed that with a wave. "I love working Sundays. I can get things done. And the office is quiet." He tapped his right ear. "Tinnitus. Too many gigs."

"It's like a ringing in your ear, right?"

"Constant sound. Sometimes it's a drone. Sometimes a whistle. I swear, this sounds nuts, but it's like I can hear the electricity in the room. I keep the sockets switched off when I'm not using them."

He was right. That sounded nuts.

"How does your job work? What kinds of things do you have to do for your clients?"

"It varies. Everybody is different."

"And for Ash?"

"He was different day to day. Sometimes he wanted me to be hands-on, other times, I needed to get out of his way. You had to kind of work that out for yourself."

"When was the last time you saw him?"

"It would have been when he first started the album. I visited the studio."

"Headspace."

"Right, yeah. See, he was in a leave-me-alone phase. So what I do, is it's more about emotional support. My job really is to get him what he needs and then step back."

"You stay in touch, though?"

"Oh, yeah. Yeah. All the time. We would talk twice, three times a week on the phone."

"Okay." I kept irritation out of my voice. "When was the last time you talked to him?"

"Couple of days before he went missing. There was going to be a party at the studio we were using, a couple of producers were arranging a big blow out to celebrate something. I don't remember. Whatever is was. Doesn't matter. But Dave didn't want to go, so I had to make his excuses."

"Was that normal?"

"With Dave, yeah. When he was in the creative zone, he didn't like to be bothered. He only wanted to make decisions about the art, and said talking about his writing ruined the purity of it."

"Was it only when he was in the creative zone?"

He grinned. "To be honest with you, he can be a bit passive aggressive. Or a lot. I do a lot of his talking for him, with people outside of his social circle."

I noticed Danny's tenses were swapping around. One minute he was talking about Ash in the present, the next in the past.

"How was he doing? Like, his mood?"

"Good. Good. He was clean, sober, happy. Married. I tell you, the album he was working on? The songs popped. Really popped. This was going to be huge."

That didn't sound like the album I'd listened to.

The music was moody, haunting. Danny was used to selling excitement. I was getting the full pitch. His hands moved with the words.

I stuck to the subject.

"You manage all three of them?"

"The Doormats, yeah. Yeah. But for the other guys it's more of a legacy deal. I manage the band, but Eddy's quit music, and Todd's session work takes care of itself."

"How long have you been with them?"

"Oh, years. I came on while they were recording *Legends*. Been with them ever since."

"They've been with Modello that long?"

"No." He smiled, it made him look like a five-year-old with facial hair. "I guess you could say I'm a legacy deal, too. I was working on my own when I signed the guys. Then I moved to Bleecker, and when Modello bought them out, the band and I moved here."

"Did they have another manager before you?"

"Yeah, yeah." I was starting to get irritated by how often he repeated the phrase. "Todd did it for a while, I think. When they were first gigging. Then they signed with Jimmy Ziskin."

Ziskin's name struck a chord.

I must have heard it back in the day, when I followed the band more closely than I had in recent years. Danny said the name in a way that didn't leave room for interpretation, like he didn't want the words in his mouth, but was too polite to spit.

"Not a fan?"

Danny put his hands out. "I don't want to speak ill of the dead."

"Yeah, you do. I won't tell him."

"He was a chancer. Made a real mess of the contracts. To be honest with you, half of the game in the music business is learning to recognize the people who are serious from the ones who just want to be seen being in the business, you know?"

I knew. The same problem existed in my old line of work. Some people were more interested in being criminals than they were in committing crime.

Danny continued. "Jimmy didn't have a clue what he was doing. Half my job when I came on was too sort out who owned what, and try to get everything on the level. Jimmy had set up companies for the band. Merch. Recording royalties, publishing royalties, one that was supposed to be paying into an investment company."

"Is that normal?"

"The companies? Oh yeah. Any serious band is a business. Touring, making albums, bands run up big debts. So they form companies to shoulder it and pay themselves salaries. It's all about moving debts around, protecting yourself from them."

"Very rock and roll. So Jimmy messed up?"

"Yeah. He had the right idea, but didn't know what he was doing. The rights and ownerships were all over the place. The guys, the band, they were still liable for everything, no protection. I had to clean it all up."

"And he passed away?"

"Yeah." It was a muted *yeah* this time. I didn't count it. "Suicide about a year ago. God, has it been a year already? You know, they had a news story on Dave yesterday, and they said it was six months, and I couldn't believe it."

I didn't know much about the music industry. I liked bands, and songs, but I didn't read rock biographies or pay attention to any inside-baseball stories. But even I knew there was a proud tradition of songwriters being screwed out of their royalties.

"Does David own his own songs?"

"Yeah. I fixed it. Well, through another company, but it's in Dave's name. Dave's and mine, I got ten percent as a thank you."

"What do you think happened to him?"

Danny sighed and settled on the edge of his polished black desk. "I don't know. He's gone missing before, a couple times. But never while he was clean. And never for this long. Every time he's mentioned in the news, they talk about him being dead. So sad. So sad."

Danny wasn't talking like someone who would have shut down investigations into Dave's disappearance. But I knew part of this was an act. Talking to people like Danny Stewart and Todd Flambé was making me realize just how much the music business had in common with my old life. Lies. Confidence tricks. Half-truths. The only real difference was, in my game, it mattered that people believed you. In show business, it seemed like everyone accepted they were being lied to, but still played along. It was routine. I needed to spot which of the lies was the important one.

"Edgar said you'd be able to get me the address for Dave's ex? Karen?"

He tilted his head to one side and gave an odd smile. For just a second there I was through the mask. I'd asked a question that had caught him off guard.

"Sure." He went around his desk to sit in front of the computer and started searching for something with the mouse. "Here it is."

There was a soft hum and I heard a sheet of paper sliding into a printer. I also saw him twitch at the noise. Danny pulled a large drawer out of the desk and I saw the machine, nestled in among bubble wrap. Danny handed me the sheet of paper when it was finished.

"She was a good kid," he said.

"One other thing. If something has happened to him, if he's gone. Control of the songs would be split between you and Louisa?"

He hesitated a couple of beats before answering.

"Yeah."

THIRTY-THREE

LOUISA

I have enough money to pay them.

Nobody knows this. Not even Ally. I keep parts of myself even from her.

When you grow up poor, you know money doesn't last. Some make up for that by spending it all right away, throwing affection around before it runs out. I had uncles like that. Gamblers. Every dollar that came into their hands went straight out again. When a horse came in I would get new clothes or jewellery. Then six months would go by without a word.

I learned the other approach. When the money started to come in, I always held some back. A stash. Ready for the moment everything fell apart. In a way, I've always been planning for right now. Even in my worst days, when I was spending stupid amounts on drugs, I never touched my reserve.

It became even more important with Dave around. Having one recovering addict in a relationship is tough, but two? That's a recipe for theft and lies. My stash wouldn't be safe if he knew about it.

After he went missing I split it. I gave some to Ally, to hold in the emergency fund. I kept the rest back. Just in case.

I wait for Gyul to arrive. It feels like forever. The minute she's in the door, I'm out of it. Back before everything went wrong, I might have been okay with leaving the kids alone for thirty minutes. Dave and I haven't always been saints when it comes to childcare. A few times, once they were tucked into bed, we'd go down to the street for a meal or to watch a show without calling Gyul or one of the previous nannies. We never left the area, and were always within a few blocks. But I don't take chances now.

Ally calls as soon as I hit the street. I start to wonder if Gyul called her.

Has Ally got people spying on me?

"How can I look after you," she says, "if you won't let me look after you."

That annoys me. Eats away inside. She's talking to me more and more like a child these days. But I don't show it. I give her the political voice, and tell her I need some air before we go to the party.

I walk down to Little West 12th.

My café. The last place I tried to improve things. The last time I thought I could be accepted, treated normally. I got bad review after bad review. Even the food bloggers wouldn't say nice things about me. The only support I got was from young women who were a bit too fascinated with me, and the kind of annoying white feminist guy who wants to tell you how right you are, right up until they realize there's no sex in it.

So the place folded. There's always pressure in this part of town to make way for new business. The building's owners have tried a few times to get me to give the space up, but deep down I'm not ready. Exiting the lease early would feel like admitting I've lost touch with who I was. I've hung onto it, and the place has become somewhere I can come to sit and be alone.

The lease is finally running out. There's another six months, and then we'll need to decide what to do with all the junk.

Isn't that odd?

Important things are starting to fade away into a fuzzy mess, but I can remember how long is left on the lease of my old café.

My childhood.

I remember my childhood so well now. Memories I thought lost decades ago are fresh and vivid.

It seems to be getting sharper as everything else gets fuzzier. I remember Astoria. Running around outside Reah's place. And Newton Avenue, where we lived. I remember how much shouting my parents did over me spending time with Reah. Moving away to Rockaway. It felt like we'd traveled half the world away.

This city. It's big when you want it to be small, and small when you want it to be big.

Focus, Louisa.

I open the box to the shutter controls and raise it up. It only takes two attempts. Inching its way up until it's level with my shoulder, and that's good enough.

It doesn't matter that this place has been closed for over a year, if I put the shutter all the way up, people will think it's some kind of deliberately trashed theme bar and try to walk in off the street.

The light switch is at the back. Closing up in summer was fine, because there's enough light filtering in to pick out the way out. But in the winter it meant walking through the café in total darkness.

I make my way across the open space where the tables and chairs used to be laid out. They're stacked along the wall now, waiting to be thrown out or given away.

Around the counter and through the door to the staff area. I don't bother with the light switches for the front. The office is on the right, and inside I see the desk still stacked with the same pile of paperwork I've been ignoring since the place closed.

The metal safe is on the floor next to the desk, and I turn the two dials around to click out the combination. Something else I'm having no trouble remembering.

Inside is more paperwork, some family jewelry, and bundles of cash.

There's a little over a hundred grand here. I count seventy out into a bag and then lock the safe.

Standing in silence for a moment, I can hear the hum of a few appliances that have been left plugged in. Looks like I've been getting one over on Con-Ed, because nobody has come collecting.

Back out on the street I roll the shutter down and check my phone.

I've broken my own rules, and logged into the Hotmail account on my cell.

I send a message. *Got the money.*

It's not even a minute later when the reply comes through with directions where to go.

THIRTY-FOUR

CON

Turned out the address Danny had for Karen was out of date. Knocking on a few doors in her old building was enough to find out she still worked nearby, as a barista on 9th Street, Park Slope.

The coffee shop looked like an independent store. The logo looked familiar. Sometimes the bigger chains will still own a store like that, and suck people in with the promise of supporting something local, but the menus and branded packs of coffee usually give them away.

Walking past the window, I caught a glimpse of a woman behind the counter. She was focused on wiping something up off the surface in front of her and hadn't seen me.

She looked to be around forty, with dyed blonde hair and painted eyebrows.

The song off Ash's album drifted into my head. "*I used to love her, but now she's blonde.*" Could it be? The most throwaway sounding song on the album was about Karen? Maybe. I'm not one for reading too much into lyrics, but men don't make for the subtlest writers when it comes to women.

There was a slight twitch to her movements, and I spotted an addict right away. City life is full of people who are functioning addicts of one sort or another. The guy in the call center who has booze for breakfast. The woman at the DMV who chases her demons away with cocaine. The college professor who can't get to sleep without a few puffs of weed. This barista had a powerful itch for something.

I didn't want to risk spooking her by going in and talking. One scenario kept playing in my head. If Ash was still alive, maybe he was with Karen? Could I learn more from hanging back and following her than by asking her questions up front?

Most of the street was lined with brownstones. There weren't many hiding places. At least, not with a view of the coffee shop. I could stay out of sight, sure, but I wouldn't be able to see her. Half a block down, on the other side of the street, was another coffee shop. Nobody ever needed to worry about not being able to get a caffeine fix around here. I walked a few blocks down. Once I was sure I was out of sight from Karen's shop, I crossed over and walked back up to the second shop. I ordered a large coffee and chose a seat in the window .

Putting my earphones in, I pressed play on Dave's album, and listened to it through again.

The fun song kicked in. The power pop, with the chorus repeating the phrase meant to be over and over. It was joyous. I'd taken it to be a loud love song. But as I listened in to the verses, I noticed darker theme. *"Hotel's the same. We can use other names."* Why would a married man be singing about hotel rooms and fake names? A touring musician, who also had a song about Karen's hair color?

It looked like drugs weren't the only weakness David Ash had fallen back on.

In the same song, a few lines later, he sang, *"They won't care who I am, you can be Jack, I'm Dianne."*

I winced at the forced rhyme. But there was that name again. Jack. The same name as the person who'd been feeding information to Dee Buana. Coincidence? I didn't want to read too much into a dumb bit of wordplay, but if Karen was the blonde of the song, was she also the Jack? I'd been assuming it was a male, but if Dave could cast himself as Diane, maybe I was wrong.

Thinking of Jack took me back to those moments at Rockaway Beach. Halliday. Seeing a dead body is never easy. I've seen a few, starting with my grandmother in the hospital when I was ten. But Halliday was different. The blood. The imprint of violence in the room. It felt like voyeurism, but there was nobody there to be watching.

Ash and Karen.

Karen and Halliday.

Why did my brain go there?

I looked across at the front of Karen's coffee shop again, and it clicked. The logo above the window. It was the same as the loyalty cards in Halliday's wallet. There had been quite a collection, the way someone might casually pick a new one up each time, never getting around to sticking to the one.

He'd been in that coffee shop, and there could only be one reason.

Did Karen know who he was? Had they talked? Or had he hung back and watched, like me, waiting for some sign of David Ash?

Louisa had a financial motive for killing Ash, but not for hiding the body. And now it looked like her husband was cheating, she had an emotional one, too. And her alibi was paper thin. Her friend, manager and caregiver Ally had already admitted to us that part of the alibi was a lie. She hadn't been there when the call happened, when Louisa was taking drugs. There was a window of time there where anything could have happened. Louisa hadn't given me her dealer's name. There were just too many things that weren't making sense.

And too many convenient suicides.

Wait.

Convenient?

Another leap my brain had made without telling me. Someone had been in the middle of trying to make Halliday look like a suicide. As it was, the cops might still be lazy enough to buy it - I'd heard no follow-up. But Halliday's death was fresh in my mind and it had taken a while to connect it with Jimmy Ziskin from, what, a year ago? Two people who were only vaguely connected, both taking their own lives a year apart? In this city, the odds on that happening were fine. Nothing to question. Except I knew one of them wasn't suicide, so…

I tried a few google searches, different combinations. Jimmy. James. Ziskin and Doormats, James Ziskin and suicide. Eventually I found the news report on his death. A small notice. The only interesting thing about it was the date.

Danny had been wrong. It wasn't a year ago. Only two months. He'd died eight weeks before David Ash went missing. Jumping from his apartment in the city. Well, falling was probably a better description. That could still be coincidence, but it felt too close for that. Like maybe there was something there. A link. A reason.

But what could it be?

If Ziskin was linked to this, then the two suicides were both in question. What could have been worth killing Ziskin and Halliday for?

Stealing his computer…

And the Carl Waltz connection wouldn't go away.

The ADA, who either owed Halliday 100k, or who had information Halliday felt he could extort for that figure. Threatening me off the case. Along with the business card for the other name. Charlie Starr. Waltz and Starr's details had been stored side by side. Were they connected?

The reason Waltz gave me made sense. Political. Publicity. A good case to help him run for his bosses job when the opening came up. But it felt too neat. In a case full of messy things that didn't fit, I had an instant distrust of something that felt easy.

A pimply kid with the barista uniform and eighty years' worth of beard walked into Karen's coffee shop.

A few moments later, Karen came out, carrying a leather jacket, and headed away up the street, fast.

I waited a few seconds while I drained my coffee, then followed.

Karen was nervy. I could tell she was worried about being followed. Looking back over her shoulder. Pausing at traffic lights to sneak glances around. But I'm experienced at following people. Back in the day I could walk right up and take a wallet without being noticed, so following from a distance was easy.

We walked down a couple blocks to Prospect Park West before Karen crossed the road and walked up in the direction of the Plaza. At West Drive she turned into the park. I slowed down to let Karen build up more of a head start. I didn't want to spook her. We walked up the slight incline as the wide road threaded between the trees, until Karen turned off onto a smaller cobbled path. The trees and bushes were close in around us. I fell back out of sight when I saw someone up ahead, facing away from us. Standing beneath a lamppost.

It was Louisa.

What the hell?

THIRTY-FIVE

LOUISA

I'm getting the F train to Prospect Park, to meet a blackmailer, to go see Dave.

I'm getting the F train to Prospect Park, to meet a blackmailer, to go see Dave.

This is how I do it.

I tell myself the story over and over.

It keeps me moving, stops the panic from setting in.

I can feel it. Deep down. The same as when I left Johnny in the park. It's like acid, bubbling away at the bottom of my gut and around the edges of my thinking. Just waiting to boil over and eat away at something that matters.

But I've taken my medication. As long as I stay calm, and keep my mind focused, I'll be okay.

I'm getting the train to Prospect Park, to meet a blackmailer, to go see Dave.

Stay in control. Stay calm. Keep telling the story.

A few people recognize me on the train. I see them taking pictures. It's always funny how they think they're being sneaky, finding ways to angle a chunk of metal and glass in my direction. I don't mind the pictures. What can they do? It doesn't matter whether I tell them where I'm going or not, they'll make something else up.

Nobody approaches me.

Good.

I don't want any distractions while I do this. I climb the steps out of the station at 7th Avenue and it takes me a few seconds to get my bearings before I walk to Prospect Park.

I check the latest email.

Enter by the arch.
Follow West Drive round to the right. At the tree stump walk across the grass to the small path.
Wait by the lamppost. Come alone.

There are people all around at the archway. Traffic is busy. The noise and fumes combine with the heat to close in on me. I walk up to the entrance to the park and follow the directions, veering right as the path splits off in two.

Walking past young families with strollers, and loved-up couples holding hands. I can't see how this is a discreet place to meet, and I start to panic. Someone will recognize me. I'll draw attention. The blackmailer will be scared off.

I push all of that away, adding it to the worries bubbling away below. I find the tree stump. It looks old and weathered, like it was cut a long time ago. About ten feet behind it, across a grass verge, is a small path with faded cobbles. I step across the grass, expecting people will be watching me. There's a bend up ahead, threading between trees, and I can just about make out the black shape of a lamppost.

I stand beneath it and wait. Without anything better to do, I start counting, giving my brain something to focus on while I wait.

There's movement behind me, coming up the path. I turn and -

I recognize the woman who stands behind me.

She's familiar. I just can't quite place her. I meet so many people, even before I got sick, that remembering names is difficult. She can see some recognition in my eyes, I think, because she hesitates before speaking.

"Bring the money?"

I nod and tap the bag at my side.

"Hand it over."

"Where's my husband?"

She looks around us before stepping in closer.

Her voice comes out hard and impatient. "Hand it over."

I'm not falling for this. I can play an idiot on television, but nobody should mistake me for one in real life. Stepping toward the grass, making it look like I'm ready to walk away, I say: "I need to see Dave before you see any of this."

She tuts. A real tut. Hardly criminal of the year. Looking around again, she pulls out a cell phone and taps at the screen, scrolling with her finger. Then she holds it up for me to see. It's a picture of her with Dave. I can tell it's recent, because he's wearing a soccer top a fan gave him on a European tour last year. Dave knew nothing about soccer, but Europe was a big market for him, and he liked to play along.

My heart tries to move in two directions at once. It wants to soar with hope, because Dave is alive and well. But I also recognize the smile on his face in the picture, and the way his arm is draped around her. The angle makes it look like Dave is taking the picture. An intimate selfie.

Dave was cheating on me.

That had been obvious, I guess. But it had been something I could ignore until now.

"Where is he?" Fighting back a knot of emotion in my throat. "I want to see him."

"You don't set the terms here," she says. "Hand me the money, then go back to the city. It's not safe for me to count it here, so I'm going to take it away and check it. Once I'm happy, I'll send you the address where you'll find him."

"No, I -"

Now it's her time to play it hard, half turning to head back down the path. It's an obvious bluff.

And it hits me.

Bluff.

Have I known all along?

If Dave is alive, and living with her, he wouldn't need to send her to blackmail me. He would have access to his own money and savings. That cash he's got saved up from the record advance. From the boost in sales he's had since he went missing.

She doesn't know where he is.

Bluff.

And with that, something else I've known all along starts to creep to the surface.

I look her in the eyes. "You don't know where he is."

She starts to panic now. We stare at each other. I see something else in her face. Heartbreak? She's crumbling. Realizing the same thing as me. Maybe we've both always known.

"You really don't -" She pauses. "I thought -"

Unspoken between us: *He's gone.*

She turns and runs, leaving me with the money.

Dave's not coming back.

I need to stop hiding from the truth.

The panic bubbles up. I can feel it. Dizzy. The world starts to swim around me.

Not now.

Hold it together.

THIRTY-SIX

CON

I followed Karen on foot down to 3rd Avenue, which I think put us in Gowanus. The murals covering every other wall in Brooklyn faded away as we walked. She moved fast. Not quite running, but close. Kept looking over her shoulder, but she wasn't watching for me now. She was watching the way she'd come.

Expecting Louisa to chase?

What was in the bag?

The smart guess was money. The smart guess is always money.

What was the payoff for?

I felt bad for leaving Louisa there. Should she be out alone? Was that something she could cope with? I sent Ramona a text, saying where Louisa was and what time I'd seen her, followed with an appropriate amount of question marks. I put the phone on airplane mode, to make sure there were no unwanted beeps or buzzes while I was trying to keep a low profile.

Karen stopped in front of a run-down building next to the elevated train tracks. There was a shopfront on the ground floor with a green awning, and a sign written in Arabic. Karen fumbled with her keys and opened a door between the Arabic store and a deli.

I hung back and waited. If it came to it I'd be able to pick the lock, but I didn't want to risk that on an open street. I waited for five minutes, and the door opened again. A young Asian woman stepped out next to me.

I had pulled my own keys out as the door opened, and made it look like I was trying to find the right one. The woman held the door for me with a tired smile.

In the hallway I saw mailboxes with the names of each tenant. *K Jesperson* lived on the fourth floor. I climbed the stairs to Karen's apartment and rapped softly on the door. I heard voices on the other side.

The door opened a crack, and she looked out at me over the chain. "Oh, I, yeah?"

"My name's Constantin McGarry. I'm a detective. I want to speak abou-"

Karen shut the door.

I waited a beat before calling through the thin wood. "I just want to talk. I'm not looking for trouble."

Sometimes, as both a con man and a detective, the best approach was to tell the truth. She opened the door again and looked out at me. Because she'd believed the truth of why I was here, she also believed the lie that I wasn't going to cause any trouble. That was entirely dependent on what I found inside.

"I'm just trying to help."

There was another hesitation. Karen looked over her shoulder at something in the apartment, then back at me. I smiled, but didn't say anything. Let her have the conversation in her own head. The door shut just enough for the chain to be slid off, and Karen stepped out into the hallway with me.

"So what are you looking for?"

Blunt. Straight to the point.

I responded in kind. "I'm looking for David Ash."

"Another one."

So, Halliday had spoken to her.

I raised my voice a little louder than needed. "And I'm wondering why you were meeting with Louisa Mantalos."

The words carried. Karen looked across the hallway at the other door, and then up at the stairs, waiting to see if anyone responded. Then she pushed the door open and motioned for me to follow her inside.

The living room was furnished with a couple of old sofas, some bookcases piled high with everything except books, and children's toys. There was an older woman sitting on the sofa. An aged version of Karen, someone who had started out the same but melted a little like a candle, spreading outwards.

"Ma, this is, what was it?"

"Con."

"This is Con. He's a detective."

The older woman shuffled forward in the seat without getting up, and offered me a hand. "Oh yeah? Do you have a badge? ID?"

"I'm more of a private investigator," I said. "Emphasis on the private."

"Okay," Karen's mother's accent was stronger; she stretched out a few words longer than there was any need to. "What are you looking for?"

I turned to Karen and raised my eyebrow. I could see from her reaction she wasn't comfortable with me answering in front of her mother.

"Ma, could you go and look after Tabby?"

The mother grumbled and got to her feet before giving me a long wary look and leaving the room. I guessed Tabby must be the child who owned all of the toys scattered around the room. Either that, or Karen was spoiling a cat rotten.

The apartment didn't look big enough for three. Based on the layout I'd seen so far, I was guessing there was only one bedroom. If there was a second one squeezed in somewhere, it couldn't be big. They were all living right on top of each other.

Once we were alone, I tried to figure out the best place to start. I decided on the most recent. We could work backwards from there.

"What was going on at the park?"

Karen was going to try and bluff her way out of it. Her eyes gave it away. "What do you mean?"

"Come on. I saw you. You tried to take the bag off her. It didn't look like a social occasion. What's going on? You blackmailing her? What have you got?"

She crumpled on the spot. It was a subtle gesture, but unmissable. Something collapsed inside of her, and she started hugging herself. "I lied to her," she said. "Told her I knew where Dave was."

"As Jack?"

She blinked, her mouth pursed into a small questioning 'o'. "What?"

"Did you use the name Jack when you contacted her?"

"No I... I didn't use a name. Why would..."

It was genuine. Karen wasn't Jack.

"Never mind, carry on, please."

"He'd been giving me money. Dave. I don't know, he kept saying it was to help pay the bills until he could be with me, but it was also hush money, I guess. Then he went missing, and I was struggling. And I thought I could get some from Louisa, trick her. I didn't think she knew me. I saw the look in her eyes, and she's just as lost as I am."

I heard movement in the next room, then a child's giggle. Karen's mother called out the name *Tabby*, but it was too late, and a young girl toddled into the room. I'm no expert on babies, but she didn't look to be much over a year old. Unsteady on chubby legs, but grinning at the sight of her mom.

She didn't have Karen's eyes.

She had David Ash's.

THIRTY-SEVEN

CON

"I didn't plan any of this, you know?"

The child was back in the bedroom room with her grandmother. I could hear a television playing. Happy voices, music. Some kids program. Karen took a seat on the sofa and invited me to do the same. She was still hugging herself loosely. Looking down at the floor as she talked.

"I hated him. For a long time. I'd moved here just to be with him, followed him all the way to New York."

"You'd been a couple back home?"

"On and off, for years. He was always really sweet back there. New York changed him."

"How did you meet?"

She smiled. It was distant. "He was dating a friend of mine. Sally. We used to go to the mall together, Sally and me, then one day she started hanging out with this guy. I met him a few times and he seemed nice. Funny and sweet, a little shy. Sally, she was moody. Controlling. When she was giving Dave a hard time, he'd talk to me, and I'd try to make peace between them, you know? Get them back together."

"And from there…"

"Yeah."

"Can't have been easy, dating a rock star in New York?"

"Oh, no." Her accent grew strong again. "There were always fans who wanted to find out who I was. People on message boards and social media. Dave was protective about it. You know Ryan Adams? Well, he had a breakup once, and some fans published the woman's name and address on the internet, and she got hate mail. Dave didn't want that to happen to me." She paused. Thinking something over. I watched her jaw move a little as she processed it. "I suppose it also meant it was easier to cut me out, when he decided to. He kept things separate, like, his life? It was broken into different groups. He didn't let people at school know about when his bands were playing. Those two groups never met each other.

Then when he moved here, it was only me and Edgar who got to stay in his life. Then when he got famous, I wasn't part of the plan." She seemed unable to settle on whether she wanted to linger on the good or bad times. Her face shifted from happy to sad, and back again. "His best songs were about me."

"Really?"

"Yeah. You know *Attentions*, and *My Side*? They were both me."

"And when did you guys hook up again?"

"Couple years ago." She smiled, answering a question I hadn't asked. "Tabby is thirteen months old. He started coming around to do the same thing he'd done with Sally. Whenever he and Louisa had a fight, he'd come to talk to me, like it was the only way he knew how to deal with it."

"Did they fight a lot?"

"Seemed like it. It was only a few times at first. He came around and bought us take-out, then pretended he was there to ask about me. He started to talk about the two of them, and didn't shut up for an hour."

"And then one thing led to another."

She nodded. "He said he was going to leave her." Karen sniffed back a tear. The water in her eyes was telling the truth. "When I got pregnant." She laughed. "You'd think I'd be used to his lies by now."

I looked around the room again. This wasn't the kind of place David Ash's daughter should be living.

"Your mom, she moved to town to help?"

"Yeah. She wanted me to go back home, raise Tabby there. But I kept hanging in, kept wanting to believe Dave."

"Are you still using?"

"No." She hesitated, but it was honest, trying to figure out how I'd spotted her drug problem. "Been clean for a year, got my NA chip last week."

"Congratulations."

I left that for a moment, let her feel good about something before getting back to painful questions. She looked fragile, ready to collapse at any moment, and I knew my questions were only going to make it more likely.

"Did you and David use the same dealer?"

She licked her bottom lip. Watched me for a second.

As much as we'd shared in a short space of time, I was still a stranger asking about something she'd rather not give up.

"I used someone local," she said. "Dave would bring his stuff. I don't know where he got it."

That seemed like the truth. Or close enough.

"And you talked to Matt Halliday, the other PI?"

"He found me. And he'd figured out the thing with Tabby, and said he had proof Louisa was lying. Said she knew what had happened to Dave, and he'd save me. Kept talking about how he'd save me. Then he stopped coming around, for a long time. Came back in the last few days and started again, saying how he'd save me, how I needed him."

"And what else did he say?"

"Well, I said I didn't want his help, and he got really upset. He was always really dramatic, I don't think he was well. Then he said, if I didn't work with him, he'd tell the press about Tabby, and Louisa would sue me. He said, if Louisa didn't care what happened to Dave, she wouldn't care about hurting Tabby."

"When was the last time you saw him?"

"Like I said to the last guy. He came to the coffee shop yesterday, when I was on shift. I didn't want to talk to him, but…. I was so scared to say no to him sometimes. He wanted to come back here, I could tell. But I said I needed to get back to work, and customers came in, which stopped him making a scene. I mean, he was so intense, I didn't like being around him. He'd be really happy one minute, then if I said the wrong thing, he'd be needy, or angry."

"You said he'd left you alone, and started again in the last few days. Did he say anything different? Any reason why he started coming back again?"

"He seemed worked up over it, but didn't say why."

"Did he tell you what he had before? The first time he tried blackmailing Louisa?"

"He said she was lying about her health, but he didn't say how."

"Wait." I realized I'd skipped past something important. "Go back, like you said to what other guy?"

I flashed back on what she'd said in the doorway. "Another one."

So caught up in connecting the dots between Ash, Karen, and Halliday, I'd missed the obvious.

"Someone else came around? Other than Halliday and me?"

"Yeah, this guy yesterday. Asking how I knew Matt."

"What time was this?"

"I don't know, late. When I was clocking off, he stopped me outside the shop. So I guess it was around five?"

Five.

Halliday died a few hours later. How did this new guy fit in? Was he following a trail that led him to Halliday, or did he always have everything he needed to know, and was starting to chase down loose ends?

"Halliday's dead," I said.

I saw genuine shock in her eyes. Sadness. "Oh, no. Oh."

"Did this new guy give you a name?"

"Charlie something? Starr?"

Okay. Working theory. Starr was cleaning something up. Covering the tracks and removing awkward players. Halliday was the one to attack Buana, and Starr had been the one to interrupt, before shooting Halliday in his own trailer. Karen wasn't safe.

This apartment was smaller than mine. I had three bedrooms. I double checked the bookings on my phone. All my guests had checked out today, and there was nobody due in tonight.

"Pack some bags," I said. "We need to go."

THIRTY-EIGHT

LOUISA

Where am I?

Street corner.

Why am I -

I'm catching the F, to go to -

No, I've done that. There was the woman. The one with the photo. I've seen her before. My memories are tearing loose. I see her eyes again. Her face. Same face? Think it's the same face. Where is she? Where am I?

This is a memory.

I think.

Yes, it is. Coming back viscerally, like I'm reliving it. The tastes. The smells. The heat. It's a July night in New York. So you know it's hell on earth. The humidity has just broken a little for the first time in weeks. There's an odd feeling in the air, like static, but there's no storm about to hit.

I'm at a club in SoHo. I can never remember the name. Just a bunch of initials. A few years ago I wouldn't have been caught dead here, but now? This is my life. A guy called Joss is doing a line off a table. They have rooms for this. Special. You can lock the door. Nobody can see what you're doing. Everyone has cameraphones now.

Trust me, I know.

Joss says something to me. He's told me who he works for. A record company, a film company, it's one of those. He steps aside and nods for me to have a go. I usually smoke it. I prefer the way it hits, and I've seen so many horror stories about people messing up their noses. But free is free.

I snort it in one pass and then wipe my nose. There's the quick stab to my head, like an ice cream headache, but that's not the coke. Whatever it's cut with has done a job on my sinuses.

Joss grins and heads out through the door.

I follow.

No. I'm on a street corner. I was catching the F.

Why am I here? I'm panicking. Why am I panicking?

Where. Okay. Get a place. I look around.

A church. I'm outside a church. Of course I am. Always keep finding my way back to these things. Which one? Saint Augustine. Okay. What street? I look to the corner, there's a sign. 6th Avenue. Okay.

No, not okay.

I'm drifting again.

Her eyes, her face. Same face? Yes.

I follow Joss through the crowd. I'm on the edge of the dancefloor again before the drug kicks in.

Oh.

Yeah.

I am alive.

And, hey, I'm dancing.

It's Todd. The rock star. He's been here the last few times. He's dressed exactly the way you'd expect. We usually end the night with long talks out on the curb while his friends throw up, and I guess maybe we're an item now? I don't really know. The rules seem different in music. It's like high school, but with more eyeliner and less common sense.

Todd's cute, but I'm not sure. I can read people. I can play people. And Todd seems to be fake, like he's trying to play me. But still he's cute, he's famous, and we're in a club, so I'm dancing with him.

He grinds. He wiggles. He slips by people without breaking his rhythm.

I'll say this, he moves well.

I drift again...

I'm in a room. There's a piano, I think? I'm with Todd, he's pressed against me, in me. When was this? I'm there and not there at the same time. High. I'm high. And he's whispering, frantic. I pull him tighter, tell him to keep going. He tells me he's about to cum, and it sounds like an apology.

Now things change again. I'm at the nightclub. It feels like the same night as before but...

I'm needing more air. I stumble outside. The bouncer reaches out to get my attention. I'm about to be kicked out.

"She's okay." Joss steps out beside me. "She's with me."

The bouncer backs off. Okay, Joss has some pull.

He heads toward another parked car, turns to me with his eyebrow raised. Hmmm. Okay. Why not. There's a guy sitting on the curb with his back to us, smoking.

There's a woman sitting next to him. From their silence, I can tell they were very much not silent before I turned up. There's an argument in the air.

She looks up at me.

Those eyes.

That face.

"How's it going, Dave?" Joss says to the smoker.

Dave looks up at us and everything fades into the background. His scruffy hair is flopping down across his forehead, and he brushes it away from the clearest blue eyes I've ever seen.

He smiles.

I'm sure of something.

Now I'm somewhere else. I don't recognize this. It feels more recent. It's right now. I'm outside a church. Yes, I know this. The church. 6th Avenue. I pull out my, what's it? My cell. Call Ally. She picks up right away.

"Where the hell –"

I say the address. I mention church.

Church.

I went to church as a girl.

I drift.

Dave says he's leaving.

Where am I?

Where is this?

Jack.

That name again.

Jack.

Where am I?

Dave is being moody. No, Dave's not here. But he is. He's on the phone. He's both here and somewhere else. No, I'm on Dave's phone. I'm reading messages he's been sending someone named Jack. Sexts. Flirting. Pictures. Body parts. I recognised Dave, but now I'm seeing naked parts of a woman I've never met. And why do I feel like the one in the wrong here? I'm looking through his phone, I'm seeing pictures that weren't sent to me, why am I doing this? I feel dirty.

No, I'm talking to Dave. Arguing. It's his voice. I'm at home, he's away. He's avoiding the issue. I push, try to find out what he's holding back.

"Who is Jack?"

"Just... oh, look. I mean... she means nothing, but I..."

Nothing? The pictures they sent each other didn't look like nothing.

He pauses. I hear the sigh. This is classic Dave. He doesn't like talking about issues head on. He'll sit on them, and a year later you'll hear a song about your argument.

"I think I'm leaving," he says.

I get a hot flush of anger. "You think you're leaving?"

The anger builds.

If he was in the room now, I swear, I could kill him.

PART FOUR

"She helps me through my disease.
Though it's make believe.
She never leaves
My side."
-The Doormats

 **TRANSCRIPT**

Don't Tell A Soul
Season Three
The Disappearance of David Ash

Episode Four: The Problem with Louisa.

Audio Clip: Hot Take ident.

Ad: *Don't Tell A Soul is part of the Hot Take network. For more information visit hottake.com and subscribe to Hot Take Plus to hear all our shows with ads and plugs removed.*

Audio Clip: *"...I don't think Louisa even knows what truth is..."*

Audio Clip: *"...she was always straight with me. I don't know. This city needs heroes and villains, and I think everyone just decided it was her turn..."*

Audio Clip: *"...There was never any real proof she was involved in the Ricky thing."*

Theme tune plays.

 Dee: Hi, I'm Dee Buana. This is *Don't Tell A Soul*, the podcast about secrets, lies, and the truths we think we know.

Theme tune fades out.
 Dee: I don't have much to say up front this week. I want to let the episode speak for itself, and, honestly, my view on it is so different now.

 This episode is very much a relic of what we knew then, and what we didn't. Anything I say would mess with your listening of it.

Theme tune fades in.
Theme tune fades out.

Dee: The problem with Louisa. That's a phrase I've been hearing a lot. More than almost any other. As I look into her past, and talk to people who knew her before she was famous, they all seem to take a moment, pause, and say '*the problem with Louisa...*'

Whether it's an old high school friend whose boyfriend Louisa stole, an old teacher who struggled to get her to pay attention, or someone who worked with her on one of the many jobs she held down for less than a week. They all seem to think there was a problem, and they all want to tell me about it.

Let's back up.

With Louisa Mantalos, it seems like there's what you think you know, and what you should know. I was the same. I thought I knew her. And far better than I knew David Ash. She was on TV all the time. In the magazines. I don't really know at what point she went from hot new thing to part of the same old problem, but I definitely feel like it happened.

So, the Louisa we all know is the one we've been given. Attractive, ballsy, likeable woman from the Rockaways, cast on reality TV as the best-looking version of all of us. Then the celebrity chef, going from cooking cupcakes in her parents' kitchen to making budget meals for the rest of us from a TV studio. Then the drama starts. The sexy photoshoots. The gossip. The sex tape. And then David Ash. And now she's a villain. And her husband goes missing.

But there's another Louisa.

What if I tell you she's not even really from the Rockaways? Maybe you know. I guess it depends on how closely you've followed the story. I didn't know.

Louisa Jade Mantalos was born at Mount Sinai in Queens, to Stavros and Mary Mantalos. They lived on Newton Avenue until Louisa was fourteen, when they moved out to the Rockaways.

I managed to track down a few people who knew Louisa and her parents. And I learned of a whole different version of her.

Elsi Tanner: Oh, she ran with the Kanellis family, for sure.

This is Elsi. She was friends with Louisa right up until the Mantalos family moved, though she admits things became strained towards the end.

> Elsi Tanner: Yeah, see, she stole my boy. Ricky. See the problem with Louisa, if someone else had something, she wanted it. The minute she had it, didn't care anymore.

> Dee: And you say she was mixed up with the Kanellis family?

> Elsi: Yeah. Yeah. She was into all that.

It's not entirely clear what all that means. If you're the type of person who already knew Louisa came from Astoria originally, you probably already know she was mixed up in organized crime. I could fill up a whole season of the show talking about the Kanellis family. But somebody has already done it. Here's a plug that stays in even if you're a *Hot Take Plus* member.

If you listen to one of our sister podcasts on the network, The Gangs of America, you'll find season two was dedicated to the history of organised crime in the five boroughs.

What you really need to know for our story is that there was a time when the Greek crime families controlled large parts of Queens. They had the lion's share of the gambling and loan shark businesses, and co-operated with the Luchese family on protection and extortion.

As immigration has continued to change New York, each new generation has had a different balance of power, and the War on Drugs changed things completely.

These days, the Kanellis family still exists on a much smaller scale, with their turf limited to a few blocks in either direction.

Reah Kanellis, the head of the family is still a well known - and generally well respected - figure locally, but much of her power is now symbolic, and based on memory.

The family was still much more active back when Louisa was a teenager. And Elsi tells me Louisa was a full part of it.

Elsi: She loved it. The status. The attention.

Dee: What did she do?

Elsi: Worked the counter, mostly. Reah ran things out of a bodega on the corner of 30th. Still does, I think. The place is still there, anyway. Different name, different cat, but it's still there. She'd get local kids working for her, on the corner selling drugs, or collecting - because people wouldn't attack kids - and if you got to work behind the counter in the store, that meant she really trusted you.

Dee: Was Louisa into drugs back then, too?

Elsi: I never saw that. She was into boys, and making noise, showing off how important she was. But I never saw drugs.

I keep giving Louisa the benefit of the doubt on this.

I mean, we all did some stupid things as teenagers, right? I have a Powerpuff Girls tattoo. But there feels like a big difference between normal teenage mistakes and being involved in organised crime. And the fact she never talks about that publicly, the way she sells the single mom from the Rockaways act, tells me she knows how it would change the way people see her. And that... feels like we're being manipulated. But maybe we take it at face value. Everybody is allowed to change. Except, as I was researching this episde, I learned that Louisa's lawyer, Ramona Cross, lives in Astoria and has represented several of Reah Kanellis' gang members, getting them plea deals.

In addition, Louisa has also just hired an ex-con from the same area, named Constantin McGarry.

One quick Google tells me he was convicted for armed robbery, and *three* quick Googles tell me that he's also linked to the Kanellis crew.

So why would somebody who has honestly left all of these ties behind be so knee-deep in hiring Kanellis people?

It was while I was trying to chase down these questions that I spoke to a retired police officer, who wishes to remain anonymous, who made me see Louisa in a whole different light.

> Anon: ...yeah, see, I don't think Louisa knows what the truth is.

> Dee: You think she's lying.

> Anon: No, I mean, I really don't know if she knows. One day to the next, I'd see a different person. Sweet one minute, obnoxious as shit the next. But the one thing I don't get, all these questions about whether she killed a guy. And nobody is talking about the problem with Louisa and Ricky Friedberg.

Ricky. This is a name I've heard a bunch of times now. Ricky Friedberg. I've done a little digging. That could be the title for the whole show couldn't it? I've done a little digging, season three.

Ricky came from a good family. The Friedbergs will tell you they're not rich. They did, when I spoke to them. One of the first things they mentioned. But they live in Queensboro Hill now, in a nice big house. I counted four cars outside.

> Max Friedberg: I just got lucky on the dot com, got in and out at the right time. But we're not rich, just comfortable.

That's Max Friedberg, Ricky's father.

The way he talks, you'd picture a tech genius, someone who knew how to make money off the dot com bubble. But Max is a city trader. Or was: he retired twenty years ago on whatever nest egg he'd landed, enough to be comfortable.

But not rich.

> Elsi: They were totally rich.

You remember Elsi from the last Louisa episode. She was Louisa's best friend before the move out to the Rockaways. Or, to really pinpoint the change, up until Ricky.

> Elsi: Even then. They lived right by us, but they had a house, not an apartment. Nice place with a drive and a fence. All us girls loved him.

Ricky didn't go to the same school as Elsi and Louisa. Nobody remembers where Ricky went, and his parents didn't want to be drawn on naming the place. Elsi tells me it was a private school. And Louisa's little group were all getting on great until Ricky Friedberg entered the scene.

> Elsi: I met Ricky at a friend's party. He was a few years older. And you could just tell, or I could, he had a little something extra about him. He talked better. He name-dropped countries he'd been to. And I had to have him.

> Dee: Sounds like it worked?

> Elsi: Oh yes. There was nobody could get in my way if I wanted something. Except...

> Dee: Louisa?

> Elsi: Once I wanted him, she wanted him. Once me and him were going out, she just had to, well...

> Dee: Did you fall out over him?

> Elsi. Oh yeah. Oooh yeah.

From what I can gather, Louisa and Ricky were the hot item in town for about two months. Much to the concern of Ricky's family..

> Max: I knew she was trouble. I told him. I wish I'd kept telling him.

Until they broke up over, well, whatever teenagers break up over.Elsi doesn't know, or doesn't want to say.

> Elsi: I don't know what it was. Probably nothing. It feels like that stuff was always over nothing, looking back. What I think is that she was never really all that into him. She wanted him because I had him, then when she had him, she was bored.

> Dee: What happened next?

The 'what happened next' is open to speculation.
Sounds familiar, doesn't it? Here are the facts.
Ricky Friedberg was found unconscious on the steps of Saint Demetrios in Astoria. He'd been severely beaten, both legs broken in multiple places, and his skull was fractured. Ricky stayed in a coma for several weeks afterwards, and when he regained consciousness, he wasn't the same.

> Max: Just wasn't the same boy. He never really came back to us.

Ricky suffered brain damage and loss of function.
He needed full-time care for the rest of his life, which wasn't long. On the morning of his twenty-third birthday, while his parents were out buying a cake and his caregiver was out of the room, Max suffered a fatal stroke.
So how does this tragedy relate to Louisa?

> Elsi: After they broke up, Ricky started saying all this mean, nasty shit about Louisa.

> Dee: What like?

> Elsi: He said she was a slut, basically. Said she seduced him, that she already knew what

to do, and had been with over ten boys already.

Dee: Was any of that true?

I should pause here just to say... This is uncomfortable, isn't it? We're talking about teenagers here. And let's not forget, barely teenagers. Louisa is thirteen or fourteen when all this is going on. Ricky was sixteen. I'm asking about the sex lives of underaged teens. Of children. But it feels like I had to ask.

Elsi: You know... honestly, I don't think so. For all the stuff I say about her, and I say a lot, I think Ricky was her first kiss. I think he made all of that stuff up to be mean. Louisa... she was always... she developed early, let's say. She was always judged on her looks. I guess that's never changed. And people always made up nasty things about her.

Nasty things might be an understatement. Though how many of them are made up, I'll leave to you. From a number of people I was given the obvious connection. A boy calls Louisa a slut, Louisa is connected to the Kanellis family, the boy gets beaten into a coma.

But I also get the feeling nobody wants to go on record making that connection. The Kanellis family might be a faded force in modern Astoria, but the name runs deep, and fear has a long memory.

Could an over-protective Reah Kanellis have arranged for Ricky to be taught a lesson? Could an over-protective Reah Kanellis have arranged for David Ash to be taught the same lesson?

THIRTY-NINE

LOUISA

Riding the train by myself always feels exciting.

Mommy doesn't like it. Says I shouldn't go past the streets around our own block on my own. Says it's not safe. Daddy, I think he knows, but he pretends he doesn't? Like, I think he used to do the same, and he's okay as long as he doesn't have to know.

I think they'd both freak right now. Getting a train into the city to come back out again. Not even sure how I knew what to do. The map was kinda confusing. Letters. Colors.

But it's fun. I feel like a grown up. Like I'm taller, just doing this by myself.

People keep staring at me.

Must be worried.

Should she be here all on her own?

No, that's not it. They're staring because they know me. They're staring because I'm famous. Where am I? I was outside the church then, no, I wasn't, that was before. I decided to get the train back home.

57th Street station.

I caught the Q. Not the F. Why the Q? What was I trying to do? I'd called Ally. She was going to come get me, why did I move? Did something scare me, or did my mind just drift? Ally's right, there's no way I can go to the party. This is getting worse. Did I take my medication today? Why is my mind going all over the place like this? Is it stress? I don't usually go like this. Is this how it's going to be now? Is this me losing my mind?

No.

It's just panic.

You get like this when you're stressed.

The train pulls in. The N. No, that's not what I need. But I'm in the way, people are shuffling around me to get on. I'll step on and off. Are people taking pictures? My social media notifications will be going crazy.

I haven't lost the bag. Still have the money. I'll turn around and head home.

Riding the train by myself always feels exciting.

I find a seat by the door. I like to be right by the door. Sometimes I lose track of the stops, and don't know it's time to get off until we're pulling into my station. If I'm too far down the car I get worried. What if there's a crowd and I can't get through them in time? What if I miss my turn, and get lost?

I'm carrying a bag.

Is it mine? I don't know. It feels big. Like, a grownup would have this. But not me, not us. My mom would never have something like this. It looks shiny. Shiny is expensive. We're not expensive. It's got-

Holy crap.

(I said crap.)

(I could get in trouble.)

It's got money inside. Lots of money. Paper money, in bundles, like in the movies.

Why do I have paper money?

The money was for the woman in Prospect Park.

She tried to trick me. I almost went along with it. Got me panicking. Spinning out.

Things are coming loose. So many things. No, not *things*. Don't say that. Use the right words. Focus. Find them. Memories. Memories are spinning out.

Don't give in to it. Calm down. Think about your boys.

My boys.

Where are they?

They were in the park, did I leave them?

No. Not the park.

They're with Gyul. At home. Safe.

Get yourself home, Louisa.

Home.

Before Mom and Dad get angry.

They don't like me being out here like this.

FORTY

CON

I got Karen, Anita and Tabby back to my place.

Mom had already turned the rooms over and left some food in the kitchen. Karen and Anita took a room each. Tabby could share with one of them. Once Anita and Tabby were settled in one of the rooms, watching TV, Karen joined me at the table by the window, drinking coffee.

"This is nice." She looked around the room. "You said it's an AirBnB?"

"The two rooms, yeah."

"You get interesting people staying over?"

"Well, they're not all hiding out, but yeah."

"You really think we need to? I mean, that he didn't…"

She was shaken. I could hear it in her voice. My mind flashed again on Halliday's body. I wondered which of the five stages of grief included "running from the killer".

"I don't know, really. No idea what's going on. Everybody is lying."

I held her eyes after that, letting the implication hang: *even you.*

She looked away, out the window. "What do we do? Call the cops?"

Karen wasn't from my world. She didn't know the rules. She needed to learn. Fast. What would be gained by bringing the police in? I had no idea what was going on, which meant there was nothing to use, no leverage to talk my way out. And if the ADA was wrapped up in it, calling the cops would just invite even more trouble.

"Will we be safe here?"

I said yes, but I meant *I don't know.*

I took the dead body as a pretty big warning in itself. And how quickly had these thoughts become the new normal? What had Halliday uncovered?

He'd hidden Charlie Starr's business card in his wallet, along with ADA Waltz's. Starr had shown up at Karen's place the same day Halliday was killed. The day after I found Halliday's body, I was tricked into a meeting with Waltz.

Was it all just about Louisa's health, like Karen had said? Halliday and Starr as vultures circling, sensing blackmail money. It was a simple answer. It worked. But still, something felt off. We needed something to work with. I couldn't figure out my next move if I didn't know where I was starting from. Karen had to know something. Even if she wasn't aware of it.

"Tell me about this other guy. Starr."

"I really don't know. He was creepy, that I know."

"Creepy how? Like Halliday?"

"No, different. Matt was... Matt was unstable. He was one of those, you know? Like I couldn't tell any minute what he was thinking. And half the time I think he believed what he said, when he was talking about protecting me or saving me."

"So what was different about the other guy?"

"You ever get the feeling someone's wearing a mask? I don't mean like, not like normal, just the way people are. But when it feels like someone's wearing a human mask, there's a layer of glass, and they got something else underneath."

I'd met a few people like that. It was best to get the hell away from them.

"What did he look like?"

"About the same height as you. Maybe a little smaller. Blond. Dressed really sharp, expensive suit."

"You can tell how much a suit cost?"

"You can always tell. Mostly it's the shoes, really."

"And what did he want?"

"Matt. How did I know him. What did we talk about."

"Did he ask about Ash?"

"No, just Matt."

"Did he mention the name *Waltz*?"

She shook her head. "Nah."

Could it be something else?

Maybe a different case Halliday was working.

He'd bitten off more than he could chew with someone else, and this was all one big coincidence. That could explain why Starr hadn't killed Dee Buana.

"I need you to think," I said. "Think back over everything Matt said. There's got to be something you know, something we can use."

"I don't know anything, I swear."

"Listen, I believe you. I know you're not holding out anything deliberately. But there's a chance you heard something that might be important, even if you don't know it. Let's go over it again, you said Matt found you?"

"Yeah. I don't know how. But I don't know how you did, either. However you did it, I think he did the same. Came to my work, tried to get me to talk there, then turned up at the apartment. Came on all tough, like I was going to get in trouble. Then he changed, tried being really nice, but he came off as weird."

"What questions was he asking?"

"Same as you. Wanted to know about my background, my time with David, Tabby. He said he'd been hired to prove Louisa was guilty."

"No. He was hired to clear her."

"Not the way he said it. He was probably lying, though." She looked down at her hands for a second. "Everybody keeps doing that."

Rule number two.

Everybody lies.

Maybe Karen didn't need as many lessons as I thought.

"Tell me who he talked to you about. The first time around, when he first showed up, started asking questions. Do you remember who he mentioned?"

"Oh yeah." Her accent got stronger the more she talked. "The guys in the band. Todd. Eddy. He mentioned Louisa and her manager, Alex?"

"Ally."

"Ally. Mentioned Danny. David's manager, you met him?"

"Yeah."

"Asked about David's drugs. Mine, too. Where we got them from."

"Where did you get them?"

"Dave let me use his hookup. He had a tab, I guess. I never paid. There was a system, I called a number, then they called back, arranged a delivery."

"You remember the number you called?"

"It's in the notes on my... hold on..." She swiped through apps on her cell. "Do you have a pen?"

I handed her a pen and the back of an envelope. She wrote the dealer's contact number down and passed it back to me. I tore off around the number and slipped it into Halliday's wallet, which had become my de facto filing method for things relating to this case.

So far, Halliday seemed to have walked the same path as me. We'd talked to the same people and asked the same questions.

"Then he came back?"

"What day is this? Sunday? It would've been Friday, I think. Maybe Thursday. Said he had something new. Said there was someone trying to muscle in. I guess he meant you."

She was upset. I could tell she didn't want to go over it, but I needed her to.

Whatever happened on that last night could hold the key to why Halliday was dead. And if I figured that out, I might crack my own case. I remembered my cell was on airplane mode, and switched the reception back on.

"When you got in the car, did he threaten you?"

"You don't get it. He didn't need to."

"Okay. Did he talk about it? Say anything at all that was different from before?"

"Not really."

"Is there anybody else he mentioned? You knew David longer than anybody in town, except for Edgar. You knew him back home. Is there anyone Halliday asked you about who I haven't mentioned?"

"No." She shook her head and sipped her coffee. "Definitely. No."

My phone started to buzz as messages stacked up.

"Wait." Karen set the drink down. "Well, yeah. But only Jimmy."

"Jimmy Ziskin?"

She nodded. "Yeah, you know him?"

I checked the screen of my cell, playing for time while my brain raced to find the right place for that new piece of the puzzle.

There were missed called from Ramona, along with a series of texts.

Louisa is missing. Call me.
We can't find her. CALL ME.

There was a voicemail from a number my address book didn't recognize.
It was from Louisa.

FORTY-ONE

LOUISA

I'm sitting near the back in Saint Demetrios. The corner of 30th Drive and 30th Street. Easy enough to remember, I guess. Somehow I found my way here.

First boy I ever kissed lived right across the street, in one of the houses on the other side of the elevated tracks. Ricky Friedberg. I think he's dead now. He was so nervous, didn't really know what to do. But neither did I, really. I just seemed to be more comfortable at it than him, and he thought I'd done it before. I remember his hands were so sweaty. It's funny, I haven't thought of him in years, but now the memory feels so fresh, like I'm in the moment again.

Life is just weird. Fame is even weirder. My life, it's a *before* and *after* of fame. It was supposed to be the answer. All my debts, all my problems. Waking up every day and thinking of bills, of mistakes, of health insurance for my parents, of all the things that were out of my control. If I could just get on that TV show. If I could just get the world to see me. One big deal, that's all I needed. One big paycheck. And life would all be okay.

Now look at me.

Life is very much *not* okay.

Con walks in. I see him hesitate, mid step. It almost becomes a dance move. He spots me and smiles. There's stress behind it. He steps over and slides onto the wooden pew beside me.

"Thanks for coming. You called Ally?"

"Ramona."

"She'll call Ally."

"I figured."

I put my arms out on either side, resting on the back of the pew. Reflexively, my hand brushes the bag full of money on the way past. I've touched it every few seconds since I calmed down. I can't help it. Some part of me needs to keep checking it's still there.

"It's nice here," I say, softly. "Quiet."

"Yeah."

"Do you go to church?"

He pauses before answering. "I don't think I've earned it."

"I never knew how much I missed being around here. I was just thinking about this boy I kissed, right across the street. It's funny how these things come back at you, isn't it?"

"When did you move away?"

"Fourteen, I think. My parents wanted to get me away from Reah Kanellis, the whole scene. You know Reah?"

"Worked for her when I was a kid."

"In the shop, or on the corner?"

"Both. I was a spotter on the corner first, call out when the cops were coming. Then she saw I was good with my hands, said I had natural talents, brought me inside and put me with some guys who taught me."

"That's exactly the kind of thing my parents didn't want."

"Mine didn't want it, but we never moved. They just tried raising their volume. Mom and Frank tried to scare me out of it, didn't work."

"Frank?"

"My stepdad."

"Is that where the McGarry comes from? Because I'd figured, with a name like Constantin…"

"My mom's side. They're all Greek. I was named after her uncle."

"And what about your real dad. Your father, I mean?"

There's a long gap. I see uncertainty. I've touched something. "I don't know. Mom's never told me anything about him. Could've been Greek, could've been a Martian. I have no idea."

"I think you'd look a bit greener if you had any Martian in you."

And I think, *Martians don't look so cute.*

Then bite down on that.

Where did it come from? *Not now*, Louisa. Maybe not ever. Is that a side of me that needs to go away? How can I l be with anyone, if I don't even know how long I'll be myself?

Another thing to put in the 'not now' box. Think about it later. "So, McGarry. Your stepdad's Irish?"

"He'd tell you he was. Born and raised here, never been to Ireland, but he's Irish."

"I think roots are important. Probably. I mean, I guess they are. I feel like it matters my family was Greek, though I couldn't say why. And I think that's maybe why I called you first, not Ally. Your first name, the Greek in it. There was something familiar. That makes no sense, right?" He opens his mouth to answer, but doesn't have anything. "And I think it should matter to me more that I was raised in the church, you know? I only really remember about it in the bad times, but I always feel like it should be more of a thing in my life. But then..." I give him a quick smile. "I'm not sure I've earned it, either."

He nods. Doesn't seem to have anything to add to that. He knows the value of silence.

I do too, but I need to keep talking, keep in control of myself. *Roots.* "I almost went to see Reah. You know, standing outside her shop, that was the moment my mind started to quieten down, the focus came back. How bad is that? Standing outside a criminal's place is when I started to feel like me again. So came here instead." I laugh. "The other choice. Were you raised religious?"

"Kind of. Frank goes to church still, when he can. Don't know how much of it he actually believes, but it seems important to him to go. Tried hard to get me to care about it, but it didn't take."

"Catholic?"

"Yeah. But my mom, she's Jewish."

"If your mom is Jewish -"

"I am too, yeah. Well, I guess. I don't know. I've gone around on that over the years. I was confirmed, so I guess I'm Catholic, but the Jewish wiring is in there, too. I'm Jewish when I call my mom, I'm Catholic when I argue with Frank."

"Which of those do you do most?"

"Arguing with Frank."

"The rest of the time?"

"I don't think much about it."

The conversation is so easy. Relaxed. I know I'm just coloring it with the knowledge that we grew up so close together. Feels like we have the same roots. Know the same people. If my parents hadn't moved, and I'd stayed working for

Reah, Con and me might be old friends now. There's a feeling here, I can't get it anywhere else. Everyone else is fake. But Con, even Ramona, they're *from* here.

It feels...

I touch the money again, then turn in the seat, pulling my right leg up under me, to face Con. "You still see Reah?"

He hesitates. I can see there's some lie in what he's about to say, but not an important one. "I got out of all that."

"You and Ramona, you go back a long way?"

"Right back to when we were kids, yeah."

"That's sweet."

"Not really, we're not an item. That didn't work out. We're just friends."

We're. Just. Friends.

The worst lie in the English language. How often has anyone said that, and meant it? I can tell he doesn't. And I know she doesn't either. Someone just needs to hit them each in the head.

He seems to read my silence, filling it with another excuse. "We're too different. She sees the best in everybody. It's why she does what she does. I see the worst."

"Do you see a killer when you look at me?"

Because I don't know now. That memory. The anger I felt at Dave saying he wanted to leave. It was bright red. Hot. I could have killed in that moment. And Ally wasn't there until later.

I don't know.

I just don't.

But maybe I do?

Con looks at me. He doesn't blink, or hesitate. "No." Now he turns in his seat to match me. "What happened today?"

"I think it's getting worse now. Aggressive. I can feel it." I put my hand to the side of my head, like he needs an illustration of where the illness is. "There's this other person in here, and I don't like her. And she's pulling at me, stealing my brain. Then I was here, and the first thing I thought, call you."

"Not Ally."

No. I don't want to think too much about that. And the thought of the woman in the park, I feel the tearing at the end of my mind. I need to avoid that. "How are you getting on with the case?"

"Do you know Jimmy Ziskin?"

Hell, do I.

I snort.

"Jimmy. Yeah. Piece of shit. Almost ruined Dave's career. He was years before me, but he kept coming back, always asking for money, trying to get Dave to invest in some stupid scam, or bail him out of trouble."

"Dave ever give it?"

"No, he wanted nothing to do with Jimmy. But I think he felt a bit of guilt, leaving him behind the way they did, so he always heard him out before saying no."

"When was the last time you saw him?"

"Oh, Dave kept him away. Wasn't allowed around our place, I put my foot down."

"I still need to meet your dealer."

That's odd. I'm sure I gave Ally the number to pass on. But with my memory, who knows? I'm not confident of anything. I cover for it instead. "Yeah, I'll get you the number. There's a system. You call it, they hang up, call you back from a different line."

"What's Ally's boyfriends name?"

My head almost rocks. He's got me totally off guard with that one. "I keep forgetting. Uh, Zeke? She told me, I think. Yeah."

"But you don't remember him?"

"After today, you're going to ask me what I do and don't remember?"

It's meant as a joke, but I can hear the words are coming out harsh, defensive. He nods an apology.

There's movement in the doorway. Ally strides in. No pause. No dance move. She heads straight for us, her white coat billowing out behind her like, *get out of my way, I have shit to do.*

She stops and looks down at Con. There's something there. A coldness? I don't know. It's different from before.

"Con."

"Ally."

She looks at me, tilts her head toward the door. "Come on, let's get you home."

Ooooh she's mad.

There's going to be an argument as soon as we're in the car. Can't wait.

I lift up the bag. Touch Con's arm on the way past. "Thank you for coming. And I think it's the same thing. What you said about you and Ramona. Seeing the best, seeing the worst. It's the same thing."

FORTY-TWO

CON

I walked up to Hallets Point.

The route took me down to the end of 30th Avenue and along the paths that thread between Astoria Houses, the run-down apartment buildings that local politicians had been promising to replace for years. Vacant lots across the road were covered with boards showing pictures of what the new neighborhood would look like, if they ever got around to building it.

Condos, a library, a new waterfront.

Were they Edgar Malmon's handiwork?

I'd believe the development was serious on the day I could walk up and touch the buildings.

Ray Yorke answered the door on the first ring. There was no crying this time, and he wasn't wearing any breakfast cereal. He smiled and nodded me inside. Matty was on the floor in front of the television, watching a show about a street magician doing card and tumbler tricks. He beamed when he saw me, asking to see something.

I ran him through a basic trick. Shuffling the deck, I picked the card off the top to show an ace of diamonds. I shuffled again, and produced the same card. A third time, same result. I let Matty shuffle, and still the ace was on top. He laughed and applauded, and I showed him how to do the trick.

In the back room, Ray loaded up his laptop and brought up a bunch of windows on the screen.

"His lawyers have a lot of stuff," he said. "Savings, checking accounts. He owns a couple of houses in Minnesota, and I guess he bought his parents a house in Jersey, because it's in his name but a search of the address brings up their details."

"Nice idea, have them close but not too close."

"Right. He has a joint mortgage on a place in the Meatpacking District."

"The Village."

"Whatever. The mortgage is paid from his account, but money is coming in from somewhere else each month, a few days before the mortgage goes, and it covers half of the value. I figure that'll be from his wife, but haven't checked."

"Strange they're paying a mortgage when he owns, what, three other properties? Doesn't he have enough saved up to buy it outright?"

"The prices over there? No." He tapped one of the windows, it was a property listing website. "I checked. There were two apartments sold in that building recently. One went for two and a half million, the other for four."

"And he doesn't have that?"

"He does now. Or will have, if he's still alive. But not back then." He pointed to bank statements. "I guess since he went missing, all his sales have gone up. But it's not going into his own account, it's being stored with these companies he formed. He's been smart. So these companies make the money, and then he gets a salary."

"But if he owns the companies..."

"Ultimately the money is all his, yeah. His, and the other people who have stakes in the companies. But it's not cash readily available to him, he wouldn't be able to just go down to an ATM and withdraw it."

"What's his estate worth right now? What will Louisa get if he's dead?"

He pressed a few buttons and a chain of emails filled the screen. "Two different answers. Check this out."

Ray's finger traced across the right order for me to read the messages. Ash had been talking to his lawyer, Andrew Case, about a new version of the will. He'd asked for the estate to be split between the two boys and his parents. There was no mention of Karen or Tabby. No mention of Louisa.

He'd cut her out.

Did she know about that?

Something else hit me.

My conversation with Elizondo. He'd said Louisa *thought* she would get the money, Not that she *would*. So he knew about the change of will.

"She wouldn't get anything?"

"Well, I don't know. I'm good with the numbers, you'd need someone else for the law. She's his wife, so maybe she could contest the change, maybe she'd entitled to a share by law, or maybe she'd be entrusted with the money for the children, I don't know. But it seems pretty clear he didn't want her to get anything."

"And assuming that held, who stands to get the most?"

"Well, take your pick. His kids, his parents. The band members would still have their current stakes in the companies, but sharing it with his family, not Louisa."

"Is there anything else that stands out? Something strange? Any big payments to people, something I can use?"

"There's one odd bit. Hang on." He moved the windows around on the screen, looking for the ones he wanted, then lining them up in the right order. "This is a 401(k). He's a paid employee of one of the companies, so he's been paying into a 401(k). Last September he took out fifty thousand dollars."

"You can take money out like that?"

"Sure, but if you don't put it back within a certain time, it gets reported."

"Did he put it back?"

"Nope. The money vanished. There's record of it going to his bank account, then he took it all out in a branch one day, one big withdrawal, then it's gone. I can't see any signs, any changes in pattern later on, nothing that suggests it's the same money being returned, and it never went back to the 401(k)."

"Do you know if the cops have seen that?"

"Yup." He tapped another email. "Here's his lawyer talking to his own lawyer, confirming they'd handed information over to the police, and asking if he needed to take any extra precautions to protect himself."

David Ash withdrew fifty thousand dollars in September and went missing two months later. There was no trace of the money showing up. It had, like the man himself, vanished.

Could the money have been for Karen?

For drugs?

Jimmy Ziskin died between the withdrawal and Ash's disappearance.

"Wait, go back. You mentioned the other people who had stakes in the companies. Do you know who they are?"

"Sure. Edgar Malmon. Daniel Stewart. Anthony Preston."

I'd spoken to each of them. They all stood to gain financially from Ash's estate, but none of them seemed to be gaining anything extra from his death than they could have gained in life. They would still own the same share of the company, with Ash's percentage passing on to his family.

"How about a Jimmy Ziskin," I said. "Is he listed anywhere?"

Ray looked up at me. His expression told me he knew the name. "Jimmy? Why would he be involved?"

FORTY-THREE

CON

The way Ray explained it, Jimmy Ziskin wasn't from the band's world. He was from mine.

"Knew him for years," Ray said. "Surprised you didn't. But I guess you didn't know me before Watertown, so maybe it's not that strange. He was always trying to insert himself into the cool scenes in the city, wanted to be money, but there was always the smell on him, that he was too keen to fit in."

"Desperation."

"Yeah. Nobody liked him. It's funny, I was going to say he wasn't as good as us, but then, we both got caught, and he didn't. So he won, I guess."

I wanted to point out I was caught for driving.

My record as a grifter was spotless.

"What was his thing?"

"I knew him through poker. Those big games in the city. You know the one they made the movie out of? That one, and others. I'd play in them, always losing but I didn't care, it was about mixing with the right people, you know?"

"Like who?"

"All kinds. Movie stars. Politicians. Mob guys. I made a few connections there that kept me safe in Watertown later, and got me out early."

"Jimmy was in these games?"

"A little, sometimes. He was like the guy trying to come up from the little leagues, you know? Come across the river, sit at the big table. That's why it's funny you don't know him, he played in the same circles you did. I mean... no offence."

The more we talked about the name, and the games, the more I started to think I did know Jimmy.

Or had played with him a few times, at least. But memory is weird that way, you can talk yourself into remembering anything you want.

"I got kicked out the scene pretty early, as soon as I got a reputation as a mechanic."

"Yeah, must be that. So, I got to know Jimmy quite a bit. Know his story."

"Which is?"

"Started out with local bands. First thing I heard he did, anyway. Took a few on, called himself a manager. I guess that's where the Doormats come into it. That makes sense. He never told me who the bands were. I think he'd wanted to be a rock star, for like five minutes. But then he started ripping them off, trying to take their money. Except," Ray grinned, "he told me, the problem was, bands didn't have money. They had debt. So he was moving debt from one place to another, finding ways to cut himself in on the money before it vanished into the black hole, but it was hard work."

"So he got out."

"Yeah. Moved over to movies. Called himself a producer and went around convincing writers to give him their options for free. Or he'd do this thing where he'd say 'give me your book for one dollar, and then when I get the movie set up, I'll cut you a real check'. And then he'd sell the rights around. Make it look like he was setting up film deals, go into meetings armed with artwork, or a poster. Some letters he'd faked from actors saying they'd be in the film. But nothing would ever get made. All he was doing was selling and reselling the same thing, over and over, and it wasn't really his in the first place."

"Selling the Brooklyn Bridge."

"Exactly."

"He didn't get caught?"

"Nope. He said everyone in that business assumes everyone else is cheating, so it's like the perfect place to get away with it. It wasn't that people didn't figure out what he was doing, it was more like everybody knew and just left him to it. The big players wouldn't touch him, the sensible middle players wouldn't touch him. But there are always people looking to get into the business, easy marks, and there are always people floating around who want to invest money."

"So what happened?"

Ray paused. "Don't know, I lost touch with him when I went inside. The next time I heard his name was when he took a header off his balcony. He was living over there, Upper East Side. Got drunk, stepped off into the air."

Ziskin steps out into the air a month after David Ash had taken fifty thousand dollars from his 401(k). Halliday winds up with a gun in his mouth the day after warning me off the case.

"Does the name Charlie Starr mean anything to you?"

"Nope."

"Could you take a look?"

"Sure."

The connections were there, but something was missing. That something was David Ash.

How did he fit? What was the one thing that would make everything click into place?

"Did David Ash ever show up at the poker games?"

He shook his head. "Not that I ever knew. I wouldn't have been looking for him, but I tended to remember everyone who was there, they were all business opportunities for me."

"Would there be a way to find out if Ash invested in one of his dodgy movie schemes?"

"I can try. Jimmy's finances would be easy, they'll all be historical records, nobody will be keeping an eye on the activity. Give me a few hours."

"See if there are any ties you can spot to Ash. Does the 401(k) money show up, were they in any business together, anything like that."

"On it."

I showed him the picture I'd taken off Dee's phone, the contact details for Jack. "Anything you can get me on this number. Who it's registered to, anything." He nodded, taking a note of the number. I tried one more thing, pushing my luck. "You're going to say no. But is there any way you could get me a look at Carl Waltz's finances?"

He leaned back and put both hands on his belly, giving me a fake laugh. "You're funny."

I showed him the Post-It with Waltz's name next to the 100k figure.

"Are you sure you have the right one?"

What?

"What?"

"Cody Waltz."

The minute he said the name, I felt like laughing at myself. Something I should have known all along. Something I think I did know.

What had run through my mind at Karen's coffee shop? Too many convenient suicides. I hadn't really known why my thoughts had gone there. I'd known Halliday wasn't a suicide, so it had been a huge leap to connect it to Jimmy Ziskin before I'd really known any details about Jimmy.

But there was another one.

And it had been in my mind ever since the first night, talking to Ramona at the bar on 8th and West 12th. Carl Waltz's son, Cody. It had been all over the news at the time, the son of one of the city's most prominent figures.

Ray typed in the name then turned the screen to show me all the hits. The stories, the social media, the message boards, Cody Waltz had jumped off his balcony. He'd died the same way as Jimmy Ziskin. Two weeks before Jimmy's own tumble.

Too many convenient suicides.

"Did Cody play poker?"

He grinned, cat with a full bird in his mouth, "He did. Very well. Chopped me up a bunch of times."

"Who ran the game?"

"Give me five minutes, I'll hook you up."

FORTY-FOUR

LOUISA

The boys are away with Gyul. I don't know where. Probably at the movies or getting burgers and ice cream. The easiest ways to buy their silence.

Usually I feel a little heartsick when they're away. Even if it's only for a short time. But right now, for once, I'm glad of the space.

I couldn't bear the thought of them seeing the way Ally and Ramona are glaring at me. They might ask questions. Like, Mommy, are you in time out?

Ramona met me here, after Ally drove me home. And we've been sitting in an awkward silence ever since.

The quiet is worse than if they were shouting.

It's like they know nothing they can say is worse than what's going on in my own head. The voices whispering to me, telling me this is how it ends. Today is the worst I've ever been. For a while there, I genuinely didn't know where I was. What year it was. How old I was, or how young. I never lose track of who I am. I'm always Louisa Jade Mantalos. That's the easy part. But everything else seems to be up for negotiation with my own mind, and I don't know the rules.

This thing, this thing is taking everything away from me, one bite at a time. It's stealing my identity. How can I be the same person if I don't remember the things that made me who I am?

We are our memories. We are the people we've loved and the things we've said. And those are fading.

And yet.

And yet, some memories seem to be coming back to me, and they're not the ones that I want. I'm remembering seething anger at Dave. The night he went missing. We argued. I felt that rush of pure resentment. The hot flash, which always came right before a violent outburst.

I'm remembering the drugs. I'm flushing them down the toilet. But what's that thing I'm feeling while I do it? Is it high?

Have I already taken some, before changing my mind? The one thing I fought hardest for, to be clean and sober for my family, for a second chance, and I threw that away.

What kind of an illness is this?

This Alzheimer's?

It's taking away the things I treasure, the things I fought for. It's leaving me the bad moments. The angry moments. It's trying to make me cold and mean.

I've fought something like this before. Addiction tries to take away all of your successes and leave you with the failures. And now my own damn mind is trying to do the same thing.

"Where did you get the money?" Ramona says, finally.

"I have a stash. Emergency fund."

"What happened to you out there?" Ally is pissed. Barely holding it back.

"I'm fine," I say. "Just got confused."

But I'm not fine. The voices get louder. The illness. It's coming for me. It's taking me. From here, life is over. My memories are fading. I'm fading.

And I don't feel ready.

I don't want to go.

It's not fair.

"I really think it's time," Ally says, turning to Ramona. "We need to talk about it. I've been telling Louisa we should draw up some paperwork. I've had a couple meetings with Lori."

For Ramona's benefit she adds, "My own lawyer. And I think we need to look at power of attorney, for me. Just something to protect her." She turns back to me. "So you've always got me in your corner."

I feel a flush of anger again. "Because we need paperwork for that? You're not in my corner now?"

"That's not what I..." Back to Ramona. "Do you see what I'm meaning? Could it help keep Dave's family away, if I'm involved in a more legal sense?"

"It won't make a difference to their case," Ramona says. "In fact, I spoke to their lawyer earlier."

I try for the name. "Andrew something."

"Case, yeah."

"Okay."

"The thing in the park yesterday," Ramona says. "It's really messed us up. Dave's family is all over it. They're using it, and if they push that, they can use social media, TV. Half the city was talking about you being an unfit mother yesterday. Case is going to call our bluff on the stalling tactics. Push ahead with the custody challenge, get your medical records."

"Will it work?"

"Honestly, I don't know. Things like this are really more about political will than any legal precedent. If there is the will to get it done, it gets done. And right now, it feels like all of the will is against us."

"And they'll get access to my health records. They'll know."

Ramona goes silent. There's something more. I can read it in her face. In her hesitation. She's holding back.

I push. "What is it?"

"Why are they doing this?" she says.

"For custody."

"No, I mean, why this? Why now? Asking for your health records is a very specific challenge. We know it's their ace card. But how would they know that?"

It sinks in. I know what she's saying.

"They already know?"

"Yeah. They know about your illness. I'm sure of it. This is their way of showing their hand. They're letting us know they've got it, but they'll need to come by it officially to be useable."

"You think they want to do a deal?"

Ramona pauses again. "Maybe. It's possible. I'll talk to Case again. Try and figure out what the game is."

"How can they have it already?"

As soon as I ask the question, I know the answer. Ramona says she doesn't know, and gets up to leave. I let her go without putting voice to what I'm thinking.

I know.

I know how.

Andrew Case is the Ash family lawyer. A friend of Dave's father, they go way back together. He was Dave's lawyer in the old days, before the band got famous.

Another memory flashes up, hard and cold, of Dave

telling me he's seeing a lawyer about separation. I'm only remembering this now, but it's been buried in there for a while, because I've known all along he'd taken that step.

And to keep it quiet, he'd gone to the family lawyer.

Dave went to Andrew Case.

Dave leaked my health records.

FORTY-FIVE

CON

Leysa Wayne greeted me with a reserved smile. I'd been met at the door of their Upper West Side brownstone with a similar smile by Leysa's wife, a British woman named Carina. They both had a serious air. I could picture each of them running million-dollar businesses with the same ease they pretended to welcome me with.

Carina led me up a flight of stairs to a well-appointed office at the back, looking out onto a small yard decorated with potted plants and pear trees. Leysa had been sat at a desk, talking on the phone in a quiet, clipped tone. She'd put up a hand in greeting and gestured for me to sit in a leather sofa along the opposite wall. Carina asked if I wanted anything to drink and, when I declined, said she would leave us to it.

Leysa's call lasted another couple minutes, during which I didn't seem to exist.

Firmly put in my place, I looked out the window at the yard until she was done.

"Mr McGarry?" That reserved smile, a polite handshake.

"Thanks for agreeing to this."

"Ray vouched, told me you know the rules."

Never call the cops.

"He's a good friend."

"He's an asshole," she said, with the same smile. "But he was a good customer."

"Well, thanks all the same."

"What are you looking for?"

"I need to talk about your game."

She nodded. Obviously she'd already known that, but we still had to talk our way in, figure each other out. "There's only so much I can say."

"I understand."

Poker in New York was big business. The city always had three or four regular games on the go at any one time that could be referred to as the game. The meeting place of A list actors, investment bankers, CEOs and, ultimately, predictably, criminals. One of the games had been made into a Hollywood movie, and several others had been the subject of gossip. I'd tried to get into one, early on, before my reputation with cards preceded me.

"How did yours start?"

"Naturally. It just seemed to be my turn." She tapped at the desk for a moment, rubbing her hand on a blemish in the smooth wooden surface. "I'd been involved in the one before me. The famous one. I was an investment manager, and when that game went down, some of my clients had been involved in the sting. So I knew about the game, knew it had ended, and saw the gap in the market."

"How long did you run it?"

"Ten years."

"That's a good run."

"I went in with a plan, treated it like a business, never took anything personally or got involved in any of the... extras."

Extras. Every version of the game ultimately seemed to go the same way. People would get into it initially to play with the famous people and make connections with politicians and business leaders. That would always be the draw. But over time, and usually very quickly, the game would also attract drugs, professional sharps and gangsters. Once the pros or criminals got involved, the game was effectively dead.

"You never got into the drugs?"

"Never. And I vetted everybody, never allowed any professionals to sneak in, never got involved with the clients."

"The mob?"

She shrugged. "The trick there was to know what we were dealing with. High level guys were allowed to play, as long as they knew to leave their business at the door like everybody else. The low level guys were kept out, because it was always about ego for them, wanting to muscle in or show off."

"You never had any problems?"

"Of course we did. But we dealt with them."

"And you got out at the right time?"

She paused. "I stayed a few years longer than I wanted to, to be honest. I found it hard to give up in the end. The plan had always been to make five million, just about enough to never have to worry about money in this damn city, then get out. But..." A genuine smile now, nostalgia. "Power is hard to give up. I mean, I knew *everything*. You run that game right, you're the most connected person in town."

"So what made you give up?"

"Part of me knew it was past time. Most of me knew. But the part that wanted to stay...that's the part that screws everyone over. That's the part that gets them raking games, doing drugs, waking up next to baseball players."

Somewhere above us on the third floor I heard a baby starting to cry. Leysa looked up at the ceiling. We sat in silence as someone else, I assume Carina, climbed the creaky stairs and started soothing the baby. The tears slowed, then stopped.

"That's why I stopped," Leysa said, after a deep breath. "I remembered the plan, and what I'd wanted. And I had a choice, start to make all of those bad decisions, or make one good one."

I nodded, felt a pang of jealousy. I wasn't sure what it was for. I've never wanted children, and I was already out of the criminal circuit. But she had something else here that called to me. Certainty. An answer. She knew what she wanted out of life, and she'd made the choice to take it.

"If you never raked the game," I waved my hand at the room, "How did you make a profit?"

"It was easy enough to let the general understanding get out that it was considered appropriate to tip the host somewhere around ten percent of your winnings."

"And the losers?"

She shrugged. "Had no need to be generous. And I was a great host for them. We rented a suite at SoHo House, I laid on everything they could want. Free drinks, free food. Free drugs. Free escorts. If you came to my game and lost, aside from whatever you'd paid for the buy in and thrown at the table, you could get yourself a good time in every other way and it seemed like they were free gifts."

"Because you still got a cut of their money."

"I did."

"How high did the pots go?"

"Usually a hundred thousand or so, sometimes more."

"Millions?"

"Sometimes. But I lasted so long because I had ways of controlling the mood, keeping people from being dumb, protecting them from themselves."

"And they let you just walk away? With everything you have on people?"

"It's not usually that easy. That's something else that traps people. You become an inconvenience when you leave, walking around with all that dirt. But the world helped me out." She paused, waited to see my confused expression, then continued. "Covid. When everything shut down, that was my chance. The game stopped and I conveniently just didn't start up another, left a gap in the market for someone else to fill. And with everything else that was going on in the city, I wasn't a priority. People just let me go."

"Good timing."

"But understand, the whole reason I stay this way, and why I was so good at the job, is people knew they could trust me. Ray has vouched for you, but I'm still not giving anyone up. I'm not naming names, I'm not here to gossip."

"I hear you. I don't want that. But maybe I can give you some names, people I already know or suspect, and you can decide whether you're okay confirming them?"

She watched me in silence for a moment, ran a tongue across her bottom lip, then nodded slightly. "Go on."

"I know Ray played, obviously. I don't care about him. I'm thinking Jimmy Ziskin played?"

"He's dead, so, yes. He did, sometimes. But I started to smell he was cheating, and was there fishing for something big, like an angle on other players, so I cut him out."

"Was he ever there on a high pot night?"

"Medium, I'd say. Won some, lost a lot."

"Did someone named Charlie Starr ever play?"

"No."

It was a very fast answer. Firm.

"Is there a story there? If he wasn't involved in the game, you wouldn't be breaking any confidences?"

She seemed to think it over. "Charlie was... not someone I wanted swimming in our pool. Others in the game had warned me off."

"Other criminals?"

She smiled in a way that said yes without saying yes.

"Cody Waltz?"

Her mouth opened, then her lips pursed and she didn't answer.

I pushed. "He's dead too, there's no confidence there."

"And we both know someone else who isn't dead, I'm sure you don't need me to explain that part."

"Okay," I held my hands up. "No details, no amounts, but Cody did play?"

A pause. "Yes."

"Was he good?"

Another pause. "Very."

"Did David Ash ever play?"

"No."

"Louisa Mantalos?"

"No. I know Louisa, we used to be friends, but she was never involved in the game."

"Why *used to be?*"

"People grow up, they grow apart, friendships run their course. But there's no story there for you. Louisa was just never... a long term bet when it came to friendships."

"Did you ever meet a guy named Matt Halliday?"

She turned to the ceiling and barked out a loud, forced, HA. "Now him I don't mind trashing."

"There's a story there."

"I don't know how he found out about the game, but he did. And he kept trying to offer his services. Collections. Enforcement. Security. He seemed to be under the impression he was more impressive than he was. But you swim in the pool I was in, you don't see the Matt Hallidays of the world to be all that appealing. Or intimidating."

Interesting. Jimmy Ziskin and Cody Waltz both played. Charlie Starr and Carl Waltz were intimidating, and Matt Halliday wasn't. Halliday was someone who didn't know his own level, constantly getting in over his own head. Ziskin was someone who was maybe on my level as a card cheat, always looking for a new hustle. A solid shape was starting to form. I could see the story, it just wasn't one that seemed to involve David Ash or Louisa Mantalos.

Which game came next?

"You say you left a gap in the market for other people to fill. Do you know who filled it?"

The baby cried again. This time the soothing voice came straight away, in a sing-song lilt, and I got the impression Carina had stayed in the baby's room. The sound was enough to pull Leysa out of our conversation, I got the feeling things had come to an end.

"I'm out of the game," she said, returning her attention to me. "That's all I care about."

FORTY-SIX

CON

I was starting to feel fried. Running close to empty.

I knew finding Halliday's body had affected me. That was something I was still pushing away, to be dealt with later. But the strangeness with Ally, the threats from Waltz and the moment with Louisa. What was that moment? Did I imagine it?

I was stuck in a non-argument with Ramona about a case I should never have taken on, and it was starting to look like some kind of hitman or mob fixer was tracking down people who got too close. I had half a notion, more than half, that Halliday, Ziskin and Starr were all linked by the poker game, but there was no link between the game and David Ash.

I was in way over my head. I should have known this would happen. I *did* know this would happen. Why did I take the case?

Ramona.

Always Ramona.

I needed to tap out, but I was too close to finding the connections. I could feel it, right in the air in front of me. Hovering. Waiting for me to grab them.

It was time to figure out which lies were important.

I headed downtown to The Last Drop.

Sunday evening, the place was in the last throes of weekend bro bar status.

Drunken and loud young men, almost all white, being right about everything and confusing stupidity for flirting.

There were a few punks and indie kids in the corners, judging the rest of the crowd, regretting their life choices.

I pushed through to the front. The same bartender was working. She told me her shift was only just starting. She hesitated when I asked if Todd was around. Must have been used to fending off that question from music tourists and hangers-on. She leaned in to talk quietly.

"He's down in his pit," she said. "Recording."

"He has his own studio?"

She paused again. I could see her realizing this was new information for me and questioning whether she should have said it. I smiled to let her off the hook, but inside my head raced. Todd had his own studio.

Would he have ever let David record there? Could that be where he'd cut the demo tapes?

"I don't think he'd -"

I didn't give her the chance to finish. If you don't want someone to say no, it's best to ask a different question. I pointed at the door at the end of the bar. "Through there?"

She looked at the crowd waiting to be served, then back at me. I'd put her in a tough spot. She made a show of sighing, and then waved me toward the door. In the small hallway at the back of the bar I found a staircase leading up, and a heavy-looking door set into the opposite wall. I pulled it open. There was padding on the other side, and it was stiff in the frame. There was a flight of stairs leading down, and I could hear muffled sounds drifting up toward me.

I took the steps slowly, straining to hear what he was playing. I was expecting some kind of bass-driven rock, or old school punk, but did I hear piano? It was accompanied by a stylized, out of tune Tom Waits growl.

I pushed open a second heavy door at the bottom, and now the full music hit me. Or whatever was left of it in the air, as Todd stopped playing to stare at me.

He was sitting at a battered old piano, with an assortment of cables trailing over the wood and under the hood. There was a computer on a desk beside him, and I could see something on the screen moving, recording.

"What the hell?" He spoke fast and agitated. His voice was a little lighter than last time, lacking the gravel. There was alcohol fraying the edges of his words, and a large glass of red wine was sitting on the piano in front of him.

Todd looked around at the room, and then back to me. The walls were adorned with jazz posters, and there were shelves full of albums that looked too old to be a collection of 80s indie or 70s rock.

I realized I'd got him. The real Todd Flambé. Maybe even Anthony Preston.

The slip wasn't going to last long. I could already see the wheels spinning behind his eyes as he tried to regain composure.

"That sounded cool," I said. Trying to tease out a little more time with this version of him. "New stuff?"

His hands fidgeted. I could read his thoughts, deciding whether to push me out or answer the question. Trapped between two different versions of himself.

"I, uh. This is just for me," he said. "It's not what people want."

"I liked it."

He blinked. "Uh, thanks."

He fidgeted again for a second, and a shy smile crossed his lips. He stood up and waved me in. This wasn't the *yeah, cool, cool* guy I'd spoken to upstairs. I just needed a little more time.

"Maybe you could release it under a different name?"

Another smile. This one suggested maybe he'd already done that. I wondered if there were whole albums out there from the real person, Anthony Preston, under another name. Free of whatever trap he'd built up for himself with the Doormats.

He drank the wine down in one go. "It's all stupid," he said. "Whole thing. Anyway. You didn't come here to give me career advice."

"I wanted to ask you about Jimmy Ziskin."

He tipped his head to the side, shook it, and let out one single laugh. He turned to a small cabinet low down next to the piano and lifted out a fresh bottle of red wine. He opened it and filled his own glass, then found one for me. I took the drink. I could sip it. No need to throw up extra barriers by saying no.

"That fucking guy," he said.

"Danny told me he managed you for a while."

"Yeah. I tried. I was doing it at first. I know money and contracts and all that. It's..." He paused. Gave up holding onto something. "It's what I'm from. My family, my parents, they live off capital gains. So a few small contracts? I could've handled that. Plus half the clubs and bars at the time were owned by people like me, people pretending not to come from...you know... so I had contacts. We skipped whole steps because of me, we didn't tour in a shitty van, sleep on students floors, none of that. We got good bookings. Because of me. But then Jimmy muscles in, making all these promises. They wanted him to take over, so we signed his contracts."

"You didn't think he was on the level?"

"People always want a piece of what you got. In any business. In music, part of what we got is cool. Jimmy wanted a piece of that. I didn't think he was going to cheat us or anything. I just didn't think we needed him."

"Did you get the sense after that he'd tried to screw you guys over?"

"I dunno. Maybe. Depends who you ask. His contracts were a real mess, it was hard to follow all the trails to see who owned what. Danny thinks Jimmy was trying to con us. Me, I think he was just an idiot who wanted to be part of the cool kids club. I mean, we were in debt right up until Dave's solo career took off, so it's not like we had anything worth stealing."

"Did you stay in touch?"

"With Jimmy? Some. I saw him at poker games here and there, and he'd come round to see me sometimes, trying to talk me into investing in one of his things, or asking for a bailout if he'd gone in over his head."

"You never did?"

"Bailed him out a couple times, but you soon learn to turn that tap off. Never invested. Like I said, I know what I'm doing with money. I want advice, I go to my dad, not to someone like Jimmy."

"Did you play in Leysa's game?"

He slow-grinned. "You heard about that? Yeah, I played a few times. I like poker, but the egos get involved too fast, once that happens, the game is done."

"Too many egos in Leysa's game?"

"Too much of everything by the end. If I join a game, I go in thinking I may well lose a few grand, I may win a few. But towards the end - the end of when I was going, I mean - every pot was over a hundred grand, and I just couldn't throw that kind of money away. I didn't have it to throw."

"Really?"

"Things are different right now. I hate it, but anything with Dave's name is becoming a license to print money.

Before he... before all this, most of my money was from family connections, or invested." He turned his palms up, waved at the room around us. "This place. Stocks. The band's companies. I'm not saying I was broke, I was rich, but none of it was liquid. I couldn't go to the bank and put my hands on it. So I just didn't have cash to throw into a stupid game where everyone wanted to show how big their dicks were."

"You saw Jimmy at them?"

He held up a single finger. "Only once. I told Leysa after, steer away from Jimmy, he's here to muscle in. He never showed up after that."

"You ever play Cody Waltz?"

He opened his mouth but paused a beat before answering. I could see the light go on. "Waltz? Well, that all kinda makes sense now, yeah. The things he'd talk about. Jokes other people would make. I figured he was someone important, but he was kinda young. Does make more sense if he was related to someone important."

"You didn't know?"

"Just knew him by his first name. Cody. Yeah. Maybe I was told his second name and it didn't stick, I don't know. I know who Waltz is now, did I know all that much then? Probably not, you know?"

"Was he good?"

"He was aggressive. Loved to mess with people, force the pot higher, force people to go all in. But he didn't have the extra thing you need, to know when it's not worth playing. That's what makes you really good."

"Did Dave ever play?"

He laughed, seeing where I was going. "You're barking up the wrong tree there. Wrong forest. Believe me, I thought the game had any link to this, I would have been shouting about it. Dave hated gambling. Hated it. Always struck us funny, you know, this guy, loved everything. Booze. Drugs. Whatever else. Give him a new thing, he'd find a way to need it. But he always hated gambling. I think his parents scared that into him, maybe there was a family member or something, I don't know. But we'd play poker on tour, the rest of us, with the crew, with Danny if he was there, whatever bands were in the same hotels. Have some fun and party, and Dave would just vanish off with whoever his local girl was, or sit in the corner shouting about how we were all wasting our time."

"Do you think he ever invested in Jimmy's schemes? Or bailed him out?"

He knew where I was going with this. "I don't think so. Dave hated Jimmy. He agreed with Danny. More than that, really. Danny agreed with him."

"Jimmy was stealing?"

"Yeah. Dave was – is - a kind of secret control freak. He lets other people do the dirty work, but he's always calling the shots. If he decides he doesn't like you, then you're cut off, but you'll never hear it from him. Danny or I would be the ones to actually tell people to go away. Dave would just delete them from his mind, ignore them."

"When was the last time you saw Jimmy?"

He smirked. "The funeral? Sorry, that's mean. It was sad. I mean, he was a jerk, but it's still sad, right? I went to the funeral. Weren't many people there, and it was a weird crowd. Like, there was some of us from the old days, the bands. There were a few film people. A bunch of shady types who I guessed were his investors. Seemed like there wasn't a single person there had a nice word to say about him, but we went."

"David went?"

"Oh no. Just me, from the band. Jimmy didn't exist in Dave's world anymore, and Eddy basically always does what Dave wants, so it was just me."

"Anyone else stand out to you at the funeral? Anyone who might be connected to David, or who felt out of place?"

"Could say that about any of them, really. I knew half the people, didn't know half. Maybe recognised a few without knowing them, from poker, or just from parties in the city or back in the old days. The people Jimmy tended to get investment from, they weren't really connected, you know? Not in the business. He got money from people who wanted to be involved, not people who were already in."

There was a clear line forming. Cody Waltz and Jimmy Ziskin either losing money they couldn't pay, or winning enough off the wrong person, bruising a dangerous ego. Charlie Starr cleaning up the mess. Carl Waltz covering for his dead son. Maybe he genuinely believed it was suicide, and wanted things to be as simple as possible. Didn't want any links to the game being exposed in a messy investigation. How hard would it have been for Halliday to find out about this, just as I had? Maybe he tried to blackmail Waltz, or Starr, or both. Got himself a ticket to the boneyard for his troubles.

But that still didn't give me a connection to David Ash.

I was closer to solving two murders that nobody seemed to even know were murders, and no closer to finding my missing rock star.

"Do you think there's any way Dave would have got mixed up in the game, or bailed out Jimmy?"

Todd shook his head, once, emphatically. "No."

He looked down at the piano. His fingers twitched above the keys, playing a tune somewhere at the back of his mind. I was losing him. He drained off most of the glass and refilled. The wine spilled over the sides as he poured. He offered me the bottle, but I shook my head, showed I still had the first drink.

"Do you think David could have just deleted everyone, the way he did with Jimmy? Just decided he didn't want any part of this life anymore, moved on somewhere else?"

Todd looked back at me. I couldn't read his expression. The wine in his system was making it impossible. Was it grief? Remorse? Or jealousy?

"Not a bad idea," he said. "I bet half the guys in the business would like to do that."

I didn't have anything to add, so I waited him out. He settled down onto the piano stool with a heavy sigh. His knees creaked. "We all come here to be young in the city. That's really all we want. To be young, and cool, and here." He played a few sad notes. They held in the air around us. "What do we actually do, though? Really? We dress up, pretend to be someone else, and help to drive up the rent in whatever part of town we're drinking in."

I started to feel like a voyeur. Todd wasn't really talking to me now, he was arguing with himself.

I'd gotten all I was going to get, and the longer I stayed, the more I felt like I was intruding on something private.

"Did you ever play in the next game? The one that came after Leysa?"

"Nah." He was somewhere far away now. Lost in a mood, wrapped up in red wine. "I didn't want to play nice with Ally."

WHAT?

"Ally? Ally was involved?"

He nodded, not looking at me. It felt more like he was talking to a ghost now, I was barely in his room. "It was her game. She muscled in on that just like everything else."

I hesitated, looking at this new piece, trying to move all the parts around and see if this new information helped me or was just a curveball, a pointless surprise.

He filled the silence with notes from the piano. A mournful, bitter, energy. "Wrong tree, man. Wrong tree. Dave hated Ally almost as much as he hated Jimmy. He just couldn't delete her, because she'd worked her way into their life so much."

There was an obvious question here. One I was annoyed I'd never asked. "How long have Louisa and Ally been friends?"

"I don't know. Couple years? The apartment they're in now? That was Ally's. They got a good deal because she had some big debts I think, needed a quick sale. But then she stuck around, just never left."

And he was gone. Leaning away from me. His head moving with the music.

I pulled open the door. I mumbled a thanks to no response and closed the door on my way out. Halfway up the stairs, I heard tentative, slow singing. Songs played and never heard. A performer choosing to have no audience.

FORTY-SEVEN

CON

Charlie Starr was waiting for me at Sharkey's.

I got a call from Frank telling me someone had walked in off the street asking for me.

"Weird guy," Frank said. His voice was muffled, like he was leaning into the receiver, talking low. "Asked for a Shirley Temple. Insisted on choosing the glass, made me wash it in front of him, so he could see."

"Did he tip?"

"Ten bucks."

"Did you wash it naked?"

"Just get here, will you?"

I texted Ramona on the way.

I decided against a call. Somehow, it felt like this case was putting more distance between us. Piling pressure on the old unresolved issues. There had only been one part of our shared history that had caused any problems before, but a lifetime of loose threads had been trailing out from that crack, waiting to pull everything apart.

She'd been lying to me. Now I was withholding from her not only that David Ash had been cheating and had a daughter, but that they were hiding out in my apartment.

I thought back to our conversation outside my apartment. When I'd said she hired me to do things she didn't want to know about. The hurt in her voice when she'd responded, "*Is that really what you think?*"

What was this case doing to us?

I didn't put the full details into the message, because I still didn't know what was relevant. I said I was on my way to the bar to meet someone related to the case. I left out mention of Ash's secret family staying at my apartment, or high-stakes poker games, or Ally.

Ally.

What did that mean? I had assumed she'd been on the scene for a long time. Louisa's best friend. The only one standing by her. But now it seemed she'd inserted herself into the story more recently. But even still, she was the one friend sticking by Louisa. She took over the card game, but that only worked to solve mysteries nobody was asking me to deal with.

It was quiet when I got to Sharkey's. There were only four people there, including Frank. He didn't need to point the guy out to me.

He was standing at the bar. There were empty stools on either side of him. Karen had been right about his suit. It was a three piece, in the kind of blue that doesn't exist for less than four figures. His blond hair didn't look like it had ever been out of place in his whole life.

The Shirley Temple was in front of him, sitting dead center in the middle of a napkin on the bar.

He turned to me and his thin lips spread out into what I assumed was a smile. "Constantin, I presume? I've heard a lot about you. My name is Charlie Starr."

He didn't offer a hand to shake.

"What can I do for you, Mr. Starr?"

"Charlie, please."

There was a hint of the south to his voice. But not full-on. He spoke softly. A man who was used to being listened to. I would bet he'd never had to raise his voice. Most of all, I knew exactly what Karen had meant when she'd said he'd been wearing a mask. I was looking at a calm, well-mannered front.

There was something else beneath the surface, and I didn't want to find out what it was. The back of my neck started to itch.

"I was hoping we could talk somewhere a bit more private," Starr said.

Frank had a back office that he let me use sometimes, but there was no way I was talking to Starr behind a closed door. I was already thinking, for the first time in my life, that maybe the first rule should be more of a guideline.

Never talk to the cops….unless the alternative is talking to someone who scares you more.

I took a step back and tapped the bar. "Here's fine."

"You seem to know who I am. Well, that answers one of my questions, at least. I'm sure you understand why I'd like to be able to talk discreetly."

"And you'll understand why that's not going to happen." I pointed to the table at the back. "My office is right there."

Starr pursed his lips, looked around at the two other patrons. He gestured for me to lead the way and said, "Please."

At the back of the room I took my usual seat, facing forwards, able to see the door. I figured this would put Starr further on edge. A man who probably valued that position even more than me. He stood looking down at the seat next to him for a second. He stooped to wipe it with a napkin, then eased himself down, lifting his pants at the knees to avoid creasing.

"I've been asking around about you," he said. "You help people out for money. Everyone says you're discreet, never go to the police."

I didn't say anything. He sipped at the drink and placed it down on the napkin, turning the glass until it lined up exactly on the previous watermark.

"Two associates of mine took their own lives. One only yesterday. It's all very sad."

He smiled, I wondered if he was daring me to point out I'd been there, in the same lot, outside Halliday's trailer. But I couldn't read him the same way I could almost anyone else.

"Only two?" Was I holding back my fear? Could he see it? "You've forgotten about Cody Waltz so soon?"

His head twitched. "Interesting."

He said the word as if I'd surprised him, maybe he'd underestimated me, or expected something different.

"Why are you here, Mr. Starr?"

"Charlie. I'm here to help. These friends of mine -"

"Say their names."

"Certainly. Matthew Joseph Halliday, Cody Dustin Waltz and James Kenneth Ziskin. They've brought a premature end to our business dealings and, more important, I'm sure we both agree, more tragic, the world lost two bright lights. I was looking into Matthew's affairs, seeing if there are any loose ends I could tie up. I know he'd rest easier knowing someone was doing that for him. And I found out you and he had some unfinished business."

He slipped a wad of bills out from his inside pocket. They were fifties. A lot of fifties. He set them down on the table.

"I gather you're looking for a missing person. That's quite exciting. But my concern is, you may think what happened to my two friends is linked."

"You want me to stop looking into them."

"I want you to find your missing person. I hope David Ash is safe and well. But I want to be clear that there is no connection. As tragic as all three deaths were, they were nothing to do with your case. And, above all, I want to preserve their memories, their dignity in death."

With another fluid move, he produced a passport and handed it across to me. There were two boarding pass stubs bookmarking a page. I opened it to see a stamp for Russia the day before David Ash disappeared.

The first ticket stub was dated for that day, and the second was for a week later.

He said. "I'm really not worth looking at."

I flipped to the passport ID page. Starr's picture was almost identical to the way he looked sitting across the table from me, but the suit was a different shade of blue.

"Easy enough to fake these. Nobody has a boarding pass stub these days unless there's a reason to have one."

"Oh, absolutely. We both know people who could forge them. If you like, I could introduce you to the very best. But, really, why would I bother? I would have other ways of dealing with the problem." He paused. "Please, excuse me. I want another of Francis' fine Shirley Temples. Would you like something?"

"I'm good."

He stood up and headed back to the bar, where Frank pretended he hadn't been watching us the whole time. Starr waited while Frank washed another glass in front of him and prepared the cocktail. Starr walked back to the table, sipping the red liquid through a straw.

"Wonderful," he said, sitting down. "Now, where was I? Oh yes. Let me put it like this. If I thought we had a problem here that necessitated I lie, or fake a passport, I would have much easier ways of dealing with the problem. But I don't like mess, and really, all we have here is a bit of a mess, something we can clean up. I'm saddened at the passing of these friends. I wish I could have changed their minds, but I respect their choices. The business I had with them is not related to your missing friend." He tapped the stack of bills. "And really, I do hope you find the man you're looking for. And I want to help, by removing myself from your enquiries."

The message was pretty clear.

He was all but admitting to having killed Halliday, Waltz and Ziskin, but telling me he'd had nothing to do with Ash.

And the craziest part was, I was believing him.

Even though it had the signs of a classic con. Tell the mark the truth up front, to mask the lie. But two murders would be a hell of a truth to throw out there as a gamble.

I realized I hadn't seen him blink since we started talking.

Was that even possible?

"Did you lose to them all in one night, or over a series of games?"

His ran his bottom lip beneath his top teeth. "From what I've been told, you got behind the wheel of a getaway car despite never being a wheelman. We've all let our egos get the better of us sometimes. Made mistakes. I lost myself for a few hours, one night. Carried away with the moment. Now I need to fix my error."

"You went *on tilt*."

Tilt is the dream ticket in a mark, at the poker table or during a con. It's the moment when they stop thinking straight, led by luck, emotion ego, or adrenaline. The chemicals rushing to the brain start to make the decisions, reason goes out the window. At the card table, someone on tilt can start to make some very bad choices, and then follow them up with several more, each compounding on the previous one.

He raised an eyebrow in acknowledgment.

I said: "How much did they take you for?"

"I find it vulgar to talk about money, don't you?"

"We can leave the numbers out. But I'm wondering whose money you lost. Your own? You're going to a lot of effort just to clean up your own mess. At some point, you're spending more to fix the problem that you spent on the problem. But maybe it was someone else's money?"

"Money is relative. I'm self-employed. Gig economy, you could say. I'm in the human nature business. Who I am, how I make my living, rests on my brand. On what people think of me. The people who seek my services, I need them to remain confident in my abilities."

"You can't afford to be embarrassed."

"But I *can* afford not to be."

"And who do you work with?"

"Are you religious, Constantin?"

"I don't see what -"

"My uncles were priests. My father built the local church. I was raised in the faith, but I never had it. I learned to lie by praying every Sunday. And I learned not to care about it after all the worried, sleepless nights, wondering why I was the way I was. Why couldn't I just believe? How could I know whether there was a God? And then, one morning, I woke up, and the pain was gone. There was no answer. I accepted there never would be. Some questions were above my reach."

I got the message.

He finished the drink and stood up.

Behind him, I saw Ramona walk in.

I wanted to signal to her, to say stay away until Starr was gone. But I knew I couldn't do it without tipping Starr off that she was important to me. I saw Frank put up his hand, wave for her to pay attention to him, and shake his head. She turned toward the bar instead.

"It was pleasure meeting you, Constantin." Starr gave me that thin, cold smile again. I felt like I was talking to a great white shark in a suit. "Please don't take any offence when I say I hope we never need to talk again."

He turned on his heels and walked out, saying goodbye to Frank on his way past.

It was five minutes before the hair on the back of my neck relaxed.

FORTY-EIGHT

CON

I handed Ramona a gin. The back office at the bar was small and cramped. A desk piled high with invoices, a laptop that had seen better days and a couple chairs. Ramona had taken a seat opposite me and, at first, she hadn't wanted a drink. After I'd started to give her the edited highlights of the last day, she'd asked for *all of the gin.*

"Dave has a daughter," she said after a long sip of alcohol. "And was having an affair with the mother."

"Yeah."

"And they're in your apartment."

"Yup."

"And that guy you were talking to is some kind of mob fixer -"

"Let's not rule out Satan as an option."

"And he just admitted to you, without admitting to you, that he killed Ziskin and Halliday. And the ADA's son. Or had them killed. And he did this while telling you he had nothing to do with David."

"Right."

"And we think the ADA is putting pressure on the cops to prove Louisa guilty to make sure no focus ever comes to his son."

"Right."

"So now I'm sitting on information about two homicides. And can't do anything about it.":

"Looks that way."

"And this is all over some big card game, run by Ally, where Ziskin, Halliday and Waltz's son all won big off your Satan guy on a night he got carried away."

"Halliday was involved, but I'm not sure he was part of the game. He might've just tried to muscle in, or he figured it out like I have, and tried to blackmail Starr."

"But Dave wasn't involved in the game, and Starr says he didn't kill him."

"I think I believe him? Something feels right about it, something feels wrong about it, I don't know. I'm not seeing what he would have to gain by lying to me. Why wouldn't he just kill me? And Dee?"

"Dee, by the way..." She did the thing where she cocks her head and hip to the side at the same time, pretending to be annoyed at me. "Has messaged me three times today, because someone promised them an interview."

"Why would he speak to me at all, unless he was telling the truth? Basically the only solid proof I have that he's involved at all is conversations he just had with me, and he never really confessed anything."

"So why did he talk to you?"

"I guess he's used to buying people off. And in the city, really, how hard is it to believe it's just crossed wires? A bunch of people who know each other, all unrelated to Ash."

"But Ally?"

"Feels wrong, doesn't it? Did you know how long they've been friends?"

Ramona clucked her teeth. Breathed out. "I always assumed it was a long time, they went back, you know? Why would she stick by Louisa if it was just..." She clucked her teeth again. "It's not a motive though, she'd have the same issues as Louisa, no real reason. She doesn't gain anything by killing him, doesn't gain anything by covering up his death. No financial motive, no emotional motive."

"There's something going on there, though. She came to see me last night, after you left."

"What?"

"Yeah, she was drunk. I think she was coming onto me."

"What?"

Ramona was hooked in.

Was it anger?

Jealousy? At any other time I would have played the game, teased more of that out of her as payback for her moving on with her own life. But I was too tired, too distracted by the case.

"Nothing happened. But she was acting strange. Kept talking around the issue, like there was something she kinda wanted to say but couldn't bring herself to."

"Maybe it was just the game, she wanted to tell us about it but didn't?"

"But then there's her hiring you, and Halliday, which isn't the move she'd make if she was completely on the level here. She'd use her contacts book in the city."

"Her own lawyer is pushing for power of attorney, to give Ally control of Louisa's affairs."

"Is Ally's lawyer pushing for it, or is Ally pushing for it?"

"Well, yeah. Good question. But that doesn't feel like a reason to hide anything about David. If she knew David wasn't dead, she wouldn't have spent six months playing this game. If she knew he was dead, she would have had many easier ways to control Louisa's situation. And she'd be a Bond-villain level of genius to have planned far enough in advance to kill him and hide him just to someday get power of attorney and *maybe* make some money."

"Which brings us back to no clear options. I think we need to focus on the finances. Forget the card game, forget the other murders. Louisa is the job. If we can work up something based on the 4019k0, it might be enough to throw doubt on the case. It could help us get Louisa some breathing room."

"Or get us killed."

She wiped some alcohol off her lips and looked up at me. "I don't vote for that one. What do you think happened to Ash?"

I exhaled slowly and stared at Frank's cork noteboard, buried under receipts, Post-Its and insurance paperwork. I hoped the answer would leap out at me. It didn't.

"David was cheating on her. He had a kid with someone else, and he might have been planning to leave. Or maybe he was going to string them both along, I don't know. But either way, all that does is give us an emotional reason for Louisa to have killed him."

"Yes."

"And if he's dead, Louisa thinks she gets control of his Doormats material. So there's a financial reason. Unless she knew he changed his will, which would eliminate the financial reason, but still give an emotional one."

"The financial motive doesn't make sense. There's no body. If Louisa was going to kill him to profit, why would she hide the body and stop him from being declared dead?"

"Objection sustained," I said. "And we could say the same about the band members. None of them really seems like they'd profit any extra from his death than his life. They still get the same share either way."

"Share of more money, though. The way his sales have gone up. Everyone knows a rock star becomes more popular after they die. Maybe someone in the band just wanted to push that forward a few years."

"True. But that seems like a lot of effort. Todd's from a rich family. I think if he was going to bump anyone off for cash it would be his parents. And Edgar seems pretty happy with the life he's got, earns money from art. And, again, if they wanted to profit from his death, they wouldn't have hidden the body."

"True."

"And there's Ally."

"With basically all the same issues."

"Or we're back to Charlie Starr, and back to us both getting killed."

"We're still both saying we definitely think Louisa is innocent?"

"I don't think she's lying. Seems like she's having a hard enough time keeping hold of things she wants to remember, maybe it's not difficult to let go of a few things she doesn't. Especially with the drugs involved."

"She's given me the dealer's number, I have it here. There's a system, we need to -"

"Call a number, and then they call back." I finished the line for her. "Same system Karen used, must be the same dealer."

I fished the number Karen had given me out of Halliday's wallet. Compared it to the one Louisa had given Ramona.

Same number.

Same system.

I looked again at the chaotic mess of the corkboard, and what do you know? An answer did jump out.

Frank had no filing system. He made it up on the fly. And maybe, just maybe…

I laughed, thinking back again to my conversation with Elizondo. Telling him he focused too much on motive, and on things needing to make sense. I'd been ignoring my own advice.

Ramona read my expression. "What?"

"I keep waiting for it to make sense. Maybe it doesn't have to. I mean, most crime is spur of the moment. Opportunity. Motive. Maybe she just lashed out in the heat of the moment, and then she's been lucky enough to get away with it this far. If there was no planning involved, then there's no plan for me to find."

Which would take it back to Louisa being the main suspect...

Great.

A knock on the door saved me from following that thought. Jake, the barman from the Dark Star Lounge, leaned in. "Your old man said it was okay to come back here. Listen, I kept thinking back on when we talked." He handed me a USB stick. "I wasn't fully honest. You were just a stranger, like. But the whole Ash thing, it's not right, I think we all want to know what's happened."

"Sure."

"It's the security footage. There's three videos on here. The first two, like I said, the cops and the other detective took. The third one, they didn't know about. And since they didn't ask for it... well, all cops are bastards, right?"

"Where's the third camera?"

"There's a room in front of the bogs, like a small passageway, right by our back door. We had some trouble years ago with people leaving the back door open, taking crates of beer out, so we have a camera in there. Hidden, like. Mostly we just see musicians snorting coke out there, who cares. We kinda have a rule, we don't snitch. We need the famous people to trust us, so we don't report on what they get up to. But, uh..." He was growing nervous. "You'll see."

"You want to talk us through it?"

"No. No. I really... I shouldn't be doing this. Just... take a look."

He looked like he wanted to say more but offered a nervous smile that took several inches off his height, bobbed his head and left.

I loaded the files on Frank's computer. Three movies. In the first I could see Dave sitting at the bar. Jake had obviously clipped the videos down to the relevant parts. Dave sitting at the bar in the foreground. Jayar, the kid from the recording studio, was talking to him. Jayar's body language was tentative. He knew his place in the pecking order, and expected to be brushed off by this famous musician at any moment. Jake kept appearing at the edge of the frame, chatting to Dave and walking up the bar to serve other people. He stood for around five minutes talking to a blonde woman with her back to the camera, and a man whose head was just out of shot. I pressed fast-forward. After five more minutes, Jayar left. I guessed to head to the party down the block. With around three minutes left on the footage, Dave slid off the stool. He offered a one finger salute to Jake and walked out of shot.

I clicked on the second video. The same scene from a different angle, behind the bar, focused on the cash register with the people just on the edges of frame. I clicked on the time bar and scrolled forward through the footage to the end, when Dave got up and left.

Except he didn't.

Now from this angle I could see the difference.

"I've been in there," I said. "He's not walking towards the door, he's going to the bogs."

I turned to Ramona, but her eyes stayed on the screen.

"Wait," she said.

This video carried on a few seconds longer. The anonymous blonde walked out of frame not long after Dave, in the same direction.

I clocked on the third video. High up, angled down, pointing towards a locked fire exit. The camera hidden in a corner. Dave walked into shot, headed straight for the fire exit and leaned his back against it, facing the camera without seeing it. The blond entered the shot. She did a little shimmy as she walked towards him, and it was clear from the slight movement of her head, and from watching Dave's mouth, that they were holding a conversation. That ended when they kissed. It was hard to tell from behind, but it looked like she kept alternating between kissing and talking. We watched as her right hand snaked its way down the front of his pants, messing around with what was inside. Dave's hands hitched up her skirt slowly, then one gripped her butt while the other vanished from shot, in between them.

Ramona reached out to take the mouse, "I think we should…"

"Hang on." I scrolled forwards. The encounter lasted around three minutes. Afterwards, Dave, walking stiffly, pushed though the toilet door, leaving the woman on her own to correct her dress. She turned, leaning her own back against the door, and pulled a cell phone from the bag that had stayed on her shoulder the whole time. Between the light of the phone, and the dim overhead bulb, the camera captured Alison Oliver's face in fine detail.

"No way," Ramona whispered. "No fucking way."

"I guess we should have seen it coming."

"That's Louisa's alibi completely gone."

"Is it?" I tapped the screen. "Was Ally giving Louisa an alibi, or was she using Louisa to give herself one?"

FORTY-NINE

LOUISA

It's time to let go.

Of Dave.

I see it now.

Even through all of the pain. Through all of the questions. The fights. The doubts. Through all the cracks in our marriage, I still hadn't quite let go of the idea. The idea of the two of us. Of the mythic *us*. The story you tell yourself when you build a life with someone else.

Sometimes it feels like it would be easier for a meteor to strike and wipe us all out, rather than actually give voice to the *end*. To admit, out loud, that we're broken beyond repair.

But now I'm broken, too.

I can't be fixed.

I can't be saved.

I need to own what's happening to me.

What has been happening, what will happen

Dave betrayed me. He leaked my health details to his lawyer. Regardless of whatever's happened to him now, whether he's alive or not, there's no going back. The story is over. We can't be put back together again.

Marriage is marriage. It's a promise. I know people think celebrities get divorced all the time, but it still hurts. It still feels like failure.When I broke up with Peter's father, I promised myself the next one would be right.

And I went through many guys who weren't, but none of them had any chance of sticking around. They didn't count.

Then I met Dave, and he was the one. He was the man I would hitch my future to. And then, one day, somehow, he wasn't.

To have one divorce in understandable. People get married young and grow apart. Shit happens. But to have two? I might as well get a tattoo on my head saying failure. Nobody wants that. You ignore the feelings.

Bury them away.

Pretend like time really does heal all wounds, and the next week, or month, or year, will bring the love back.

But I'm free from that now.

Free from one prison to get trapped in another.

I open up the window and lean out with a cigarette and lighter. I could spark up here, have a smoke. This is how I used to do it at my parent's house, hanging half out of my bedroom window and puffing away. When you're a kid that seems like sound logic. You don't think about how your parents' room is the next window along, or that the cigarettes don't smell as bad as the smoke that clings to your clothes and fingers.

My boys are in bed. Will they still be able to smell this in the morning?

Look at me, I'm the adult in the house but I want to sneak around, scared of what my children will think. This is pathetic.

I close the window and head up to the private rooftop balcony.

The lighter is cheap. Plastic. I move it into place in my palm, holding the cigarette in my other hand, and try to click it into life.

Something catches my eye.

Across the street. Same as before. Someone is watching me. Someone leaning against the railings of Jackson Square. Standing beneath the one streetlight that blinks on and off. I keep my eyes on the lighter, but now my hands shake.

My skin crawls. Burns.

It's definitely a man.

Dave?

I bolt downstairs. The door slams shut behind me. I push out through the door and he sees me coming, turns to run. He cuts left onto Horatio Street. I know the area so I head straight through Jackson Square, which will bring me out onto the same intersection.

I can see his shape moving along the street, and I'm gaining.

At the other side of the square I vault the fence. Good to see I'm still in decent shape, because as I was approaching it there was a voice in my mind telling me I was going to fall and look stupid.

You're running, you already look stupid.

He heads down Greenwich Avenue, but I'm already close enough to see it's not Dave. He's built differently. His frame. His ass.

It hits me for the first time, I'm chasing a stranger through the city. I have no idea who this is, or why he was watching me. What the hell am I doing? I'm even still holding the cigarette and lighter. I feel a slight movement in my back pocket, followed by the sound of something hitting the sidewalk.

Damn. My cellphone.

I reach out to him, but my hand misses his shoulder by a few inches. I can hear him panting. Slowing.

Just a couple more -

Got him.

We both hit the ground. He turns to look at me, out of breath. Trying to speak, but only managing ragged breaths.

Todd.

Todd Flambé.

Why?

He looks ready to cry.

I watch as he climbs to his feet and takes off again.

PART FIVE

"Who are you seeing, in my dirty eyes?
Who am I hearing, in your dirty lies?"
-David Ash

 **TRANSCRIPT**

Don't Tell A Soul
Season Three
The Disappearance of David Ash

Episode Five: About Jack.

Audio Clip: Hot Take ident.

Ad: *Don't Tell A Soul is part of the Hot Take network. For more information visit hottake.com and subscribe to Hot Take Plus to hear all our shows with ads and plugs removed.*

Audio Clip: News Bulletin: *"...from outside the sixth precinct, where we understand Louisa Mantalos has just been arrested in connection with the disappearance of her husband, David Ash, six months ago..."*

Audio Clip: News Bulletin: *"...suicide, suspected to be in order to avoid the murder charges..."*

Audio Clip: Voicemail: *"It's Con McGarry. I know who Jack is. Gimme a call."*

Theme tune plays.

Dee: Hi, I'm Dee Buana. This is Don't Tell A Soul, the podcast about secrets, lies, and the truths we think we know.

Theme tune fades out.

Dee: I've made a decision. I want you to know straight up front. We're not going to play the confession.
I know we said we would, and a lot of the initial buzz about this season was based on hearing the full recording. But you know...this season has... well, I guess I'm looking at all of this differently. Even just editing the episodes together and putting them out, realizing how close I came to getting killed and just...

I watched a true crime documentary last night. Nothing new there, right? I've watched loads. I host a true crime podcast. But this time something happened. When they got to the killer's confession, and he's talking about driving his daughters to ther spot where he killed them, I had to turn it off.

This wasn't entertainment.

It was a dark, private thing.

Crime hurts. It's grubby.

And so....yes, I have the confession. But I think what was said in that room should stay in that room. And there are people, names, mixed up in that recording who have their own lives to lead. I'm already thinking about how David and Louisa's two boys might see this show come up in Google searches when they're older. Even though I've never mentioned their names. I'm thinking about those boys and the lives they need to be allowed to live. Do they need someone like me to come in and decide, on their behalf, whether the world gets to hear that confession?

But I'm working extra hard here not to let you down, too. I'm not feeling as guilty as I would have done at the start. You had the episode about me, you got to hear my pain and fear. That wasn't part of the news cycle.

You had the episode on Louisa's past, again, that's not stuff that had come up in the news. I have a real surprise for the final episode, next week. An interview I never thought possible. And today? Today, we reveal who Jack is.

But not yet.

Let me back up a little first, give this to you in the right order. So you already know I was getting tips from someone called Jack. And then, when they told me Louisa was still using drugs, they offered to hook me up with the dealer. And that's what led to this.

Jack Halliday: Back off Louisa.

Dee: What? Wait... how... no get... no please....

Loud noises. Scream.

I was sure I wouldn't hear from Jack again after that. And I was also sure I wouldn't respond even if I did. But then, early the next morning, and I'm talking three AM, I got a text:

> Jack (Dee reading): I'm sorry. That wasn't me. I didn't know.

Followed by another, an hour later:

> Jack (Dee reading): Still friends?

And twenty minutes after that:

> Jack (Dee reading): Fine.

And around noon that day, I got a voicemail:

> Jack: It really wasn't me. The guy who attacked you, I'm so sorry. But he stole your details from me, I didn't give them to him.

So the night I was attacked, those voices you heard, the ones that came to help me, they belonged to Ramona Cross and Constantin McGarry. Ms. Cross is Louisa Mantalos's lawyer. Mr McGarry is the PI they hired to look for David Ash.

They were never meant to be my enemies. The point of this show is to look for truth, not pick sides. But something had happened, along the way, and by the time of the attack it was very clear that Louisa didn't want the show to happen, and we became two different sides.

But that didn't stop them helping me. And McGarry offered me an interview. I tried to follow up a few times the next day, after the hospital and a few hours' sleep. I wasn't getting any reply, so I was ready to write the offer off, when I got this voicemail:

> Voicemail: "It's Con McGarry. I know who Jack is. Gimme a call."

I called him back straight away, and we talked. And I think I liked him? He was talking about being close to knowing what happened to David, and he told me he knew who Jack was, and it might help the case if I confronted them, forced a response. I replied to Jack's messages and agreed a phone call to, air quotes, clear the air.

Here's how it went. I went into the conversation you're about to hear, with Jack, already knowing who I was talking to, even though Jack continued with the voice distortion.

Theme tune fades in.
Theme tune fades out.

Jack: I just want to clear the air.

Dee: Sure.

Jack: The thing that happened to you, that wasn't my fault.

Dee: Whose was it?

Jack: There was this guy, he's dead now.

Dee: Is this Matt Halliday?

Jack: ...Yeah.

Dee: So how did Halliday know to attack me?

Jack: I was working with him. Thought I could control him. But he went, he went off.

Dee: So it was your fault.

Jack: I didn't want that to happen, is what I'm saying. He was off by then, I wasn't controlling him.

Dee: Why did you contact me in the first place?

Jack: I thought this would make a good story for you.

Dee: But why?

Jack: What do you mean?

Dee: You seem to know a lot about the case. About Louisa. You've been feeding me information all along, and I'm wondering why?

Jack: I...

Dee: Did you think all along that she was guilty?

Jack: No, I... I didn't know. But I thought...

Dee: You like to be in control.

Jack: I don't know what... how do you mean that?

Dee: This thing was dropped into the middle of your life, like a bomb, and you weren't in control anymore. And hooking me in, manipulating me, it was a way of feeling in control.

Jack: I mean, doesn't everyone like to be in control? But that's not... the way you're putting it -

Dee: Was Halliday part of the card game, or

did you use him as your collector and security?

Jack: ...What?

Dee: Is this just how you show love, Ally?

Jack: (inaudible)

Dee: Is it just about control, or is this, is this your way of showing love? I guess I'm asking, did you know you were manipulating Louisa, or did you think you were helping?

Jack: What?

Call terminated.

FIFTY

CON

I don't like guns.

Especially when they're pointed at me.

This one was small. Hidden beneath an expensive brown leather satchel. You'd only see it if you were looking. And I was looking. The gun's owner was a blond man of just over six feet tall. He was beautiful, in a way very few people ever manage. His features were clean, and rolled like a natural rock formation. His eyes were of a blue pale enough to look like ice, and his hair was neatly swept back. It almost didn't look gelled. His clothes were expensive. The lines were crisp. I didn't know whether to feel nervous about the gun, or inferior about his looks.

I settled for both.

Ramona made a noise next to me, a sharp intake of breath, caught in a similar dilemma.

He looked out across the rooftops, from where we were stood on the High Line, then back to us.

"Sorry," he said. His voice was as polished as his appearance. "Nothing personal."

I was being threatened by a male model.

Ramona took a step back beside me.

Back at Frank's bar, she'd called the number to set up a meet. I'd said: "Mona, there's no way I'm letting you walk into a meeting with a drug dealer."

She'd said: "It's sweet how you think I'm giving you a choice."

Ramona drove us across the river. She took a few wrong turns, where the GPS somehow seemed to not understand the road layout of the most famous city on earth. I couldn't help thinking of films like The *French Connection* and *Serpico* with GPS added to the driving scenes.

Ramona parked in a spot we'd been instructed to use, on Horatio Street, outside a laundry that advertised itself as *Mean Green Cleaning Machines*. A door opened next to the laundry and two young women stepped out. They were both blond, and attractive in a poised, unemotional way. They both wore black clothes and light jackets.

Ramona rolled down the window, and they asked for her by name. We climbed out of the car. One of the blonds moved her jacket enough to show us a gun tucked into her waist.

"Just play nice," she said in a Midwestern accent.

The second stepped in close with a small electronic device, about the size of a cell phone. She swept it around our bodies. It beeped when passing over our own cells, and she took both of them. She then nodded for us to follow, and turned without a word. They led us around the corner onto Washington, and then one block up, to the High Line steps.

"Go on up," the chatty one said.

The silent one gave us a head start, then followed.

The High Line was quiet. There were a few tourists wearing masks, a few young couples. We kept walking until we got to the point where it passes beneath a building, and that was when the male model stepped out in front of us. He indicated for us to step over to the side, where it was quiet, then showed us the gun.

The quiet blond carried on past us a few yards, taking up a position leaning against the railing. She held the electronic device in her hand, pointing it in our direction. I could hear a faint white noise coming off it. It had to be some kind of sound canceling gizmo, in case we had someone taping the conversation from a distance.

The male model slipped the gun out of sight beneath the satchel.

"Okay," he said. "What are you looking for?"

Ramona hesitated. She didn't know what to say, so I took the lead. "What can we call you?"

"Anything you like."

"Okay, Sven."

He smiled. "That'll do."

"I'm Con. This is Ramona, she called you."

"I know who you are. You wouldn't be here otherwise." To Ramona, he said: "You mentioned a client of mine on the phone. I checked with her, she vouched for both of you. That gets you five minutes."

I made a point of looking to the blond, then back to Sven. "Are you a drug dealer or a Bond villain?"

"I like to have beautiful people working with me. It's good for business."

"They deliver?"

He nodded. "Yes. My customers like to see them. It gives the business a certain aesthetic."

"Sounds like you should be working in modeling."

He smiled again. "I used to. We all did. But we all earn more working this way. Set out own hours. Total control."

Delivery partners. He sounded like a tech startup.

"Who delivers to our mutual friend?"

"Any of my partners can do it. Depends who is working on any given night. I let them choose."

Ramona spoke for the first time since leaving the car. "You know the night we're talking about."

"Yes, I do. I made a house call myself. I wanted to make sure she really wanted it."

I asked, "How do you mean?"

"We had coffee, talked. I wanted to make sure it was the right thing for her."

"Why?"

"She hadn't used my services for a long time. Then suddenly she wants treatment."

I was getting tired of talking in such vague terms, but there were more important issues. "No, I mean why do you care?"

Sven paused. Caught off guard. He hadn't expected that question, and it made him drop the code. "Well, we're talking about addiction here. If a client of mine gets clean, then calls out of the blue, it can be a suicide run."

"And you don't want to lose a client."

"My business depends on treating people well."

"How did she seem?" Ramona asked. "You didn't think she was a risk?"

"No. She was fine. Agitated, but fine. I didn't think she was a danger to herself. Just needed to relax, have a good time."

I took over again. "What did you sell her?"

"A significant amount of Ketamine, coke and heroin."

"How much?"

"A significant amount."

"Enough to OD, if you'd been wrong?"

"Yes."

"Ketamine. That affects the memory, right?"

"It can do, yes."

"She asked for it?"

"Yes."

"Think she had anything she wanted to forget?"

Sven didn't answer.

Ramona went straight for the point. "You might be the only person who can place her at home, give her any kind of alibi on the night David Ash went missing."

Sven stepped back, self-consciously putting distance between him and the idea. "That won't be happening."

"If she goes away for murder," I said, "you'll be losing a client."

"I already hope to have lost her. As I said, I care about the wellbeing of my clients. It was a mistake for me to sell her that last shipment. I hope she can stay clean."

I changed gears. "Okay. Was David Ash ever one of your clients?"

"Yes."

Ramona said, "Didn't they know? That you served them both?"

"They wouldn't have heard it from me."

"And they wouldn't tell each other?"

His shoulders flexed slightly. It was a very stylish form of shrug. "Addicts tend not to be honest with themselves, let alone each other."

"Did anyone deliver to him on the night he went missing?"

"Yes."

I tried for the million dollar question. "Where?"

FIFTY-ONE

CON

I noticed more details about the building on our second visit. The first time around, I'd been too focused on Louisa, and on what she was going to tell us at the end of the cab ride. This time I took a look around at our surroundings.

Louisa's café was on Little West 12th. In a two-story red brick building nestled between two more modern structures. The metal shutter was down, and there were no alleys or fire escapes on either side. There weren't many people walking by. I could hear the noises of the restaurants and bars, but they were drifting over from the streets around us.

Ramona stood behind me, giving some degree of cover, while I picked the lock to the metal box. There was a second keyhole inside. I used my pick to turn it, but nothing happened. I turned it three times. Nothing.

"Keep it turned," Ramona said.

I tried, and the shutter started to rise up.

There would be no living with her after that.

I kept the key turned until the shutter was at head height, then focused on the lock to the door.

We could have called Louisa or Ally for the keys, but decided not to on the walk down. We still had to deal with the possibility one of them had killed him. There was no real financial motive for either to have played this long game, but now that we knew Ally and Dave were fooling around, there were clear emotional motives.

Louisa could have found out and killed Dave in a fit of anger, spur of the moment. Ally could have argued with Dave, maybe demanded he leave Louisa, and killed him when he refused.

If there had been no grand plan, that would explain why there were so few *signs* of any grand plan.

And still, through all that, the slight doubt... *was he even dead?*

Everything said yes.

But if he wasn't, and he used this place to hide out, he'd have some explaining to do before we brought Louisa or Ally in on the news.

The café was dark inside. I could see the chairs where we'd left them. Their shapes were solid in the gloom, but everything else was indistinct shadow. Ramona switched on the flashlight setting of her cell, and I followed suit. The room was cast in an electronic half-light. Aside from our feet on the dusty floor, all I could hear was the hum of a few kitchen appliances coming from the back.

I found the light switches behind the counter. Then we stood and got our bearings as the overheads flickered into life. There was a door beside me that led to an office. Ramona nudged me and pointed to a staircase next to the kitchen door.

"You look around down here," I said. "I'll take upstairs."

I figured if there was anything to find, it would be on the top floor. And it should be me that got there first. Ramona had been messed up enough by finding Halliday.

I took each step slowly, feeling for creaks. The light switches behind the counter must have been master controls for the whole building, because the bulbs burned bright when I reached the top.

The first door was the bathroom. There was no sign of recent use, but the seat was up. The last person to drop anything off had been a man. Next I pushed open a door to an empty room. Completely empty. It felt like I was directly above the kitchen.

Turning toward the front of the building, above the café area, was a large open room.

There was a table off to the side with three computer monitors and a mixing desk, the cables trailing beneath the table to a tower computer. Curtains, towels and egg cartons covered the walls. On the floor I found plastic bags with traces of white crystals, and a small camping stove.

There were musical instruments scattered around the room.

Lots of them.

Fender.

Gibson.

Gretsch.

A battered red drum kit was set up in the corner, flaked with paint. Four different microphones pointed at it, set up for recording. And, on a guitar stand in the center of the room, taking pride of place, was an age-worn Les Paul Junior.

This was Ash's studio.

The place he'd been recording his personal, introspective album. He'd taken a huge delivery of drugs here on the night he disappeared. Was that why he'd left the Dark Star? To come here and meet the delivery partner?

I heard something from downstairs. It wasn't quite a scream. More of a strangled cry. Something that had died in Ramona's throat because she wasn't willing to let herself give in to whatever had startled her.

I took the stairs three at a time on the way down, rounding the corner into the kitchen.

Ramona was hunched on her knees in front of one of the large chest freezers. She was dry heaving.

David Ash was in the freezer.

His skin was pale. Frosting covered the tip of his nose. Small flecks of red were gathered around the pupils of his dead eyes.

FIFTY-TWO

CON

It was Ramona's turn to stall on us calling 911.

I was fine with that.

Ramona may have tried to throw up, but I was the one to go all in. The contents of my stomach pooled in the doorway. The inside of my mouth tasted like a twenty-year-old carpet. The back of my throat burned, and my teeth felt like they belonged to someone else.

Something about the sight of David Ash completely unnerved me. It wasn't just that he was dead. I'd seen Matt Halliday's body. It was the way he was frozen, stored like a lump of meat. The thing you find in the bottom of your freezer, without a label. That's not how a human should be treated.

Ramona ruffled my hair and offered me a tissue to wipe my lips.

I climbed to my feet and coughed away the burning sensation before saying, "This is going to be a mess."

I asked which of us would get the honor of calling it in, and Ramona hesitated.

"We should tell Louisa first," she said. "She's my client."

I reached for her phone, stopping Ramona as she searched for Louisa's number. "We need to be careful here. Someone killed him and covered this up. All we've done here is find solid evidence it was Louisa. If you call her before the cops, and your phone records are ever checked…"

"I'll be seen calling the main suspect to warn her."

"Exactly. A dead rock star in a freezer, and the two people who find him are an ex-con and the lawyer of the main suspect. Second time in as many days that we're first to a dead body, too."

All the signs pointed to Louisa.

As far as we knew, she was the only person who still knew about this place until I got involved. Ally hadn't known. I couldn't see a way Charlie Starr would have found it. And if he did, why would the body be hidden away in the freezer?

He would have had a million ways to make the corpse disappear, and everyone else he'd killed in this case had been made to look like suicide. This was amateur hour, not a seasoned killer. Somebody had stuffed David into the box in a moment of panic.

Like a piece of meat.

Louisa was the only one who made sense.

Ramona said: "I'll call Ally. That doesn't look as bad. And she's the one who pays me, so it works out. What she does with it…"

Ally didn't pick up. The call rang out twice before going to voicemail, on the third attempt it went straight to voicemail. Ramona dialed 911. The conversation had a lot of *yes really* and *here right now*. Somewhere between the call and the first car pulling up outside, Ramona took my hand in hers. Years dropped away for one moment, and we were two kids against the world again.

Two uniformed cops were the first to arrive.

Neither of them seemed pleased to see us.

"Well, fuck" were the first words out of the mouth of the more experienced sergeant, as he stepped in my puke.

"Crap," said the younger one, catching sight of Dave.

"You might want to -" I started, but it was too late. The younger cop was adding the contents of his own stomach to the collection I'd started.

They put in a call to the night watch desk. I was expecting a night shift detective. One of the NYPD's late-night firefighters who caught calls for the whole of Manhattan and handed the case off to the precinct the next day. Instead, Henry Elizondo himself walked in. I made a crack about him having nothing better to do with his time, which prompted a glare as he led us through to the old eating area of the café and told us to take a seat. He pulled up one for himself and left it sitting in front of us while he wandered off to the side and made another phone call.

Making us wait.

Trying to make us panic.

After finishing his call, which seemed to get quite heated, he dropped down into the chair with an exaggerated old man sigh. "What's going on here?"

"I was hired to find David Ash. I found him."

"Funny guy." He looked down at his cell, shaking his head. "I was in bed. I'm still wearing the underwear I was sleeping in. You know the funny part of all this?" He paused long enough to see if I'd make a joke, before answering his own question. "It wasn't this call that got me out of bed. I was already up, looking at another dead body."

I shared a look with Ramona, neither of is knowing where he was going with this.

"Alison Oliver," Elizondo said. "Apparently took a dive out of her window tonight. All the way down."

The inside of my head started to shake. I don't know if the outside matched it, but everything felt loose and warm, very very warm.

Ramona's voice cracked, "what?"

"Lived on the fourth floor. I guess you knew that. To be honest, it's all a bit of a gamble at that height. I've seen people fall from higher and survive with broken ankles. I've seen people who've tripped down the curb and broken their neck. I think Ms. Oliver would have to have been very sure she'd gotten the angle right, head first, just to make sure. That's a lot of work."

Ramona said again: "What?" Then looked at me, "I don't..."

I shook my head. I didn't either.

Too many thoughts were fighting for my attention. None of them were breaking all the way through the white blanket of shock wrapping itself around my head.

Why would Ally...

Well, she surely wouldn't, but then she'd died in exactly the same way as Jimmy Ziskin and Cody Waltz. Charlie Starr's fingerprints were all over that.

But why would he kill Ally?

And what if Louisa had known about Ally and Dave?

Where was Louisa right now?

I became clearly aware that we had no idea, we hadn't tried to contact her. Would she have any kind of alibi for tonight, if her last alibi had just been taken out?

Or what if -

What if Starr had been working for Louisa this whole time? Could that have been the connection I was missing?

And then one even worse thought, for me. What if this was genuine? I'd put Dee up to calling Ally and confronting her with the Jack information. What if Ally had taken that call tonight, and then taken things further once her emotions spiraled out of control?

Elizondo was still talking. "How did you find Ash?"

"It's my job."

The café was filling up with people.

One team taking care of the forensics, another photographing every square inch of the place. Someone else was walking around with a tape measure, and I started to wonder if he'd decided the building was a great fixer-upper opportunity.

I felt my cell buzzing in my pocket. A call or message. We hadn't been arrested; we hadn't been searched or read any rights. As far as I knew, right then, we were just witnesses. But I didn't want to take my phone out. And still something else. A thought trying to push through the chaos and shock. I couldn't place it. I felt like I'd seen something obvious, something I'd been looking for, and walked right passed it.

What had I seen?

Elizondo stifled a yawn. "So, how did you get in? A ladder onto the roof or something?"

I wasn't concentrating on the moment. Too busy trying to think. Before Ramona could stop me, I answered, "It's what I do."

Damn it.

"Okay." Elizondo flashed us a grin and waved to the nearest uniforms. "Ramona Cross, Constantin McGarry, I'm arresting you for breaking and entering. Anything you say…"

FIFTY-THREE

LOUISA

I watch from the corner of Christopher Street as Petey runs in through the large green doors of his middle school. Most mornings it's Gyul who takes them to school. Ally's done it a few times. But today, it felt important for me to do it. I waited for Gyul to turn up before giving her the day off. Felt a bit mean, but my cell hasn't worked since I dropped it last night. One more thing to fix. Or, one more thing for Ally to fix.

If me and Ally can be fixed.

Every time I think of her, it comes with a raw flash of anger at the way she's been treating me. Almost gaslighting me, but still with the idea that maybe her intentions are good? That cools off the anger, leaves me thinking I should call her, just get back to normal.

Though *normal* hasn't existed for a long time, and I'm about the change it all over again.

The boys don't know it yet, but today is when everything changes.

After school, I'll take them for food, somewhere they like, and tell them about Dave.

They deserve to know what's happened. And it's my job to tell them. I understand now that the real reason I've been keeping it from them is my own doubts. My fears. My own inability to accept what was going on. If I didn't have to say it out loud to them, maybe it didn't have to be true. Maybe it's the last day when they get to be innocent. Detective Elizondo was right. Learning you can't always trust your parents, that's part of growing up. You lose a piece of yourself when that happens, and you never get it back. Today Johnny and Peter will learn that their daddy is missing, and their mommy has been lying to them.

Where we go from there? I don't know.

Petey won't let me walk him right up to the gate. On the walk down he told me not to call him *Petey* now, because it's a little boy's name. He wants to be *Peter*.

I was spared from feeling upset by Johnny, who seemed to have sensed his opportunity and acted even more like a child than usual, filling the space. Johnny was wearing his coat inside out. He refused to turn it around before we left the house, and I didn't want to be late so I left it as it was.

Now on the street, walking to his school, I'm feeling paranoid. Am I getting more looks than usual from the other parents? Are they judging me because I'm famous, because they think I killed my husband, or because I have this fizzing bundle of energy next to me wearing his coat inside out?

I feel more vulnerable than usual this morning.

No phone. No contact from Ally. Feels like I'm out here all alone for the first time.

I turn to head back up Hudson Street, and see Detective Elizondo crossing the road.

"Well hello, young man." Elizondo looks down at Johnny. "You having an inside-out day?"

"Like the color."

"Well sure. That's a good color. Got one just like it."

Johnny squints up at him. "You?"

"Yeah. Exactly the same. Well, it's wrapped around my boiler at home, but it's basically the same thing."

"You're weird."

"Ain't that the truth, young man." He looks at me now. "Hi Ms. Mantalos. Could I have a couple minutes?"

I gesture down at my son. "I have him with me."

Elizondo turns to face back the way he came and points up Hudson Street. There are two cars parked at the curb near the corner. They're unmarked, but I know right away what I'm looking at. A woman gets out of the first car and starts walking toward us.

He's still talking. I'm not listening. I hear the tone in his voice. I read their faces. I know what this is. I just know. It's Dave. Somehow. Something's happened. Have they found him? I snap back to focus at the mention of Ally's name.

She's...

Dead?

What's going on?

He's asking me where I was last night, and now I'm trying to think how I explain the thing with Todd.

Elizondo is still talking. Dave's name now.

"...news hasn't got it yet, but I gotta be honest, that's pretty lucky. Someone's going to make a call to them sooner or later. They could already be on the way here. Listen, I'm sure you want a quiet few minutes with your boy, and to call someone for him. We can go handle this in private."

I hate this man so much.

But in this moment, as I hold back tears, all I can do is say, "Thank you."

FIFTY-FOUR

CON

The officers who had been first on the scene were the ones to drive us into the precinct. They made us wait while they changed their shoes from spares in the trunk. On the way in, Ramona whispered to me to stay silent until I spoke to my lawyer. I knew that meant waiting for Ramona to talk herself out of trouble to come represent me.

They booked us both in and separated us. We were taken to the precinct holding pens, a smaller, and marginally cleaner, version of what we would face if we were moved on to central booking. I was sure we wouldn't get that far. The cops didn't care about how we got into the café, Elizondo was just flexing. If Ramona was still locked up by the time they contacted Louisa, they had a shot at getting something from her before she spoke to her lawyer.

And, like an idiot, I'd given them the excuse.

My need to run my smart mouth. My need to poke authority. I stuck to the plan. I gave only one-word answer to every question for the rest of the stay. Lawyer. I knew they had my lawyer in custody, and they knew they had my lawyer in custody. That didn't stop me playing the game with a slight smile.

After a couple of hours I saw Carl Waltz show up, and he stood talking to Elizondo for a long time, pointing to me occasionally.

Waltz was the first to walk over.

"Breaking and entering," he said. "You really don't like your parole, do you?"

There were a million things I wanted to say to him, but none of them while I was in custody.

"Lawyer."

"I wouldn't worry. I think you've actually helped me out here. Done what the cops couldn't."

This started the game. For the next few hours, Elizondo would come back and hold one-sided conversations.

He chatted away in monologue about his dog, his ex-wife and the Mets. Nominally, he was filling in the gaps of what had happened in the years since we'd met, as if we were old friends, catching up. He wanted me to get comfortable around him, even friendly. To open up before Ramona could get back to represent me. I'd already been read my rights so, as far as he was concerned, if I decided to start talking, he was ready to listen.

When he wasn't with me, I guessed he could have been trying the same thing with Ramona. Or maybe he'd stay away from her, not wanting to give the lawyer anything to use against him. At some point, the exhaustion of the last few days caught up with me, and I drifted off.

I was woken up by Elizondo tapping my leg.

He led me through to the interview room. The clock on the wall said it was six in the morning. The smell of his cheap deodorant filled the air, but he probably smelled better than me.

He asked a few seemingly innocuous questions. Things that weren't tied to the case, at least on the surface. I opened my mouth as if to answer, then made a show of zipping my lips.

He laughed. "You know, I should thank you. I told you before, I haven't had a good night's sleep since this all started. I think after today, I'll be able to sleep like a log."

"I don't think logs sleep," I said.

"What was that?"

"Lawyer."

We stayed in the room while I drank coffee and ate a couple of stale cookies he said had come from the office. He led me back through to the holding pen, where I could see the sun spilling in from the high window.

I was in the pen for another couple of hours. Ramona came to see me somewhere after eight. She was out, and said they'd already brought Louisa in.

The three of us – Ramona, Elizondo, and me - headed to the box one final time as I gave my official statement. I bent the truth only slightly, saying that I'd learned David Ash was recording material at his own studio and that someone had given me the address. I didn't mention Sven, or impossibly attractive drug couriers.

We went over it three times. Once Elizondo seemed satisfied, he said I was free to go.

Out at the desk, I took back my phone, wallet, keys and shoes. I thought of the collection of business cards and papers I had stashed in the safe sleeve of my wallet. A whole load of proof, some of it taken from crime scenes, and the cops didn't even know they'd had it.

My cell battery was dead. I asked the desk sergeant if I could use a charger, and he gave me a look that said I should try being somewhere else. Ramona handed me one of the charger packs she kept in her bag.

I asked Ramona for an update while I waited for enough power to receive my messages.

"Louisa's been arrested, but she's still here. They're moving fast. Not only Dave, but they're angling to get Ally…" She paused, caught out by her own mention of the name. "They're trying to pin Ally on her, too. I think the ADA wants to make a show of getting this done quick, to prove they got it right six months ago."

"How's she doing?"

"Not good. Once they move her on to central booking, I'm scared what that'll do to her."

"What about the kids?"

"The nanny is with Johnny. Peter's being pulled out of school now. I need to make some calls, get Louisa…"

She trailed off, but it didn't matter. I knew what she'd been about to say. This was the stage she was supposed to step off. Hand the case off to a more experienced trial lawyer and walk away. Same for me. I'd done my part. Dave was found. Ally was dead. Louisa was the only one left standing. It was time for Ramona to go back to her cheap office in Queens, and me back to stealing rings back for old friends.

"Have you told Louisa about Ally and Dave?"

Ramona shook her head. "Not yet."

My phone beeped. There was a voicemail from the night before, while I'd been at the café. I headed out onto the sidewalk to listen to it away from the cops. Ramona followed.

"Hey, Con?" It was Ray. "You should drop by."

Ray didn't like to leave messages. He never sent information by email or phone. The flip-side of him being so good as a hacker was he was hyper aware of how easily he could be hacked. For him to leave a message, even one as innocuous as that, I knew he'd found something important.

What do you have, Ray?

And there was still that thing. Whatever it was. The thing I'd seen back at the café. The element I'd overlooked, but not missed, sitting somewhere at the back of my mind, shouting for me to notice.

Elizondo came out and headed to the corner of the lot, away from us. He lit up a cigarette.

I touched Ramona's arm. "Delay them. Stay with her. Whatever tricks you got, just stall. Stop them from processing her."

I walked across the lot towards Elizondo. He was pretending not to notice me, but that became impossible as I stepped right to him.

"You want the truth?" I said. "All your talk about trying to be one of the good ones. We both know the real reason you're not sleeping at night, and it's not some noble itch."

He blew out smoke, tried to look defiant but I could see his eyes darting around, looking to see if anyone was in earshot. "McGarry, I really think -"

"Your problem is you're not an idiot. That's why you couldn't let go of my case, because you knew there was a driver, and you knew there was someone next to the driver in the front seat." I slipped in the real question he'd always wanted an answer to, with no intention of answering it, just to keep him hooked. "You're no idiot on this either. You've figured out all the same things I have. You know who is covering what, and why, and you know exposing that would be to lose your job, which is the only thing you've got left. So you stay quiet. And that is why you don't sleep."

"Be somewhere else."

I didn't want to give him the satisfaction of the last word, so I paused before leaving and said: "Sleep tight."

What do you have, Ray?

FIFTY-FIVE

LOUISA

"I just want you to understand the process," Elizondo says. "What's happening right now is my boss, the ADA and the DA are locked in the mother of all conference calls. They're talking over the evidence. It's all stacking up on one side. But what the DA really wants is a confession. If you say you did it, then everything becomes easier. For both of us. The state of New York isn't going to need to spend a fortune proving what we already know, and you're not going to need to be exposed to a big trial. Your boys won't need to see you dragged through the mud."

My boys?

That gets my attention.

I sit up in my seat. We're in the interrogation room. Or *the box*, as Elizondo called it. Ramona is sitting next to me. She touches my arm.

"Detective," Ramona says. "My client won't be commenting at the present time."

"Oh sure. Sure. I know that. You've got her well drilled. But, the thing is, we all know how these trials go. Public spectacle. Peter and Johnny will see you on television every day. They'll listen to the talking heads. The press will speculate over the details of David's death, and where his body was found. Whatever relationship issues you two were having, they'll be talked about in the court, and in the media. And then we layer in Alison Oliver's death on top. I mean, I don't know, but my gut says it won't be hard to imply there's a connection. People like drama, the jury will like the idea that maybe David and Alison, well… you know. Or," he pauses, leans in closer, like he's offering me a tip, "if you confess, we can probably get you a quick deal. A lenient judge might look favorably on a confession, and I'm sure you had your reasons."

I know it's a lie.

Ramona told me to expect this. With all the drama, all the speculation of the last six months, the DA will want the trial either way. They put every chip they had on me for this, and they'll need to show it was a good bet. The DA or ADA will want to use my name a lot during the next election.

Elizondo continues. "After here, you'll go to central booking. You'll be in the system, then on to Rikers. General population. Maybe they're watching all about you on the news right now, waiting for you to show up there. But if we got a confession, maybe we could make things easier on you."

"You're not going to break me," I say.

It sounds convincing.

I'm a good actor.

Truth is, I don't know what I'm doing. My whole world had flipped around. The boys are with Gyul, and Dave's parents are on the way to pick them up. And Ally is...

Ally is...

Why?

Did she think I did it?

Do I think I did it?

Dave was in my freezer, in my café. Who else knew about that place? Could I have put him there, and just totally blanked it?

Could I have put him there and decided to blank it?

I start having flashes. Images in my head, of doing it, of hitting him or stabbing him, of looking down at him in the freezer. But are these memories, or ideas? Is my memory putting back together what happened, or creating what I'm being told happened?

Ramona touches my arm again. "Don't say anything."

"I'm not trying to break you," Elizondo says. "I'm here to help, Louisa. Can I call you Louisa? It's time. I'm the one person on your side right now. The DA isn't. My boss isn't. Your lawyer? You're paying her to be on your side. Con McGarry was paid to be on your side. I'm for real. The media are after blood. But I can help make things easy here. The truth is, you broke yourself, when you killed your husband. And something like that can eat away at a person. Maybe make them start to forget things." He pauses again to give a look saying he's been holding that card for the right time. "But all of that goes away if you just tell me what you did. It's time, Louisa. I can help you feel a whole lot better about yourself."

Ramona leans forward. "Detective, I'd like a moment alone with my client."

Elizondo leans back in his seat. He makes a clucking sound with the roof his mouth, puts down his pen, and says "sure", like it's the hardest thing in the world. He looks up at the camera and says the time and date, before leaving the room.

Ramona looks up at the camera before speaking. "We need to give them something. We need to stall, slow this whole thing down."

"What could we give them?"

"I think —" She looks at the camera again. Leans in close. Lowers her voice. "We need to go all in. Let me tell them about your thing."

I sit back. Give up my secret? Tell them about my Alzheimer's? The one thing I've been holding to myself. It's coming to define me. Not the illness, but the fear of it. The thought of it. Keeping it from people, trying to control how the world sees me.

And haven't I done a stunning job of that....

Ramona's talking. "I can hold them off. Buy Con some time. He thinks he has something. I can show your medical records. Insist that you need to see your doctor before they even think of moving you. They might need to find an independent consultant to come in. The DA will start to panic, worried about lawsuits if they handle it wrong. Probably, we could throw doubt on whether you were in a fit state for Miranda. All kinds of things."

"David's family are already getting the boys. What have I got to lose?"

Ramona touches my shoulder, then looks through her bag for some paperwork. She tells me she'll be right back and leaves the room.

I lean back in the seat and breathe out slowly. As my lungs empty, I feel lighter. I could float. The one last secret that has been pressing down on me. All the energy and effort to keep it. The stress. The worry. It's gone.

Ramona comes back in. She has this odd look on her face. Confusion? She seems in a haze.

"Todd's here," she says.

"What?"

"From the band. Todd. Apparently he walked in a few minutes ago. I think he's talking to them about the night David died."

FIFTY-SIX

CON

There was a moving van outside Ray's house. Two large guys stepped out through the open front door, carrying the sofa between them. Either one of them looked like they could have done the job solo. They looked at me without any kind of greeting. I watched them walk around to the back of the van and start loading the sofa.

I stepped into the house and knocked on the door on my way past. The living room was almost empty. The television, furniture, any of the toys I could remember seeing, they were all gone. There were a couple of packing crates in the center of the room.

"Ray? Hey, Ray?"

Through the doorway to the backroom I heard movement.

Charlie Starr stepped into view.

He was wearing blue surgical gloves and drinking a carton of Capri Sun through the straw.

"Constantin, what a nice surprise."

I didn't turn to leave, because I could feel the doorway behind me fill up. One of the two big guys, maybe both.

"Boys," Starr said. "Would you be so kind, give us a couple minutes?"

I felt the obstruction move behind me. Turning, I could see the open door, and the way out. I guessed they would be standing out on the sidewalk, waiting to stop me. And I needed to know what had happened to Ray and Matty.

Starr tilted his head for me to follow, and stepped back out of sight. I walked through to the back room slowly. I didn't want to let Starr see my fear, but something bad could happen the minute I was through the doorway, and my skin knew it. It was trying to rip off my bones and run away. The back room, where Ray's equipment had been—the desk piled high with mess and computer parts—was now empty, save for one chair. Starr had spread plastic across it, and eased down into it now to look up at me.

I aimed for the bravest front I could put up. "What have you done with them?"

Starr stared up at me while he finished the drink, letting me hear the sucking noise as the carton collapsed in on itself. "You think I go around dropping bodies like in the movies? That's no way to do business."

"You've dropped four so far."

"I only dropped three of them." He gave me the thin smile. "Apologies, that was in bad taste. But you set me up for it."

"Why Alison? What did she do?"

"It's more a case of what she didn't do. Killing someone is a sign of failure. It means all other options have been exhausted, and that you've made a series of bad decisions. The trick is to stop the problem long before it gets to that point."

"Bribes."

He nodded. "Business deals. Incentives. It's no different from every other kind of business. Usually, the more money you show people, the more control you have. And I don't recall you rejecting my cash yesterday."

I'd been avoiding thinking about the bribe. It was in the safe in Frank's office. Not accepted, but not exactly rejected, either. Someone puts money in your hand, where I'm from, you take it. But those bank notes felt heavier than usual.

"Did you try to bribe Alison, or did she try to bribe you?"

"I told you yesterday, I find it vulgar to talk so much about money."

"So where's Ray? Matty?"

"He's an interesting young man, Matthew, isn't he? Those card tricks. He could go far in our line of work."

That wasn't an answer. The absence of one filled the room. I kept my voice calm. "Where are they?"

"I didn't ask for specifics. I asked Raymond what the value of this house was, gave him cash. I believe he's on his way out of state with Matthew."

"You bought a whole house to hush this up?"

He gestured toward the back window, but all I noticed was the glove on his hand. "I've bought the whole street. For some clients. I suggested they get in on the regeneration of Hallett's Point. Might as well turn this situation to my advantage."

"How did you know to target Ray?"

"He targeted me. Searching my name. My records. There are only half a dozen people in the tristate with his level of skills."

"Why are you here? If everything you've said is true, you weren't involved in Ash's murder. Why are you still mixed up in all of this?"

"Well, in the first place, I'd say you've already confirmed I'm not involved. You found him. And, from what I'm hearing, there's only one suspect. But you know I had dealings that were tangential to your case, and I wouldn't want any of those tangents to show up in the course of a police investigation into the tragic death of David Ash."

Right.

He was still covering the same tracks as before. Ally had been linked to the game, it was her game. But he'd been okay leaving her alone this long, something had changed in the last few days. Could it just be a concern she would talk to the cops, or to the press, about the game?

I could buy that.

"You don't want the cops poking around your business."

"Honestly? The law is as flexible as anything else. I can always persuade people to look the other way."

I saw it. Right then. I could see exactly why he was going to the trouble, and, in a twisted way, it made sense.

I grinned. For the first time in his presence, I didn't feel anxious. I was in control.

"You're scared." I took a step forward to emphasize my new confidence. "For all your big talk. For all your hints of big clients, and trying to intimidate me with tickets to Russia. You want to scare me, but this is all about who scares you, isn't it?"

He didn't respond, so I continued. "Your whole job is built on an image, the big scary fixer in the expensive suits. But you're just another mark. Someone else who was turned into a fool by poker. And you're just terrified, absolutely terrified, people above you will find out how you got hosed. Because if they don't believe in your myth anymore, you become another problem for them to solve. And someone else like you knocks on your door."

He waited until I finished, then waited some more. He

was good at using silence, and it drained away my bullishness. His expression was calm, even friendly. But his dark eyes made me think of Quint's speech in Jaws.

"We don't knock. Are you done grandstanding?" He tapped his fingers on the plastic that covered the arm of the chair. A sign of impatience. "I made you a good offer yesterday. I'll note you didn't return the money. And I also know, from talking to Raymond, that you asked him to do the work before you met me. So, in all good faith, I can be reasonable and assume you didn't break our agreement. But then you show up here at the door…"

That was the second time he'd circled back to the bribe. Yesterday he'd said he was in the *human nature* business. I guessed this was his tactic. Always coming back to the green, seeing how many times he needed to do it before his target fell in line.

"I think we need to be more specific about the agreement you were offering."

"Really?" He crossed his legs, waved as if to say, bring it on. "What are you unclear on?"

"Did you kill David Ash?"

"No."

"Do you know who did?"

"Aside from what's being said in the press? No."

"Have you ever met Louisa Mantalos?"

"Yes." Pause. "A couple days ago. She was dining at Tribeca Grill with Ms Oliver and I introduced myself, pretended it was to set up a business meeting."

"Why?"

"It was targeted at Ms. Oliver. I wanted to make eye contact with her. Remind her I was in the world."

"You were worried she would talk about the game."

"Alison had agreed, long ago, that what happened at the game stayed at the game. But then her trained ape tried to shake me down. She assured me last time we spoke that he'd gone rogue, but by that point my patience was gone. It's a finite resource."

He was telling me that resource was running low once again. I started to wonder if there was a window high enough for me to fall out of.

Starr leaned forward. "Now, may I ask you something?"

"Sure."

"Why are you still looking?"

I opened my mouth, closed it again.

It took another second for me to find an answer.

"It's my job."

"As I understand it, your job was to find David Ash. You have done that." He stood up, took a step toward me. His nostrils twitched. "Those are the same clothes as yesterday?" He moved back. "Everything seems fairly clear. His wife killed him, panicked, stuffed him in a freezer. You've done the job you were paid for. So why are you still following this?"

I stood my ground. "I believe her."

"*Belief*. You interest me, Constantin. That's the truth. That's the real reason you're still breathing, and I hope that you will continue breathing past this conversation. My patience lasts until people stop interesting me. And belief is the most interesting thing of all. People pretend to be whoever those around them need to believe they are. The preachers at my family church? I looked in their eyes. They didn't believe the things they said. But the town needed them to pretend, and so they did. Everybody lies to everybody else, but what really excites me, is how everybody lies to themselves. I like to see how much it takes. How much is a person's self-delusion worth to them, in round numbers, or in threats. In people's final moments I see the exact second they give up on the lie. The moment James Ziskin stopped telling himself he was a player. The moment Cody Waltz stopped telling himself he was untouchable. The moment Alison Oliver stopped telling herself she was in control. I became their mirror, the first time they'd really seen their own reflection."

"Nice speech."

He slipped his wallet out, opened it.

"You still interest me. I know I could make you see the truth if I killed you. But what I'm wondering is: what is your self-delusion worth to you? How much would I need to offer you, to stop pretending to care about other people?"

FIFTY-SEVEN

LOUISA

Todd.

Of course.

I think back to last night. Todd watching me from across the street. Running away when I approached. That's not normal, right? Not exactly romantic. Why can't guys tell the difference between love and desperation?

It all falls into place, as the memory comes loose.

The Friday night. After the call with Dave. I talk to my dealer. I can feel his hesitation. A dealer who doesn't want to deal. Imagine that. He comes round and we talk for a long time. I should pay him extra for counselling, but instead he gives me a discount.

On the way out he says, maybe what I need is to get laid? Get even with Dave, find someone to make me feel good about myself.

I know it's his own clumsy version of making a pass at me. That's a ball I'm not interested in catching. After he's gone I go straight for the coke. I rub a little across my gums. I'm holding back, still not ready to go all-in on this. I want a little tingle. The buzz to ease me into it. Fifteen minutes later, instead of the buzz, my brain does a strange thing. It says, hey, he was right. It says go for it.

I feel something crawling up my spine. An itch I've been holding down for a long time. I rip a page out of Dave's autobiography, the one he's never even read. I roll the paper up and take a long hit off the coffee table.

Coke table? That's not funny, but I laugh anyway.

The boys are asleep.

They'll be fine for few hours if I slip out.

Okay, I'm not going to win parent of the year, but I'm about to go jump someone's bones, out of revenge for my husband doing the same. Leaving my boys in the safety of their own home is the least of my problems.

I giggle at that, too.

There's a white noise humming away at the base of my skull. I get that with coke sometimes. I have to be a louder version of myself just to be heard over the droning. I take some of the Vitamin K, too. The way the two drugs talk to each other, love it, never gets old.

There's a hoodie I use when I want to head out without being noticed, hangs down over my forehead and comes in tight around my face. I slip it on and head down to the street. I don't consciously think about where I'm going, but only so I can act surprised at where my feet take me. Deep down I know. I've always known this option was available, after all. Down Greenwich Avenue. I stop at a store that always has the best selection of wine. All those colors. And I giggle at myself again, because why am I looking at alcohol, like I'm not going somewhere that already has it?

In less than half an hour I'm at the Drop. I walk in, keeping my hood up.

Todd spots me right away. He's sitting in the corner, looking lonely. Any other day he gets to hold court, but tonight it's a bro bar, sweaty, macho, full of annoying kids. The people who really pay the bills in these dives. The only people who are going to talk to Todd are wanting to say how much they love Dave's solo songs off the film soundtracks.

I smile.

The smile.

Take his hand and nod at the door behind the bar. I know about his room downstairs. It's soundproof. He showed me before, and he's never told Dave or Eddy about it. I know that it means something to him, to share a secret with me that he's kept from the guys. But I also know the truth about Todd, that even Anthony Preston doesn't accept. Todd only came into existence as a foil for Dave. Todd likes me, Anthony loves Dave.

I lead the way down. Then I lead the way for everything else, too.

And the whole time, I'm thinking about Dave.

No, wait. There's another memory here. Buried in the memory. The thing I've always known. The thing...

Jack.

I'm back staring at those images.

The pictures Dave and Jack have been sending each other. And a precise arrangement of small moles above Jack's breasts. The same ones I've seen dozens of times on Ally.

Ally. Jack. Jack. Ally. Like an introduction in my mind. The thing I'd been daring Dave to admit when I asked him who Jack was.

And now I'm back in the room with Todd, thinking about Ally and Dave the whole time.

Until the end, as Todd finishes and I don't, and all I have is buyer's remorse.

This hasn't solved anything.

What have I done?

To Todd.

To myself.

Mostly to myself.

I leave Todd there. Naked.

I can see he knows the score, too. He's having the same regret as me, but wrapped up in something deeper .

I'm sorry, Todd.

I walk home. Fast. Almost running. I'm at civil war with myself. This is me. This isn't me. Which version am I playing right now? I can't blame the drugs. Coke doesn't change me, it turns up the volume on who I really am. So, is this who I want to be?

I take a few more belts of cocaine. The heroin sits there, untouched. It calls to me. Then I feel the crawling sensation under my skin. The itch. I'm looking for roll-up paper, to get a smoke on the go, but there isn't any. Through the white noise in my head, I feel the familiar lurch of rock bottom racing up at me. Ketamine. Make like go away. Ketamine. Make my brain go away.

I look at the sofa. The one I bought with my first real money. The thing that was new and mine. I think of home. My parents. I think of who I really am.

I flush the drugs. Through anger. Pain. Frustration.

The white noise is growing. It's wrapping around me.

Oh man, the come down is going to be *epic*.

FIFTY-EIGHT

CON

I didn't think I could feel any lower, climbing the stairs to my apartment.

Each step took effort. The events of the last few days adding up to a burden that pressed down on my shoulders. Without Ray, what could I prove? What leads could I find? I was out of ideas, and out of juice. I had Ramona stalling for time in the city, for a miracle I couldn't deliver.

Then I opened the door and found a whole new level beneath me.

Karen and Anita were sitting in the living room, watching the news on TV. Tabby was asleep, curled up beside Anita on the sofa. I read both Karen and Anita's reactions as shock. They were pale, unmoving. Karen's eyes were red, with a rawness to them suggesting she was all out of tears.

On the screen, a local station was cutting between a reporter stood outside the Precinct house, and old video clips.

Louisa on *The Biz*.

David Ash on stage.

A Doormats video.

I recognized one of the clips as *Nothing Always Happens*. The video I'd discussed with Todd, the one Ash had refused to appear in. Was somebody at the TV station wise to the joke of choosing that song, or was it just a cruel irony?

Karen looked up at me. I knew questions would be coming. I wanted to be anywhere else, to be doing anything else, to avoid answering them.

"Is it..."

Her words trailed off and she turned back to the screen.

"Was it you?" Anita said. "Found him?"

"Yeah."

"And it's true what they're saying? That woman?"

I didn't have an answer. There weren't any words to help untangle the knot of emotions I could hear wrapped up in the question. Deep down I believed Louisa was innocent.

But I had no idea where that belief was coming from. All the evidence said she was guilty, and all my work had done was to help stack the case against her. I eased down onto the chair by the window, pulling it slowly from under the table to avoid waking Tabby with the scraping noise.

On the screen they were now playing another clip of the band. It was odd now, to see the Doormats on screen in their prime. Todd looked the way I used to picture him, young and full of that sneery punk cool. Edgar bashed away on his battered old drum kit. And David Ash? Well, he wasn't a frozen lump of meat.

He stared out of the screen at us. Big eyes, ruffled hair. A message from the past.

"He was alone?" Karen spoke softly. "He was all on his own?"

I nodded.

She looked at the screen, then at the floor, before turning her head up to the ceiling as if to tip tears back from her eyes. "All this time, he was right there, all on his own. I kept hoping, I guess, you know, I just wanted..."

I tried for a gentle smile. "I know."

"Why would she do it? Why do that? Was it... was it me?"

For half a second, after all the days of doubts and questions, I thought she was asking if she had killed him. Some part of me was ready to see a cruel joke, in having another person not remembering what had happened. Then I realized what she was really asking. Had Louisa killed Ash because of her, the affair, maybe even Tabby.

"None of this is your fault," I said, sounding sure of something for the first time that day.

"He's right," Anita squeezed her hand. "Whatever happened, you can't blame yourself."

Karen's lip wobbled. I knew what was coming next and didn't feel comfortable being there for it. But I felt the responsibility. Ash's death might not have been on Karen, but the discovery of it was on me. A whole chain of events I'd set in motion. Three lives here that I'd ruined. Plus Louisa, the two boys. Ally.

Halliday.

Would Ally and Matt Halliday still be alive if not for me?

Ramona brings me in against Ally's wishes. Ally sets Halliday on me. Halliday has a second go at getting money out of Starr. Halliday gets himself killed, and sets up Ally to meet the same end. But still, like Starr himself, that was a different puzzle. It didn't tell us anything about David Ash.

Tabby opened her eyes and turned to look up at me. David Ash's eyes. Father's eyes. Fathers. My brain fizzing connections. Like Waltz the father protecting the memory of Waltz the son. All this pressure just to keep his dead boy's name from being linked to gambling debts and a poker game. But Waltz did seem to believe his son's death was suicide. Could I blame him one last act of protecting his son?

On the screen, the band were running around, goofing off, having fun. Young and alive. Edgar looking slightly awkward and out of place, Todd looking at David, David owning the screen. And right there, with everything lined up my mind, with all the right thought muscles working, the answer hit me.

I knew what it was I'd seen the night before.

I knew Louisa was innocent.

I knew the missing piece that would explain the whole thing.

Ramona's cell went straight to voicemail. She was busy, naturally. Probably in with Louisa that very moment. How long did they have before she was booked, put into the system. Once she was in, even if proven innocent, the system can keep a person in processing for days. Delays in court papers. Delays in decisions. Delays in which Louisa would be in Rikers, falling apart, maybe never fully coming back. I flicked through the business cards I had collected in the last few days, all stored in Halliday's wallet. There was one that I could try. It was the longest shot. If Ramona was busy, so was this person. But I needed a little luck to roll our way, to give us a glimmer.

I prayed to Saint Expedite as I typed in the number.

Carl Waltz answered straight away,

I looked up at the ceiling, thanking whoever.

"Hello?"

"Carl Waltz," I said. "Con McGarry."

"What -"

I didn't give him time. "I get the lengths you go to for a

memory. But what If I tell you you've not gone far enough?"

I could feel the temperature drop on the other end of the line. "What do you mean?"

"Your son didn't kill himself. Just like you already suspect Alison Oliver didn't. Just like Jimmy Ziskin didn't. Matt Halliday. You're really not connecting them all the way back?"

There was silence on the other end. Except... did I hear a sniff? Was he crying?

I pushed home the gamble. "Whatever you need to do, you're going to put a pause on processing Louisa. Whatever bit of information you need to conveniently remember or find, you're going to ease off her and give me some time."

"Why?"

"Because then I'll tell you who killed your boy."

The pause was telling. "A new piece of information may have just come to light."

"I'll bet it has."

I hung up, found another number in my collection, and called.

"Hey," I said when it was answered. "Want to solve this?"

FIFTY-NINE

CON

"Oh, hey."

Edgar Malmon blinked. I'd buzzed his door five times before he answered, and he looked out into the sunlight like a mole forced up out of its hole.

"Have you checked the news?"

"No, I was, uh." He scratched his chin. It sounded like striking a match. "No."

Malmon didn't invite me in right away. He pulled his phone out of paint-flecked jeans. "Oh. Oh, wow. I mean, oh." He looked up at me, then down at his screen again. His face showed just about every emotion I could imagine. "Um, so, it's true? Louisa?"

"That's why I'm here." I looked around, made a show of it. Conspiratorial. "I don't think Louisa did it."

He got halfway through a shake of his head without fully committing to the move. "What?"

I took a step forward. "Can I come in? I need to talk to you about Todd."

"Todd?" He paused. "Uh, sure."

Edgar opened the door wider and nodded for me to come in. I followed him up the stairs. At the top I could see a new canvas in the middle of the room, with the vague forms of three figures in the center. The image was still taking shape, but it looked like one of the Doormat's more iconic images, from an early photoshoot.

Malmon said, "I felt like painting us. The band."

"Looks good."

"Hey, can I get you some coffee?" I didn't get a chance to comment in the time before he followed up. "I'm going to need a gallon of it." He paused again, shook his head. "Just keeps hitting me, you know?"

"Take your time."

He went downstairs and I heard him grinding beans, then muttering to himself as he filled the coffeemaker.

I took a look around the room again, at all the paintings and digital art lining the walls. The odd mix of crazy and commercial.

Malmon came back up carrying two mugs of black coffee. He settled down onto his stool and looked down at the floor in thought for a moment before scratching the back of his head. "So, was it you? I mean, found him?"

"Yes."

"How was - No, never mind. Dumb question."

"It's okay. Strange situation, there aren't really any dumb questions. I didn't come here to break it so bluntly, to be honest. I just need to clean a few things up. See, when I was talking to Todd the first time, I was getting this weird vibe. Like he was holding back on something."

"I remember you picked up on him having an act. But that's just Todd."

Edgar picked up his paintbrush. He didn't move to start painting.

"I know. I spoke to him again, after, and I saw the real him, I think. Maybe the guy you and David met the first time. So I know where the act is. But there was more, like I felt him avoiding something. Now I know what it was. He didn't want me to know where he was on the night Dave died."

"Hey, come on. You don't think - This is Todd. He couldn't kill anybody."

"I never said Todd killed him."

He gave me a confused look and set the paintbrush down.

"See, I just got off the phone with Louisa's lawyer. Turns out, Todd was with Louisa that night. He just turned up at the station to alibi her."

He looked around for his stool, pulled it closer. "What?"

"Yeah, I know. When I was talking to you guys, I was all about David. I asked Todd when was the last time he'd seen him, and I knew there was something off about his answer. I was just missing the real point of it. He was more worried about the last time he'd seen Louisa."

"Are you sure?"

"Seems that way. I guess, while she wasn't under arrest, he could sit on it. Pretend it didn't happen. But once the cops arrested her, he needed to step up."

"So… she's off the hook?"

"Too soon to tell. He can only vouch for part of the evening, the rest is still up in the air. They'll still see her as the best suspect, and they've been convinced of that for six months, so they won't give up on it easy. Plus they fancy her for Ally's murder."

He took a step back, like his weight had gone from under him for a second. "Ally…"

"Thrown out her window."

I looked around at all the same canvases I'd seen before. He still had the one I'd commented on. The mishmash of colors, sitting in a ball in the center of the image. What had he said before? A caterpillar liquefying.

"I guess all of this is in the interpretation, right?"I pointed at the painting. "I mean, you tell an art critic that it's about the soul of a butterfly or something, that's all they're going to see. It could be a Twinkie. Hey, when was the last time you saw one of those?"

"Been a while."

"What if we said it was a dead body in a freezer, think people would ever see that?"

Edgar's eye twitched. The same tell I'd seen on my first visit. But this time, I knew what it meant.

His voice came out shaky, emotional. "How did you know?"

SIXTY

CON

"You know, I've got to say, you'd be a great grifter. I read people for a living, and you had me fooled. I think it was Todd and Louisa. I was so busy trying to figure out what they were holding back, you just sneaked right past me."

I stood up and sipped at the drink, made a show of examining the art on the walls. I walked over to the commercial work we'd talked about on my first visit.

The sports car. The buildings. Production art on a poker movie. The artist's dirty secret, he'd called them.

"Jimmy ever come to you for his movie art?"

"He came over a lot. Especially early on. Always wanted help. I drew film posters for him, some concept work."

"You knew he was conning people?"

"I guess. I don't always know what I know. I suppose I did, but he had this way, he'd make you feel like you had to help him. Like his superpower was filling you with a sense of obligation." He paused to laugh. "Just like Dave."

I pointed at the poker art, "Was this one of his? Jimmy's?"

"No, different deal."

"You like to play, though?"

A nervous laugh. "A little too much. It's... the thing that always separated me and Dave, really. Gambling. He was really into everything else. I liked the other stuff, but gambling was where I went crazy."

Edgar wanted to talk. After all this time, he wanted to open up. I could feel it in the room, building.

"Did Jimmy come to you about the game, or were you already in?"

He laughed.

It sounded wet, emotion welling around the edges.

"We used to play on the road. It was this, it was like a game. I mean it is a game but..." I waited, letting him ease past his self-consciousness. "The thing was to mess with Todd. He always fancied himself the player, talked strategy and read books, and he'd get super competitive about it. I wasn't great, really, but I was good enough to lose a certain way."

"What way?"

"We never talked about it. Back then. We never... it wasn't an agreement. But I knew Jimmy was good with the deck, I knew he could do things, keep track of who had what. And we both wanted to take Todd down a little, cut him up, give his ego a kick. Me and Jimmy, we just fit together well on the table, we both felt it."

"You worked together."

"Without ever saying it, yeah. Then after Jimmy was gone, I worked on getting better. I had to keep having this thing to hold over Todd, to keep taking him. But that's when I started to go nuts with it. Take trips to Vegas, tournaments, blow money I didn't really have."

"Ever need bailed out?"

"Dave helped a couple times. He was always a dick about it, always told me I was the only person he'd do it for, and I needed to grow up. But he still helped, so I just accepted the attitude. And it wasn't like he was a saint himself, you know? Who always picked him up when he fell down? And I never had an attitude about it."

"When did Jimmy come back on the scene?"

"You gotta understand, Jimmy had never asked me for money. When he was managing the band, he talked money with Dave and Todd. I stayed out of all of that, just signed my name, took whatever my cut was. I just wanted to play, didn't want to talk numbers. So I hadn't really seen that side of Jimmy, apart from at the table, which we'd never talked about. Then after the band, I knew Jimmy would go to Todd and Dave for money, and I knew they didn't like to give him any. But he never asked me for it. He only ever talked to me about art, movies or poker. I helped him out with paintings and drawings, we never talked cash. I guess, I mean, I guess it never really felt like I was buying into whatever he was doing. I was just helping out a friend, favors."

"Sure."

"So when he came to me about the game..." He sighed. With it, I could hear the dam break. "It just worked. He got me, I never felt like I was being roped."

"Which game was this, Leysa's or Ally's?"

"He told me about the first one, but I was on the wagon hard. Dave had helped me out of a tight spot, and I'd promised to clean up. And I knew Todd played at that one, and I just figured I'd stay away, make sure not to fall into old habits. Then he came to me about the second one, and he said Todd didn't play because of Ally."

"He didn't like her."

"None of us did, really. She'd just forced her way into things. That's how we felt, anyway. Louisa had felt the same way, but she was with Dave so you always make room for that, you know? A girlfriend, boyfriend, whatever. They come on the scene and you resent them, but you're an adult, you also know some of your resentment is just dumb teenage crap, you make room. But Ally was different, she wasn't with any of us, she was just there one day, involved in everything. We didn't... I guess we didn't handle that well."

"But you were happy enough to join her game?"

"You have good times and bad times, when you have a problem. Just like Dave with the drugs. There are times when you're fine and make smart choices. And times when you're dumb, and none of your choices make sense, you can't rationalize them." He paused before adding, in a low voice: "Though you spend all your time doing just that."

"This was one of the bad times."

"I was spiraling. Yeah. Making all the old mistakes. I'd go out to Atlantic City, Vegas, go on tilt, lose everything I'd won, then get up and do it all again, and it's like... I don't know, not that I enjoy it, but you get to this place where you just think it's what you deserve. You're not even thinking about winning or losing now, you're just doing, and hating yourself, and then doing again."

He was pretty worked up, talking fast. He paused to breathe in deep, then drank some coffee, which wasn't really helping.

"So when he came to me about the new game it was..." He stopped, laughed. "See, looking back on it even now I can't figure out. Did he know I was spiraling, and did he come to hook me? Or did he not know at all, did he mean well, just Jimmy being Jimmy, you know? I can never work out, did he know he was cheating his friends when he did it, or was it just who he was? Even saying it now, I'm trying to let him off the hook. I know, right? It's like, how much more of a mark could I have been?"

"It happens. It's okay to be fooled. That's what they do."

"Good of you to say, but yeah. He totally fooled me. He was just setting me up. Maybe it was revenge for not sticking up for him against Dave and Todd. Or maybe he was taking it out on me because they wouldn't play."

"How did he sell it to you?"

"It was the first time we'd really talked about the trick we used to run on Todd. He came to me and was like 'hey, we worked well together didn't we, really cut him up. We could make a fortune, you and me, doing that at this new game.' And I got sucked in. I just wasn't thinking right."

"How would it work?"

"You ever played with a silent partner?" I hadn't. I knew the game, but wanted to hear their version. "You just have a patsy, someone else at the table who, ultimately, is happy to lose to you, but is working with you, you keep an eye on each other's hands and pots, help drive the pot up at key moments or help keep it restrained. Jimmy was great at that kind of play."

"So this was Jimmy going into business against the table, Ally didn't know what was planned."

He shook his head, a firm gesture. "Definitely not. She was running it honest. I didn't like her much, but I'll give her that. She just… didn't really know what she was doing. Not the way the others had. She didn't control who was allowed in, she just wanted the status of it, I think."

"She let the mob in."

"She let anyone in, if they looked flush."

"And Jimmy went into business against the wrong people."

"Yeah." He watched me in silence for a second, like he was trying to read how much I knew. "Yeah, so he got in over his head. It was always going to happen, I guess. But first he went in against me."

I'd jumped ahead, ruined the flow. I waved for him to go at his own pace.

"I figured out two or three games in. I was already over a hundred K in at that point, basically wiped out apart from this place. And it took me until then to see it, that he was conning me. The whole time, I'd been thinking we were working together, right? Helping him. And because I was spiraling, I just wasn't thinking. I'd be up quite a lot at times, and those moments I'd be all, well this is our system working. Then I'd lose big and I'd blame that on bad luck, or bad cards. I never stopped to notice the patterns. That he had another silent partner at the table. No, that Jimmy was someone else's silent partner, he was helping to drive money to someone else."

"And they were conning you."

"Well, Jimmy was. I don't know if the other guy was." A tired laugh. "And even now, like I said, part of me wants to let Jimmy off the hook, say he didn't mean it, maybe he just wanted insurance, wanted two partners at the table, me to support him while he supported someone else."

"But no money came your way. The other partner, Cody Waltz?"

He nodded. "So I quit. When I saw it, I quit. I told Ally what was going on, left it up to her to decide whether she wanted to fix it, and keep the game honest. But I was out, I walked away and got help, went into rehab."

"Did it stick?"

"Every day since. I hope it will tomorrow."

"Congratulations."

He took that with a nod. Didn't say anything.

"So then what happened?"

"Ally had been letting in the wrong people."

"Charlie Starr."

He watched me in silence for a few seconds. I saw fear in his eyes. He didn't even want to say the name.

"My last night, the night I hit rock bottom and figured out I was a mark, I crashed out early that night. Went all in on a stupid hand, done. And I was already... I'd already got the idea in my head of what was happening, but wasn't sure. So I stuck around for about an hour, watching, chatting, enjoying the food. Mostly watching. And that's when I watched the way Jimmy and Cody were both playing, and saw the connection. But the other guy -"

"Starr."

"The other guy was there that night, and I could see it man, he was about to go full tilt. It was in his eyes. You could just see it. Everybody at the table could see it. Most people cashed out early, I think they didn't want to be there or cross that guy. But a few stayed in. That's when I warned Ally and left."

"Did he figure it out?"

"I think Ally told him, after."

"How much did they take him for?"

"From the story I heard, the guy went in about six hundred."

"Thousand?"

He snorted. "Of course."

"They took him for over half a million."

"Not just Jimmy and Cody, of course. By the time all the hands were played and the pots had gone around, everyone left in the game had taken some of him. But Jimmy and Cody were the ones cheating him."

"And he wanted their cut back."

"I think he wanted the whole lot back, and everyone else decided to pay."

"Not Jimmy and Cody."

"He came to me. Jimmy. Really scared. Or acting scared. He was saying how he'd messed up, taken money from some mob guy, and they were going to kill him if he didn't give it back. And, this was the thing, he said he already didn't have it to give back."

"You believe him?"

He was crying now. "No, I said, how can you not have it? But that was always the thing with Jimmy. Always looking at new ways to make money, always talking about future investments, big ideas, but he never seemed to have any. Money came in, he moved it straight out. Even in good times. But then, this time, he's screwed me out of a fortune and we both know it, and he's coming to me for help?"

"What was he asking for?"

"He said his share was a little over a hundred. Cody's was three. And I said to him, go to your new friend. Ask this magic Cody kid to bail you out. He said Cody was ghosting him. That Cody had family connections, didn't give a shit what happened to anyone else because he knew he'd be okay."

"You said no."

"I said no." The tears were steady now. "First time. Then he showed up all beat and messy, his arm was broken. He said they were serious, and if he didn't give this guy the money back, they were going to kill him. And then, then, he says, and what if they find out there was another partner?"

"Blackmail."

"Well, he never out and out said it like that. It was just implied, really, for me to pick up. And it makes no sense, I know. I was a mark at the game. I walked away from it with nothing, cheated. But the threat was just enough to scare me, and this was always my weak spot, I always get all mixed up over it, when to feel guilty, when not to. Addiction does a real number on you. And he got me all thrown around because he told me the other kid was dead. Cody, the untouchable one, had been touched. But I didn't have money. I had some, I'd had a couple decent royalty checks in the time since I quit the game, Dave's solo career had pushed the band into profit. And some good commercial art deals. You know," he paused, gave a sad smile, "it wouldn't be problem now. After all of this with Dave, I could get that kind of money fast. It's just piling up. But then? I had some money, but even with that Jimmy was still short."

"By fifty?"

He gave me the appraising look again. "Yeah."

"Keep going."

"I couldn't go to Todd. I mean, I could, he's got the most out of all of us, with his family. His parents could have solved this over breakfast. But he's always such a dick about money, always quick to hold things over you. I went to Dave. He made more off the band than us, with the songwriting and everything. I asked for help. And he gave me the rest."

"Just like that?"

"Just like that. It was amazing. He didn't judge. Not at that point. And he knew what it was for, I'd told him about the game, about the psycho, about Jimmy. I'd told him this money was to save Jimmy's life, that it was to maybe save mine, and Dave just...made it happen."

"Okay, so you gave Jimmy the money to pay off Starr, but then he still took a jump..."

"Yeah."

"You never went to the cops, told anyone what you knew?"

"I was scared. Dave, too. You ever messed with those guys? We were both in over our heads, and what did we know, really?"

Had Jimmy been honest about how much money he'd taken from Starr? Had he paid him back, and still been killed? Or had he come up short, and paid with his life?

People being turned stupid out of ego.

People killing out of ego and money.

People hiding the truth out of ego and fear.

If every man in the world stopped caring what other men thought of them, every conman would be out of business, half the murders would stop, fraud would cease to exist.

That filled in all the gaps on one side of the story. But I still needed the rest. "There's no music stuff here. You've got nothing to say who you were. I thought that was odd, but it helped sell me on your act, this guy who wanted nothing to do with the old life. But when I found David, I saw his Les Paul."

"Only thing he was ever really faithful to."

"Your drums were there. The red ones."

He laughed, and through the tears it was a nasty sound, almost animal.

"Back when we were kids, back home, we had this club. It was just the two of us, and we'd sit in Dave's basement, his parents' basement, and smoke weed, get drunk, play music. We called it music club. The two of us against the whole fucking world. Then, I don't know, life got weird. Suddenly we're in a band, and there are lawyers and managers, contracts, advances. Music wasn't fun, and we all started to hate each other. We changed. I was becoming someone I didn't like. So was Dave. And Todd, well, I'd never really liked him, but he got weird. Then Dave got famous, and Louisa happened, and it all went away."

"You guys missed playing together?"

"Yeah." There was a genuine sadness in his eyes. "I'm not sure what started it. We were talking after Jimmy died, and it was like we were trying to talk about everything except that. And one of us, I don't know if it was me or him, one of us said, 'we should do music club again.' So we did. Got together and jammed."

"Music club was back on."

"It was so good." He smiled. The sadness was still there, but it was thawing with a warmth beneath the surface. "Just like being kids again. The world went away, and it was just us, making noise, talking about life, having fun you know? Fun." He wiped at the tears that were sliding down his face. Blew his nose. "Then, he got the idea that we should record some of his new material. That it'd be a fun inside joke, his new album would have me on it, and nobody would know. Those were the kinds of ideas we'd throw around early on, before the band became a business."

"Were you both doing drugs?"

"No." He scratched his arm. I don't think he knew he was doing it. "No, I put that stuff down a long time ago, it was only the gambling I couldn't shake. Dave was hitting it hard. I've always figured that was my fault. I was always a bad influence on Dave. I have this way. I'll plant an idea and walk away, knowing someone else will take credit and run with it. A lot of the stupid things Dave and Todd did, they were my ideas. But I'd just plant the seed and watch. And it was the same with drugs. I was the first in the band to take them, but also the first to kick them. I'd do a thing, then a while later Dave would do it. But whatever I did, he needed to do bigger..."

Oh god.

The last piece fell into place.

I'd turned up at Edgar's place knowing he'd been involved in Dave's death. Everything lined up. But even though I knew the where and the who, I was still missing the why.

Why would Dave's oldest friend kill him?

Now I knew. He hadn't killed him.

He'd done something maybe worse.

"Overdose," I said quietly.

"Yeah. We'd arranged to meet for a session. There was a party at his main studio. He said he just wanted to record, no drama. So I headed up to our jam space, but when I got there, he was already...he was a mess. All contorted up on the floor, gunk coming out of his mouth. I tried to..."

He trailed off as a larger crying fit overtook him.

Again I waited until he was ready to continue.

"I tried to help him. His heart stopped and I was trying CPR, but I've only ever seen it in movies. I don't actually know what to do."

"911."

His mouth opened and closed, but no words came out.

"Why didn't you call them?"

"I panicked. I don't know why. Look —" His voice rose. "I know how it sounds. I know how it is. But it wasn't like a plan. You know, you hear about all these criminals in the news, and in films, and it's always like they're these schemers, planning everything out. But I wasn't thinking straight. I just thought, time. I wanted time. I just needed air, and to think, and to calm down and figure it all out."

There was another answer waiting to come out. I was happy to let Edgar get there in his own time. He was talking as if I'd just caught him dropping a cherry bomb down the toilet. Like it was a prank gone wrong.

On some level, I don't think he'd processed the reality of what he'd done until now. The problems had been locked away, in a freezer.

"The money," he said, after a pause. "There's two different...when I look back now, it's like when I talk about Jimmy, and I try to remember things differently to make him not cheat me. Ands with Dave, like, there's the version where I was just too late to do anything and then panicked. But there's another version, where all I could think about was the money. The problem would go away. Dave was the only person who knew about me thinking I was Jimmy's partner at the game... Oh god, I sound crazy."

"Did you go back?"

"You ever do something stupid, but then realize right away it was so dumb you couldn't go back on it?"

I flashed back to sitting behind the wheel of a getaway car. And I remembered sitting in the box at the police station, confessing to Detective Elizondo, and wondering why it was fair my whole life could turn on one stupid decision.

Edgar continued. "The minute I got outside, into the air, I knew I could've called 911 and maybe saved him. And what I'd done was this huge thing, that I'd put him in the freezer, and how the hell do I explain that rationally? How do I tell the cops that and not come off like a killer?"

"So you walked away."

He nodded and buried his head in his hands, circling back to answer my previous question. "I went back to pick up the Con-Ed bills. Each time, I'd tell myself on the way, this was when I'd fix the mess. But then I'd get there, and it all felt too big. How do you fix *that*?"

"You should know, Jimmy, for all that he did to cheat you, he didn't give you up. I've met Charlie Starr. If he knew about your part in this, you'd know it by now. For all his faults, Jimmy went off that balcony without saying your name."

After another couple of minutes of muted sobbing, he seemed to pause.

I said, "Feels good to come clean, doesn't it?"

He looked up at me. He swallowed a few times, and sniffed. "Yeah, actually."

"You know, talking to me is one thing. But there's a woman on her way to prison for this. She's got kids. Todd's stepped up to help, going to drag his own name through the mud. But if you talked, officially, all of this guilt will lift, all the crap you've been carrying around."

I pulled my phone out, along with Elizondo's card.

First rule.

Never call the cops.

Unless...

I dialed the number, and when Elizondo answered, I said: "You still looking for that good night's sleep?"

After a quick introduction, I handed the phone to Edgar and told him I'd wait down on the street for the cops to show up. I took the stairs slowly at first. Just enough to listen in on the start of the conversation and make sure he was confessing.

It would be the first of many. The cops would make him go over it all again at the station, multiple times, checking every detail until they were happy. But that was between him and them. I'd done my bit.

Dee Buana was waiting for me out on the street. They were leaning against the wall, looking at a small handheld tablet. The screen was showing audio, it leapt as I spoke.

"You get it all?"

Dee nodded. Tears in their eyes. Listening to the confession had been as hard as witnessing it. I opened my jacket, and waited while Dee reached in and unclipped the microphone and followed the lead around my back to the battery pack tucked into my jeans. The recording was backup, in case Malmon was willing to confess to me but not the cops. I didn't much care what Dee wanted to do with it now. Maybe I'd helped with an episode of the podcast.

I sucked the cool air in as we waited on the sidewalk. I needed it. What was I supposed to feel? Edgar hadn't murdered Dave Ash, but he hadn't saved him either. He'd made a series of mistakes, and topped them off with a moment of stupid panic. I could choose to believe him and think that the fear and emotion had gotten in the way. Or I could decide he'd acted out of selfishness, deliberately, throwing both Jimmy Ziskin and David Ash onto grenades to save himself.

I wasn't even sure if Edgar himself knew the truth.

He'd spend the rest of his life trying to figure it out.

That's when I heard the gunshot upstairs.

Just one.

SIXTY-ONE

LOUISA

I'm exhausted.

It's a good kind of tired, though. This is almost over. All of it.

The cops have changed. Now it's all smiles and coffee. Someone even asked if I wanted anything ordered in for lunch. I've been moved. Now I'm in the same room we used the first time I came in six months ago. Comfortable seats, nice lighting, a television in the corner.

I resist the temptation to find a news station and see what they're saying.

Ramona has been in and out. First she came back to tell me they'd been informed of my condition. They've called my doctor, and he's on the way.

Then, with Ramona at my side, I told Elizondo my side of the thing with Todd. He was quick to point out that "*even if this checks out*" it's not an alibi for the full night, and they haven't got a time of death for Dave yet. There's a big window there, and it will be easy enough to make a case that I still did it. But I can read in his eyes that he knows the game is up.

I feel lighter.

Things are finally going my way. Maybe this is my reward for telling the truth. I say a few silent prayers. How long has it been since I went to church? Really went, I mean. That visit with Con doesn't count. I can't even remember. I started going a lot when I was kicking the drugs and alcohol, and I've been to a few church basements since then for meetings. But the last time I went for real?

I'll put that right once I get out. Take the boys with me. They can light a candle for their daddy.

Another hour goes by. Elizondo sits with me to talk about sleep. We're both craving it. He seems to think I'll admire his commitment to the case, like he hasn't been haunting my every step for six months. The only difference between him and a stalker is the badge he gets to wear.

Elizondo is sipping coffee when his phone goes. He excuses himself to take the call, and then everything goes crazy. I hear shouts. A sudden burst of activity across the station. I sit with Ramona. She keeps going to try to find out what's happening but comes back each time with no further information.

And then I'm free to go.

Just like that.

"What's happened?" I ask both Ramona and Elizondo. Nobody is talking.

At the desk they start running through paperwork with me, like checking out of the worst hotel in history. Handing back my bag, my keys. I start to ask for my phone, then remember I smashed it chasing Todd.

That little slip of memory makes me worry a little. I can feel the illness. I can feel the blank spaces and the faulty connections. They're so big now. I breathe in, I breathe out, and I thank whatever has pulled me through this.

Con walks out of the box. He looks shaken, and just as exhausted as the rest of us. Ramona gives him a long hug and they hold a hushed conversation. Then Con fills me in on what's happened.

Eddy?

Eddy killed Dave?

Or didn't save him. Or, I don't know.

It's his fault. And now he's dead, too.

This is all such a mess.

I'm too numb to know how I should react. The news just washes over me. I'll deal with it later. One thing at a time.

Elizondo pulls me to one side. "I'm going to miss our chats," he says with his hangdog smile. For a second I think that's as close as he's going to get to admitting he's been wrong. But he takes my hand in a firm shake and says. "I don't say sorry all that much in this job. I don't really know how."

I hold back a tear. It's not for him, it's for the whole thing. His half-apology feels like the period at the end of the story.

Then Elizondo and Con share some kind of moment. I don't really understand all of it, but I know they have a whole extra bit of history between them.

Elizondo says: "I guess you were right about the fruit."

Con smiles. "Maybe. Or we just need time. Everything makes sense later."

"Like why you got behind that wheel?"

"Goodbye, detective."

A uniformed officer drives Ramona, Con and me to my apartment. There are press waiting outside both the station and my place, but we ignore them. I invite Ramona and Con up for a coffee, and we sit there. None of us has anything to say. Which seems crazy. So much has happened. So much to talk about, but none of us seem to want to start.

I get a tense call from Dave's parents. They ask if it's okay if Peter and Johnny stay with them overnight. I want to see my boys. So, so bad. But maybe a little space will be good. Time to think. Time to gear up for whatever comes next. His parents know the truth now. All of it. They know I didn't kill Dave, but they also know about my illness. Will they still try to fight me? I want at least one night without drama. To figure out what my new world is.

So far, my illness is still mostly under wraps. The police know. Dave's family knows. But these things never stay hidden. I'll take control, do a couple of interviews on primetime, sell the rights to someone I can trust. I'll be in control of the message, and I'll have what's left of my family beside me.

Ally.

Ally is dead.

She was my only friend for so long. But she was also never my friend, was she? I don't know. She'd been pushing hard for power of attorney. Had I really wanted her to produce the TV show about me, or had she manipulated me into asking her? She's done so much to help me since Dave... died. But she's done so much to cheat me.

Like they were cheating on me...

Both of them.

Was it a game?

I don't know.

I'm letting go. It's over. I don't care.

I'm all out of care.

SIXTY-TWO

CON

Two weeks after we found Dave's body, Ramona was putting in twenty-hour days just to meet demand. The way she'd handled the media, plus the fact she'd stuck by her client and not given up, had turned her into a mini celebrity. The same law firms who'd turned her away in the past were now making her offers involving corner offices and company benefits. Everybody wanted to be associated with her.

I slipped in through the door to see she was talking to a young family at her desk. They were speaking loud and fast in Spanish. There were other people waiting on the benches she'd put in by the door. I wondered how lawyer/client confidentiality works when other people can listen in, but trusted she had it figured out.

I caught her attention and signaled I would come back later. She nodded, mid-sentence, and focused back on the family.

Down the block and round the corner, I walked along to Sharkey's. Frank started mixing me a Shirley Temple as soon as he saw me. I'd developed a taste for them.

Three days after Dee handed the confession over to Elizondo and Waltz, Charlie Starr was killed in a drive-by shooting outside a restaurant. The news described it as a gangland killing. The links between Starr and Ash's death had not come out in the media. The suicides were all still officially suicides. The trail was messy enough that I was convinced people would connect a few dots eventually, and Dee was free to include it in the podcast, but so far the David Ash story was just one of infidelity and overdose.

I didn't know who had pulled the trigger on Starr. Whether it was Elizondo, Waltz, or an off-duty patrol unit. What I did know was he'd learned not to mess with the biggest gang in town.

I wondered what truth he saw reflected back at him, right at the end.

The world didn't care about any of this. They were too busy paying attention to Louisa.

Two days after being released, she gave an exclusive TV interview, talking about the ordeal of the past six months, and coming clean about her Alzheimer's diagnosis. Her children sat with her for the first half of the show, as she talked about still being a mother, and how important her family was going to be. For the second half she sat alone, so the interviewer could get more into the challenges and realities of the condition without upsetting the kids.

Alzheimer's had owned the news cycle for a couple of days after that. People spreading awareness about early onset. Medical experts coming on to discuss whether a cure was close to being found. Louisa was praised in most places as a positive role model, as someone who had moved the conversation forward. There were already rumors about a Hollywood movie. The same news outlets and TV shows that had been calling her a killer were now showering praise and calling her an inspirational figure. I would have loved to have sat in on some of the meetings behind the scenes, to see just how much dirt those people were made to eat.

Not all of the news was good. She was still heavily criticized in some of the expected places, and social media was split evenly between people supporting her and tasteless jokes. For all the people who realized they'd been wrong and backed off, there were others who now wanted to spread the notion Louisa had murdered her husband *and* her manager, and the cops were covering it up. I was sure that when people finally started to link all the suicides into some half-baked conspiracy theory, Louisa would somehow be the mastermind behind it. She didn't care about that. It was all part of the game, and now it was a game she was back in control of.

She even agreed to record an interview with Dee, for the last episode of the podcast.

She looked amazing on screen, for the tv interview. Confident. Calm. Sexy. For some reason, I didn't have trouble reconciling the two different sides of her anymore. She was both the hot woman on TV, and someone with a severe illness. I could see them both at the same time. I didn't know whether that was a sign that I'd grown up, or that my libido could overcome any challenge, but I didn't beat myself up about it.

I introduced Louisa and the boys to Karen and Tabby. Things were tense at first, but the boys bonded with Tabby, and that seemed to thaw relations between the two mothers. I couldn't read how that one was going to go, but maybe Karen and Louisa need each other now.

Louisa's financial situation would be complicated for a long time to come. David Ash was now officially dead, but it would take a while for all the loopholes and technicalities to be sorted out. She'd received big payments from TV companies in the wake of the news. Exclusivity deals. Sponsorships.

She used some of that to pay large bonuses to both Ramona and me.

Todd was falling apart. The public's interest in the Doormats was higher than ever. Spurred on by the double tragedy, the album sales went through the roof. In the middle of it all, Todd posted to social media that he was closing the bar and wouldn't be doing interviews. I didn't know if Anthony Preston would ever be able to break free of Todd Flambé, but I was rooting for him.

Ramona continued to see her new mystery man, and I continued to pretend I was fine with it.

Elaine Blatt picked up her ring from Sharkey's

Best of all, Frank paid out on the bet.

Everything was closed out.

So why wasn't I happy?

Without telling anybody, I'd taken a few trips over to the church where I'd sat with Louisa. I never went in. I still didn't feel like I'd earned it. Each time, I would then walk up the block to stand outside Reah Kanellis's shop. Wondering if I'd earned entry to that, instead. Then I would turn on my heels, make my way along to Sharkey's, to hang out with Frank.

Frank, for his part, kept watching me. Even now, when he thought I wasn't looking, he was sneaking glances in my direction.

"You did good," he said, before taking a few steps away, leaving the thought on its own.

"I cost you a bet."

He turned back, a silent laugh coming out in short

breaths. "That's true."

We sat in silence for a few more moments, as I finished my drink and he made me another. I felt the same tension I'd had at the end of Edgar's confession, when I'd said to him, feels good to come clean, doesn't it? Edgar had looked so relieved to get the words out, finally. Stop the demons running around inside. But even now, right up until today, there were still things I was holding onto.

"You and Ramona," I said, quietly. "The only two people who've never asked why I drove that car."

He smiled. It had the look of a confirmation. We'd both been wanting this. "You think I don't know, my boy?"

There was more coming. I could tell. I waited.

"I didn't drop out of high school, you know," he said, after more fake cleaning. "I was expelled."

I tried to ask, what, but I only got as far as forming the word with my mouth. No sound came.

"I was never very smart. Smart enough for a job, you know, but nothing special. I already knew where I was going to work. My old man, your grandpa Joe, he'd sorted that out. I was going there whether I graduated or not. Both me and your uncle Liam. But I had this friend, Brian, he had something. Looking at colleges. He wanted to be a marine biologist because of Jaws."

"I think the real money was in being the shark."

"He went out and got drunk with the football team one night. He was always looking to fit in. He wasn't a total nerd, he wasn't a jock, he was just a normal kid. He kept trying to find a group who would accept him. So the football team, they took advantage. Egged him on to do something stupid. He broke into the school and threw cans of paint all over the principal's office. Ruined the furniture, wrecked paperwork. Came to me the next day, scared out his mind. He knew he'd get expelled for sure, and arrested. So I went to the principal and made a deal. I told him I knew who did it, but that the kid was scared of being arrested. I'd say who it was if the cops were kept out of it."

"You turned your friend in?"

He shook his head. "I told them I did it. Spun a version of the story that kept Brian out of it, made it like he was never there. I was expelled and went to work with your grandpa and uncle. Brian went to college."

"Did he make it as a marine biologist?"

"Changed his mind three times, then dropped out. Turned out he had a drinking problem, and I picked bad friends. But good or bad, you still look out for your friends."

We shared a look after that. Holding it for a moment. Nothing more needed to be said. I told him I was off to see Ramona and he smiled, told me to call Mom more often.

Back along 28th and up Steinway. Ramona's office was closed, but the light was on. I rapped on the glass door and she stepped into view to unlock it. Her jacket was off and she had a glass of wine in her hand, She had the overall look of someone who's happy to have let a little pressure our of the tyres at the end of a long day.

She gave me a tired smile. "Hey."

She motioned towards the refrigerator. "Want a drink?"

"I'm at my limit."

Another smile.

We sat either side of the desk and made small talk for a while. The latest on Louisa. Some of Ramona's cases. She told me about the drug addict father who'd been trying to cut a deal. The one who stole a computer to pay for a birthday present. She'd managed to get him community service on the understanding he attended rehab and stuck to an NA program. Her phone screen flashed a few times, bringing up little green boxes. Messages from her mystery partner.

As we began to lull into silence, I could feel the same moment building as back with Frank. The same small knot in my gut as when I was seeing Edgar's relief.

I had one more push to make.

"I said to Frank. You and him are the only two people who've never asked why I was in the car."

"I've never needed to know why." She shook her head, with a look that said, *Oh, you idiot.*

"I ruined what we had," I could feel my throat dry up, and wished I'd taken the offered drink. "I've never apologized for that."

"You've apologized hundreds of times."

"I've never meant it."

She smiled again. "I know."

I paused, wiped my thumb across my upper lip, and realized I'd swiped the move from Elizondo. "I'm sorry, Ramona."

She swallowed something back. Her eyes almost glistened with tears. "Thank you."

She reached and took my hand. More messages were flashing up on her screen, but she was ignoring them, giving me full focus. And now, as with Frank, I could feel there was more coming. It was a day for clearing things out.

"The other day, after... after we found Halliday. You said I hire you to do bad things."

"I know. I didn't mean it the way it sounded."

"I think you did, but that's okay. That's not why I was upset. The reasons you gave, they're all true. When I hire you, it's with the added benefit that you can do things I don't need to know about. But that's not *why* I do it."

"I know."

One last pause. "I never cared about why you were in that car," she said. "What killed me. What killed us, was you didn't take the deal. I know you were offered one. All you had to do was give them one name. Give them the one name they didn't have. And you would have walked away free. You threw your life away over some stupid little boy's code, and whoever was wearing that mask, you put them above what we had."

She wasn't saying the words with any anger. That almost made it worse. She was saying it calmly. Like it was the simplest, most obvious thing in the world, the way I had ruined our relationship.

And it *was* obvious. We'd both always known this, but in the way that meant we never addressed it.

I breathed in deep and let it out, nodding, hoping she could see I'd understood what she'd said, and was thinking about it, feeling it. "You're right. But the truth? Real truth?"

Her head twitched to the side. "Please."

"It was never about who was in the car with me. That name doesn't matter. I mean, it did to the cops, but that wasn't the point. It was all about who wasn't in the car."

Her mouth opened, closed. No words. She nodded for me to continue.

"Liam."

She repeated the movement. Her mouth opened. Closed. This time she found something to say, "Frank's brother?"

I breathed in and out again. "He'd run up a gambling debt with the Kanellis family. And he was a good driver. I don't think Frank ever knew any of this, or he chose not to know, maybe. But Liam when he was younger used to do street races, and then later on did a few favors for people. So when he owed this money, he was in a tight spot and they gave him a way out. Drive the car on this one job, and the debt would be cleared. But Liam is Liam. You know how he is. Opposite of Frank, he can't hold his shit together for five minutes. He got scared, got drunk. I think maybe he figured if he was drunk it could all be called off, but things don't work that way, and he was getting called in to do the job, and threats were being made. Legs. Arms. Homes. The usual."

"And you knew about it."

"Well I knew enough. I was on the inside of the Kanellis business."

"You stepped in."

I didn't reply. Didn't need to. The whole story was pretty clear from there, I thought.

Ramona wasn't done, though. "And Frank knows none of this?"

"I don't think so." Thinking back on the conversation I'd had with him before heading here, I wasn't sure just how much he knew, or chose not to, "I'll never tell him."

"And you did all of that, all of this, for Liam?"

I waited a long time before answering, looking for the simplest way to explain it.

"No. I did it all for Frank."

I watched every emotion roll across her face. The tears that had threatened before started to form now. She excused herself, and went to the bathroom. I heard deep breathing, and a few sniffs. I got up and let myself out the front door, using those damned skills of mine to lock it without the key.

Rule five, always have a way out.

SIXTY-THREE

LOUISA

"Is this a happy ending?"

Dee smiles at me over their glasses. They know, this is an impossible question.

We're sitting in my living room. On my sofa. My sofa. The first thing that was brand new and all mine. I watched Dee set up a mini studio right here. There's a portable sound baffler, we both have headphones and expensive-looking mics and the laptop is recording, with two additional digital recorders linked into each mic.

No chances taken, Dee wants to get this one nailed.

How can I answer this question?

"What is a happy ending?" I say.

Dee smiles again. It's a fun game, I've thrown the ball back, can they catch it. "Do you feel like it's the right ending?"

Now we're getting somewhere.

I finally know I didn't kill Dave Ash. My husband. Six months of doubts, gone.

But I didn't do much to save him, either.

When did the final crack appear in our relationship? Was there one comment or deed that broke us apart? If I could locate the moment, have it over again, would a different approach save us?

And if it did, would I want to?

I don't mean I wouldn't want to save his life. But could he still be around if we'd seen the problems sooner?

Good marriages don't end in divorce. And marriages don't always stay good. There's no defeat in that.

We both relapsed. Fell back into old habits and did something stupid. For Dave, it was fatal. For me, I get to limp on. But I'm not going to blame the drugs. Heroin didn't turn Dave into a bad husband. Coke didn't turn me into a bad wife. We did that ourselves. We are the choices we make. Dave made his. I made mine. Difference is, I'm going to live with them.

And Ally.

I know how Ally fits into it all logistically.

But where does she fit emotionally?

She lied. She manipulated. Do I want to decide she was the evil one and seduced Dave? Do I want to go with the idea it was all Dave's doing? Were they just two adults who did something stupid? Were they even thinking of me at all?

I don't know.

For all I know, Ally had some grand scheme. Saw an opportunity to set herself up for life by managing, and then eventually taking over, my estate. There would be at least one decent paycheck in it for her, in film or TV rights. Or maybe she thought she was helping. Her own family screwed her up so much, did she even really know what love was by the end? Maybe she just showed affection by controlling people. She was helping me and she was betraying me. I enabled her to do it, every step of the way, because I wanted to feel like someone was looking after me.

Who doesn't want to feel looked after sometimes?

It will take time for my emotions to settle on how to feel about her, and by then I may not even remember her name. The hardest part is accepting I let someone so damaged into my children's lives. I spent too long doing that. Too long defining myself by the affection of others.

It's making it hard to look at Karen.

Too soon to know what exactly we have. How our relationship will settle. Do we like each other? I don't know. But I could have been her. She could have been me. Maybe she is. Maybe we need each other. It feels good having someone else around to help with the things Ally used to take care of, but she can't be an employee. My boys have a little sister now, and I don't want them seeing Tabby's mother as my assistant, as just another person I pay.

And Tabby.

That girl.

When Con introduced me to Karen, I wanted the wall to go up. I wanted so badly and urgently to close off and push her away. But the minute I looked into Tabby's eyes, I felt the pull. Like looking at one of my own.

But are we a family now?

I don't know.

I guess, like 'happy ending', 'family' is what you need it to be. It's whoever's left when everyone else has walked away. Or it's a choice. Family is who you choose. That's my working theory. And I'll need that as my illness sets in. And Dave's parents. What do I do with them? How can we ever trust each other, after everything? They still haven't said whether they still want to push the custody battle, now my illness is out in the open. They could win. They could take the boys. But I'd rather we choose each other as family.

It's messed up, but I'm going to make it work.

My memory is failing me. Jumping around. The connections are all messed up. Just the other day, I woke up and turned to talk to Dave in bed. I'd forgotten he was dead. And then I didn't know, was that my illness or just grief? I'm spending time each day trying to rebuild the connections. Trying to piece together all the moments that make me who I am. For the most part I think I get them right, but what if I'm wrong? Am I still the same person if I have different memories?

I spent so long worrying about that.

You know what? If one memory goes, I'll make another.

In whatever time I have left.

"My mind slows,
attentions come and go,
but my heart stays."
-The Doormats

ACKNOWLEDGEMENTS

First, and always, this book is dedicated to my wife Lis. For full support in all my bad ideas, and fixing my mistakes.

This book wouldn't be in your hands without the help, advice, or insights of Adam Croft, Bart Lessard, and Stacia Decker.

Thanks also to Jess Lourey, James Oswald, Eva Dolan, M.W. Craven, Mark Edwards, Hilary Davidson, Steve Weddle, Dave White, Chantelle Osman, Johnny Shaw, Antony Johnston, Jacque BZ, Blake Crouch, Matt Iden, Steve Konkoly, Russel McLean, Franz Nicolay, Angel Colón, Todd Robinson, Andrew Case (who is not the evil lawyer he appears to be in the book, he's actually one of the good 'uns) and James Ziskin.

ABOUT JAY STRINGER

Jay Stringer was born in 1980, and he's not dead yet.

His crime fiction has been nominated for both Anthony and Derringer awards, and shortlisted for the McIlvanney Prize. His stand-up comedy has been laughed at by at least three people.

He's English by birth and Scottish by legend; born in the Black Country and claiming Glasgow as his hometown. Jay is dyslexic, and came to the written word as a second language, via comic books, music, and comedy. Alongside Russel D. McLean, Jay was the first to bring Noir at the Bar to the UK.

Jay won a gold medal in the Antwerp Olympics of 1920. He did not compete in the Helsinki Olympics of 1952, that was some other guy.

Lightning Source UK Ltd.
Milton Keynes UK
UKHW011056270721
387842UK00004B/774